The Great Big Fairy

Fourth book in The Fairies Saga

A Novel by

Dani Haviland

The Great Big Fairy and *The Fairies Saga* are works of fiction. Names, places, characters, and incidents are the product of the author's imagination or used fictitiously for the reader's entertainment. Any resemblance to persons living, dead, or fictional, events, business establishments, or locales, is entirely coincidental.

Copyright 2011 by Dani Haviland
Published by Chill Out!
All rights reserved

~ The Fairies Saga ~

By Dani Haviland

In chronological order:

Naked in the Winter Wind

Aye, I am a Fairy

Dances Naked

The Great Big Fairy

Fairies Down Under

ISBN 978-0-6159847-2-8

(Front cover by www.TheKillionGroupInc.com)

SOMETHING SPECIAL

Just so you won't get confused about who's who, I put a cast of characters on the last page of the book. I figured that was the easiest place to find it.

And if while reading, you find that someone is narrating the story—that it's in the first person—that's just Evie taking over. Sometimes that old lady in a young person's body just won't shush!

(If you want to know more about Evie and her experience with time travel and rejuvenation, read NAKED IN THE WINTER WIND)

Contents

B illy was finally finished with his paperwork. It had been a long night. James and Leah had left only an hour and a half ago and unless something drastic occurred—and he didn't even want to speculate on that possibility—he would never see his newfound brother or sister-in-law/best friend again. But, now he, Billy Burke the lifelong orphan, had a mother, and that blessing he had stopped hoping for about fifteen years ago. He also knew who his father was and, although he may never be able to meet the elusive Marty Melbourne, he could find out more about him from his mother, the sweetest woman in the world, Bibb Stephens.

There was no reason for him to delay his final task. It was time to head out of town and pick up his going away present from James: the 'Beast,' the classic 1964 red Dodge pickup truck. He'd get one of the officers to drop him off near the site; he wouldn't have to give him an explanation. That would make the task easier, but he still wasn't ready to admit the finality of their departure. He already missed them both and actually hurt physically from their absence. The ache of emptiness went from his shoulders to his kneecaps and made it feel like his spine was an iced up rope, just dangling down through his midsection, holding his pelvis to his collarbones. He snorted; Leah would have told him that that was anatomically impossible, but that *was* how he felt.

He gathered up the piles of reports, straightened the edges by banging them just a little too hard on the top of the desk, and tugged at the drawer with more force than necessary. It felt like his left hand had four thumbs as he fumbled through the dividers. He finally found the file for the case and tossed it in like a shovelful of coal into a furnace, messing up the neat pile

1

that he had just put it into. "That's enough of you!" he said. Hopefully, he would never hear the name Atholl MacLeod again.

"Sir, there's someone here to see you. He says it's very important," Dyane called over the intercom.

"Have Sergeant Carter take care of it, will you? I'm off shift now," he replied with exasperation. He realized it was the wrong tone, but it was better than the one he was holding back. He didn't know if he wanted to scream or cry or laugh. But he did know that work was not the place to let loose. He stood up to leave then scanned the remaining papers still on his desk, making sure they were devoid of anything that would remind him of his time traveling family when he came back to work that evening.

"Sir," Dyane called back, "He says it's about someone named Evie and her daughter Leah, the nurse. He says you'll know who he's talking about."

Billy went weak in the knees then everywhere else. Fortunately, his chair, strategically placed, caught him as he plopped down in a solid, controlled fall. He swallowed hard, started to speak, but only an embarrassing squeak came out. He tried again. "Send him in," he said, this time, the words coming together and finding a way out of his mouth.

Dyane opened the door for the large visitor. Billy stood up and his eyes widened as they watched the man duck his head in order to enter the office. He wasn't the tallest man he had ever seen—he had met a couple of the gangly basketball players with the Hornets—but he was the biggest in terms of being a proportionately built man. Billy quickly tipped his head down when he realized he was staring. He walked around to the front of his desk and shook the hand of the huge man with auburn red hair. He glanced up again and the gentle giant grinned and whispered, "Six seven," like he was sharing a secret.

Billy pointed to the chair, offering his congenial new acquaintance a place to sit, then walked back around his desk, touching its surface as much for reassurance that he was awake, as for physical support lest he fall down from shock. He sat down slowly in his seat, his head bowed down, concentrating on the desktop. He didn't think he could make the transition from standing to sitting while looking into the face of this big man.

"I didn't mean to stare," Billy apologized as he looked up again. "It's just that you remind me of someone. All you're missing is the Scots accent." Billy couldn't help but think of the man's resemblance to Jody Pomeroy of the *Lost* novels. If James and Leah had just gone back to his time, the 18th century, could

2

it be that Jody Pomeroy had come back here, to this time? He fought back the urge to shake his head 'no' in answer to his own unspoken question and smiled nervously.

"Weel, I guess I lost a bit of the accent since I've been back here in North Carolina. Now, that bein' said, are ye the one to talk to about Leah and Evie?"

"Who *are* you?" Billy asked incredulously before he answered the Jody look-alike's question.

"I'm sorry. I dinna introduce myself. I'm Benjamin MacKay, but ye can call me Benji."

Billy nodded his head slowly in answer to Benji's question about being familiar with Leah and Evie. He didn't even try to talk lest the sounds come out as the 'baa, baa, babble' that were coursing through his brain. He'd read all the Lisa Sinclaire novels at least once. Benji was Jody Pomeroy's grandson and he was now sitting in front of him, all grown up. He was supposed to be a fictional character!

"Weel then, I hope it's not too late to catch a ride back with Leah. I got distracted with a couple of unsavory characters. But, it seems that ye've helped me quite a bit and have the MacLeod brothers out of my hair now. I, um, *heard* that Leah was goin' *back* to see her mother soon. I understand she knows how to, um, *travel* safely and without a lot of pain involved?" he asked rather than stated, focusing on Billy's eyes for his reaction.

Benji could see by the detective's wide-eyed and slack-jawed appearance that Billy understood what he was talking about. He waited for his reply, but the stunned police officer just sat at his desk, palms flat as if he was holding down the wooden furniture, and shook his head back and forth slowly. "You're too late," he whispered, his head still moving at the same, slow pace. "About two hours too late. They've already gone."

Benji winched, shut his eyes, and shook his head with a look of sadness and frustration. "Jest two hours..." He exhaled. "Um, do ye happen to know how they traveled?" he asked tentatively.

Billy pinched the bridge of his nose then spread his thumb and index finger out over his eyebrows, rubbing them back and forth in a nervous manner. He wanted to delay the answer. He didn't know if this Benji, this 21st century Benji, was a good person or not. Could it be that he was in with the MacLeods? Before he could answer, he heard the cautious question.

"Are ye related to Marty Melbourne, per chance?"

Billy's head snapped to attention, the fog of indecision blown away with the hurricane force of the shocking inquiry. "Why?" was all that he could think to reply.

Benji chortled. "Weel, ye must be then or ye woulda answered 'who' or 'no.' Ye look jest like him, have his same nervous habit of pinchin' yer eyebrows, and I'll wager if ye had the English accent, ye'd sound jest like him, too. But, yer not his grandson James, are ye? I mean, yer an American and an officer of the law. He's a member of parliament and a businessman."

Billy drew a deep breath, making the snap, gut decision that this was a good man and could be trusted. "James is my brother and Marty is my father," he said. He started to say more of their relationship but stopped. He'd let Benji talk and see how much he knew.

"Ye said 'they' went back, not jest Leah. Who went with her?" Benji asked.

"James did. He's her husband now. I don't think he would have let her go by herself. He was quite smitten with her. They only knew each other two weeks, but as soon as I saw those two together, I knew it wouldn't be too long and... Hey, how did you know Leah went back?" Billy asked, losing his original train of thought. This man was sharp and didn't miss a word.

"I read about it in a letter," Benji said plainly. He opened his mouth to say more then decided he'd wait to see if this American was going to let something slip. He wanted to know how much he knew before talking about time travel to a total stranger.

But, Billy was smart, too. He was also playing the 'show me your cards and I'll show you mine' game. "So, how do you know Marty Melbourne?" he asked with a glint in his eye, letting the big Scot know that they were playing mental poker.

Benji grinned and replied, "Ye make a livin' out of this, aye? I mean, jest any little thing a man says ye can use to find out more about a situation."

Billy pointed to the first part of the nametag on his desk. "It says detective, aye? So how do ye ken him?" he asked, mimicking Benji's accent.

"He came to our place when I was much younger. He and my father talked fer quite a while. Ye see, my father had read a letter about a James Melbourne and was tryin' to find him. He dinna ken much about him or his family, but what he kent was enough. It turns out that both men were lookin' fer each other. My father was writin' a book about, um, writin' a book that

4

interested Lord Melbourne and the two actually took a trip here to North Carolina in the early 90's. Young James and I came with them."

Billy decided to lay out a card and see if he could gain Benji's confidence. "So was the book about," he paused then made eye contact with the large red haired man, "about time travel?"

"What?" his new acquaintance laughed, "Do ye believe in that nonsense?"

But Billy could tell that Benji was just having fun with him. The walls were down and they were both now comfortable. "So, does this mean that you've traveled and it was painful? I mean, you mentioned Leah finding a way to travel without pain."

Benji rolled his eyes. "Ye have no idea how painful. I was only a lad, but I get the cold goose flesh jest thinkin' about it. I guess this means ye never went, um, back?"

"No, I'm sort of new to all of this. Have you had breakfast yet? I'm just getting off work and I think we have a lot to talk about."

1 They Might Be Giants
August 17, 2013
Greensboro, North Carolina

"Ye said I jest missed them?" Benji repeated, hoping to get more information out of Billy before they went to breakfast.

"Benji, I'm afraid that Leah and James left at dawn. I know how they did it; I can tell you all about how they managed it, the time traveling secrets as it were but..." Billy suddenly changed the subject. "Can you drive?"

"Anythin' with wheels, wings, or tracks!" Benji boasted.

"Good; I have to go just outside of town to pick up my truck. Come on; we'll go get some breakfast first. I know a sweet little place that has an all-you-can-eat breakfast buffet."

"Um," Benji paused then looked down in embarrassment.

"My treat, of course," Billy announced as he slapped the red headed giant on the upper arm. He couldn't reach the place behind the shoulders where an 'atta boy' was usually administered without reaching up awkwardly. The man was huge!

"I appreciate it," Benji said as he held the door open for the man who he was sure would become a good friend. He could already tell he was a decent person.

As they walked through the lobby Billy admitted to Benji, "Actually, I'd like you to come with me out to the site for another reason, not just to drive the truck back to my place. I'm *sure* that they made it but if something *did* happen to go wrong, I certainly want someone to be there with me. Are you game?"

Benji grinned, sniffed under his right armpit, made an ugly face then laughed as he said, "Aye, I'm a bit gamey, but if ye'll let me use yer shower after we get back from the site, then maybe I'll smell a bit better. In the meantime, ye might want to drive with the windows down. It's been a while since I've had the pleasure of bein' intimate with a bar of soap."

"No worries there. I'm sure that I've smelled worse but having the windows down will feel good, too. Now, do you have your bags or luggage or whatever?" Billy asked.

"Nothin' fer me," Benji said as he opened the door. "The only bags I have are under my eyes from lack of sleep so let's get this show on the road. After we get done with the chores, I'd like a quick shower, maybe give these clothes a quick scrubbin' so I dinna cause the weak of heart to pass out from the smell, and then I want to go back, too!"

Billy didn't know what to say so didn't say anything. How was he going to tell him the bad news? Instead, he addressed the immediate task. "That's my car there: the blue Vette." Billy looked over at his new acquaintance. "Six seven?" he asked although he was sure that those were the first words the man had spoken to him.

"Give or take half an inch and whether 'tis morn or evenin'. I tend to shrink durin' the course of the day if I've been workin' hard."

Benji cocked his head as he looked at the compact accommodations of the passenger side of the vintage Corvette. Billy came up next to him, unlocked the door, and said with almost a straight face, "I can go back to the maintenance department and get some grease if you think it would help you to squeeze into it."

"Nah," Benji joked back, "I'll jest suck in my breath and poke the parts that dinna fit out the window." He squeezed into the seat, brought his knees toward his chest, wedged his raggedy shoes into the narrow foot space, and hunched his shoulders forward. He reached his left arm under his right to pull the door closed and managed to roll the window down, too. He twisted his upper body toward the door and placed his right arm out the window, his left arm still crossed in front of him, his hand gripping the door since it was either that or hold it straight up in the air. "Ye did say it was jest a bit down the road, aye? I feel like a bear hangin' out o' the front seat."

"It's not too far," Billy replied then crowed like Jim Carrey in The Mask, "Hold on to yer lug nuts; we're on our way and in style." He popped the transmission into reverse, spun the car backwards in a half circle, crammed it into first gear, revved the engine, and then proceeded to enter the highway cautiously and at the speed limit. "We won't get there any faster with speeding, getting caught, and having to stop for a ticket than if we just go the limit and hit all the lights. Besides, the boys'd never let me live it down. I only go fast when I'm out of this jurisdiction and when the roads are cleared. Are you going to make it?"

"I'll bide as long as I dinna smile."

"What?" Billy shouted over the road noise.

Benji turned back toward him and answered, "If I smile, I'll git bugs in my teeth. And I hate bugs!" then faced straight ahead and grinned with his mouth shut, just in case.

2 Breakfast for the Boys

"I sure hope these people dinna go out of business from feedin' me," Benji said as he polished off another plate of bacon, grits, and scrambled eggs. "It's been quite a while since I could eat my fill and, weel, with such a spread, I kinda felt it hard to stop."

"Don't worry about them. I just came into a few extra bucks and I'll leave a generous tip. Now, just let me get rid of some of this coffee and we can hit the road." Billy excused himself with a nod and left the table to go the restroom.

Benji leaned sideways in the booth and stretched his legs out and his arms up, fully satiated and hopeful. It looked like Billy was a man he could trust. He turned back around and waited for the dark haired and mustached police officer to return to the table.

"Ready?"

Benji climbed out of the booth then held up his index finger. "That musta been Indian coffee; it kinda crept up on me. I'll need to make as much room as possible before I get back into that wee car of yers."

Billy waited outside for Benji. He unlocked the passenger door of the classic blue Corvette and looked under the seat mechanism to see if there was a way to override the glide on it. Even with the seat scooted all the way back, Benji's knees were in his face. Benji came out and saw what Billy was obviously trying to accomplish. "If ye have a socket set, I can probably jest remove the stop. I'll put it back when we get to wherever it is we're goin'. I've done this before. It works fine as long as I dinna stretch out too much. I dinna want to wind up with my neck stickin' out the rear window," he said playfully.

"Here ye go," Billy said in a Scots accent. "Emergency tool kit; dinna leave home without it."

Plop, plop, scoot and the non-automatic adjustable seat was modified to fit the mountain-sized man.

Billy noticed the raggedy shoes Benji was wearing, held together with duct tape that looked like it was ready to lose its hold. Benji noticed his observation but didn't respond to it. After all, it wasn't as if he could do anything about his shabby attire.

And, he knew Billy wasn't judging him, just being a detective, taking in the physical aspects of his new acquaintance.

"Here we are," Billy said as he pulled up behind the red '64 Dodge pickup. He exhaled sharply. "Just where they said it'd be."

Benji extricated himself from the front seat, stood beside the car, and arched his back, a pop pop emanating from his lumbar region. He looked over and saw Billy glance back to make sure everything was all right. "Jest a bit stiff and sore. It's been a long week." He snorted and amended his statement. "It's been a long decade!" then mumbled, "at least!"

Benji walked over and stood beside Billy. He pointed with his chin toward the trees. "That's where they went through, aye?"

Billy nodded but didn't speak. The tears were quickly filling up behind his lower eyelids and he knew that his voice would betray him. "Do ye think it hurt them?" Benji asked.

"God, I hope not!" Billy replied in shock. He had never thought about that. But, now he remembered what Benji had said when they first met: they could travel without pain.

"Ach, I'm sure that's the case or someone surely woulda mentioned it. It isna somethin' ye keep to yerself." Benji saw the confused look on Billy's face. "I think we need to talk. I'd say yer place or mine but since I dinna have a place, I suppose we'll have to go wherever ye want. I'm still a bit new to this town."

"Come on; we'll go to my apartment. Here, I'll draw a map of how to get there." Billy bent over and picked up a stick, and used it to sketch a rough map. "Just follow me but if you get lost or held up by a light, my place is easy to find," he said, tapping the big X he had drawn for their final destination. He turned and walked the few paces back to the truck and reached under it with his writing stick. He dug behind the right rear wheel, excavating a pair of keys on a circle of twisted wire. "Here, you drive 'the Beast,'" he said, offering the metallic behemoth to Benji. "It looks to be more your size anyway."

Benji took the keys and unlocked the door. He scooted the bench seat back as far as it would go, adjusted the mirrors, and started the engine. "Sweet," he commented softly as the engine roared to life at the first turn of the switch. He always did like the sound of the big muscle engines.

He looked up and saw that Billy was already in the Vette and ready to lead the way. "After you!" he called out to Billy, in an American accent.

Billy sighed as he looked in the rear view mirror then waved, putting on a fake smile for his new acquaintance. Now what? How was he going to tell the big guy that he'd have to wait a whole year before he could go back?

3 Benji

Benji enjoyed driving the old Dodge pickup to Billy's apartment. Even though the day was young, it was already hot but it didn't bother him today. With the windows down and the breeze blowing through his hair, it felt like oxygen was being pumped directly into his bloodstream through his pores. He could feel the raw power of the 318 engine through his hands on the steering wheel: true carbureted, unrestricted by smog controls or electronic sensors, high torque, spark-ignited, gasoline horsepower.

The drive without any A/C was actually refreshing. Benji didn't like air conditioning. A Freon modified atmosphere always made him feel like he was trying to breathe through only one nostril. Science might not back him up but his body could sense the reduction in available oxygen in an artificially controlled climate. He'd bide the heat and keep his health.

Billy was one traffic light ahead of Benji. He had already parked and was out of his ride when he saw Benji pull in. He pointed to his assigned covered parking spot, indicating that that was where he wanted the truck parked. It was a tight squeeze in the long bed pickup. He usually had to back up at least once to negotiate the tight corner and the inconveniently placed post that seemed to be in exactly the wrong place. Benji waved back and pulled straight in on the first try. "Ho kay," Billy mumbled. "Maybe he is an ace equipment operator. At least he seems to have the gift of parking in tight quarters." Billy started chuckling to himself. "Yeah, but then again, that might be because he's had to learn how to maneuver that huge frame of his."

Both men were mute as Billy led the way to his apartment. As he unlocked the door, Billy saw Benji stoop and untie his shoes. "What are you doing?' he asked, although it was obvious that the man was taking off his shoes.

Benji quickly had both shoes off. He used the toe of one foot to hold down the heel of the sock on the other foot, pulling it off effortlessly then repeated the process on the other side. Both feet were quickly bared, toes wriggling in the fresh air and soft grass. "I'm countin' my toes to make sure I dinna lose any on the ride over," he joked then said, "I got in the habit of removin' my shoes when enterin' a house. It was more than respect when I was in Alaska. In the winter, it was snow and slush on yer boots and in the summer, *both weeks*," he chuckled, "it was mud. Takin' off the footwear saves on the floor and rug cleanin' but I like to do it 'cause takin' my socks off jest feels so good."

"Well, if it makes you feel more comfortable, go ahead. Peter will vacuum whether the carpet is dirty or not. Or at least that's what he says. He's my, um, roommate. Go ahead and sit down. *Mi casa es su casa.*"

"*Gracias,*" Benji replied. "I appreciate the hospitality." He looked around and chose the long couch to sit on, letting Billy take the overstuffed chair. By the placement of the reading lamp and newspaper, it was either Billy's or Peter's favorite chair. He'd take the company couch.

"So, are you ready to talk about this? You look a little beat."

"Little beat; there's not much about me that *is* little," Benji laughed. "I'm a *lot* beat. But I need to know how," he said seriously, "how do, or did, they go back?"

Billy sat back in his chair then realized that he couldn't be relaxed when he related the story. He scooted to the edge of his seat, elbows on his knees, each hand massaging the other as he began his dissertation on time travel, as he knew it. "Well, as far as we know there are four factors: focus, location, time and um, jewelry."

"Okay, ye have my attention. I'm sure ye need to elaborate or I could be out of here with a pop-bead necklace."

Billy chuckled, "Well, actually the jewelry was an ancient Greek drachma coin with a couple of strategically placed holes, threaded on a piece of ribbon. At least I think they were strategically placed. Anyway, rather than chance it, James found two drachmas and had them drilled in identical places at the jewelers. He strung them on a cord so they would be discreet and they'd be able to touch them while they concentrated on their walk through the trees at dawn. Leah had noticed that Evie wore an identical one strung on black ribbon when she went left."

"Then there are the other three factors. Focus: they focused on Evie, the younger version of Dani, as she was known when she lived in this time. She's Leah's mother by the way and that's *very* complicated. I'll show you the video later."

"Time: James was told by his, our, father, Marty, the man you said you met years ago, to come through on August 17th at daybreak. And, the last essential part is location: through those specific trees. The Trees are markers for a portal, probably magnetic."

Billy held up his fist and enumerated as he reiterated the factors. "James said they had to," one finger up, "focus on Evie while," second finger up, "holding onto their drachmas and," third finger up, "walking through the trees," fourth finger, "at that certain date and time."

"Hmph," Benji said. "Do ye happen to know where to drill the holes in the wee Greek coin and do ye think it would be too hard to find one?"

"James got four of them before he left: two for them and one for me and Mom in case Dad didn't come back. She wanted to be with him at any cost and well, if all my family was back there, I wanted the option to go back, too. Oh, by the way, I just found out they were my family last week. It's a long story, for another day. But, we know where The Trees are. You were there with me when we picked up the truck."

"Aye, I recognized them," Benji said then sighed and sank back into the sofa. "And I'll show you the video so you can see who Evie is, so you'll have a person to focus on, and I'll let you have one of the coins. But, I think you're going to have to wait a year."

"Weel, I've waited this long, I suppose I can find somethin' to fill up the next three hundred and sixty-five days," Benji said with resignation. "Now where's the video?" he added with a spark of hope, adjusting his position on the couch. Billy brought out the smartphone that had been back and forth through time twice. "This is one of those fancy solar powered jobbers. That's why it worked in the 18th century. Leah took hers with her. This one was her mother's. She, rather someone else, inadvertently made a video. You can see her as she is now. I guess that's right since this is how she looked a few months back. She was pregnant in this but had triplets a few months later. At least she's doesn't look like the sixty-year old woman who disappeared a year ago."

Billy shook his head; he was confusing himself and he knew the story of what went on. He didn't need to make it tougher on Benji. "Here, scoot over. I'll just shut up and show you the video. That's what James and Leah did for me and it worked. Words fail when trying to explain this."

Benji scooted over and Billy sat down next to him, briefly shocked at the man's body heat; he was a furnace. *Focus, Billy!* "Can you see it or do you want to hold it? I've seen it already but, if you have a question, I want to be here."

Benji looked down at him and said, "Yer not scarin' me by sittin' close if that's what ye mean," then laughed. "Nah, get as close as ye need; I'd rather have ye nearby than over there," and nodded to the overstuffed chair Billy had been in.

Billy snuggled up to Benji and did the taps and slides to open the video file. "Here it is," he said as if he were announcing an eight-legged dog. "Let me know if you want me to pause it at any time."

Benji didn't say a word as he watched the mini movie, but Billy was close enough that he could feel the big man's shudders. He didn't look up but knew that Benji was crying. He had to be emotional: he was viewing his grandfather, the man he wanted to go back in time to see. Billy paused the video when Jody's face came into view full screen. "You look just like him," Billy said.

Benji laughed and cried at the same time, "Pretty scary, eh?" then the laughter stopped and the tears took over.

Billy pulled away from his big new friend and grabbed the box of tissues from the bathroom. "Here, blow ya big baby," he ordered then realized that he was crying, too. "Well, at least they're tears of joy," he explained as he pulled out a double fistful for himself.

"Aye, they are," Benji said. "How am I to keep busy fer a year? I thank ye fer showin' me how it's done, but now it's even worse, or rather stronger: the cravin' to go back to him, to where I belong. I, I dinna feel like I belong here."

"Well, you were born back there, weren't you?" Billy grimaced and thought fast. Didn't Benji say something about it earlier? Hopefully he had, otherwise how would he explain to him that he knew who he was, at least all about his family back in the 18th century?

"Aye, I was," Benji said, not looking at Billy but staring at the frozen image of his grandfather. "Maybe that's why I feel the pull, the draw to go back." He shut his eyes and reached over to give the smartphone back to Billy.

"Well," Billy said as he accepted the phone and stood up. "I don't know about you, but I'm beat. You can take a shower and wash the clothes you're wearing. The washer and dryer are in the bathroom. Help yourself to anything you need. I don't have any clothes that will fit you, but you can use one of those big bath towels for decency until your clothes are dry. Now, don't leave without tellin' me, okay?"

"I'll be here when ye wake," Benji promised. *He wasn't going to promise any more than that, though. He'd leave when the time felt right— just like he always did.*

Ж

Billy awoke from his nap when he heard Peter come in the door. He got up and started a pot of coffee.

"Who's *that!*" exclaimed Peter when he saw the pair of men's very long, bare legs poking out from the end of the couch.

"Oh, him," Billy said nonchalantly then turned away so Peter couldn't see the smirk he was hiding. "He's just a stray I picked up."

"Uh, didn't he come with clothes?" he asked, a little uncomfortable at seeing the near naked man asleep on their sofa.

"Yes, he did but I didn't think he needed them in the shower." Billy was teasing Peter and beginning to enjoy the little repartee too much. His grin was giving him away.

Peter could see that this was a totally innocent situation that only looked provocative, and that Billy was messing with him. "Well, gee, I just thought the Incredible Hulk had busted out of his pants and you threw him a towel to save him from embarrassing himself in front of the ladies," Peter drolled then changed to a serious tone. "No, really; who is he?"

"Really, he's just a stray I picked up. But, he's sort of a friend of the extended family. He came to see James and Leah. They left this morning and won't be back for a while," Billy explained. *'Quite a while, if ever,'* he wanted to add but didn't. "So, since he's broke, needs a place to stay, has great character references, and is skilled, I said he could hang with us and help out around here." Billy saw the shocked look on Peter's face and quickly added, "That is, of course, if it's okay with you," and put a hand on his shoulder.

Peter patted the hand then picked it up and kissed it. "If you trust him, I trust him. But, he looks familiar. I know I've seen that huge body and red hair somewhere before."

Just then, Benji awoke with a shudder and quickly composed himself as he realized where he was. "Weel, it looks like I have an audience fer my nap takin'. Is this what ye do fer entertainment?" he joked as he adjusted his bath towel and sat up, rubbing his hands through his long hair with a frown. He'd have to wait for a haircut unless Billy had some clippers he could use.

"That's where I've seen you!" Peter exclaimed.

Benji's face immediately paled and his jovial smile evaporated, a fog of fear replacing it. He wasn't sure, but he

16

would have bet a million bucks that these two men were a gay couple. They wouldn't, couldn't have seen it, could they?

"Didn't you wrestle as The Flying Scotsman?" Peter asked with a glint in his eye. "I mean, you sure look like him..." he smiled as he teased. He was sure of it now.

Benji breathed a huge sigh of relief. "Aye, I had to do odd jobs to make ends meet." He shrugged his shoulder. "Some jobs jest werena as 'respectable' as others although those were the ones that usually paid the best. At least this was one that people enjoyed watchin' and no one got hurt, not really. It was fun, but I got tired of bein' the bad guy. I managed to save a bit of money so moved on. Billy, do ye think the laundry's done? I dinna hear it thump, thump, thumpin' in the dryer." Benji got up, inadvertently flashed his hosts, said, "oops," then pulled the towel closed as he chased his laundry, closing the combination bathroom laundry room door behind him.

"I thought that those scars on his back were make-up," Peter said softly to Billy. "Ouch!"

"Yeah, ouch is right. For someone who appears to have had a rough life, he sure has a good outlook," Billy said. "And a great sense of humor. So, you agree then? He's decent enough to watch this place and then help take care of me while you're out of town?" Billy asked as he walked up for his 'welcome home' hug from his partner.

Peter gave him a hug and a squeeze, and a quick kiss. "Oh, he'll be fine. Gee, I've got The Flying Scotsman sleeping in my living room. My little brother will be so jealous!" Peter saw the frown on Billy's face and realized that this was a situation requiring discretion. "Well, I won't tell him but just *knowing* how jealous he'd be is good enough for me. Paul isn't gay, but he had the biggest crush on him when he was fifteen."

Ж

"So, how long have you been in North Carolina?" Peter asked Benji as the three of them sat at the table, drinking coffee.

"Jest a month or so this time. The last time I was here, hmm, was when I was in my late teens, I expect. The years kinda ran together. Ye see, I had been abducted and shuttled around from place to place, pretty much had my services as a laborer sold to the highest bidder without my say so."

"You mean you were a slave?" Peter asked.

Benji nodded. "Not much I coulda done about it. I mean, I dinna volunteer fer it!" he added with a laugh. "Ye see, there were a bunch of us..."

"They had slaves here twenty years ago?" Peter asked incredulously. "White slaves? Oops, sorry; I didn't mean to interrupt."

"I dinna think they cared about the color of our skin, but now that ye mention it, I think we were all a bit on the pale side. Maybe it was jest because we were slower...Nah. We were the ones they couldna get a ransom fer...or not enough ransom. Some of the lads had family who paid and paid, but the thugs still wouldna let them go. At least as long as their folks kept sendin' the money. We boys kinda became our own family."

"Like an orphanage without the housemother..." Billy suggested, remembering his youth and the comfort he felt with his unrelated brothers.

Benji shook his head rapidly. "No, we were family, but it wasna like any orphanage I'd ever heard of; in the last century, at least. We had no beds to speak of, no schools or medicine and the whip wasna spared if we spoke our minds or dinna work fast enough. No; nothin' like an orphanage."

"But the other boys were like your brothers..." Billy offered, a little meeker this time.

He shrugged his shoulder like there was a bit of truth in the statement. "I protected them, sort of. Ye see, they ken I had a big heart...and everythin' else, too," Benji couldn't help but laugh at their uneasiness then patted his right hand over his left fist and changed the subject. "Ye see, they kept us in old slave quarters. We were three to a little room, or cell, or whatever ye want to call it. Anyway, we had to plant, hoe, harvest; dependin' on what season it was, and tend to a set number of sections or rows every day. They didn't watch us work; jest had their guards watchin' us on the monitors in their air conditioned trailers, makin' sure no one tried runnin' away or smokin' the stuff."

"Pot?" Peter mouthed. Benji nodded then continued his story.

"They dinna ken it, but there were only two in our little shack. Wee Michael was only about yay high and had little bitty hands. But, he was a good cook so they let him work the kitchen rather than the fields. He always made sure that he made up a tray for himself, me, and our other roommate, Casper. Ye see, they werena too diligent in doin' the bed checks. I shoved my pallet next to Casper's and used a bundle of rags to stuff under the blanket so it looked like he was early to bed and late to rise. As long as the work was done by the cabin as a unit, they dinna care if the lad was lazy or no. I did the work of two people. Wee Michael kept the secret. He kinda liked me, and as long as I'd let

18

him brush my hair every once in a while, he made sure that I got Casper's food and that the beds werena checked too close like."

"He brushed your hair?" Peter asked. "Was he, well, you know?"

Benji shrugged his shoulders. "I dinna ken and I dinna care. I kinda liked havin' someone touch me, like a friend or a brother," he tilted his head to Peter to make sure that he understood that was the extent of his attraction to other men. "It got kinda lonely and in the winter we scooted the pallets together and I kept him warm. Not that he had enough body heat to keep me warm but it was comfortable. And, as long as I was there, the others dinna bother him. Ye see, he was kinda pretty and they dinna have women and, weel, I guess he got, um, assaulted before I got there. So, I dinna mind what the others thought about us: he was safe and I was well fed. They never did catch on to our ruse. And, when I left, I made sure Wee Michael came with me. I left a note fer the 'goons' to tell them that Casper had escaped and we were chasin' 'im down fer 'em."

"And they believed you?" Peter asked with eyes wide.

"I dinna ask," Benji replied. "We never went back and they never caught up with us. We wound up in Asheville. I got a job bustin' tires at a junk yard." Benji saw the confused look on Peter's face and explained the job. "That's separatin' the wheels from the tires. Wee Michael got a job at a salon, washin' hair," Benji laughed. "He'd come back to the shelter, his hands all sparklin' clean and soft, and mine; weel, it took about two months fer the black to come off of 'em *after* I left that place."

"What happened to Wee Michael?" Billy asked.

"Oh, weel, the lady who owned the hair salon took a likin' to him and decided to teach him how to cut hair. Last I heard, they were marrit and had a bairn who stayed with them there at the salon, off in the corner play area, while they washed and cut hair all day. I think it worked out jest fine fer both of 'em." Benji sighed, "They had each other, a bairn to see to, and made money doin' what they loved. We should all be so lucky."

"Blessed," corrected Billy.

"Excuse me?" Benji asked.

"There is no such thing as luck. We all have tough times: trials and tribulations, obstacles, whatever. Even though it doesn't seem fair at the time, if we are good people, and you seem to be one, then we get blessed. We just have to be patient. God will reward us in His time."

"Weel, I dinna mean to be rushin' the Lord, but I wish He'd hurry up. I'm tired of runnin'. I dinna mind protectin' the

19

small and weak but," he shook his head, "I'd like to have a place to call home and someone to come home to," he sighed as he looked over at Peter and Billy and sucked in his bottom lip. He bucked up, sat up, and added, "But, if what ye say is true, I guess there's a bit more that the Lord wants me to do before I get my blessin'. I'll bide and do my best not to get bitter in the meantime."

"Well, you're more than welcome to stay here as long as you want. You see, I'm going to have surgery day after tomorrow and Peter has to go back out of town so, I'd actually appreciate it if you could housesit for us, even if this *is* only an apartment."

"I think I can manage that," Benji grinned as he looked around. "Although I dinna ken what I'd do all day. I'm used to workin' to earn my keep. I guess I could read. It looks like ye have quite the library."

Billy gulped as he looked over and saw the colorful collection of Lisa Sinclaire books, the 'fictionalized' history of Benji's grandfather, Jody Pomeroy, and his family. He'd have to make sure they got put away.

"Um, didn't you say that you could operate anything with wheels, wings, or tracks?" Billy asked to change the subject.

"That I did. I've had quite the opportunities to learn a lot about them in the last, *phew,*" he added in exasperation, "too many years. And, if they're not runnin', I've a bit of skill in repairin' 'em, too. My mother was quite gifted that way and I guess I got a bit of the talent from her. At least, I'd like to think that I got more than jest the red hair from her."

"Well, you got the height, too," Billy said casually then blanched. How was he supposed to know that?

Benji cocked his head at Billy's revelation. "Ye ken my mother?" he asked.

Billy answered boldly and truthfully, "Never had the pleasure. But I seriously doubt that either of your parents would be petite. So, who's taller: your mother or father?" Billy hoped he had plugged his *faux pas* with feigned curiosity, then changed the subject a bit, "And I hope that she's not taller than you. She'd have a heck of a time buying shoes!"

"No, she's a bitty thing," he put his hand out flat at his chin, "only six foot even." Benji laughed then looked over at his own raggedy shoes in the corner. "But, getting' them in my size is plenty hard. And, they dinna come cheap, either. Size sixteen secondhand shoes or boots jest arena out there."

"Well, I'll tell you what. You can run a Cat, right?" Billy stated more than asked and looked to Benji who nodded that, yes, he could operate a bulldozer. "We, that is, I, can rent a dozer and we can go out to my mother's property. She has some old buildings that she wants razed. You can do that while we're recuperating."

Billy saw the confused look on Benji's face then explained who 'we' were. "My mother has liver cancer. They're going to yank it out and I'm going to give her half of mine. Both halves will grow to full size in short order. I'll be up and at 'em, catchin' the bad guys again in a month or two. So, you can use the truck for commuting and I'll make sure we go to the big and tall men's store and get you set up with some work boots and jeans this afternoon. Sound fair?'

"More than fair, mate, more than fair."

4 Greetings

Peter and Benji sat at the kitchen table playing chess. "Was that blood real or fake?" Peter asked. "I mean, I always heard that wrestling was just bad acting but sometimes it looked so real!"

"Weel, sometimes it was real. They'd tell us what they wanted us to do, kinda give us an outline like 'ye tell him his mother's an ugly cow and he gets mad and starts throwin' chairs or whatever at yer heid. He'll chase ye around the stage, up into the arena then ye knock him down when his back is turned.' We got to ad lib and sometimes it was fun. But, some of those guys, and I willna tell ye who, took lots of steroids. Ye coulda looked cross-eyed at 'em and they woulda tried to take off yer heid, or worse. No, that was real blood too many times," Benji admitted then bent his head down to concentrate on the game. "How long have ye been playin' chess?" he asked to change the subject. He didn't want to talk about his sleazy and embarrassing past with the affable but inquisitive man.

"Just a few, um; well, I cannot tell a lie," Peter admitted then sat up straight to tell his brief board game history. "I was going to tell you just a few weeks so you'd have pity on me, but I've been playing chess since I was three. I competed for a while when I was younger. My father was quite pushy," he said in exasperation. "Always trying to live his life through me..." he added dejectedly as he bent forward over the game, settling his chin onto his knuckles to reevaluate the move he had just made.

"The sport of kings, or something like that," Benji said as he castled a knight and got in position to capture Peter's queen. "But I canna see ye as anything but yer own man now. Hopefully yer father grew out of it and realized that yer a great person on yer own and that he is, too. Nobody can be him but him; not ye nor anyone else."

"Hey, you're trying to get my queen," Peter exclaimed then touched his white game piece, trying to figure an escape route. "But you're right. I never thought of it that way. I'll have to tell him next time I see him," he said then grimaced and bit his bottom lip. He looked up and said, "He has Alzheimer's disease and is in a home. I doubt he'll know who I am, much less what I'm saying, but I owe it to him to at least try to put it into words."

"Nae, ye owe it to *yerself* to tell him if he canna remember who ye are. Now all ye can do is forgive him and love him. He may not ken ye but he ken him. Let him be a mirror to reflect yer love back to yerself if he canna give it to ye on his own, aye?" Benji said gently.

"Wow, aye," Peter replied then looked down at the board again, surreptitiously wiping the tears that had spilled out of the corners of both eyes. "My queen is out of danger—give it your best shot," he said with a false bravado. His relationship with his father had always been an issue but now he could see it for how it really was. Yes, he'd go see Dad tomorrow and have the son to father talk that was long overdue, even if his father didn't know who he was.

"Weel, ye can keep yer queen, but I'll take the king. Checkmate," Benji announced then added gently, "but ye really werena into the game. I wasna playin' fair, talkin' about yer kin like that. Sorry."

"Shoot, fair or not, you gave me insight that fifteen years of therapy couldn't. Now what's for dinner, Love," Peter called out to Billy.

"We're going to Mom's for dinner. I called her and told her to make enough for an army. It's been a long time since breakfast and coffee and cookies don't count as a meal. Let's take the Beast," Billy said as he grabbed the coffee cups off the table and set them in the sink. "You two can play another game after *my mother*," he gloated at the title, "feeds us."

Ж

The three men rode to the mill in the truck with the windows down, Peter squeezed between Billy, the driver, and Benji, the mellow passenger with his right elbow hanging out in the wind. "Those are the buildings we want torn down," Billy said as he pointed to the unpainted and weathered sheds, "and then we're going to build a big house right there. We've got some preliminary plans drawn up and I'd like to get your input on them, and then here we are," Billy announced, segueing from drafting to dining in the same sentence.

Bibb came out the front door of the little apartment at the side of the mill, waving cheerfully at the trio as they piled out of the truck. "Benji, this is my mother, Bibb Stephens. Mom, this is Benjamin MacKay," Billy said in introduction.

"Benji," he said to clarify the name.

"Bibb," she responded. "Just Bibb; not Ms. Stephens or BS; just Bibb.

Peter started laughing at the exchange.

23

"What's so funny?" Bibb asked.

"Oh, even if I hadn't known Billy was your son, I'd suspect it. When I first met Billy, he introduced himself as 'Billy Burke; not Billy Bob or Billy Joe, just Billy.'"

Billy chuckled as he recalled their first meeting. Peter was an insurance adjuster, new to his job at handing out checks for claims. Both his and best friend Leah's apartments had just been damaged in a major fire. "Yes," Billy said, "and I sure had the hots for you!"

"Well, it was an arson case," Peter drolled then they all laughed together.

"Who would have thought that one month later we'd be a couple, sharing tea with my mother and..." Billy shut up quickly before he said something about Benji, the odd man out in this reunion. But he was neither odd nor out: he was here because he wanted to go back to be with his family, both of their families, back in the 18ᵗʰ century. Peter didn't know about his time traveling family and Billy didn't want him to know, at least not for a while, and maybe not ever. Trust was still hard for him to share.

Benji picked up the dead spot in the conversation. *He knew that he could discuss time travel with Billy but not with Peter around. Billy had alluded that Bibb was aware of all that was going on, or a lot of it, but Peter was being protected. Well, protected was a better way to think of it than shut out.* "So, yer both goin' to the hospital tomorrow and yer gonna donate half of yer liver to yer mother? Willna ye miss it?" he asked as he looked to Billy.

"Nope, the doc said my half will grow back in a month or so and hers, I mean, the half I give to her, will grow to full size in short order. I just, well, we'll both, have to take it easy for a couple of months and then we'll be ready to take on the world. What *do* you want to do, *Mom*?" Billy asked with a grin. He still loved to use that name.

"Well, I'm still trying to figure a way to get all the pieces to fit. I already told you about razing those old dilapidated storage shacks. If we can clear that area and get some local contractors and building material suppliers to donate goods and services, we can build a home for unwed mothers. Every time I hear the word abortion, I get the shivers."

"Yeah, me, too," Billy agreed and Benji and Peter nodded that they felt the same way. Billy added, "It's bad enough that the baby doesn't even get a chance to grow. I mean, the child didn't ask to be created but God thought it was right or sperm wouldn't have met egg, no matter what the conditions. No one has the right to end a child's life. That malarkey about a woman's body being hers to do with what she wants, would be just fine and dandy if she could remove the baby and let him grow to term without hurting or killing him! So if being pregnant is inconvenient for the mother, let's help her. If she doesn't want to keep him after he's born, there are loads of people hoping and praying for a child. I mean, they're waiting for years to adopt one!"

"But it's not just the child that's lost with an abortion," Bibb said sadly. "I lost you, well, I lost watching you grow up, but I knew you were safe. But the mothers who choose abortion lose a part of themselves, not only the child. I worked with quite a few abortion recovery groups through the years. Alcoholism, drug addiction, and suicides follow right on the heels of abortions; that and a wide variety of mental illnesses including severe depression. No, abortion kills a child and wounds the mother, sometimes taking her life, too."

Benji spoke out, "What about the fathers? Dinna they get a say? They're jest as much a father before the bairn is born as after, or can be. Give 'em a chance to claim their own, I say. I dinna ken what I'd do if I found out I had fathered a child, but I sure wouldna suggest the lass get an abortion! That is, would be, my child, and I'd raise him the best I could with or without the mother!"

Bibb added, "An abortion kills one and wounds the other for life. I'm not proud of hiding my pregnancy from your father. I mean, I'm pretty sure that life would have played out differently for all three of us if I hadn't been so prideful thinking I could handle everything myself, but I *am* glad that I didn't choose the, ugh, easy way out. I don't think I could have lived with myself if I did. And I know from the counseling center that there are many attempted, and some successful, suicides within a year after a woman has an abortion."

Bibb looked up and saw that all three men felt the same way she did. "And don't even get me started on letting young girls get an abortion without parental consent. That is positively insane! The girls aren't old enough to smoke a cigarette and yet the law says she can kill her unborn child...ugh!" she shuddered. "If a woman can't or won't or is just afraid to get emotional support for herself and her unborn child, then I want to be there. It's my dream that no female should feel helpless. She and her unborn child can, will, be safe here. And regardless of whether she and the baby wind up staying together or not, that child will still have life. Hmph!"

"Amen to that," Benji said sincerely.

Bibb changed the subject, sort of. "I've decided to sell the mill to the employees. If it hadn't been for them, I wouldn't have been able to keep it going all these years. But there's more out there: the mill is on just a small part of the land." She snorted, "I'm going to have to do something with the rest of it. Those land developers just won't leave me alone!"

"What *do* you want to do with it? I mean, don't let money get in the way. James left me in charge of all of the Melbourne assets. He said it was for us to use and not to worry about spending it all...wisely. He trusts my judgment."

"Well, I, I mean we, could build a home for unwed mothers and not wait for the donations to come in. I can talk to the businesses and see if they're interested in the project. I'm sure that many would like to give back to the community. I'm sure there are more than a few fathers of daughters out there who would like to see options for women. I mean, a woman shouldn't feel like she *has* to marry a man...even if she does want to...but so many times families aren't supportive. And, Lord knows I don't want the poor girls, or women, to think that abortion is her only way out. No, this way a woman can choose to keep her body and her baby safe. If she decides to adopt out the child, that's fine. But, I want to have resources on hand so the gals can learn a trade, build a network so even those who can't work can help those who can by taking care of the babies...at least until they're on their feet. I don't want this to be a destination but a means of transporting a woman and her child to a safer, happier life."

"Where do ye want me to start?" Benji asked. "There willna be much to do while ye are in the hospital so I can start the razing and land clearing. Then, if ye have the plans, I can be yer contractor. I jest need yer permission to act on yer behalf."

"Do you mean *you* could be the general contractor?" asked Billy.

"Weel, act as one. I'm not sure of the local regulations but I can do jest about anything that needs done with constructing a building. I mean, excavating and pouring the foundation, the plumbing, electrical, framing, drywall..."

"I get it, I get it," Billy said with hand held up. "If it has wings, wheels, or tracks you can operate it. If it has wires, pipes, or concrete, you can build it."

26

"Pretty much," Benji said with a full-faced grin. "But I think that ye need to have the building plans on file around here. I wouldna want ye to be doin' anything illegal now..." he commented to his policeman friend with a wink.

5 Mother Knows Best
Barden Hall, Scotland, 1985

*M*ona and Gregg MacKay had made the difficult decision several years earlier to leave their life and her parents in 1772 and to travel forward; to return to their native-born time of the 20th century. They had lived with her mother and father, Sarah and Jody Pomeroy, for seven years back in the 18th century. There, their two children, Benji and Rebecca, were born. It was only because of a medical crisis that they made the physically painful journey through 'The Stones' to go back to the 20th century. The ancient standing stones in North Carolina, like the ones at Stonehenge and scores of other sites around the world, were portals through time. This method of time travel, the secret of the centuries, was precarious and also caused the travelers intense physical pain. But, the trip had been necessary so Benji's infant sister, Rebecca, could receive the modern cardiac surgery needed to save her life. Becky was fine now, completely healed, and thriving.

The parents had decided to remain in the 20th century. The horrific pain of traveling was their only deterrent to returning to their 18th century family, but it was enough. They re-adapted quickly to their former lifestyle and were a traditional Scottish family. Both parents held respectable jobs, their seemingly fantasy life 200 years previously, a closely held family secret. Thanks to some creative estate planning by Sarah before she returned to her husband and the 18th century, the land and buildings of Jody's family estate of Barden Hall in Scotland now belonged to their daughter, Mona.

Life was almost perfect for the MacKays. There was still a hole in their lives though. Mona missed her mother and father terribly and, even though life in that era had been rough on Gregg, he, also, enjoyed the simpler times. The change to a modern way of life was hardest on young Benji. He only had good memories of his life before running water and electricity, cars and televisions. He tried telling his classmates about hunting with Grandpa, how when he was little, there weren't radios or airplanes, but they responded with taunts and name-calling, alienating him and deeming him crazy.

Grandpa Jody had been his mentor and best friend. Even though Benji loved his father and, even though they spent as much time together as a father and son could, it wasn't the same. Grandpa was special to him. And, he was determined that he was going to find his way back to him, one way or another. No one could change his mind although, after a year, he stopped telling his parents of his plan. He didn't like the way it made his mother sad and his father frustrated. He wouldn't bother them with it anymore. But, he would go back.

Ж

January 2, 1989
Barden Hall

"I want to read them all," Mona announced suddenly to her husband. Her eyes were brimming with tears as she stroked her greatest treasure, the inlaid box of letters. These were the written diaries, histories of a sort, sent to her and her family by her parents. The letters had been held in trust for two centuries by God only knows whom, when they were discovered amongst Gregg's deceased father's vast boxes of historical records. She and Gregg were reading one every month, or every few weeks if she was antsy, and now her curiosity had the best of her. Again. She wanted them all, now—she wanted to read all of the letters right away.

"Uh, I dinna think so," Gregg replied. "We agreed that we'd savor them, space them out, and read them over time. There are a finite number and once we've read them all, we willna have anything else to look forward to."

"Well, I've changed my mind and I want to read them all, every last one of them, this weekend. And, I'm not changing my mind back again. Now, you can read them with me or I'll read them by myself. I'll put them back in the same order when I'm done and then you can read them, one a month, until *you've* read them all." Mona stuck her chin out and crossed her arms in front of her chest; she was determined and not going to change her mind. Again.

It was early Saturday morning; their children, Benji and Becky, were in town with their friend Maura for the weekend so they could remodel the bathroom without distractions. Mona had said the same thing at least three times in the last two years, but they always went back to their 'ration the letters' agreement. Gregg rolled his eyes. He'd seen the jutting chin and heard that tone more than once. He could argue with her, but that would only eat up their limited time. He decided he'd simply say okay

29

to her and then she'd change her mind, again. Just like she always did.

"Go aheid; open all of them, right now. If there's anythin' interestin', let me ken. Otherwise, ye'll ken what's in them and I willna. I'll have a treat comin' to me the first of every month and ye willna," Gregg said, biting off the urge to say, 'nanner, nanner, nanner!'

"Okay, fine," Mona declared sharply then snorted. "Sorry about the attitude," she amended quickly. "It's just, well—call it women's intuition or mother's intuition or whatever. I just *feel* like there's a warning in there for me. I'll savor the words later. Right now I'm, well, searching for something."

Mona wiped her nose. Although he hadn't seen any tears, Gregg could tell that she was definitely emotional about something. "All right, ye win or whatever. But let's do it together. I hate it when ye ken more than I do about somethin'— at least when it's pertinent to both of us. I'm glad ye ken more than I do about engineerin' and plumbin'. And, speakin' of that, ye agree that we'll only buzz through these—just scan through them fer now? We can go back to our once a month readin's later for further appreciation? We still have to get the bathroom replumbed, ye ken. I want to be able to take a hot shower, not a warm dribble."

"Okay, you stoke the fire and I'll bring a couple of tall lattes and a plate of biscuits. There are at least two dozen letters here. Let's get comfortable."

"I've got an idea," Gregg said as he brought the coffee table closer to the couch where they were seated. "I'll just scan them, or ye can, fer bold writing: somethin' that looks like a warnin'. That shouldna take too much time. If we find somethin': great, or not great. And, if we dinna, we can go through them slower or...maybe just go back to readin' one a month again?" he suggested cautiously.

"We'll see," Mona answered in the same tone, "we'll see."

Gregg handed Mona a letter. She unfolded it gently, scanned it for obvious warnings, then refolded it and put it aside. They didn't find anything extraordinary until the sixth letter. Gregg noticed the small note enclosed even before he gave it to Mona to open. He pulled it out. "Look," he said as he pointed to the writing, "It's written with a ballpoint pen!"

"Let me see!" Mona shrieked as she reached for the letter.

"Together," Gregg announced then put the note in his right hand and opened out his left arm for her to snuggle close so they could both read it at the same time.

'Mona, Gregg: Benji will disappear but he's fine. He's here with his Grandpa and Grannie. Do NOT look for him or you will endanger him and yourselves. Take care of each other, Evie (your sister-in-law).'

"What the fu..?" Mona exclaimed. "Benji...gone?" she gulped. Her original furor and shock had segued into fear and desperation.

Gregg took the note out of her hand and turned it over, looking for more clues. There was nothing but the short and to the point warning by someone who they didn't know about, at least yet. "Sister-in-law?" Gregg asked. "Does that mean that Wallace...that Wallace has acknowledged Jody as his father?"

"Hell if I know. But Benji...how, why, when? There isn't a date on it, is there? Can't we protect him? Do you think that we should move from here? Would that help? And why can't we look for him?" Mona's questions were popping like a case of Jiffy Pop in a bonfire.

"Slow down," Gregg said as he wrapped his other arm around her and held her tight.

"There has to be a reason why we're not supposed to look for him," she said. "Shit, he isn't even gone. Oh, crap, he's with Maura. But, I'm sure he's fine. He and Becky are both fine. But if he disappears..."

"When he disappears," Gregg corrected.

"*If* or when he disappears, he'll be fine." Mona sighed deeply. "So I guess all we can do is keep him near us, let him know how much we love him, and trust that he'll enjoy his life back with his Grannie and Grandpa. Are we supposed to say anything to him?"

"NO!" Gregg screamed. "No," he repeated, bringing it down a few decibels. "God, he'd be terrified, afraid to go out into the daylight, afraid that anyone or everyone will grab him..."

Mona snorted. "Not hardly; he'd try to find out who was trying to kidnap him and challenge him: dare him to try and take him away from his mother, father, and little sister."

Now Gregg snorted, "Or he'd search out whoever was gonna take him back to Grandpa and tell him to hurry up." Gregg inhaled deeply, slowly letting out his breath and his confession, "If I dinna love yer father so much, I'd be jealous. Those two have a surreal bond and I wouldna dream of subjugatin' it. But, I will start teachin' him self-defense."

31

"Well, I guess there's a bright side to this note. My father can claim his son and now Benji has an uncle and an aunt." Mona's tears were flowing. She grabbed the napkin and started blotting the wetness. "I knew I'd have to let my son go eventually, but I thought it would be to college or another woman. I never thought it'd be to my own father in the 18th century!"

"Well, Evie said he's fine so let's jest hope he finds someone there to make him happy. And maybe he'll send us a note..." Gregg and Mona both grabbed for the pile of unread letters. "We're just lookin' fer his handwritin', nothin' else," Gregg scolded.

"Right," Mona said as she took the seventh letter in the series. "And unless his penmanship improves, it shouldn't be too hard to spot. It looks like his granddad's only worse."

Ж

"Okay, I'll admit defeat," Mona said as she put down the last letter. They had scanned over every one twice, not reading ideas, but looking for the name Benji and his handwriting. They had found references to Benji, but only Jody speaking fondly of him when he was a child, with the hope that he would grow to be a fine man, one who would make his parents proud.

"I dinna think that it was some sick joke," Gregg said, voicing the concern that they both felt. "Who would have access to those letters except for a member of the family or someone verra close? And who would ken who Benji was? Well, anyone who kent yer father fer verra long would have heard him brag about his grandson..."

"No, I think it's legitimate," Mona said with a sigh. "I'll just make sure he knows how much we love him while he's with us. At least he's going back to a time, a place, which he's always missed. I just wish we knew more."

"Well," Gregg said gently, "if neither yer father nor Benji wrote about him bein' back there in these letters, and we ken that this is a comprehensive set, then it's because they dinna want us to ken. Sarah wouldna have written anythin' if Jody dinna want her to. But, it looks like yer brother got himself a sassy wife. I wouldna doubt that they have a child or two: she's warnin' ye like she would want to be warned. Come on; let's go check out the plumbin' situation. Ye tell me what ye need and I'll hand ye the tools or hold the flashlight, yer choice."

6 Surprise, Surprise
October 17, 1781
Pomeroys' Place

Sarah didn't complain as a rule, but I could tell something was bothering her. She didn't have any spark and sat down every chance she got. When I asked her what was wrong, she'd say, "Oh, nothing," or "I just don't feel quite right." She wasn't sick, but couldn't explain the fatigue or queasy stomach that had plagued her for the last two weeks.

"Lie down," I told her when she came in with an armload of kindling. Her non-specific frown of fatigue was just too much for me to ignore. It was time for me to confirm or dispel my suspicions.

She gave me a look that said, 'who's the doctor here?' but lay down on her bed and didn't say a word. I felt her forehead just to eliminate the possibility that she had a flu bug. Nope, she was fine. It was early autumn and the daytime temperatures had dropped. It was nice not being in a constant state of bake.

"What are you doing?" she asked indignantly as I felt her lower abdomen.

I grinned and said, "You stopped having periods quite a while back, didn't you?"

"You know I did," she replied curtly. "I told you how great it was. The hot flashes aren't any fun, but not having a monthly is a fair trade."

"But you haven't been having hot flashes, have you," I asked. I was enjoying this.

"No, not really; just a warm minute or two when I'm fatigued which, now that I think about it, happens all the time... Oh, crap," she said as realization hit. "How could that be?"

"I really don't think I need to tell a doctor how babies are made," I said.

"I mean, I'm 59 years old for God's sake."

"Yes, and according to my lovely eldest daughter, who is 24 by the way, I was 36 when I had her. That means that I was 60 when I had these lovely creatures. Remember, I told you to be careful, that the Fountain of Youth serum had certain, um, side effects, like fertility enhancement..."

33

"Yes, but I was careful," she interrupted. "I went and found the wild carrot seeds the very next day."

"Okay. I believe you. But, what was the first thing Jody did when he woke up after taking the, um, elixir?"

"He, we, oh, Lord," she said, and turned onto her side, hiding her head in her hands in a combination of embarrassment and disbelief.

"And, that was a short two months ago. So, I would say that you're having twins," I said, then paused for the full effect, "at least." I grinned at her and was glad to see her roll over onto her back and give me at least a seed of a smile. "Oh, you have no idea how sweet it is to tell you that," I said as I patted her on the shoulder.

"Yeah, well now I know how you felt," she carped. "I'm getting too old for this shit!" she grumbled as she sat up.

"Oh, no you're not," I argued in a singsong manner.

"What shite are ye gettin' too auld for?" Jody asked. He walked in with the rest of the firewood, set it down, and looked at Sarah, concerned and worried about her.

"I think I'm going to have to tie a bell around your ankle, my dear brother-in-law father-in-law," I said brightly. I grabbed a dishtowel and headed to the well. "I think Sarah has something to tell you. And, I think it would best be done without an audience."

7 The Best News

Jody set down his load of firewood and walked over to Sarah's side. "So, what is it that yer too auld fer?" he teased as he squatted down, moving as if he was going to lie down next to her.

"No, no, you don't," she admonished, her hand held high to stop his progress. "I'm getting up." She grunted as she struggled to rise, "if I can make it. My back seems to have come unhinged."

"Aye, I remember ye had that problem with Hope. Dinna ye say that the ligaments loosened up when ye were pregnant."

Jody saw Sarah's face drop at his words. "What? Are ye pregnant? Ye have been a bit peekish lately..."

Sarah didn't say a word, but Jody could see the answer in her face: the glow of pregnancy that he had subconsciously remembered when he mentioned their first child, Hope, was all about her. "Yer with child!" he whispered proudly, and reached over to help her rise. He gathered her into his arms and held her close. "I thought those days were behind us," he crooned into the hair behind her ear, rocking her back and forth with contentment.

Sarah basked in his comforting hold, glad that she didn't have to find the words to relay the shocking news that even she was having a hard time believing. "Those days *were* behind us," she said as she pulled her face away from his chest, "but that 'magic' water Evie gave you, and then me, two months ago, that 'Fountain of Youth' elixir, did a biological rewind."

Sarah could see the confused look on her husband's face and explained. "It was the same elixir Simon used on her when she had a fractured skull and broken back when she first came 'here' a year or so ago. Evie gave you the Fountain of Youth elixir to repair your body after the blood loss. I had given you a transfusion of Leah's blood, but it couldn't repair your renal—kidney—failure. So, Evie brought out that wee blue bottle she had 'lifted' from Master Simon. She dosed you with several drops of the elixir. She said that since age reversal had occurred when Master Simon had given it to her, she wanted me to take a few drops, too. If you *did* get younger, I would, too. Remember when we woke up..."

35

"Aye, I remember," mused Jody with a grin of satisfaction. He remembered it well: waking up alive, whole, and with his wife lying next to him, ready, willing, wanting, and now that he recalled it with his newfound information, more wet than normal. Her menopause had caused her to have vaginal dryness, but she was certainly moist and ready that warm afternoon two months ago.

"So, we made a baby that day?" he asked. "How can ye be sure it was that day? I mean, it isna as if we havena been together more than a few times since then..."

"I, I've been taking the wild carrot seeds since the day after. Evie warned me that enhanced fertility might result with the elixir. I didn't know if it was even possible, but I didn't think we needed to have a baby this late in our lives. I'm sorry; I should have discussed it with you first. It's just I thought of it more as a health issue, for both me and the baby. I mean, after the difficult pregnancies with Hope and Ramona... I mean, the only reason I was able to carry Mona to term was because of modern medicine. I didn't want to go through another loss like we had with Hope."

"Ach," Jody cajoled, "if the good Lord meant fer ye to be with child, I dinna think He means to take him away before he even has the chance to draw a breath."

"Well, that's the other thing," Sarah explained reluctantly. "According to my good sister Evie, it's going to be twins," she huffed and added with a smirk, "at least."

"Weel, I think we can handle as many bairns as the Lord sees fit to bless us with. I mean, we do have land, crops, and animals, a house, and family here to help us. It's more than we ever had before, aye?"

"Yes, that's true. If I can just keep the baby in me until term..."

"Babies," Jody corrected using the foreign name, to him, for bairns. "Ye'll be fine whether ye have one or two or, may the Lord bless us, three bairns in ye. Now, dinna despair, but remember the words ye gave yer sister: eat well, drink plenty of water, and put yer feet up several times during the day. Evie did fine, and so will we, I mean ye."

"We is right: you're just as pregnant as I am. It's just that I get the *pleasure*," Sarah rolled her eyes at the word, "of carrying the next generation of Pomeroys."

Jody gave his glowing wife a kiss then sighed in utter contentment. The Lord *did* work miracles, and Evie hadn't even had to sing for this one. "I'd better get back to work. If I stay

36

here, I'll be kissing on ye all day, and then, weel, ye ken how I tend to get carried away..." he said with a glint in his eye.

"Well, at least I won't have to worry about getting pregnant," Sarah snorted. "I'll give all my wild carrot seeds to Evie." Sarah saw the shock in Jody's eyes. "I know, I know," she explained. "You want Wallace to have his own biological children, but Evie needs a break, both physiologically and mentally, from being around so many babies. She's young enough, or at least her body is, that she has time to have at least a dozen more children, even if she has only one at a time."

"Aye, yer right, and it isna any of our business. Jest because ye give her the seeds fer birth control, doesna mean she has to take them. But yer wrong," Jody said then paused, waiting for the argument he was sure would come. But, Sarah was mute, and only dipped her head to him to suggest he finish his remark. "Wallace doesna care about the biological part. He jest likes havin' more children. Havin' five of them in the space of three months, and one of them fully grown, was a gift, he said. I'm happy with havin' so many bairns around, too. And, me a father again at nearly sixty!"

"Yeah, well, remember, I'm older than you. Just don't go making jokes about Sarah and Abraham," she remarked, and patted him on his back, urging him out the door.

Ж

Jody left the house with a spring to his step, almost skipping. He was making loud, almost scary, noises as he made his way to the barn. It was obviously his attempt at singing a psalm of praise. The words of thanksgiving were recognizable, but any semblance to a song was nonexistent. Jody knew he couldn't carry a tune, but was letting the Lord, and everyone else in a two-mile radius, know how happy he was.

"So, what am I going to do now?" Sarah whined when I reentered the house.

"Well, I suggest you eat right, drink lots of fluids, get plenty of rest, and stop wearing that corset! No, really, we probably have at least a few weeks before you need to find better clothes, or at least more appropriate to your condition, but the corset can't be good."

"Hmph," Sarah answered and turned toward the window, as if the sky held the answer to her new condition.

My flip explanation at what to do about her condition didn't remedy her bitter mood. "What's wrong?" I asked.

"I've been pregnant twice before. The first one didn't turn out well; I mean I didn't—couldn't—carry Hope to term.

She, she…" Sarah started to get choked up. She held up her hand when I started to tell her that she didn't have to continue. "Mona came out just fine, but they had to give me meds to relax my uterus so I wouldn't go into pre-term labor. Evie, what am I going to do? I'm already inadequate as a baby-bearing female, plus I'm old enough to be this child's, or these children's, great-grandmother! And that's the other concern. Twins cause extra stress on the womb and are often born early. How, what, I mean…"

Sarah's steely demeanor had buckled. "Hey," I counseled, "you forgot to add the equalizer into your unbalanced equation. Both you and I were enhanced, repaired, rejuvenated, all of the above…" I put my index finger under her chin, lifted her face, and looked into her bleary red and amber eyes. "I was fine and had three babies. You'll be fine with two. And remember, you've got lots of help now."

Sarah sniffed and wiped her eyes then ran her fingers through her hair in her classic gesture of trying to compose herself and her hair at the same time. "Besides," I threw in, "what are you going to do about it? I still believe that if God didn't want me to have these three babies, and you to have those two, *at least*," I grinned, "then you wouldn't be in this condition. Babies may be surprises at times, but they are NOT accidents, *capisce?*"

"*Capisce*," she said, slightly humbled, but no longer depressed.

Ж

"Sarah, where did you stash the FOY water?" I asked. We were alone, and I had a theory I wanted to investigate.

Sarah looked around and made sure Jenny hadn't sneaked in. "Yes, we're alone," I verified.

She reached up and pulled out a piece of the stone façade on the fireplace, almost dead center above the fire pit. "Here," she said as she put the blue facet cut bottle containing the Fountain of Youth water in my hand. "You don't want to take any more, do you?" she asked.

"Hell, no! I mean, heaven's no," I said, and then brought my sound level down a few dozen decibels. "It's just that I know approximately how much I initially consumed, at least from what Master Simon told me. He said I sucked down almost a whole bottle. I only dosed you and Jody with a few drops each. However, I'd swear this bottle was almost full when I had you put aside for safekeeping last summer when I came back from my hospital trip to 2013."

"Yes, at least that's what I remember," Sarah confirmed.

"Look, it's almost gone now. I think that storing it near the heat concentrated the elixir. That would explain why the small dose I gave you and Jody had such profound results. I only meant to heal him, but your dose was so if he got younger, then you would, too." I opened the bottle that was barely one quarter full and pulled out the little glass rod I had used as a dropper. "See, it's almost caramel-colored now. I think you'd better find a more temperate hiding place. I don't want it to freeze either."

Sarah sighed, then grinned, happy that she had an answer to her own dilemma. "I had Jody make a hollow spot in the footboard of our bed for some of his, um, precious items. Only he and I know about it, but I think someone else should know, too. I'll put this in here. I don't think our bedroom area will get down to freezing. Or at least I hope it doesn't."

"Okay; here, you're the keeper of the juice again," I said and handed back the youth and health enhancing elixir.

"And you, dear sister, are the keeper of the secret of the coins and nuggets. Jody managed to obtain some rare coins and a few sizable gold nuggets a while back. We've managed to turn them over in the last ten years or so. Sometimes there are more, like if he makes a good wager or profits in some other way. Other times, we've been essentially wiped out. We use them for emergencies, like to buy arms or someone's freedom, or for major purchases." Sarah shirked her shoulder and admitted, "Well, that's how we got this place. If Jody is ever held hostage, he told me to let him have a moderate amount of time to get himself out of his predicament, but if it looked dire, I was to use my own judgment on how much to use to keep him from the gallows." Sarah shuddered at the thought.

"The nuggets are nice because they're different sizes, and their value is pretty straightforward. The coins, well," Sarah looked at my pendent, the one Wallace had made from an ancient Greek silver drachma, the token that had allowed me to travel forward to the 21st century, and then back to my family in the 18th, "we didn't know at the time that they had other merits. We have a few more just like those, and they're not going anywhere, at least in that format. Jody would melt them down and use them as teaspoons before he'd allow just anyone to have one. But regardless, unless something horrible happens, they're safe where they are. We're fine with the goods that God has allowed us to have. We work hard and He rewards us. And, that's how it should be."

8 What's a Woman To Do?
Late spring, 1782

The months went by quickly for the lady in waiting. Sarah never puked once, although she admitted she got queasy when she smelled bacon or sausage cooking. "Okay, we're having grits and eggs in deference to the babies," I announced then laughed. I added, "I wouldn't doubt that those kids—I mean children—you're carrying will want a pet pig instead of a dog. The smell of cooked pork seems to upset them."

I designed and constructed a day coat, sort of a dress, for Sarah. "See," I bragged as I pointed out the extra seams. "This will grow as you grow. Just a few snip, snips, and the gown will be one size larger. I've allowed for four increases. I hope it won't be too bulky in the side seams for now, but I guarantee it's going to make you feel better later. Shoot, you probably won't even have to cut the seams—they'll probably pop apart by themselves. I only used basting stitches.

Ж

Sarah was now well into her eighth month. She asked me several times a week, sometimes even a couple of times a day, to listen for the babies' heartbeats. Of course, I always obliged her. I knew all was well with the physical aspects of her pregnancy, but her mental health was just as important. Her confidence level was definitely under the influence of hormones. "Would you check again," Sarah would ask, always using the same words and same gestures, a nod to the rolled up parchment, then a weak, insecure smile.

"Okay," I replied again this morning. I spent the next five minutes playing submarine hunter, using the improvised stethoscope as a sonar detector. "I can hear two rapid heartbeats, clear as a bell. They're both strong, but about half a beat off of each other in rhythm. That one little guy sure moves around a lot. You ought to name him Neptune. He's sure at home in the water. And no, one of the beats isn't yours. I checked your pulse, and it isn't nearly as fast as theirs."

"Well, it least that part's normal," she said with *reliefignation*, her own custom mixed emotion of relief and resignation.

40

"Duh! Everything is normal *and* healthy with this pregnancy. Now, your body was 'rewound' enough to get pregnant," I began again with the same speech I gave every time...

"And stay pregnant," Sarah added with a voice of confidence, her lines spoken like a pro.

"And stay pregnant," I continued my part of the speech, "so I'm sure the delivery will be a snap. Come on," I said, taking a break from my 'it's all going to be fine' routine, "do you feel good enough to take a walk? It's a beautiful day out."

"Sure," she replied as she put her hands on the arms of the new rocking chair Jody had crafted for her. She leaned forward and I remained at her elbow, ready to help her stand. "Uh, I feel a draft," she said as she stood up all the way. "Oh crap, I think my water broke."

"No, it's too early," I argued, "I mean, it's only March, right?"

"It's April first," replied Sarah dismally.

"Right," I said, "April Fool's Day, hardy har har..."

"No, really," she explained, "I have the lower back ache and..."

I moved behind her to look at the back of her skirt. "Oh shit, I mean, oh amniotic fluid," I said, and then started to giggle.

"I can't have the babies yet—it's too soon!" Sarah whined, as if she begged me for it not to be so, then it wouldn't be.

"Let's see, you got pregnant about August 20th. Subtract three months and add five days so...May 25th due date and crap, Sarah: today is the last day of April, not the last day of March. You're only about three and a half weeks early. That's not too bad for twins. But, you stay put, just the same, and I'll get you some clouts. I remember how irritating, I mean frustrating, it was to have that mess dribbling down between your legs..."

"Is Grannie gonna have her babies today?" Jenny asked as she popped in the door, "'cause if she is, I want to help. I never saw people babies comin' out, just dogs and goats and baby chicks."

"Chickens are hatched, not born," I corrected.

"Well, they sure come out makin' a lot of noise, more than baby dogs..."

"Puppies," I interrupted in order to correct her.

"Uh, huh, that's right. I forgots. Hey, can Grannie have the babies without Grandpa? Isn't he supposed to be here? I mean, I'm sure he'd want to be here..."

41

"Well, he was here for the most important part," Sarah said, softly enough for me to hear, but hopefully not by my little Miss Perception.

"Did he share his present with you?" Jenny asked. "Is that why you're gonna have the babies?"

The look of innocent awe and wonder on her face was priceless. Sarah took a deep breath, hoping to say something profound, or at least convincingly evasive. She looked into Jenny's inquisitive eyes, and was deflated by her pure and undemanding curiosity. "Yes," she said simply. "Now, would you get me a drink of water?" she asked. "I'm real thirsty all of a sudden."

"Yes, Grannnie," Jenny trilled, then grabbed a cup from the sideboard, and filled it from the ewer. "I'll get some more water, too." She hustled out of the room, but paused once outside and carefully shut the door behind her so she didn't wake the babies.

"How long do you think it would take you to ride to Julian's?" Sarah asked, "I mean, if you rode as fast as you could?"

"Shoot, I don't know, an hour and a half, why?" I looked at Sarah, but she wouldn't lift her head to look at me. "Why?" I repeated firmly. Now I was playing the role of doctor and big sister.

"Because I think he can be of help here. He did great with you when I burned my hands and, and..."

"And you don't think I can handle delivering you of twins while watching out for my three plus Jenny? Duh! Remember, Jenny is the helper in this. She can do just about anything I can with those babies but nurse them. And, they all can sip from a cup, and are doing a great job with eating solid food. Shoot, I only nurse them three times a day anymore. And, that's for birth control as much as anything. I mean, I gotta admit, I like the way it feels, and the bonding is nice and, crap, I'm rambling. Sorry. What I *can* do is have Jenny ride over to get Leah and James. I don't think he wanted to go into town with the other men since she's so close to her time, too. If she can ride in the wagon, she can be here in fifteen minutes, tops. Now do you feel better?" I asked, although I could already see that she did.

"That damned town hall meeting!" Sarah cursed. "Why did it have to be now? I swear those, those, *assholes,*" she whispered the designation, "set up the election for now. They knew we were having a baby."

"Babies," I corrected with a grin.

"Well, Jody didn't let on that we were having twins..."

"At least," I interrupted with a laugh at the slim possibility she was having triplets, then backed it down a notch. "No, I'm sorry, I shouldn't make light of it. I'm positive everything will be fine. And, I doubt the next generation of Pomeroys will be here too soon. I mean, I would guess you're going to have at least six hours or more of labor. You haven't even started the real thing yet, have you?" I asked, although I was pretty sure I was correct. I could see her belly firming up with fairly regular contractions, but she didn't look miserable enough to be in true labor yet.

"No," she said crossly. "I want to get it over with, but I want Jody here, too. He wasn't able to be with me with the first two..."

And then Sarah broke into a thousand pieces, each one wetter and more trembling than the other.

"All I can do is help with the clinical aspects, but I'll send Jenny to the Melbourne's right away," I said. "If James believes that Leah can ride in the wagon with Jenny for assistance, then he can go into town and get Jody. I'm sure Wallace can speak for the two of them, if needed. I doubt there is any political issue in this new America, or in the world, or anyone or, or *anything,* that would keep Jody from being here with you for the delivery, *capisce?*"

"*Capisce,*" Sarah agreed then started to compose herself, wiping and sniffing away her outward signs of weakness.

"What's *capisce?*" asked Jenny as she walked in with fresh water and a basket of eggs. She set them on the sideboard and waited for our answer.

"Do you understand," I answered, meaning that was the definition of the word.

"No, I don't understand. That's why I asked. What's *capisce?*" she asked again, this time with a slight tinge of frustration.

I was beginning to feel like I should start the 'who's on first' dialog with her a la Abbott and Costello. "Depending on what inflection you use, *capisce* means 'do you understand' or 'yes, I understand.' *Capisce?*"

"*Capisce!*" Jenny declared. "Oh, and I got the eggs before my brothers could get them. Leo and Judah found one this morning and were trying to eat it, shell and all! But, don't worry, I got it before they could put it in their mouths or even break it. But, they sure cried when I took it away," she explained.

Before Jenny could catch her second wind on the tale of the two toddlers and the egg, I interrupted. "Would you ride over

43

to your Big Sister Leah's and ask her to come help me with Grannie? And, have your Big Brother James go to town to get Grandpa Jody."

I liked to use family designations with the given names whenever I spoke with Jenny. She never dimmed in her delight of having a family. Pride may be a sin, but in this case, it was pure happiness, was based on the love of her new family, the close-knit group she had been deprived of in her younger years.

"Okay, I'll take Prince Charles and ride over as fast as I can." Jenny ran to me and grabbed me around the waist, "I love you, Mommy," she said, then bounced over to Sarah. "I love you, Grannie." Then she put her face down to her grandmother's belly and spoke to the wee inhabitants within, "And I love you, too, my little aunts or uncles!" She waved broadly, grabbed a cookie off the plate on the table, saluted us with it, and bounced through the doorway, pulling the door shut softly in consideration of her napping siblings.

In all of about thirty seconds, Jenny was back. "Mommy, Mommy! Grandpa Julian is here, and he brought my sister Leah with him!" she shouted, obviously forgetting about her sleeping brothers and sister.

I scurried down the steps to intercept Julian and my eldest, and very pregnant, daughter. *What was I thinking when I asked Jenny to go get her? Leah was huge and looked ready to foal at any time, too.* "Leah," I scolded aloud, "you shouldn't be out riding!"

"Well, maybe not horseback riding," she puffed as she approached the steps, "but I thought a wagon ride would be acceptable. I had Wesley ride over to get Julian so he could bring me here." Leah looked right at me, and then I could see there was another reason she was here. "I wanted Sarah to, um, check me, that is if she's up to it."

Julian helped Leah to the porch bench seat then took the break in conversation as an opportunity to excuse himself. "Well, if you don't need anything else, I'll be getting back to the ranch. I sent Wesley back to Leah's place since James is with Wallace, and Jody's in town. He can take care of their stock while they're gone. I don't want to leave José by himself. We have two nannies ready to kid."

"Well, I'd appreciate it if you'd stay here, for a few hours at least," I asked. "Sarah's water just broke, and I might need a hand. She's ready to 'kid', too!" I joked nervously.

"You didn't burn *your* hands, did you?" Julian asked, recalling his forced indenture as midwife at my delivery when

Sarah burned her palms. She had grasped a hot pot while I was in labor. Julian, the man with the smallest hands among my three attendants—Jody and Wallace being the other two—was drafted into helping me bear two of my three babies that evening.

"No, my hands are fine. But, four hands are better than two," I argued.

"Yes, and you have Leah here to help you," Julian countered as he watched Leah move awkwardly from the bench into the house.

"Yes, and with her we have the potential for another 'kid' popping out real soon. Now really, Julian," I argued, "How close do you think she could get to Sarah to pull out a baby? Did you see that gut, I mean baby belly? She's almost as big as Sarah, and she's only having one!"

Julian sighed, "Okay, once again, you've won me over with one part logic and two parts passion; I'll stay."

I walked with Julian to the barn to unhitch the wagon. Neither of us spoke nor needed to. I was glad I didn't have to convince him to stay and that he hadn't argued that he should be allowed to return home. I put out some hay for his horse while he took off the leather and brass accruements. "But, understand this," he said suddenly, "I'm only here as the backup. I'm sure that between you and Leah, you'll be able to take care of this. I'll just boil water or help Jenny with the babies. Where is my godson by the way? I haven't seen him in a month, at least."

"It's only been two weeks, but he misses you, too. James let him have that laminated photo of your portrait. He showed it to him when he was fussy. It calmed him right down. But, when he took it away, Judah screamed and cried so much that James let him have it back. He sneaked it away when he was asleep, but you're not going to believe this, Judah searched for it when he woke up. 'Poppi, Poppi,' he screamed, and wouldn't stop. I finally had Jenny ride over to James's place to get it back. I made him a little pocket in his blanky to keep it safe. I'd like to take it out and put something less intriguing in its place, but he'd know the difference."

"Yes, he's pretty bright," bragged Julian as he leaned on the ledge of the wooden half door, looking out at the corral.

"Yes, bright and passionate, just like his Poppi," I replied with a smirk.

"Evie..." Julian scolded, his voice stretching the two syllables of my name into a mini lecture on propriety and good manners.

"I know, I know," I replied, then moved over to plant a big kiss on his cheek. "But, there isn't anyone here but the two of us. Now," I whispered close to his face as I looked around to make sure that my second-generation silent spot, Jenny, hadn't crept in without notice. "I want you to know that if I had come here as a gay man, I would have given José a run for his money..." I said lustily, and smacked him on the behind.

"Evie!" Julian blurted out, totally surprised and shocked. He hadn't expected flirtation from a woman, any woman, much less his daughter-in-law. Julian had long ago accepted that I was unpredictable and had a very progressive set of morals, totally alien to this time period. But, I guess I had stepped over the line with the much too familiar fanny fanning.

I turned away from him, not wanting to hear a lecture or even see the stern look that would be the abbreviated version. "Julian, you're hot," I said sassily. "I just thought I'd remind you in case José hasn't told..."

I froze. "I'm sorry," I whispered as I paled, suddenly aware of what I had just said and done. I turned around to beg forgiveness, my mouth moving open and shut but the words stuck in my throat. The tears started to flow. "I, I don't know why I said that. It was totally inappropriate. I, I guess I'm stressed. I mean, I meant what I said, but I shouldn't have said it. I guess the filter on my brain mouth connection failed. Will you forgive me?" I asked with complete sincerity, my hands clutched together under my chin, essentially begging from a foot away, slowly lowering myself into a kneeling position.

Julian looked around and saw we were still alone and that I was not only distraught, I was panicked. He reached out and pulled me up from my half-lowered position, unclenching the hand I had tucked in front of my neck. He placed one arm lightly around my shoulders and pulled me close, but a respectable distance close. I heard my father-in-law tell me, "I don't know why, but yes, I forgive you." He released his open aired hug and looked me in the eyes, bringing up his thumb to gently wipe away the tears from my cheeks. He didn't add anything to his words but leaned in again and placed his left hand on my right shoulder. This time, it was my peer who wiped the hair off my brow and gave me a firm and, if it was possible to be given there, passionate kiss on my forehead. His hands dropped to his side and he stepped back, ending his gesture with a nod, a wink, and a smile. I think he felt the same way.

Ж

"I'm sure glad Leah decided to come and visit today," Sarah told me when I came back in. She had set out a tray of fresh clouts, medical alcohol, and a small jar of oil on the little table next to the window.

"You forgot; Leah *knows*. She's faster and more reliable than a cell phone. At least her powers aren't affected by sunspots," I added with a smile. "Now, if you think you could bend over low enough, would you check her? That's why she came, or so she said. I've never done a pelvic and don't know what to feel for."

"Go get her," Sarah instructed with a shrug. "She's out there with Jenny and the babies. I'm doing fine, but I'm definitely feeling the contractions now." My eyes opened extra wide at the new revelation. "But, I'm not ready for the breathing yet," she answered in response to my slightly fearful stare.

I didn't have to go far to find all of my girls in one place. Leah was making over the cute little spit curl that Jenny had put in Wren's hair. "Jenny, I need to have Leah come with me. Now, she's probably going to spend the night here so you'll have lots of time together, okay?"

"'Kay," she replied as she picked up Leo and ran her fingers through his sparse hair, obviously evaluating the chance of getting his hair into a fancy 'do.

"Okay, up here, young lady," Sarah called to Leah when we came in. "This is where your mother had her babies and where I'm going to have mine, God willing, and yours, too."

"Well, I hope you have yours first," Leah remarked as she adjusted her skirts. "I'm not ready for this, I mean..." Leah looked over to me with absolute terror in her eyes as she stopped in midsentence. I saw that she was 'reading' again.

She had done it many times before and told me about it just days after she got here. "It's spooky, Mom, knowing 'stuff' about people. I don't want to 'peek' into the private parts of their lives, but it's just 'there.'"

"But, it happens to you all the time, doesn't it?" I knew Leah was psychic to a degree. Of course, there was no way I could know what it was like for her.

"I subconsciously tune out most everything, but this is different." She leaned in to tell me what I already knew. "I 'read' about her in books!"

I nodded and added, "I did, too. I remember everything, I think. The first memories I had when I got to this house were of her and Jody, just like I had read in the Sinclaire novels."

Sarah hadn't noticed Leah's insecurity. She had other concerns. She sighed and said in exasperation, "Now, if you'll excuse me a moment, I *thought* I was ready. I'll be right back. Damn, that'll be the best part of not being pregnant. I'll be able to hold my water for longer than twenty minutes at a time!" She steadied herself on the doorframe, then walked toward the privy with an exaggerated waddle that I was sure meant that one of the babies had dropped down further into the birth canal.

"What's wrong," I asked Leah when I was sure Sarah was out of earshot.

Leah said, "I almost asked her about her first delivery. God, I didn't want her to have to recall it!"

"Well, she probably already has. I mean, she's been frightened about this pregnancy ever since she found out about it."

"Well, I definitely didn't want her to know that I knew about the first one!"

"Yes, but since she knows that you have 'the sight,' she wouldn't be shocked, at least not much, if you did know. Now, relax, okay?" I said, and helped her lie back on the chaise.

Sarah came back from her potty break. "Sorry for the delay. Looks like you're ready." She placed the stool at the end of the chaise between Leah's raised knees. I held her hand as she sat down carefully.

She was willing, but not necessarily able, to perform Leah's evaluation. She bent forward and found that her belly was in the way. She stood up again and nudged the stool with her foot to the side of the chaise where I helped her sit down again. She sat parallel to Leah, then reached in sideways, finally able to perform her awkward pelvic exam.

I stood at the head of the couch and looked in awe at Leah, my eldest, and very pregnant daughter, as she got checked. I didn't remember her as an infant, but the bond was still there. And, now she was going to make me a grandmother. I watched as her hazel eyes widened in shock. I followed her stare. She was looking at her midwife doctor, Sarah.

Sarah never could hide her emotions, ever, and right now, she wasn't even trying to.

"What?" I asked. "Don't tell me you found a fist!" I hissed in fear. That had happened to me. Judah came out fine, but that wasn't always the result.

"No, no fist," Sarah said slowly, "but we have a lot of centimeters, about five."

"How much effaced?" I asked.

48

"Um, fifty percent, I'd say. It's kind of hard to get in there just right. I'm not used to doing an examination sidesaddle," she said as she wiped off her hand.

"But, I could stay this way for days," Leah argued, but with no one save herself. "Shoot, for all we know, I've been this way for days, weeks even!"

"Have you been having sexual relations?" Sarah asked clinically, her eyes unblinking and callous.

If I hadn't heard the change in her tone, and seen that Sarah hadn't moved, I'd swear another person had come into the room and swapped bodies with her.

Leah blushed, gulped, looked at me in embarrassment, and then up at Sarah.

"Never mind," Sarah said coldly. "It doesn't make any difference now, does it? But I hope you enjoyed it at least six weeks' worth, because that's the last time your husband's..."

"Sarah!" Leah and I screeched at the same time, interrupting the completion of her description of James's genitalia and report on their recent intimacy.

"Oh, I'm sorry," Sarah said, then froze.

"Did I really just say that?" she asked after a very long moment, her face still scarlet in embarrassment.

"Well, you started to..." I replied, then paused, filling the air with an awkward emptiness. Evidently, I wasn't the only one who had an alter ego taking over with the stress of babies coming.

I took a deep breath to recover. "Hey, Leah, get up," I announced to change the theme and atmosphere of the conversation. "Turnabout's fair play, eh, Sarah? Let's see if she can check you. I mean, Leah, you see how dilated and effaced, or whatever, she is, then scoot over and I'll see, or rather feel, what all this measuring stuff is all about. I mean, I know what a centimeter is, and effacement is the thinning of the cervix, but I need a baseline..."

"Ugh," Sarah carped, "the ultimate indignation: having my yah-yah felt up by my daughter-in-law and granddaughter."

"Or sister and niece," I suggested, "depending on which hat I'm wearing today. Actually, I'm feeling more sisterly than daughterly," I said, then punched her in the upper arm.

"Well, that makes it easier. I forget sometimes that you're really the same age as me."

"Yeah, well try it from my point of view," Leah interjected. "She's my mother, my 'biological, I came out from

49

between those thighs' mother, and she looks like she's my little sister!"

"How about if I grab a few pieces of charcoal and draw old age wrinkles on my face, and maybe a wart or two; would that make you two whiners feel better?" I asked.

Sarah and Leah shared a look with each other, nodded, then answered, "Yes," as one. Leah waddled over to the fireplace and kicked out a small piece of burnt wood. She leaned to the right, then to the left, and then tried to squat down to get it.

"Forget it!" I said after stifling my giggles for a full half minute. She looked like a monkey in a fat suit trying to reach a handful of nuts on the ground. "You'll just have to remember who I am, because I am *not* painting on a mask. We don't want to scare the babies when they come out now, do we?"

Leah tried one more time to squat down and grab the charcoal, then winced and yelped, biting off a scream of pain.

"What happened? I asked.

"I think I pulled a muscle. I can't move. Oh, shit! That's what I get for trying to make you put on the mask. Shit, shit, shit! I can't move!" she cursed through clenched jaws.

"Hold on," I said. I ran to the door and called, "Jenny, come here, stat!" then came back to Leah's side to see if I could help her move to the chair.

"No!" she screamed. "Sorry, I'll just stand. It's just a muscle spasm; it'll pass."

"How are you going to check Sarah then?" I asked.

"Uh, ooh, shit, I mean shoot. Jenny, what are you doing here?" she yelped, embarrassed at being caught cursing in front of her little sister, the great 'appearing act,' who had suddenly popped into the room.

"Mommy called me and told me to come stat. That means right away. I know lots of words. Mommy and Daddy teach me new words all the time. Daddy's even teaching me Latin and José teaches me Spanish. "*¿Como estas?*" Jenny asked, showing off some of her new language skills.

"*Tengo dolor, mucho dolor,*" Leah replied haltingly. "That means I'm in a lot of pain. Would you help me to the chair, *la silla?*"

"Okay," Jenny said, and moved in next to her arm. "Are you okay?" she asked. "Your face looks funny. Is the baby hurting you? Grannie says her babies kick her something fierce. But, they don't hurt, not really."

"No, my baby isn't hurting me any more than usual. I just bent over the wrong way and pulled a muscle. Help me sit down over here, would you?" Leah asked haltingly in between yelps of pain.

It took Jenny and me a couple of minutes to get it accomplished, but Leah was finally seated. "Nobody talk for a minute, please," she asked, her face flushed from the pain. She shut her eyes, cautiously straightened her back, then carefully set the back of her hands on her knees, or as close as she could get to them. She touched her middle fingertips to the ends of her thumbs in the classic yoga pose of peace. "Ah ohm, ah ohm," she chanted between deep, calming breaths.

Jenny was standing by the door, both of her hands clasped over her mouth to contain the giggles that were trying to squeeze out. I didn't know which one was more comical, Leah or Jenny, but they were both cute.

Leah finally stopped her mantra, took what I recognized as her final deep cleansing breath, and then smiled, evidently pain-free, as she opened her eyes. "Doing yoga breathing for practice?" I asked. "You know, it won't be too long and you'll be doing the Lamaze breathing," I added.

"Yeah, I know, don't remind me," she answered with a face contorted between a grin, grimace, and a glare at me for bringing up the inevitable.

"Hey, you're only bringing one into the world. You have it easy. And speaking of bringing into the world, do you think you can check Sarah now?" I asked.

"Climb on board the BBB," Leah intoned like a cartoon character train conductor, adding a mimed elbow pull of the train whistle. "The Baby Birthing Bed, two babies, coming up!"

"At least!" I added in a high-toned comic voice as I held onto Sarah's elbow.

"Can I watch?" Jenny asked, unintentionally bringing the silly mood back to seriousness.

I looked at Leah, then we both looked at Sarah for the answer. "Come up here by my head," Sarah said. "You can watch from up here with me. Besides, I want you to hold my hand," she added, and put the back of her right hand on her shoulder in an invitation for Jenny to join her at the head of the chaise.

"Okay," Jenny chirped, and we all relaxed, the tension released.

"Alrighty now, how close are your contractions?" Leah asked Sarah as she arranged the skirts over her knees.

"I don't know? I wish I had a watch with a second hand. Every time I start to count, I lose track. Ooh, there's one now."

51

Leah's hand had been on Sarah's belly. She felt the contraction and immediately moved her hand up between Sarah's legs to check her cervix.

"Shit, I mean shoot; that hurts!" Sarah yelped.

I snorted, but didn't say a word. Her eyes cut to mine. "You're enjoying this, aren't you?" she said sternly.

"Oh, yeah," I drolled, "but you told me that you 'had' to check for dilation during a contraction, right?"

"Yes, right. Leah, why don't you change places with your mother? She needs to see, or rather feel, what's going on. How many centimeters am I?"

Leah replied with widened eyes, "Five and about fifty percent effaced."

Sarah's face fell as fast as mine did, I'm sure.

"What's five and fifty mean?" Jenny asked.

"That's, uh," I stuttered in shock, "Um, that's how 'ripe' your sister and Grannie are. I mean, how ready their bodies are to let the babies go. They're both going to be ready at the same time, I think," I answered aloud, then prayed silently, 'but I hope not.' "Would you go check on your siblings?" I asked in order to dismiss Jenny. I didn't want to field any more female physiology questions.

"Isn't this where we make bets on who pops first?" Leah asked, a false lilt in her voice.

"Yeah, a pool with bets on times, weights, and genders. Although, we have more possibilities to bet on than people to bet," I said.

"I still say you're going to have a girl," Sarah told Leah. "Didn't you say that there hasn't been a son born to any of your maternal ancestors since..."

"Since anyone can remember, at least until my baby brothers," Leah said.

Sarah saw the sad look on my face and said, "Sorry, I forgot that you don't remember."

"What?" I mocked brightly with feigned jocularity. "You forgot that I forgot? Ah, don't worry about it," I said sincerely. "It's true. I don't want to know anything about my past life, but anything before that, like ancestors who I never interacted with personally, is fine. No, Leah is mine, and that's all I need to know. The life the two of us share as mother and daughter started a year ago, and that's good enough for me."

"You're afraid to remember, aren't you?" Leah asked gently.

"Hey," I said defensively, "how would you like it if you suddenly found out you had an adult daughter, an ex-husband, and God only knows how many skeletons in your closet, that someone else knows all about them, but you don't, and probably never will? How do you think James would take it? Aren't you happy now? With this new baby coming, a new home, a, a..."

"Sorry!" Leah blurted out. "I wasn't trying to bring up old shit...Jenny! How do you do that? I swear," Leah huffed when she saw that Jenny was back.

Sarah and I nodded in agreement: yes, Leah swore too much. Leah saw us and shot the two of us a dirty look then continued. "I think, I think...that every time a cuss word comes out of my mouth, you pop up," she said to Jenny.

"Grandpa taught me to be real quiet. At least he told me about me dragging my foot. He said that being quiet might save my life sometime." Jenny giggled. "But, he said sometimes it was good for other stuff, too, like hunting and fishing, and catching Grannie sneaking cookies..."

"I did not!" Sarah blurted. "Well," she admitted, "maybe just a few. The babies were hungry."

"So, Leah," I asked, in order to change the subject, "how about you do the counting so we can find out how far apart Grannie's contractions are?"

"I wish I had a watch with a stopwatch function, even a second hand would be nice. I left mine..." she said, then stopped suddenly before letting on where the watch was: back in the 21st century.

"Is the second hand the little skinny red one on Brother James's watch?" Jenny asked.

"Yes..." all three adult women answered at the same time. "Why?" I asked.

"Because he let me borrow his watch for a science experiment. See," she said, and pulled it out of her pocket. "He wanted me to see how fast I could run back and forth from the porch to the barn and back again. I'm supposed run every hour to see how many seconds it takes. I'm supposed to write it down here." Jenny took out a scrap of paper and a small pencil like the ones they gave out at miniature golf courses. "I'm supposed to let him know if I'm faster before or after I eat, or earlier in the day or later. Then he says he's going to show me how to make a graph or gaf; I can't remember the word exactly."

"Yes, the word is graph, but could you do the science experiment later?" I asked. "We need to use the watch."

"Here," Jenny said, holding out James's Rolex. "Do you need me to help? I can time stuff. I timed how many drops of sap came out of the trees in the spring so we could figure the rate of flow. I also timed how fast a stick floated from the big rock to the bridge. That was measuring speed or rate per second. Brother James said I'm real bright with some of my studies."

"Okay, you can time Grannie's contractions. Now, when her tummy gets hard, you note what time it is, including seconds. Here, she's having one now," I said and nodded to her to check the watch.

Jenny placed her hand next to mine on her Grannie's belly, and then announced, "She's all done," at the end of the contraction.

"Fine, do you remember what time it was?" I asked.

"10:30 and twenty seconds," Jenny said. "Now what?"

"We wait for the next one. The time that it starts is what we need to know. From the start of one contraction to the start of the next one is the time between contractions...how far apart they are. They usually start at about fifteen or twenty minutes apart, and then get down to one minute or less."

"There it is!" Jenny announced when she felt Sarah's next contraction start. "It's 10:35 and 25 seconds. That's, um, five minutes and five seconds apart, right?"

"Right," I said. "Now, Leah, are you having regular contractions yet?"

"I don't know about regular, but yes on the contractions. I thought they were just Braxton Hicks, though," she said.

"Braxton hiccups?" Jenny asked, her face contorted in amazement.

"No, let's just call them false labor pains," Leah said. All three adult women realized that misters Braxton and Hicks, or was that Dr. Braxton Hicks, probably weren't even born yet.

"Labor pains?" Jenny asked. "Do they hurt?"

"Not yet, but they probably will later," Leah huffed.

"Most likely will," Sarah said dejectedly. "I never had a spinal, and I know it's not possible now, but a small part of me would like that option."

"I agree, but I'll pass on the needle and take the discomfort, not pain...remember, that's what you always said about labor, Mom. Oops, sorry."

Leah grimaced, realizing too late that she had just brought up my past life again.

54

"I mean, I'll take the discomfort for a few hours rather than be away from you and you and here," she said, proud of all her female family members gathered in the room.

"So, am I the designated nanny?" Julian asked as he walked into the house, Judah in his arms, toddling Wren and Leo clutching his pant legs.

Julian was smiling, radiant with love at being in the presence of his grandchildren. He saw the apprehension about the coming events in the women's eyes, and his face fell. He recalled the difficulty Evie had delivering Wee Julian who had decided to come into the world fist first. He gave his godson an extra squeeze of thanksgiving and said a silent prayer that Sarah's twins would arrive without complications.

"If you don't mind, yes, would you and Jenny see to the wee three?" I asked. "It's going to be a long day. I'm not sure, but it looks like you're going to be a great-grandpa today: Leah might be in labor, too. Only time will tell, but she's not going to be a lot of help here."

"Sorry!" Leah blurted out angrily, then added with absolutely no sincerity, "I didn't do it on purpose!" She sniffed back the tears she hadn't planned on shedding, then added humbly, "At least delivering early. I did want to get pregnant. I just didn't think that it would happen so quickly, both getting pregnant and then going into labor."

We were all stunned by Leah's surprisingly emotional eruption. I walked over to her and held her diagonally, my belly pressed to the side of hers, our faces close to one another. "Honey, I think we're all going through a very stressful time here today. I mean, your little outburst, Sarah's, ahem, personal remarks, and even I haven't been myself today," I said.

I glanced over at Julian and gave him another look of apology. He nodded that he understood, and I took a deep breath. "So, if Poppi will watch the babies, I'll get my little crash course in midwifery. Maybe we'll have a couple of babies, or more, by sunrise."

"What about me?" Jenny asked, her face full of frown. "Don't you need me?"

"Of course, we do," I said. I brought her over to her sister's other side and we shared the Leah sandwich hug. "You get to run back and forth, to be the expediter, and can even help Poppi cook."

"We still have some potatoes left. Can I chop them up and make hash browns? Huh? Can I?"

"You can talk to your Poppi about the menu. In the meantime, would you time your sister Leah's contractions? I want to see if they're consistent."

"Okay. Are you ready, Leah? I have to wait for the contraction before I can time it," Jenny said with administrative authority.

Well, Jenny waited and timed Leah's contractions while I took Sarah for a walk. Sarah's labor was progressing rapidly. At least we didn't have to worry about timing her. I never got my lesson on what to feel for with dilation and effacement, but it really wasn't too hard to figure out. Sarah got to the huffing and puffing stage, and even the foot massages weren't helping. "We have to wait for Jody," she shouted, "Shit, this hurts!"

"Shut up and breathe," I ordered. "In, out, in, out. Focus."

"Focus, schmocus, son of a bitchin'..." she huffed.

"Shush! Jenny's here," I said. "If you talk during a contraction, you'll pay for it in pain. There, it's done," I told her when her belly softened. "Now, next time, listen to me. Here," I bent down and picked up the elusive charcoal piece that Leah had tried to retrieve earlier in the day. "When a contraction hits, I want you to breathe in and out slowly, and concentrate on the dot inside of this circle." I drew a small circle within a bigger one on the hearth then wiped my hands on a cloth. "Jenny, how's your sister doing?"

"She says she's all over the charts, whatever that means. She can't talk now because she's having another 'traction," Jenny said.

I hastily poured alcohol over my hands and rushed to her side. "Let me check you," I said, pushing her skirt back over her knees.

Leah continued her huffing and puffing. Her concentration so intense that she never acknowledged my presence. She realized I was there, though, when the extra pang of pain caused by my finger on her cervix brought forth the word, "Shit!" from her mouth.

She finished her breathing regimen, and blew out a quick sentence. "None of my contractions are consistent, some are ten minutes apart, and some are like now," she groaned, and started again with her Lamaze breathing.

She was having a rough time, so I went to her feet and pressed in on the labor-easing pressure points. I could see the relief in her eyes immediately. "Sarah, how are you doing?" I called back.

"We're doin' fine," Jody announced. "It looks like yer a bit busy there, so I'm doin' the coachin' here. How much more time do ye think she has?" he asked, his hands quickly moving to press her feet to counteract Sarah's pains.

"I don't know, but I'll check her on her next one. Leah's whippin' right along here. She's at eight centimeters already. Did James come back with you?" I asked as I washed my hands in another alcohol rinse.

"He'll be in soon. My horse was faster than his. We left Wallace in town to do the speakin'. There's talk of turnin' the regulatin' of the town over to the Crown. I dinna think it'll take much convincin' fer the townsfolk to realize that we're better off takin' care of our own needs right here. Oh, here, she's done fer a minute. Go aheid and do what ye need to do," he offered as he got up from the stool by her side.

"Am I too late? Is the baby here yet?" James blurted out as he pushed open the door. His intensity toned down as soon as he saw Leah. "How're you doing, sweetheart," he said tenderly.

"Ugh, I'm not sure why women keep getting pregnant after they've been through this once, much less multiple times," Leah carped.

James sat down next to her and used a cloth to wipe her face. "God, you're beautiful," he praised. Leah huffed and gave him an exaggerated frown. "I know, I know, you feel rotten," he said, "but you are positively radiant. Is there anything I can do...and don't tell me I already did my part."

Leah's face contorted between a grin at the fact that he had read her mind, a sneer because that really was how she felt right now, and a frown because she knew that many more contractions were imminent before their baby arrived.

"I feel lost at sea. Sarah's over there, having contractions regular as clockwork. Or at least like a clock that's gaining half a minute every hour or so. Me, I don't know when they're going to hit. I just told Jenny to take a privy break. She's been at my side for four hours, at least. She was supposed to help Poppi with the wee three, but didn't want me to be alone. I mean, Mom's here, but she's doing double duty with taking Sarah for walks, cleaning up messes, oh, shit..."

Leah quit talking and immediately started her breathing. James knew what to do; he had been taught well. He didn't say a word, but went to her feet and immediately applied thumb pressure.

I was performing a pelvic exam on Sarah while James took care of Leah's needs. "Shit, shit, shit!" Sarah screamed as I touched her inside.

"Sarah, it's going to hurt more if you talk. But I don't think you have too many more contractions in you—it's time to push. Jody, get behind her shoulders and help support her. Baby number one is crowning. I can work his shoulders out, but I want you ready with a swaddling cloth."

"It's a boy? Ye can tell already?" Jody asked as he positioned himself behind Sarah, excited at hearing me refer to 'his shoulders.'

"No, not yet. You can push with the next contraction, Sarah." I could tell by the feel of the soft spots that baby number one was face down, the correct position for delivery. I put my hands inside and urged him out. "Baby's a red head and...." I slipped the shoulders out, then pulled him out the rest of the way, "It's a boy. Here, Jody, take him and clean him up, would you? Sarah, just chill a moment. The other guy isn't in position yet. Lord, help us and bring him face down, too."

"Amen," James, Leah, Jody, and Sarah chorused as the youngest Pomeroy added his own squall of agreement.

"Can I see him?" Sarah asked, and turned her upper torso toward her first son.

"Aye, he's a good lookin' lad and hearty, too."

"Mom?" Leah called urgently through clenched jaws.

"Dani, I mean, Evie, I think she wants to push. She doesn't know if she can yet or not. Can you see if she's at ten centimeters?" James asked.

I gulped at his Freudian slip of calling me Dani, my older 21st self who he first knew me as. Evidently, his inner-self wanted an older person to take charge, not the very young-bodied me. He was also speaking for Leah. She had told me they had developed quite the psychic communication rapport just before they married, his latent ability showing itself as soon as she opened up to him. I shook my head and snapped out of my momentary trance. I felt Sarah's lower abdomen: the second baby wasn't down in the birth canal yet.

Before I had a chance to answer James, Jenny popped in the room. "Do we have any babies yet?" she asked , bouncing up and down of her toes.

"Ye have an uncle here. And, he has red hair jest like yer little brothers and sister. Here, do ye want to hold him? He's a wee 'un, but seems to have a good set of lungs."

"Jody, keep track of Sarah and baby number two. I'll be right back," I said, and scooted away to kneel down at the foot of the pile of quilts that Jenny had put together for Leah. She refused to lie on Jody and Sarah's bed lest she stain it, and insisted that Sarah have use of the chaise since she was having twins, and it would be easier for me to help the babies come out.

"How ya doin', honey," I asked as I put my left hand on her belly, waiting for it to harden before checking her.

"I was tired, but all of a sudden, I'm wide awake. At least, it feels like it's time..." Leah stopped talking, immediately started panting, and then held her breath.

"Don't hold your breath! That means you're pushing." I was multitasking, lecturing as I felt to see if she was at the magic ten centimeters dilation. "Ho Kay...go ahead and push; you're ready. It'll probably take a while because this is your first one."

Leah's contractions were coming on top of each other. She pushed and she pushed, but got nowhere. She was in tears, and James was getting weepy, too. "I'm sorry, I'm sorry," he kept saying over and over, trying to comfort her, but unable to find a place to touch her that didn't result in her shaking her head 'no' and shrugging away from him.

"Try squatting," Sarah called breathlessly from her birthing bed. "And Evie, can you come over here for a quick second. I..." Sarah stopped talking and started panting.

"Oh, brother," I puffed as I stood up and rushed to the foot of the chaise.

"Or oh, sister," Jody joked. "I think the other one is ready to come out."

I got in position on the stool and spread Sarah's knees apart, letting Jody support her shoulders. "Number Two is in the chute. Great work, Sarah, this one's face down, too. See, I told you the delivery would be perfect."

Sarah took a deep breath and pushed hard enough to get another child out to the shoulders. One gentle tug, and baby boy number two was announcing his arrival to everyone in the room.

"Wow!" Jenny exclaimed.

With all of the excitement, none of us had remembered that she was in the house, much less that she was standing quietly behind me, cuddling her uncle, bouncing him gently to keep him quiet. "Another boy; he looks just like this one, only bigger, I think," she said as she looked back down at the bundle in her arms.

"Uh, a little help over here, if you can," James called. "I think the baby's stuck."

I looked away from the happy grouping of Sarah, Jody, Jenny, and the two small, but perfect, baby boys and saw the terror on both James's and Leah's faces.

"I can't do it, Mom. She won't come out; she's too big."

"No, she's not; you're just too small. Here, James, lay her back down for a minute. Jody, hand me that oil, please. I am so sorry. I forgot to use the oil and stretch you out. Will you forgive me?" I asked as I pulled back her privacy cloth and lubed and stretched, trying to work around my dark-haired grandchild's head that was crowning.

"I'll forgive you as soon as she gets out. Oomph, here we go again..."

Leah was having a major contraction. She wanted to push, but was doing her best to control the urge. "No, no, no, not yet, no, no, not yet," she puffed, her own chant to try and control her body. The contraction subsided, and the baby pulled back up just a little, at least enough that I could get a finger inside to tug rather than rub the opening.

"Okay, James, let's try to get her vertical again before the next contraction. Squat like the squaws do, Leah."

"Huh?" she asked, but assumed the position just the same. "Oh, yeah, 'Dances with Wolves,' right. I don't need an Academy Award for this performance, just my baby," Leah said, then tried to laugh, her chuckle interrupted by another contraction. "Oh, shit! Here she comes; catch!"

I flopped down on my side and looked up to half pull out, half catch, the baby. "Cloth, please," I asked as I cuddled my white vernix-covered granddaughter to my chest.

James reached over, grabbed the swaddling cloth, and wrapped it around her, taking care not to touch the umbilicus. "When do you cut it," he asked.

"Oh, boy," Leah breathed softly, forgoing her customary curse word. She stood up halfway and let the placenta drop to the pile of quilts beneath her. "Oops, sorry," she said about the mess she had just made.

"Here, you can cut it now," I told James. "Cut it right here and Leah, don't worry about the mess," I said and handed her an oversized clout to put between her legs. "Everything's washable. Man, for being early, she sure is big. You were, too; eight pounds, four ounces. James, how big were you?" I asked, then suddenly realized what I had just said.

"Ten pounds," he answered, his eyes narrowed, asking me without words how I knew how much Leah weighed at birth: I didn't remember her early years, or so I had told everyone.

"Leah, you never mentioned how much you weighed to me, did you?" I asked. "I mean, I just popped out with that weight. I don't even know if it's right or not, or even if you ever told me. At least, I don't recall talking about birth weights."

"Yes, you're right, and no, I never told you. So, do you remember if she looks like I did?" Leah asked cautiously.

I beamed at my granddaughter as James brought her over to her mother to see. I looked over Leah's shoulder. "Oh, yeah; gotta be. Either that, or I've known what she's going to look like forever. I mean, she sure looks familiar. And don't worry; she won't be bald for long. If I recall, you were bald, too."

9 Too Soon for Babies
Summer, 1782

"When can I have a baby?" Jenny asked.

"When, when, when you're as tall as your father," I stuttered. I was busy preparing green beans and she took me completely off guard. I didn't expect to hear that question from her for years!

"But you have babies and you're not as tall as Daddy," she argued. "And Grannie has babies and she's not as tall as he is either. Or does she have to be as tall as Grandpa 'cause he's their dad?" Jenny stopped justifying and started calculating. "No, wait, that can't be or no one would have babies. No woman is as tall as Daddy or Grandpa, or even Brother James. 'Sides, Rachel had babies and she was little. Hannah said they was the same age as each other, too."

"Were the same age," I corrected.

Jenny didn't say a word, which was a relief. I was uncomfortable with the topic of conversation. However, one look at her face and I could see it was because she was waiting for me to answer her initial question.

"Okay," I answered reluctantly, "you can have a baby after you're married..." I looked at her to make sure she understood that very important requirement. She must have; she was positively radiant at that prospect.

"But, no babies until after you're married and have finished school, okay?"

"Okay. And you told me that school was out in a few days because we had to work more outside in the gardens? So that means I can have babies real soon!"

"No! No, you can't. You're still too young. Besides, I said 'finished school' not just out of school. You'll be 'out' of school in a few days, all right, but you won't be 'finished' with your schooling until you know as much as your father, or at least me. And that includes reading and math, *comprende*?"

"What's math *comprende*?" she asked.

"Well, if you knew, then you'd be closer to being finished with your schooling." I looked over at her pensive face and added, "And remember, you have to be married, too. Don't forget that. And a good man isn't that easy to find. Just because there are a lot of good ones around here, doesn't mean that all men are worthy. So don't just marry any man so you can have a baby, okay?"

Jenny smirked and nodded her head. I didn't know what that meant and didn't know if I *wanted* to know. I put down the bowl of snap beans and put my index finger under her chin. "Promise me," I commanded with a serious tone and look that I had never used with her before. I wanted to make sure she knew how important this life lesson was.

"Mommy, I promise you that I will not marry a man just so I can have babies. And, I promise you he is, I mean, will be a good man," she answered sincerely.

I could tell she was telling me the truth. It looked like she accepted that lesson easily enough.

Ж

"Well, look at what the cat dragged in," James said as he walked up to the longhaired youth coming in from the mill road. Wee Ian was back, and it looked like he was traveling solo.

"I think ye have it wrong, *cousin*," Wee Ian said with a grin. James was his secret brother-in-law, but they referred to each other as cousin. "The cat dinna drag me in, but I *did* drag a cat in," he said as he lifted up a leather pouch with a kitten paw reaching out. "I brought Jenny a gift. But I think I should ask Wallace first if it's all right. I mean, with all the mice in the barn, I dinna think there'll be any reason he'll need to feed this wee critter, but it is his home and his, um, daughter," he said, stumbling on the last word.

"You like her, don't you," James teased when he saw the uneasiness. "You brought her a cat just so you could see her..." James stopped the silliness and said plainly, "Hey, she's a great girl. If I were your age, I'd want her for a girlfriend."

Wee Ian blushed at the revelation. He wasn't going to deny it. He wasn't going to acknowledge its truth, either. Instead, he changed the subject. "Where is everyone?"

"Oh, here, there and everywhere. Wallace and Jody are clearing some more land south of here. We're planning on putting in more crops next year since I'm here to help. So, are you going to stay for a while? You're welcome to stay as long as you want. There's plenty of work to spread around."

The young man sighed wistfully. "I'd like to, but I want to see if I can make somethin' of myself first. I mean, I want to be a man of worth," he said as he stood tall, his skinny chest stuck out in pride.

63

"There's nothing wrong with being a farmer," James said. "I've had money and 'worth,' back before I got here," he nodded and gave Wee Ian a wink and a 'look' to remind him that he had a life in a different world before he came here, "and believe me, *this* is better."

"Aye, but ye still have to have money or goods to trade fer the land, the tools, the stock, the seed, and anythin' else ye happen to be needin' to get started."

James heard Jenny out in the back garden, calling to her little siblings to get out of the carrots. He noticed Wee Ian look dreamily toward the sound. He grinned and said, "Boy, you have it bad, don't you?"

A frown replaced the young man's smile. "Have what bad?" he asked as he checked his chest, arms, and legs like he was inspecting himself for lice.

James laughed. "I mean you *really* like her, don't you? Is she why you want to 'make somethin' of yerself'?"

The boy inhaled sharply, but didn't reply with words, only nodded dejectedly.

"And stay there!" Jenny scolded as she put Wren in the enhanced playpen that looked like a low profile corral with vertical slats added to keep the toddlers from free ranging into places they weren't supposed to be. She looked over and saw James talking to a stranger. No, not a stranger: it was Wee Ian, the one she had renamed Scout.

"Scout!" she screamed as she ran toward the men. She threw her arms around the smaller man's waist, picked him up, and hugged him fervently, spinning him around at the same time.

"Um, put me down!" he grunted with a mixture of embarrassment and annoyance.

Jenny did as she was told, and then put her arms down at her side. She bowed her head slightly then bobbed it back up. She opened her mouth as if to speak then shut it quickly. James noticed that she was breathing in and out so rapidly that it looked like she was panting. She was a good-natured child, but he had never seen her so radiant and bubbling over with joy.

Scout looked over at James with full on embarrassment then back at Jenny with what could only be described as adolescent desire unwillingly held in check. "Go ahead and kiss her," James teased, certain that he wouldn't.

Scout leaned in and gave Jenny a brotherly kiss on the cheek then pulled back, chagrined, but obviously wanting more.

"Whoa," James said, "I was only joking."

Jenny looked at James, gave him a mischievous grin, then took one step closer to her secret husband, and put her hands on his shoulders. She looked Scout in the eye then shook her head. She brought her right index finger to her mouth, tapped her lip then moved the finger away and pointed it at his face, wagging it in admonishment. Wee Ian/Scout glanced over at James as if to ask, 'what should I do?'

"Go ahead and kiss her again," James said, "I won't tell anyone."

Scout looked deep into Jenny's eyes, slipped his hands around her waist, and held her close. He leaned in and gave her a kiss that would make any high school senior jealous.

"Uh, I think that's enough," James interrupted. "I mean, it's not as if you're married."

Jenny and Scout broke off the kiss and looked at James as one, both of them grinning with the smile of a shared secret.

"Scout?" James asked, suddenly recalling the name she had screamed when she had seen him. "You called him Scout, didn't you? Oh, shit."

Scout took one hand off of Jenny's waist, looked at James with mild disgust, and asked, "Why is everythin' 'oh, shit' with ye?"

James shook his head. He was looking at his ancestors. The mystery of who Scout Kincaid was had been answered. He had traveled back in time last year to assure that Ian Kincaid was saved, or at least that was what he thought. He only knew for sure that he was to insure the life of a Scout Kincaid, the man who would marry Jenny Pomeroy-Hart, his great-grandmother many times over. James shook his head as disbelief whipped into realization. "You married her last year, didn't you?"

Now it was time for the young, innocent couple to blush. "Aye, we did it the Indian way," Scout explained.

"But we're still married or marrit or however you want to say it," Jenny blurted out then added, "oops, sorry." She didn't want to start talking too much again; her husband didn't like that.

"Well, I won't tell anyone about it, and I don't think you two should either," admonished James. "And, don't go making any babies; for a few years at least, quite a few. I mean, she's still my little sister-in-law, even if she is your wife. You haven't been 'doing it' have you?" he asked.

Scout straightened out his shoulders and answered, "Nae, we will wait until I can build us a proper home. I willna be plantin' my seed in her until her breasts are big enough to feed babies, and I can put a roof o'er our heads."

Jenny looked down at her slightly budding chest and stuck it out with pride. Scout saw the gesture and shook his head at her: no, not yet. She sighed in resignation then giggled in relief. Good, she wasn't ready to share her gift yet. Mommy said she had to finish school first. She'd make sure she did that. Maybe by then Scout would be able to build them a home.

"Well, you two lovebirds," James said then saw the look of confusion on their faces. He shook his head in the universal sign language of 'no, never mind; it's not important.' He started again. "Well, Mr. and Mrs. Kincaid, please don't let anyone else know about your marriage. I don't think your parents or grandparents would be as understanding as I am. As long as you're, um, keeping your private parts to yourselves, then it's nobody else's business. And DO NOT go sharing those parts, okay, little brother and little sister?"

They both nodded to James, and then looked at each other. Scout's face lit up. He bent his knees slightly, wrapped his arms around Jenny, and spun her like she had spun him. He set her down and they shared another long, but more reserved kiss. They pulled apart and smiled at each other, both of them glowing all the way down to their curled toes.

"And, don't go kissing each other when anyone else is around, all right? And if, or when, you *have* been kissing," James said as he looked down and saw that they were now holding hands, "I suggest you think of sad things before you see anyone else. Those smiles you're wearing will give you away, for sure."

James opened out his arms, walked up to the couple, and wrapped his arms around his many times over great-grandparents. "I sure love you two," he said, a tear dribbling down his cheek. "Now let's get down to the house. I'm sure that Evie would like to see you again, 'Scout.'"

10 Gimme Shelter
2013 Greensboro, North Carolina

"Weel, what are ye gonna do now, Mac," Benji said to himself. "Yer job here is done; at least as far as the construction work goes. Ye dinna have anythin' to keep ye here and, shit, man," he cursed as he punched the tree in front of him, "buck up and go home!"

He had thoroughly enjoyed working long, hard hours building the combination house and school for Bibb, helping her fulfill her dream four months ahead of schedule. Work therapy is what it was called, he knew that, but when the task was completed, the old emptiness returned. He always had, or made up, an excuse for not going home to Barden Hall and returning to his family. The longest-lived excuse, the threat of the wayward and elusive MacLeod men and their thirst for treasure and revenge against his family, seemed to be gone. At least the last time Billy checked, both Eight and Niner were still in prison.

The trip through The Trees last August would have delayed his return to his parents and sister. No, say it like it is, dammit: it would have put a total kibosh on being reunited with, or even seeing them, again.

He was physically strong and would like to believe he was of at least average intelligence, but he couldn't figure out how to handle the onerous task facing him—admitting to his parents and sister that it was he, and he alone, who had let them believe that he had been dead for decades. Yes, it really would be easier to continue to let them believe the lie. But, he knew with every blood cell in his body that it wasn't right. They deserved to know that he was alive, and that he'd only started the deception so the MacLeods wouldn't target them.

Missing the hook up with Leah and James and the opportunity to travel back in time with them last August hadn't been so bad. But, finding out that he now had to wait another year, until next August 17th, before he could go back by himself, was a royal boil on his butt cheek. The initial slack time had conveniently been filled in by working and spending time with his new 'kin.' The opportunity to help Bibb and Billy felt like it was the right thing to do, but he had worked too hard, been too efficient, and finished the house too soon. He still had over eight months of idle time left before he could go through The Trees to be back with his Grandpa. He sighed deeply and finally admitted to himself: it was time. He'd go back to Scotland and Barden Hall, at least for a visit.

Billy had been a definite blessing to him; he had insisted on paying him a healthy wage, although the food, lodging, clothes, and tools he supplied seemed to be more than enough to him. Yes, not only had he given freely of his money, the family money Billy insisted, he had let him use the truck. Benji didn't mind walking, but he could get so much more accomplished at the speed of traffic. He stayed at the jobsite, Bibb's Place the contractors and delivery truck drivers called it, and he really didn't 'need' to go anywhere, but The Trees seemed to be calling him. Or, maybe he was calling them, wanting them to change their rules of engagement and let him through early. Either way, when the hard work was done and he had showered and washed off the day's dirt and drywall dust, the ride out to sit across from The Trees brought him closer to his emotional cocktail of peace and anticipation. Sitting in front of them was a sweet and sour sensation for him. "Like a lemon drop," he said aloud as he gazed at the last of their leaves flittering with the light wind, just waiting for a strong blast to knock them to the forest floor to join the others. The ground was littered with the various shaped brown and yellow leaves masking the path to the past. "But, I'll pass through yer wooden thighs in August," he said lustily, "and then I'll be the happiest man in the world: back home again."

Ж

"Don't say no to the truck yet. It 'fits' you better than me. And here, since you won't take the bonus money, please take this. Jest in case ye get the urge to go faster than the speed of feet or wheels." Billy handed Benji the airline charge card. "It's good for anywhere they or any of their travel partners go. That means just about anywhere except Antarctica...and I'm not too sure about that." Billy saw Benji's blank look and added, "But, if you want to go there, just call the number on the back; I'm sure they can fix you up."

Ж

A month later, Phoenix, Arizona

"Hmph!" Benji snorted. He wasn't a big fan of lazy people, but the man on the corner looked like he didn't have much choice. Or wasn't in a frame of mind to make one for himself. The tall, longhaired, bearded, and generally disheveled man in his 40's had a glassy-eyed look that made others turn away. Or maybe it was the sign: 'Vet—Please Help. Will work for food.' Benji stayed by the side of the bus station and watched as dozens of people walked by the, well, pathetic seemed cruel, but it *was* an apt description of the sorrowful man. He was obviously homeless. He had a military-style duffle bag with angular pieces in it. 'Probably tool box, kitchen, dresser, and linen closet all in one,' Benji thought.

Eventually, an elderly man with a well-trimmed beard and perky spring to his step walked up to the Vet. He patted the downtrodden sidewalk soldier on the shoulder, evidently giving him words of encouragement by his smile, slipped him what looked like a cigarette, patted the Vet's shoulder again in parting, and called back the words, "Be safe," rather than issuing the traditional 'good luck' farewell that Benji had expected to hear.

Vet took the rolled up monetary cylinder, opened it out, and smiled when he saw that there were two bills involved. Benji couldn't see how much he had received, but from the look on his face, it was probably more than he had made all week. He rolled the bills back into their original shape and stuck them in the cigarette pack he pulled out of his shirt packet. Odd, Benji had been watching him on and off for hours and had never seen him smoke. The vet looked up at the sky and squinted so hard, his eyes disappeared into his weathered wrinkles. Benji wasn't sure, but he could just about swear he heard the man's stomach rumble from where he was. It looked like he'd have company for his evening meal.

"Hey, there!" Benji called out as he strolled up to the vet.

Vet's eyes immediately looked to either side, then he turned at the waist, looking to see if there was someone behind him. He didn't speak, but his eyes asked 'who, me?' as he glanced up quickly at Benji. He wasn't used to being addressed by strangers.

"Yeah, you," Benji said brightly. "I've seen you out here for quite a while without taking a dinner break. Would ye care to join me for a bite to eat?"

Vet immediately put his hand up to his shirt pocket, instinctively protecting his little stash of cash. "No, dinna worry; it's my treat," Benji assured him. "Ye see, I havena any friends or kin around here and weel, I'd rather eat with someone than by myself. That is, if ye dinna mind the fare over at the all-you-can-eat buffet. Ye can have yer choice of Chinese, Mexican, Italian, American, and they even have a few of those little fishy cakes; what do ye call them? Sooky?" Benji joked; he knew what they were called.

"Sushi," Vet replied. "It's not too bad if there isn't anything else to eat but, um, you don't even know me, do you?"

69

"McCall, right?" Benji asked as he read the name on the vet's oversized jacket.

"I used to be," he answered glumly. "I mean, I still am, but I'm not in the army anymore."

"Weel, we're almost kin. I'm MacKay...we're both Mac's, aye?" The vet gave a weak half grin, but didn't move. "Come on, yer legs look like they're in good shape. I dinna have a car, so we'll have to pony shanks it over there. It's only a couple of blocks, if ye think ye can make it."

McCall nodded quickly then stooped to pick up his bag, stuffing his hand scribbled sign under his armpit. Benji thought about offering to carry the man's load, but realized that the vet might take it as an insult, that he was insinuating he was either too weak or feeble to take care of it himself. By the man's stance, he still had some dignity left, even if he had to beg on a street corner for work. At least he was willing to labor for his keep, which was more than some people.

Ж

The shunning started even before they reached the restaurant door. Mothers grabbed their children's hands lest they get near the two men as they walked through the parking lot. The whispers were hard to ignore. "Make sure you stay real close to me. Don't touch anything that he's touched. Can you believe the nerve of him, coming in *here*? Come on; we're going somewhere else."

Benji heard all of the remarks and he knew McCall did, too, unless he was hard of hearing. One glance at his dinner date, though, and Benji knew; he not only heard them, but also had been subject to the scorn many times before. Benji started to apologize for the people's rudeness, but McCall spoke first.

"I never get used to it. It's like the bones in trout: you have to work around the worthless to get to the good. Ignoring what they say is the only way to handle it. They're not bad people; they just don't understand. Shoot, it's me and *I* don't understand," he said. "Now, if you'll watch my bag," he said sternly, the look in his eye making Benji feel threatened, "I'll clean up as best I can."

"I'll do more than *watch* yer bag, I'll make sure it *stays,* and I'll even see if I can teach it to *sit*," Benji joked, trying to lighten the man's dour demeanor.

McCall rolled his eyes. "It ain't much, bro, but it's all I have."

The two filled their plates three times before deciding that they had eaten enough for one meal. "This is a nice place, but I really didn't feel brave enough to come in here by myself. I told you that I ignore the whispers, and I do. At least they're easier to overlook when I'm walking. When I'm sitting down to a meal, especially the first decent food I've had in a week, it's hard not to hear the comments. I feel trapped when I'm inside as it is," he added as he looked nervously at the windows, wishing he to be again.

"So, ye'd like to work outside, but there arena any jobs here?" Benji asked, although he knew that was what he had just heard.

McCall eyes squinted at Benji in answer: you know I did; get on with it.

Benji pushed away the last cleared off plate to give himself more room to speak. He always felt tongue-tied if his hands couldn't move through the air with his words. "Ye see, I have some experience up in the oilfields of Alaska. It's mighty tough work. Ye'd be inside to sleep and eat, but out in the air most of your shift. Ye work two weeks straight, at least twelve hours a day, sometimes more, before gettin' a day off. They give ye a warm bed to sleep in, more food than ye can imagine, and even have books to read and TV's to watch if ye feel up to it after workin' all day. Now, if ye think ye could handle the long flight up there and being cooped up for sleepin', I'll make a few phone calls and see if anyone up there is hirin'. It's hard work, but I'll bet yer used to that, aye?"

"Aye. I don't think *anything* is harder than standing on a street corner with a cardboard sign, asking for work." McCall sighed. He took a deep breath and said, "Yes, if you'd make the call or calls, I'd love to work hard. And, the cold doesn't bother me. I had enough of the heat in two tours of Iraq. The one tour of Afghanistan didn't last as long, but I did find out that the cold doesn't bother me."

"I'll be right back then," Benji said, and nodded to excuse himself.

When he got to the outside door, he looked back to make sure McCall hadn't panicked and left through the window he had been eyeing so nervously. No, he wasn't getting ready to take off, but he was a little self-conscious; he had put aside four dinner rolls and was rolling them up in a napkin to save for a later meal.

Benji pulled out the disposable cell phone and punched in the digits. Hopefully his friend hadn't changed his phone number. He had a great memory for numbers and just about everything else. He credited his father with giving him the photographic memory gene, but he still couldn't just pull a phone number out of the air if his old boss had changed numbers.

"Lynn, Lynn? Hi there, this is Benji. Yes, yes, I'm still that tall. I'm not so auld that I shrunk. I'd have to be at least 200 years old before I got to normal height." Benji chuckled into the phone when he realized that he really was born over 200 years ago, but he couldn't tell Lynn or anyone else that.

"I'm sorry, I missed what ye said. Me? Oh no, I'm not ready to come back. But, if yer lookin' fer a big man with a strong back, I have a friend who's lookin' fer work. He's a vet and as tough as they come. Yes, he's smart, too. What do ye mean? Of course, he'll listen to ye and take orders. I told ye he was a vet, dinna I? If I get him to Anchorage, will ye make sure someone picks him up at the airport and shows him around? Okay, when's the next rig pass class? I'll schedule the ticket for the day before. And make sure it's one of yer buddies who picks him up. And get him into a decent motel, too. I dinna want him fallin' asleep durin' the classes. I mean, they arena the most exciting teachers, aye? No, he's nae so tall as me, but he's still plenty big. My cold weather gear is still in my locker, and he's welcome to it. Ye jest be good to him, and he'll be good to ye. And, ye willna have to worry about learnin' a new name. He's another Mac: McCall, but ye can call him Mac and he'll answer. Okay, I'll give him this phone, too, so ye can contact him at the number on the caller ID for more information. We're jest finishin' our dinner here, so give him a bit before ye call. Thanks, I owe ye one."

Benji strolled back into the restaurant, beaming from ear to ear. It felt so good to help someone. He looked over and saw McCall sitting at their little table, grinning at the cute blonde toddler strapped in a high chair, smashing her saltine crackers, watching the bits and pieces fly everywhere while her mother chatted into her smartphone, totally ignoring her little charge's misdeeds. Yes, the mother would probably learn too late that it would be wise to pay attention to her daughter and her bad behaviors now rather than wait until it was too late for the girl to listen and heed.

"Cute little lass, aye? I'll bet she's a handful," Benji said.

McCall sighed deeply, his smile falling at his friend's remarks. "Maybe if I can get my act together, I'll have something to offer mine. She's thirteen now and thinks she knows everything. My being gone overseas was hard on her and her mother. Laura never remarried, but works two jobs to try and give Shasta everything she wants. She didn't want to listen to me tell her how to raise our daughter long distance. I just hope they realize that their time together is more important than all the 'stuff' that money can buy. A young daughter quickly outgrows her clothes and shoes, but should never outgrow the love and need for her mother."

"Or her father," Benji added. "She still loves ye. She'll realize what's important soon. In the meantime, ye've got a great job to go to, and if it's the money they think they need, ye'll have it. Ye'll have two weeks at a time to go see and get reacquainted with them. It may be a month or two before yer ready fer them or them fer ye, but dinna lose hope. They are family, after all."

Benji took a deep breath and changed subjects; he had unintentionally made himself uncomfortable talking about families and the need to reconnect with them. "Now that bein' said, I got ye a job. All ye have to do is go to Anchorage and I'll have a friend of a friend pick ye up and take ye to wherever ye need to go fer the job training classes. Ye can have my phone, its good fer a couple hundred minutes of talk time, and then when ye get to the jobsite, ye can have my locker. I left all my gear up there, so yer set."

"Go to Anchorage?" McCall asked meekly. "How..."

"Oh, I got that covered, too. Right after dessert, I'll call in fer the ticket. All ye have to do is take a bus to the airport tomorrow afternoon and yer ready to rock and roll; a new lease on life, or whatever it is they call it," Benji added in mock insecurity. He didn't want to appear too cocky in front of his new acquaintance.

"Why are you doing this?" McCall asked skeptically, ill at ease at getting so much for nothing.

"Weel, I guess because I can," Benji answered truthfully. He shifted in his seat because he really hadn't thought of it that way. "I mean, if ye could help someone out, wouldna ye?"

"Well, yes, I mean something simple like getting something off a top shelf or help carry a load..."

"Aye, and that's what I'm doing: I'm helping ye carry a load. Now, if I was in yer shoes, and believe it or not, I've been mighty close, then I ken that I'd like a fairy godfather to come by and grant my wish fer a way out of my plight..."

"You're an awfully big fairy." McCall laughed and shook his head in amazement.

"Aye, that's me: the great big fairy. Now, all this work gettin' ye a job has made me hungry. How about some cherry pie?" Benji asked.

"Great idea; I'll have mine a la mode. There's a soft serve ice cream machine over there. I haven't had that..." McCall sighed

73

deeply and grinned as he realized that now he didn't have to look back all the time—he could look forward. "Well, this is the first of many desserts that I'm going to treat myself to in this decade!"

Ж

Benji spent the rest of the evening at the park with McCall, sharing with him dozens of hints on how to handle the cold weather and the attitudes of some of the men who suffered from superiority complexes. "Pile on the layers of clothes, breathe through yer nose, not yer mouth, and dinna worry if someone says the wrong words. Toward the end of the hitch, the men, and they're mostly men, get a little tense, missin' their wives and girlfriends. And, if ye dinna understand how to do somethin', make sure ye ask. The only dumb question is the one ye dinna ask."

McCall listened and took to heart everything he was told, a contented grin on his face. He reached across his chest and pinched his hand; yup, he wasn't dreaming.

"And here," Benji said and handed him the phone and an envelope with six letters written on the front of it. "This is your confirmation code and a list of names. These are folks who will help ye if jest ask. Oh, and I threw in a couple of bucks fer the bus ride to the airport. Now, that bein' said, is this where ye spend yer nights?"

"On clear nights I prefer to be outside in this place with the trees, trash, and dog poop to being inside at the shelter. That place reeks of alcohol, unwashed bodies, and frustration. It's easier to wash off the stuff you roll in here at the park than the despair that gets under your skin there." He shuddered then looked at Benji and asked with a smile, "Do you want to spend the night at my place? It ain't much, but at least we're here in the desert and not in cold country," McCall said optimistically.

"Aye, that will come soon enough, but by then ye'll have a wee small room to stay in and a nice warm bed, showers jest down the hall, and lots of food. But fer tonight, a rolled up jacket under my head in a Phoenix park will be jest fine." Benji took off his jacket and arranged it under his neck. "We have enough time fer a few more stories then we need to get some shut eye."

McCall felt better than he had in years. A friend, a full belly, and a job: a hat trick they called it in hockey, the Triple Crown in horseracing, a grand slam homerun in baseball. Maybe the nightmares would go away now. No, now the nightmares 'will' go away he decided emphatically. Those were based on a

74

miserable past and a future that seemed futile. Now he had hope, and where there was hope, despair and depression couldn't grow.

11 Edinburgh
Late October 2013

Benji took McCall's advice and went to the Salvation Army Thrift Store for some bargains. "Oh, this is so right," he said as he picked up the drab, light brown cotton hoodie. Size 3X, too." He held it up to his chest and stretched the sleeves out, clutching the wristbands with fingers folded over. "Oh, yeah: my very own cloak of invisibility."

"That'll be five dollars, sir," the clerk at the checkout counter said.

"Really? That's all?" Benji asked then looked at the tag.

"Yes, sir; all clothing is 50% off today. Of course, if you want to pay $10, I'll just put the extra $5 in the little red bucket here, and it'll go to the shelter. They can always use the money for what food and clothing donations don't cover. You know: utilities and such."

"Aye," Benji said then handed her a twenty-dollar bill, "then today a few lights are on me. Put the change in the bucket, if ye would. And have yourself a blessed day."

Benji bit off the price tag and tossed it in the trash on the way out. Yes, people were staring at him, but it wasn't his tag tossing: it was his size and coloring. Six foot seven always got people's attention. Add to that his flaming red hair, and he was a standout in any group. But, hanging with McCall had given him some hints on how to become anonymous. Of course, that hadn't been the homeless vet's intention.

Benji put on the hoodie, scrunched down, and imagined himself in McCall's shoes when he met him: no job, no home, no family. Hold it: that really was his situation right now. Situation didn't necessarily dictate attitude. He'd have to pretend to be someone else. Yeah, right—back to wrestler/actor mode.

"Winnie the Wimp from Waukegan wooking for work— yeah, that ought to do it." Benji sighed and went back into the pit of his belly, ignoring the world as Benjamin MacKay felt it. Instead, he tuned in with the senses of an insecure, stuttering tenth grader: short, plump, and with ears that stuck out like bat wings. It was working: he suddenly had a craving for a chocolate milkshake and an extra-large order of fries. His shoulders sagged, his neck thrust forward, and he wanted to curl up in a corner with a hand held video game. Oops, too deep. Keep the Game Boy, but come out of the corner. You still have to be able to function, Winnie.

So, 'Winnie the Wimp from Waukegan' with a passport that read 'Benjamin MacKay' meekly purchased a round trip ticket to Edinburgh, Scotland. The ticket clerk noticed that he had been assigned a middle seat and took pity on the large, bashful man, switching him to an aisle seat on an exit row. "Have a nice trip, sir," she said as she handed him his boarding pass.

"Um, thanks," Benji's alter ego answered shyly, his muted brown hoodie pulled up over his deep copper hair. He could actually feel the embarrassment of Winnie when the woman spoke to him. Benji, still in character, glanced around to see if others had seen the little exchange. Nope, WWW was out in the open, and it was Benji down in the pit, surveying the works of the world through a Plexiglas navel. He'd just have to bear lying low and living in his cloak of invisibility for a few days.

Ж

"Umph," Benji groaned as he tried to get comfortable. He had stuffed the little airline pillow inside of the hood of his jacket to keep it from shifting, but evidently his body had reached the limit of how long it would stay asleep while packed and twisted into an airline throne of nylon and plastic. Oh, for the comfort of a concrete floor and a sack of rice.

The flight attendant was on another one of her 'is everything okay?' and 'can I get you a blanket?' tours. He wanted to ask her how much longer, but realized that it was Benji wanting to know, not Winnie from Waukegan. 'Winnie, Winnie, Winnie,' he chanted silently. Winnie would want to know, but would never ask. He also knew that when the plane landed, they would be at the end of their flight. Scotland. Edinburgh. So close to Barden Hall that even if he walked, he could make it in a day or less. Suddenly, Benji didn't want the interminable flight to end.

"Ladies and gentlemen, we will be arriving in Edinburgh, Scotland in approximately twenty minutes. Please make sure that your tray tables and seats are in their upright positions. Check under...."

Benji didn't hear the rest of the spiel. He was suddenly bathed in a nervous sweat. Why did he do this? What was he going to say to them? Were they even there? Mom was raised in Philadelphia, good old Pennsylvania, USA. Maybe they moved there. What about Becky? Surely she was married by now, maybe even had a family of her own. Of course, she would be living with her husband. Maybe he lived in Europe, Africa, Asia, or even Australia? Good grief, Winnie had taken over Benji, and there wasn't a stiff vertebra between the two personalities.

"Sir, sir, can you sit up, please," the flight attendant asked, smiling sweetly at the frantic passenger. "You, um, can take the pillow with you, if you'd like."

Benji realized that he had been using the foot long pillow to wipe his sweaty face and neck. "Um, thanks, ma'am," he said with an honest blush. Right now, there really wasn't much difference between Winnie and him: they were both terrified and insecure. He looked down at the pillow again and quickly assessed its potential as a barf bag. No, use slow, deep breaths, and think of video games and milkshakes. Visions of French fries not allowed until the tummy settles. Pac Man: eat my fears, gobble my apprehensions, and blast my paranoia. No one is going to see me unless I want to be seen.

Benji let everyone else leave the plane before he even stood up. His height was definitely more noticeable in the low ceiling craft than it would be in the tall, open-aired concourse. When he finally stood up, he rose too quickly and nearly fell on his face from the change in blood pressure. He managed to grab the edge of the overhead bin for support before totally losing his legs. "Careful there, sir; it was a long flight and we don't want you falling down, now do we?"

"No, ma'am," he answered softly then reached over and grabbed the bottom of the opposite overhead bin to steady himself. He nodded in appreciation for her concern, then took short, careful steps forward, this time using the backs of the empty seats to insure his upright progress. 'Winnie, Winnie, Winnie," he whispered as he walked down the portable hallway that joined the plane to the gate. "Don't stretch yet; hold it in 'til ye get to the loo."

Benji exited the snaky tunnel, almost able to stand up straight. He looked up and down the causeway to find the nearest restroom. He had been on the plane for over seven hours, including the boarding and disembarking, and had drunk two sodas. A little, no, a lot of bladder relief was needed.

And then he saw them.

Suddenly nothing mattered but finding a place to sit down, before he fell down.

"Gregg, I don't know if we should leave now. Shouldn't we wait until after Becky's had the baby?"

His parents were right in front of him.

The two of them were sitting spitting distance away from him, directly across from the gate he had just exited, life-sized and at full volume. They were discussing, almost bickering, about the wisdom of leaving Edinburgh while drinking lattes at an impromptu table made of an upended carry-on bag.

Benji spun around quickly, looking for an inconspicuous seat. The airport was crowded, but he saw an open spot near a blue-haired old lady with a critter of some sort, packed inside a plastic and wire-gated pet carrier. 'May I?' Benji asked wordlessly with a look and a hand gesture before he invaded the animal aficionado's little pet sanctuary.

"Yes, yes; here, let me move this for you," she offered and scooted aside a big bag of gifts.

Benji glanced at the plastic seat before he sat down to make sure he hit his target. Then all of his attention was back to his mother and father, suddenly twenty feet away from him. He knew the old lady was talking to him, but he really wasn't in the mood to converse with a stranger. He pointed to his ear and shook his head, hoping that she would believe he was deaf. Her mouth made the shape of an 'O' and she desisted.

"She isna due until the end of April. I'm sure she'll be fine. After all, she did fine with the first one. No, if we dinna leave now, we willna get another chance for at least a year. I ken ye, ye'll want to spend all our weekends and holidays out there at Barden Hall, addin' on to the nursery or erectin' an indoor water park for our granddaughter. Honestly, Mona, Jim can take care of his family jest fine. He seldom goes out of town anymore, and after the baby's here, I'll bet he asks for a desk job." Gregg was holding his coffee with one hand and patting his wife's hand with the other, trying to soften the tough words.

"But I know he's coming back. I can feel him, really I can," Mona argued, changing her approach.

Gregg inhaled then almost groaned. He patted her hand one more time then left it on her knee, his other hand clutching his half-full cup of latte. He had heard the words at least once a day for the last month. He didn't want to believe his son was dead. No, he really 'couldn't' believe he was dead because of the letter from Evie telling them that he was safe back in the 18th century with his Grandpa. But, now Mona was nearly driving him insane, insisting that their son was back in the 21st century.

"I'm sure he'll come see us if he returns. Now, if he's with your father like the letter said, then he's fine, and there's nothin' we can do. If he manages to come back to this time, then I'm sure he'll find a way to contact us whether we're here or in

Aruba or Zimbabwe. If, now that's a big if..." he admonished, waiting for her acknowledgment.

She gave a brief nod, letting him know she understood. Yes, she understood, just like she had yesterday and the day before and the week before. Her nod changed to a gentle head shaking. He was so tolerant of her mood swings and indecisions: what did she do to get such a great, soothing husband? She was lost in her own reflections and almost missed it. "What did you say?"

"I said I'm sure he'd head straight to Barden Hall. Becky isna goin' anywhere, except to the market or the baby doctor, so she'll call us if he comes in; okay?" Gregg said the same words with the same love and compassion as he always did, then stopped and looked around. Something did feel different. He looked down at the cup in his hand. "Here, give me that cup. I think they used spoilt milk or somethin'. I've got a knot in my waim and it must be this."

Benji didn't have to act the part of Winnie from Waukegan; he had been stunned back to insecure adolescent mode with the sight of his parents. He had heard everything they said, but it was only raw information, and too much for him to process right now. He knew he'd remember their words verbatim, he always could do that, but what was it they said about him being back with his Grandpa? His head automatically leaned forward to hear more, but the words had stopped.

His father took the coffee cup out of his mother's hand and was taking it to the trash receptacle by the big window. Now his mother was grabbing the carry-on bag and following him, out of earshot, but still in view. Even if he could read lips, it wouldn't have done any good. The two of them were leaned up against the ledge in front of the window, his father kissing his mother's hair by her ear, comforting her without words.

Two minutes later, the two of them were at the gate, tickets in hand, boarding the flight to Amsterdam.

And then they were gone.

The spell was broken. Benji heard a yipping noise. He looked down and saw the little snub-nosed Pekinese housed in the beige plastic pet carrier adorned with little pink crowns and stars and the name Princess across the opening. All of a sudden, he felt intense pain in his belly. Not only was he gut-struck in shock, the two sodas and the long flight had caught up with him.

He took a deep breath and looked around. First order of business: get rid of excess body fluids so he could stand up straight. Second order of business: to be determined after first order of business.

12 Benji's Disappearing Act
October 25, 2013

Billy couldn't stop thinking about Benji. He had hoped he would stay at the new house with him, Peter, and Mom until next August, when the time was right to go through The Trees. Benji knew the offer was open, but they hadn't talked about it: the big man always managed to change the subject when the topic came up. It didn't make much difference, though. Billy had seen the look in Benji's eyes: he was going to bolt.

It was only last week that they had done some preliminary planning for the trip. Billy wanted to make sure Benji had the coin and everything else he needed, including immunizations, before he flew the coop, or house, or whatever it was. They were trying to be discreet, but Peter could tell something was going on.

Peter had gone on a shopping spree after he incorrectly deduced that all of the talk about travelling meant that Benji was going on an extended camping trip. He bought him an elaborate, oversized backpack and something new: the latest and greatest in modern fabric technology. "Look at this," he crowed to his red-haired idol as he pulled the camouflage fabric from the bag, presenting it to Benji like it was a royal cape. "You can take this anywhere and use it for just about anything. It's windproof, waterproof, tear-proof, and even dirt resistant. You can throw it over bushes to build a quick hunting blind, poke a few sticks underneath it for a tent, wrap it around a timber frame for a boat, and could probably cobble together a little basket and hibachi to make it into a hot air balloon!" He lifted the edge of the sheet and held it in front of his own khaki-covered loins, "Or even make a kilt out of it," he laughed and nodded at Benji's jeans.

"Yer too good to me," Benji said, his voice squeaking just a little as he swallowed his embarrassment. "Thank ye."

Billy knew what it was. He hadn't meant to find a new family, but he had. If he was going back to the 18th century in nine months, he didn't want to have a strong bond to break in the 21st century. No, it wasn't the bond that was in danger; it would be his big heart that would break. Leaving for Benji was self-preservation.

82

Benji had disappeared last week, leaving only the flimsiest of notes. 'I'll be back through when the time is ripe.' "Funny man," Billy said softly. "Not the time is right; no, he's speaking of the plum time to travel. The time will be 'ripe' next August 17th."

Billy sat down in his big, overstuffed chair and mused aloud, trying to sort it out. "I still don't understand why he didn't take the truck? I thought he had changed his mind about it. He did say it would be faster and easier than 'hoofing it.' Well, he must have had a good reason. I doubt it was pride. From what I've seen, no task was beneath him. He was very gracious when accepting help, too. There must be something eating at him. Well," he sighed, "at least he stayed on until Mom's place was done. It would have been nice for him to be at the house warming party next week, but, oh, well."

Peter walked in on Billy's conversation with himself. "He's gone for good? I thought he was just going camping, then going to stay in North Carolina for a year. Isn't that what he said?"

Billy paled. Peter was home a day early. Had he overheard him talking with Benji about the August 17th window for time travel?

Peter spoke up, "I thought he wanted to work for a year or so, and then go see his grandpa or something. I know you offered him money." Peter saw the look of shock on Billy's face. "No, dear, that's fine with me. I know there's nothing 'like that' going on between you two. If I didn't know better, and I don't, I'd believe you two were brothers. But, since I've met your real brother and you two look so much alike, I doubt that Benji could even be a long lost cousin. It's just that he was so, how can I say this? He was just so comfortable to be around."

"Yes, he fit right in, at least emotionally. I know Mom sure loved him," Billy sighed.

"Well, I think he may have liked her a little too much," Peter said cautiously.

Billy gave him 'the look,' so Peter explained. "Didn't you ever notice? When Bibb would do something for him, whether it was to bring him a glass of water or a give him a hug for fixing the mini blinds, his eyes would tear up? I think he has, or had, a mother and he's missing her, missing her a lot!"

Billy didn't say anything lest he say something he shouldn't. Peter picked up on his partner's reluctance to continue the topic of conversation, so changed the subject. "When do I get to meet your father? It seems like he just got here and now he's gone. I hope he didn't do it on purpose. You did say he was happy for us, didn't you?"

"Shoot, Peter, he trusts my character judgment; if I love you, he loves you. It's just that he's going nuts, taking care of all the legalities back in London. He said he didn't give two hoots in Hell about the title for him or James. I mean, it defaulted back to James when he left and returned to him after he found those papers. It's a good thing James left me that letter with all of the people to trust in the UK, and who to look out for. He was darned smart to have Ladmo, or whatever his name was, make another copy of his hiatus papers from Parliament or whatever those documents were. Both the original and original copy just 'happened' to disappear which was mighty convenient for the wrong people."

"Yeah, and the warning about James Bradford, his buddy from The Club, was a good one, too," Billy continued. "You know, I don't think he knew that good old JB was his ex-wife's brother. And, I just found out that JB and the MacLeods have been in cahoots for years, two generations, anyhow. JB and Clotilde are at least second cousins to those slime balls. But, now that the lies and deceptions have been revealed, Dad can make a clean cut of his life in England and move here to North Carolina. He said before he left, he personally wanted to oversee the disposal of his assets. He also wanted to make sure all the fires were put out. He didn't want any old issues flaring up down the road."

"Yeah, well I was glad he married your mother and acknowledged you first, before he did the denouncing or renouncing or whatever it's called. I mean," Peter shook his head in amazement. "Wow; that was a biggie. I mean, getting rid of the title and the authority, you a British Lord..."

Billy interrupted him. "There wasn't much authority to it. They passed a law about 20 years ago that said the seat in the House of Lords wasn't going to be hereditary anymore. If Dad hadn't left and put James in as his proxy, James never would have had anything but the honorary title."

"Yeah, Lord Billy Burke Melbourne: that has quite the ring to it," Peter said then started sniggering.

Billy looked at him then they both started laughing out loud. "Well, what can I say?" Billy said in between gasps and guffaws. "I'd grown fond of the name Billy Burke. I didn't want to be a William, and Burke kind of flowed with Billy, and since Mom was going to be a Melbourne, too... Well, to hell with anyone who doesn't like that name. That's who I am, and I'm proud of it!"

"Yes, dear," Peter said as he came in for a full body hug. "And you're mine, whether we share a last name or not."

Billy gave him a big smooch, pulled back, and grinned at his partner for life. "And I pity the fool who tries to break us apart," he said, pulling Peter closer to him. "You'd be mine," he said and kissed him again more thoroughly, "even if your name was Kermit the Frog."

13 A Secondary Infection
October 27, 2013
Intensive Care Ward
Moses H. Cone Hospital
Greensboro, NC

"Here, I thought you might want to do some reading." Peter set down the blue plastic milk crate of books on the empty chair. "You mentioned you wanted to read these again. I know I've caught you staring at them a few times since your brother left. Maybe this will lift your spirits. Which one do you want to read first, hon?"

Billy winced at the weakness that Peter had seen in him. Peter saw the fleeting insecurity and moved closer to him. "I know I'm supposed to stay away, but damn it, you're not going to get better unless you feel better about yourself. Just remember, whether you're running first place in the Boston Marathon or lying in this bed with tubes up the Walla Walla and out the Yangtze, I love you. I want you to get better not only for you, but for me." Peter leaned over and placed a slow, warm kiss on Billy's forehead. "And anyone who says I can't kiss you there can just piss off. No germs are going to hurt you there, right?"

"Right," Billy said weakly.

"I know you miss your brother, but your mother needs you. And I do, too. You don't realize how special you are to us. Besides, she's getting tired of beating me at chess. You need to show me what strategy really is!"

Billy managed a weak but honest smile. "I'll work on it. The first book is the one that's on top."

"I'm sorry, sir, but you'll have to leave," the nurse said as she came in with a fresh bag of antibiotics-enhanced saline solution.

"Okay." Peter looked back at his weakened, sickly partner. "Here," he said as he handed the book *Lost* to Billy. "You can tell me all about it when I get back. They're sending me out to San Francisco for some conference," Peter rolled his eyes, "but I should be back by this weekend. That should be just about enough time for you to plow through these." Peter winked at him, blew him a discreet kiss, then smiled at the nurse as he left. "Be good to him," he warned, "he's the only one I've got."

The nurse smiled back and said sincerely, "I'll treat him like he was my own son," then proceeded to change out the IV bags.

She looked back at the door as it closed, then down at Billy. "I'd say you have at least one very good reason to get better." She poured more water into his cup and offered him the straw. Billy took a sip then looked up and said 'thanks, that's enough' with his eyes. She made sure all his invasive polymer lines were flowing in and out correctly, and each of the umpteen electrodes was secured to the various inconvenient spots all over his body. She left with the parting words, "Be good."

"Hmph," Billy mumbled. He didn't have enough energy even to be rambunctious, much less bad, and not enough strength or ambition to be anything but inert. But, he knew stressing over his situation was creating negative energy. Leah told him once that bad thoughts were the biggest hindrance to healing. He sighed and decided he'd do it Leah's way: change his outlook and let the positive attitude of faith take over.

Billy sat up, turned on the reading lamp above his head, and gingerly brought up his knees. He set the book on his sheet-covered thigh reading desk. "Sinclaire, take me away," he said as he opened up *Lost*, the first of the time traveling 'fiction' novels about Jody and Sarah Pomeroy and their family. "I may have to stay plugged in and tied up in this hospital, and they can pump me full of antibiotics and measure every heartbeat and white blood cell I have, but they can't take away my fantasies or memories. Let's see if there's something in here about *my* family that I missed. Hmph. And I'll see if I can get any insight on Benji. Maybe I can figure out where he took off to."

14 Where's Benji
November 4, 2013
Greensboro Police Station

"D etective Burke, there's a woman here who says she has some information about the MacLeods." Dyane put her hand around the mouthpiece and discreetly added, "I thought we had both of them locked up."

"Go ahead and send her in," he replied mechanically, hopefully hiding the tone of disgust that he felt. He had only been back to work one day from his second hospital stay and already had to deal with MacLeod issues!

Dyane escorted the insecure visitor to the door, giving Billy an eye roll and smirk before she left. Billy didn't pay any attention to her unspoken comment about what she thought of the girl. But, he did make sure he shut the door behind the young woman so they would have complete privacy. His own personal policy was not to judge a person by his appearance or dress; looks were not only deceiving, they often out and out lied!

"Good afternoon, may I help you..." he prompted the scared and skinny teenaged girl for her name.

"Autumn," she said with head bowed. She ventured a look up and saw that Billy appeared to be genuinely interested in helping her. "I, I, I don't know what to do," she blurted out and began sobbing. She wanted a fix so badly. She knew it wasn't a solution, but would only make matters worse. Besides, there was the baby to think of.

Billy offered her the whole box of tissues from his desktop then sat back to let her get her emotions under control. "Take your time," he said. "You are my only concern, okay?"

Autumn sniffed and wiped her face then grabbed another double handful and gave her nose a more adequate honking. She took a deep breath and started the story that she had been practicing for three months.

"He told me he was going to Greensboro, North Carolina. He said he found out that this is where the MacLeods were heading. I was kind of out of it, so he gave me this."

Billy took the worn, crinkled, and folded yellow note and recognized the large, sprawling handwriting immediately: it was

Benji's. 'Give this woman safe passage and protect her from the MacLeod clan. Benji MacKay.'

Billy looked at the severely emaciated young girl and waited for the rest of the story.

"He said he didn't know, or 'ken' was the way he said it, if it would do any good, but it 'couldna do nae harm' to have a note. He said if I went to the police, they would help me." She paused, "I didn't know you did that—help people, I mean." The confused strawberry blonde looked at Billy, "I thought all you did was go out there and bust robbers and druggies and hoe, hoe, whores." She stumbled on the last word, grimaced, then said no more.

Billy gulped as he realized that this must be what the girl did. She certainly didn't look like a high school student with parents and teachers urging her to go to college. Her body looked young, but her eyes were old, like she had lived a rough life. She was also dirty. Her stringy autumn-colored hair had dyed streaks of hot pink color that had grown out at least an inch. It looked like she had been living in the short jean skirt and spaghetti strap tank top for at least a week by the food and sweat stains on them.

"How old are you," he asked.

"Seventeen," she admitted with a huff. "I don't want to lie anymore. I've been saying I'm 18 since I was 15. I ran away from home two years ago. I thought I knew it all. But I didn't and, well, can you help me?" she asked. She turned around to look through the door's window, taking in the magnitude of the whole police department.

"Well, they might not be able to," he nodded toward the dozen or so personnel beyond the shut door, "But I can. Benji was my friend."

"Was?" she shrieked, her tears starting to re-emerge. "But, but..."

"He's fine, I'm sure. It's just he had some business to take care of. I believe he'll be back through here in a few months. I'm sure we can find you accommodations in the meantime."

Autumn shifted in her seat with discomfort. "Um, do you know somewhere I can stay that, um, has a shower? I feel really dirty and these are the only clothes I have." The detective was a polite man, he hadn't been staring at her, but she was self-conscious about her appearance. She could smell herself; he probably could, too.

"I'm sure we can find a place. But, do you want to tell me something first?" He could tell she was trying to shed an uncomfortable story, not just the dirty clothes. Reading body language was one of his specialties.

"He didn't want to do it," she blurted out. Billy jumped up and closed the mini blinds on the door window. This was definitely a private matter.

"They beat his back. They used rubber hoses so it wouldn't show, but they still did it." She sniffed and grabbed the box of tissues again. "And his wrists were bloody where they used those plastic ties to hold his hands together. I guess someone had come up from behind and knocked him out or given him a drug or something, because he was face down on the ground when I first saw him. He was huge!"

"Benji?" Billy asked, although he was sure that with the word 'huge,' she was speaking of him.

She nodded and continued her story. "'You know what we'll do if you don't do your duty,' they told him. I was out of it. I needed a fix real bad. See, they told me that all I had to do was," she dipped her head down in shame, "'screw him' and that they'd fix me up, fix me up real good for three days if I made it look like he was liking it. Well, he looked at me and sighed real sad-like. 'Only if she wants me to,' he said.

"Well, what I wanted was that fix. If I had to, um, you know, screw him, then that was fine by me. He had a stone face on him and I told him so. 'I'll do it to save ye,' he said, 'but I dinna have to enjoy it.'

"'Yes, you do,' I told him. 'If I don't make you like it, then they'll hurt me,' I lied. I didn't want to tell him why he had to look like he was enjoying, um, screwing me; that it was the only way that they'd give me the drugs.

"So he did." She shuddered as she recalled that hot summer day. "The worst part was them filming it. I mean, they were right in our, um, privates, the whole time, well, most of the time. They made him lick me all over. But, they never showed his back. The scars on his back were so, so ugly that the director—I guess that's what you'd call him, he was the man who held onto the drugs, anyways—he told the cameraman not to show the marks on his back.

"They had to stop filming once, too. Benji said he wouldn't do it without a condom, do the, um, penetration. The licking and kissing were okay, but he didn't want to chance me getting pregnant. It wouldn't be fair, after all." She snorted, "Fair: he really did, does have a strong sense of good and bad, fair and unfair.

"Anyhow, '*no way,*' the director hollered. Benji started to stand up, to stop everything, and then the director pulled out a pistol—a long, shiny one like in the Dirty Harry movies. He pointed it at Benji, but it didn't scare him none. He kept walking towards him. Then the director man pointed it at me and said, 'Snuff,' and Benji froze. 'Get back to suckin' on her tits,' he said, 'then go down all the way and make sure she's good and wet. That big thing of yours will split her if you don't. And you don't want to hurt her now, do you?' And then he waved his gun over at me again.

"'It's okay,' I said to him. Shoot, I'd say anything. I heard the words they were sayin', but I didn't care. I just wanted him to hurry up and get it done so I could get high. 'Please look like you like me,' I begged. 'Please, it will make it better.' Actually, it would, I mean, it did.

"Out of the corner of my eye, I could see the big baggie the director had in his hand, wavin' it at me like it was a big juicy steak to a starvin' dog. Well, Benji 'finished,' the director said 'cut,' and called me over. 'You did a real good job, Missy,' he said. 'You have a real nice mouth on you. Just blow me and I'll give you a bonus,' and he waved a joint in the air. 'Real good shit,' he said.

"Benji wasn't tied up anymore. He couldn't be if he was going to, well, anyway, since he was awake and not conked out, and no one there was big enough to take him down, he started to leave. But, he saw the director with a syringe in his hand, getting ready to shoot me up, right here," she said as she pointed to a place between her middle two fingers. "Benji took two long steps, grabbed that man's wrist, and I swear, picked him up in the air, feet kicking away, and broke his wrist with his thumb. Really, just placed his thumb here," Autumn illustrated on her own forearm, "and went like," she pressed a spot just behind her wrist, "and snap, he broke it. The bone popped out and everything."

Autumn straightened her back in pride. "And he said that if he ever gave me or anyone else any drugs ever again, that he would find him and break his neck," Autumn did more hand gestures, "just like that. And he meant it, too. He grabbed me by the wrist—he was gentle to me though, even though he could have broken me in two—and said, 'get dressed; we're leaving.'

"He took me to a Taco Bell, made me eat a burrito, said beans were good for me, and told me that I had to go back home, no matter how much I didn't want to. I was feelin' sassy, I mean, I still needed—I mean wanted—a fix. 'Why don't you go home,' I

91

shouted. I should have been grateful, but that came later. I think he knew it would, too.

"'Here, drink this,' he said and filled my little paper cup with water. 'And keep drinkin' water until ye canna hold another drop. Then empty yer bladder and start all over again. And eat beans, lots of beans.' I don't know what it was with him and beans, but he seemed to think that beans and water would cure me. I was mad at him because he wouldn't let me leave. I could have gone back to my street corner and made enough money to get high for at least a little bit. You see, I had an area in downtown where I'd give anyone a blowjob for $20. The pimps didn't bother with that area because it was so seedy. The men that hung out there didn't have much more than $20 and were happy to get any kind of sex. I wouldn't do anything more than that because I didn't want to get pregnant. I wasn't a virgin or anything. I, um, had, um, relations with my stepfather when I was younger, and that's why I left." Autumn snorted in disgust. "At least he had the decency to use a condom.

"Anyway, until Benji, I hadn't 'gone all the way' in two years. And now, I, I, I really need some help. I can't get an abortion because I don't have the money. I don't want to try to do it myself. I had a girlfriend who did that and she got a terrible infection, and I think she's dead now. I haven't seen her in six months, at least. I was hoping Benji could pay for it."

"NO!" Billy shouted, then brought it down a notch. "No!" he said at a lower volume, but with just as much loathing.

"What?" Autumn asked, shocked and suddenly afraid of the police detective. He had seemed like such a nice man, and now he was yelling at her.

"You're coming home with me, now," Billy commanded. It was his first full day back to work in nearly a month. He had been tired, depressed, and burned out, but now his emotional fire was raging: he had a mission.

"Don't you have to work?" she asked meekly, hoping to avoid this suddenly excitable police officer.

"I got off work ten minutes before you came in," Billy said in a gentler tone, now able to hold back his horror and fury at her suggestion. "I was staying late, just looking over some old papers. When Dyane called me and said that the MacLeods were involved, I decided we should probably talk."

"Oh, they weren't the ones who did that to me or Benji. But he did write about them on the note," she said. She didn't want to lie to a cop, that was for sure. Plus, he seemed nice. Even if he did just lose his temper, he had calmed back down in a hurry. "Thanks for listening," she said dejectedly and got up to leave.

"I said, you're coming home with me, now," Billy reiterated, but with supplication instead of bossiness.

"I appreciate the offer, but I stopped 'working' right after Benji helped me clean up. I mean, he was only with me for those three days, and I was out of it most of the time, but I promised him that I would never sell my body again for drugs. Not for drugs or anything else," she said sadly, wishing she could find some way to earn food and lodging.

"Oh, honey, you don't have to worry about me," Billy said with a swish of his wrist and a big grin.

"OH, oh, sorry, I mean, that's good. At least, for me," she said awkwardly as she realized that he was letting her know that he was gay. If that was the case, she could take a chance with him.

"Honey, it's good for me, too." Billy laughed. "We'll take care of you and this baby," he said with pride and determination.

"But *I* can't take care of a baby..." Autumn protested lamely.

"But *I* can. At least, between my partner and me we can. That is if all are agreeable," Billy said softly. Yes, if Benji was going back in time to be with his Grandpa Jody, he'd be more than happy to have his baby.

15 Meet My Mom

"We're home," Billy said as he pulled up to his apartment. "Why don't you get cleaned up here, and then I'll take you shopping."

"Um," Autumn stalled, looking down at her dirty outfit.

"Oh, don't worry about a thing, darlin'. You can wear something of mine. I have a huge assortment of Hawaiian shirts and a few pair of shorts with drawstrings that will cinch right up so they don't fall down and embarrass you. You'll be dressed good enough for the Wal-Mart. Last time I checked, they didn't have a dress code to get in."

Billy looked over at his new charge and saw that she was wavering on an emotional fence rail between grinning and crying. But, no matter which way she leaned, she was still safe. And now he was here to nurture and protect her and the unborn child she carried. "Well, at least last time I checked all the sign said was 'no shirt, no shoes, no service' or something like that. However, I would think it best if you remembered to wear something underneath, just in case a wind kicks up. We don't want you doin' a Marilyn Monroe and makin' all the other girls jealous with those pretty legs of yours…"

That did it: the tears of joy were flowing. Autumn laughed first, then cried, then managed to do both at the same time. She didn't know what to do, so sat down on the big couch and buried her head in her hands.

"Now, now," Billy said, "Why don't you go take your shower first. Then we'll sort this out. In the meantime, I'm here to protect you and," he held her hand to help her to her feet, and looked down at her barely protruding belly, "*my* baby?" he declared and asked at the same time.

Autumn sniffed back her runny nose and wiped her tears on the back of her hand. "Okay, I'll let you take care of me and *your* baby. I think I'll just find my way back to the bathroom and that shower while you find something for me to wear. At least now I have something to look forward to, even if it's just a clean body."

"Oh, you're getting much more than a clean body, darlin': you're getting a clean start. Now, get goin', girlfriend," Billy added with an affected lisp, "we're going shopping!"

As soon as Autumn was in the shower, Billy was on the phone. "Mom, I think we have our first resident or client or student or whatever. I mean...you're going to be a grandma!"

"What? I mean, who, I mean, why, I mean, how?" Bibb asked, totally baffled. She only had two sons. James had gone back in time and couldn't be 'heard' from, and Billy was gay.

"I'm going to have a baby in I'd say five, maybe six months. We have to go to the doctor to be sure. I'll have to see if I can get a referral for a good obstetrician. I mean, I don't want just anyone bringing my little red headed child into the world."

"Billy, would you slow down and speak so I can understand you? And how do you know that you're having a red headed child?"

Billy spoke slowly and deliberately. "The, mother, has, red, hair, and, so, does, the, sire. Okay?"

"Where and who are they? And, do, I, get, to, meet, them?" Bibb asked just as purposefully.

"Absolutely!" Billy said then speeded his speech up to a normal rate. "But first, the mother and I have an errand or two to run. Can you get one of the guys there to clear out the crafts room and bring up one of the bedroom sets? I think your quilting is going to have to wait until the next phase is complete."

"Can I at least know her name?" Bibb asked in exasperation.

"Autumn, like the color of her hair," he said with pride. "And I will not call the sire a sperm donor. That's beneath him. There's a story behind their situation, and I'd like to keep that confidential..."

"I understand completely," Bibb interjected then stopped talking when she realized that she had interrupted.

"It's Benji," Billy said then clenched his jaw. He took a deep breath then continued. "I might as well tell you now, because I don't think I could keep that a secret. I'm not as good as you are when it comes to that, even though I'd like to think I am."

"Well, Benji was, is, special to you, to all of us. Since he's gone, I'm glad we can do this for him."

Ж

The shower and the peanut butter and toast snack that Billy suggested had put the glow into Autumn and her pregnancy. "God, you're beautiful," he said as she came out wearing his loose fitting gray sweats.

"Um," she hesitated. "I thought you said..." she began, not wanting to tell him outright that she didn't want anything to do with him sexually. At least it sounded like he was making a pass at her.

"Oh, I'm sorry. That's not what I meant. I will *never* mean that. I'm in a monogamous relationship. You'll meet Peter in a few days. His job takes him all over the country. And yes, you'll have your own room, but not here. I'm taking you to meet my mother, the baby's grandmother! Oh, you'll love Bibb. She's a kick."

"Okay," Autumn replied, still a bit tongue-tied with all of the good fortune that was suddenly coming her way. Hopefully the saying, 'if something sounds too good to be true, it usually is,' wasn't the case with Billy. He was her last hope.

The shopping trip went smoothly. "You can buy anything you want, but I'd suggest elastic waistbands. I don't know how fast a belly grows on a pregnant woman, and I want you to be comfortable," Billy said. He was already feeling protective of her, and it wasn't just the baby. He grinned as he realized that this must be what it felt like to have a little sister.

"This is just to get you started," Billy told her as he put the bags of clothing in the back of the truck. He ran around to the passenger side and opened the door for her. "I love this truck, but I think I'm going to need to get a family rig pretty soon. Do you know when you're due?"

Autumn didn't answer aloud, but shook her head 'no.' She didn't want to tell him that she never paid attention to the months of the year much less days of the month. Periods came and went, and were just a nuisance that she had to take care of whenever she noticed that she had messed her pants. She had been clean and sober for a while, but didn't know how long. She didn't know when the sobriety started much less what the month or day was today.

Billy hadn't heard her reply, but didn't want to ask again. She probably didn't know, and he didn't want to embarrass her. He shouldn't have even asked. She was obviously in a daze with her change of life from the streets. He'd make a few calls and get some referrals for a good doctor for her and the baby. Maybe he could find out what her interests were so she could start some schooling while she was pregnant. It would give her a focus and a purpose for her life after the delivery. He wouldn't mind an open adoption, but it would probably be hard on her.

"I thought it might be easier for you if I took you over to Mom's now. She's getting a room set up for you." Billy saw the look of fear on Autumn's face. "Don't worry; if you don't feel comfortable with her, you can sleep in my bed, and I'll take the couch." He glanced over and saw her blanch. "Or you can take the couch, and I'll take the bed. I just want you to be comfortable. You've been through a lot from what you've told me. Would you allow us to treat you like a queen?"

Billy heard her slight chuckle at the remark. "Yes, dear; the queen wants to treat you like a queen," he joked. Now Autumn was laughing out loud, not even trying to contain her glee. "See, you're starting to feel better already. Now, on a serious note..." Billy looked over and saw Autumn tense. "Just listen; I want to give you a very short history lesson before we get to Mom's.

"Years ago, my mother, Bibb, was unmarried and pregnant. There was no place for her to go: she had no family and had a business that she was trying to get off the ground. She delivered her child, all alone, by herself, and took him to strangers to be adopted out. She never knew what happened to him until a few months ago. She doesn't want that to happen to other women, or girls..." Billy added with a look down his nose over at Autumn. "So, she decided to sell her business to her employees and develop the additional property she had. Before he left, Benji helped clear the land and built her an oversized house. It's a home for unwed mothers. It's an old idea that she's trying to bring back. At least bring it back without the shame that it tends to call up."

Billy changed to a bright tone, "So, you get the honor of being the first member of the extended family. You get to be my sister!"

"Wha, what?" Autumn babbled.

"Well, since Bibb is the housemother, you get to be her daughter. And, since I'm her son, then you're my sister. Oh, and by the way, that baby that she gave away was me. I spent all those years in an orphanage—which wasn't bad by the way— but she spent those same years missing me and not knowing how or if she could get me back. She's bucked the system before, and she's doing it again. And you, little sister, get to help! Come on; we're here."

Autumn allowed Billy to open the truck door for her and help her down. "I'll come back for the clothes in a minute. You're going to love Bibb."

Autumn kept her head down. She wasn't used to looking anyone in the eye. Anonymity had been a major part of survival in her past life. She could put on an old ball cap to cover her red hair, an oversized sweatshirt, baggy pants, and untied tennis shoes, and then become any teenaged kid, male or female.

She wouldn't be able to keep that up for long, though. She didn't know how far along she was in her pregnancy, but it was probably three months. She could feel the lump above her pelvic bone growing every week. At first, she thought she was just not keeping track of time very well. Actually, she never did care much for watches or calendars. But, a couple of weeks ago when she was in the bathroom at McDonalds, washing her face and cleaning up as best she, she looked up and saw the personal hygiene products for sale for a quarter. She stopped her sink-top bath and stared. She knew she had seen at least two full moons since her last period. She always thought of werewolves and fantasy characters when the moon was full. Oh, to be someone or something special. Super powers: why couldn't she have them, too? They wouldn't even have to be too special. If she could just get a decent job and take care of herself...

Herself; that had started the new panic. She couldn't take care of herself, and now was pregnant. There would be someone else to take care of if she didn't do something fast.

She was walking by the river last month when she saw it: the little yellow note from Benji. She almost lost it, but ran fast enough to stop it from blowing into the water. No, she wouldn't jump off the bridge today, tomorrow, or ever. That note flying away was a wake-up call. It was if that scrap of paper had pulled itself out of her pocket to flutter about, to remind her that there was someone out there who could, and would, help her. Even if Benji couldn't be there with her, to protect and feed her, he had given her a blank check with names on it.

Yes, she was glad she had brought it in to the police department this morning to cash it. She had clean clothes, a clean body, and best of all, hope. And now the baby had a father. Or, according to Billy, two fathers and a grandmother. Many children had started out life with much less and turned out just fine. Yes, Billy was the right person for her at the right time. She looked up and said, "Thanks, Lord. I forgot You got it all under control, but that we just need to listen. Thanks for going the extra step and pulling that yellow ticket out of my pocket."

16 Misconception
November 5, 2013

"Shit, shit, shit!"

"What's wrong, Billy?" Bibb and Marty asked at the same time.

"I told Benji that he had to wait until next August 17th to go through The Trees because that was the date you told James to come through. But, the date isn't crucial, is it?"

"No," Marty answered cautiously. "James was to come through for an event, to save the life of his ancestor. That was the only reason I told him that date. He'd be in the vicinity of the assault if he came through at that time and, well, it did turn out all right. If it hadn't, you, your mother, and your brother would never have been born."

"Benji's gone. He left a note that said he was just going to kick around the country for a few months then come back through town when it was his time to go through The Trees. He could be back there now if I'd been thinking straight."

"Well, you did have a lot on your mind with James and Leah leaving, and then the transplant ordeal..." Marty was trying to soothe his son's frustration, but it wasn't doing any good.

"Billy, I think the misconception was meant to be," Bibb said authoritatively, then paused. She giggled then tried to compose herself. "I guess that would be both misconceptions were meant to be. If Benji hadn't been where he was at that certain time, he wouldn't have 'sired' your child, and Autumn might not be alive, or at least clean and sober. And, if he were here, he'd probably take on the responsibility for both her and the baby. So, you see, it's all going to be okay. I'm sure he'll get back to where he wants to be. And this way he won't have to worry about having a child and, well, maybe a wife, in this time waiting for him. I think he was meant to go back."

"And, you were meant to have a child, son," Marty added. "I think it's pretty awesome myself. Nobody has to pretend to be someone else like Bruce did, Autumn is being taken care of and will get a good education and career training, and I'm going to be a grandpa, this time for real!"

"Well, I guess you're right," Billy said. He knew that his older half-brother, Bruce, had pretended to be James's father.

Being gay was shameful back then, and a fake marriage and an imaginary wife who died in childbirth were created to perpetuate the story of James as Bruce's child.

Bibb sat up straight, inspiration hitting her all at once. "I think I know why you feel bad. You're a great detective, and you didn't figure this one out, at least not right away. But, I really don't think you were supposed to..."

"Thanks, Mom, I needed that," Billy said with a grin. "We're supposed to let the Man Upstairs take control of some of this. Free will only goes so far. And, I think you're right. He took a bad situation and turned it into good for all of us."

"So we're all cool?" Marty asked. Bibb and Billy nodded that they were. "Good, because I want to take this lady home and see how it feels to make love to a grandma!"

"Eww; that's too much information," Billy said with an exaggerated look of disgust. "You're still my parents, you know."

"And don't we know it, son," Marty said. He reached around his son, held him close, and gave him a kiss on the cheek. "Don't worry about what you should have done, or could have done. Benji's a big boy and can take care of himself, wherever he is. And, he has given us all a great gift, even if he didn't mean to and doesn't know about it. Have a good night."

Marty turned to Bibb, "Come on, Grandma, or do you want to be called Nana?"

"Whichever one he pops out with is fine by me. Oh, and we don't have to wait for the ultrasound. I'm sure I'm having a grandson. Having sons seems to run in this family."

17 Zero Hour
Outside Greensboro, The Trees
Next year: August 17, 2014

"So it's time," Benji said softly as he stared at The Trees, his time tunnel to the past and his grandparents. He should have come into town a few days earlier so he could have stopped in to say good-bye to Billy, Peter, and Bibb. Who knows, maybe Marty had made it back, and he'd finally get a chance to see him again, too.

"Hmph," he snorted. "Or say good-bye to Wee Michael or even Autumn. Yer an evil man, Benji MacKay: makin' friends, and then dumpin' 'em, leavin' without a word, jest a scrap of paper, if ye can find one. Weel, it's too late now to do anythin' about sayin' good-byes or nice kenin' ye's. It's daybreak and time to see if this works."

Benji brought out the smartphone Billy had given him, the one he had set with a picture of 18th century Evie as the background. He had clipped a still shot of her from the video his grandfather had accidently taken. She was pregnant at the time, but that didn't matter: it was Evie's face he needed to concentrate on.

"Ye canna be usin' the picture of Grandpa fer yer focus now, can ye?" he asked himself. "Ye dinna want to be comin' back to yerself now... How can I look so much like him?"

Benji checked his backpack one more time, sighed deeply, and looked up. "It's all in Yer hands, Lord," he said. "Thanks fer givin' me the opportunity to go back to where I belong. I hope I make Ye proud. Amen."

He slung his backpack over his shoulders and fished in his pocket for the coin. "Here we go, ready or not," he said. He took one more look at the smartphone picture of Evie and started his slow, determined walk.

He had been warned about the queasiness that came with the strong magnetic pull of the site. His stomach would probably be upset either way, though. He was both scared and ecstatic that the time had finally come. Now, as long as Grandpa hadn't moved, he'd be fine. But, with as flamboyant and politically active as his grandsire was, he still shouldn't be too hard to locate. At least, if he had stayed in North Carolina...

"Focus!" Benji said to himself harshly. "Now isna the time fer waverin'. He'll be there, ye ken he will." He added softly, "I hope he will."

18 Not a Fair Trade

August 19, 1782

Benji was hot and tired and hungry after his long walk. He had been robbed his first night here; a thief had taken his backpack and most of his goods while he slept, but he still had a couple of copper coins left that he could use for food and drink. Of course, it would be smarter to keep his money and find another way to silence the growling lion in his belly. At least this town was large enough that he had options. He was deciding whether to head to the livery stable and see if they had some equine output he could shovel in exchange for a meal, or go to the tavern and try his hand at cards, when his attention was diverted to the dock.

"She's big and, if you can motivate her properly, I'll wager she's stronger than five men!" a voice shouted.

The spectators in the crowd were all jeering and laughing. Several very crude remarks were made, downright nasty suggestions that were inappropriate in any era. "It'd take a big man to get her to work if she didn't care to," said the fat man with the cigar. He started a cruel and sinister laugh. "Or a big strap. Look at those striped shoulders. It looks like she's as stubborn as a jackass with a full belly."

The crowd roared at Tubby's joke, which pleased the squinty-eyed trader. Another voice added, "Even if you couldn't get her to work, at least she could foal a bunch of big buck slaves. Look at the size of her!"

"Yeah, but who'd be big enough or dumb enough to get his dick close to her?" added Tubby. "You'd have to knock her out first. It doesn't look like the whips did much good."

"Now, now men; she's a good worker," the slave trader explained. "She's just a bit tired from the boat ride over. You know Africa is a long ways away. She just needs a little conditioning, that's all. Now, you see, I'll bet I can get her to lift those barrels of pitch and load them into this wagon and do it without the whip. See, she hasn't eaten in three days or had anything to drink since yesterday morning, so I'll wager..."

"What will ye wager?" Benji asked boldly as he walked up from the back of the all-male crowd. He looked over and got a better view of the subject of the gathering. He could tell by the talk that it was a woman, a big female slave, they were discussing. What he hadn't realized was that a human female could actually be that huge. She was nearly as tall as he was and had a broad, sturdy frame, not reedy or lanky. But she definitely had been deprived of food. He could see her ribs and just about everything else: all she was wearing was a little leather apron and a dirty and frayed rag around her head.

The squinty-eyed man who Benji had interrupted was apparently the neighborhood slave broker. His hands were full with a small book in one grimy fist and a whip in the other. But, his once overflowing mouth was now empty of words. The first sight of Benji and his height and build had a tendency to do that to everyone.

Normally the gawking bothered Benji, but this time he was glad of it. It gave him a chance to develop a plan. "I said, what will ye wager?" He scanned the crowd to determine whether he could expect help or resistance if he tried to free the woman. By the lusty leers and jeers of the shameless men, though, this wouldn't be an easy task. It appeared they wanted entertainment, not a field hand.

"Now, what would you be needin' such a big Negress for?" the slave trader sneered as he wiggled his hips obscenely. "The little ones break apart when you poke 'em, eh?" He put the whip out in front of his crotch and added an even more graphic physical representation of intercourse to the responsive crowd. They were eating it up, and he was feeling the power.

Benji ignored the crude remark rather than reply to it. He didn't want to feed the perverted frenzy. "It looks to me like ye need to load those barrels onto the back of the wagons, and this lass here is the only one strong enough to do it. And, by the looks of her back, it doesna look like she's takin' to the task," he added sarcastically. He was going to have to challenge the man...

"Oh, she'll do the work, all right," the slave trader said. "You see, I have this nice big ham bone here that will motivate her just as much as this will," and brandished the cat o' nine tails with the metal tips covered in dried blood.

Benji kept his poker face on, but grimaced on the inside. That was probably her blood. The wounds on her back were still bright red, although blood was not flowing. He knew the look and feel of lash wounds: hers were more than twelve hours old, but less than twenty-four. And, if he didn't do something for her now, she'd have more soon. The only thing worse than a flogging was another one on top of wounds that hadn't yet healed.

"So, I take it yer a bettin' man," Benji taunted as he walked closer to the greasy flesh vendor. He snorted with disgust as he looked down his nose at the peddler and his ill-fitting jacket. He'd start the intimidation process right away.

The trader squared his rounded shoulders, trying to make the most of his petite and portly self as he grandly presented his reply. "Yes, I am, if I feel that there's money to be made and that it's a sure thing for me," he crowed to both Benji and the crowd. The man was high on the support of the mob, and Benji's size wasn't bothering him. After all, he still had the whip in his hand.

"So ye think ye can get the lass to load the barrels if ye offer her the meat..."

"And a jug of water," slave trader added.

"And a jug of water," Benji agreed. "So, I'll wager that she willna do it fer either the meat or the water. And, if I'm right, I'll take her with me. And, if I'm wrong and she loads them, then I'll load the next three wagons that ye get in here free of charge, no ham bone required."

The slave trader shifted his position, moving his whip holding hand down to scratch his balls, unsure of the bet, but not wanting to be called a liar either.

"I mean, if ye arena sure, I'll jest load the one wagon and take the lass as payment. I jest think ye'd be gettin' more work outta me than her." Benji was stalling. He didn't know why he was doing this, but it seemed like the right thing to do.

The slave trader wasn't sure if he should take the bet so, delayed his decision by changing the topic. "So, what are you going to do with her after you load the barrels?"

"Now, that really isna yer concern, is it? So then, ye do agree with me: ye dinna think she'll load them even with the offer of the meat and water?" Benji grinned as if he had won the bet without even having to deal the cards. But, he knew in his gut that it wasn't going to be this easy. Hopefully, though, the man would take the wager.

Benji began playing the crowd, stretching out the anticipation of the trader's decision by walking over to the loading dock, looking at the barrels then back to the onlookers. He knew the trader didn't want to be embarrassed by losing a bet. He put one hand against the top edge of the barrel and pushed it, testing its weight. It was heavy but doable, even on an empty stomach. He turned back to face the trader. "I can jest load the one wagon and take her then?"

Benji really didn't want to load the sticky barrels, but he would do it to spare her another flogging. And, if he left her there, she'd most likely be whipped. He really did believe that she wouldn't do anything she didn't want to do, no matter how much whip, food, or drink were involved.

"I'll tell you what," the trader countered. "You can have her—free and clear, bill of sale included—if you load the next five wagons." Slave trader knew she was stubborn, but he did need to get the wagons loaded. He'd cut his losses, be rid of her, and get the wagons taken care of so he could head to the coast.

"No, I think yer right," Benji said with mock remorse, "maybe she will load the wagons fer the meat and water. Sorry to have disturbed yer sale there." There was absolutely no sincerity in Benji's apology and it was obvious to everyone. He was gambling without a wager being made. He knew the man was just a ringmaster and would be better off getting rid of the non-performing giantess than to be made out a fool.

"Okay, you load three wagons and you can have her." If he sold her today, whoever bought her would probably want his money back, too. She wouldn't work no matter how he or the other four owners had beat or starved her. She had been in America since she was a babe. Even the ruse that she was 'new' to the country hadn't been enough to keep her sold. She was back in his stable again, and he wanted to be rid of her for good.

Benji looked over at the sticky barrels, winced, and shook his head. "I dinna think I could do that today. I'm a bit hungry myself and I've worked up a mighty thirst with the long walk here. Now, if it's only the two wagons, and ye want to throw in a big dinner with all the drinks I can handle," he grinned and started nodding his head with delight at the idea, hoping the trader would be receptive to this arrangement. Yes, he would have loaded the wagons for the food and drink without the woman. But, she needed to be away from the whip more than he needed a full belly.

"Okay, okay," he said in exasperation. He looked around and saw the crowd had thinned so his embarrassment was minimal. "You can have her and dinner at the tavern if you get the wagons loaded. Hey, the tavern master's here." He signaled for the man to join them. "Here, feed him all he wants after he gets these two wagons loaded, d'ya hear?"

The apparent tavern master turned to look at the size of Benji and then back to the trader. "*All* he wants to eat?" he asked. That would be a lot of food by the size of him.

"And drink," Benji added with a smile.

The trader shook his head in resignation but agreed, "And drinks. Just put it on my bill. I'll be heading out in the morning...as long as these wagons are loaded properly. And you have to do all the loading before you get your dinner!"

"Aye, I'll stand by my word. And I'll be collectin' the bill of sale and the lass when I'm done with the task." Benji didn't know how slave trading and sales were done in this time era, but he did know that document would be good to have for her safety and for his.

Ж

The crowd had dissipated and the tall woman and the tacky barrels were all that were left of the earlier fracas. The wagons pulled up next to the cargo. Two young black boys, one driving each wagon, sat on the seats, sweat pouring off their brows, holding still except to swat at the occasional biting fly.

"Go ahead and take yer rest under the trees over there," Benji told them. "Ye can get water to drink down there at the creek. I willna be too long."

The two boys looked at each other, but didn't move. "I willna say anythin' to anyone. The man willna be back fer a bit. He went to take his food and drink. Ye can wait jest as well in the shade as in the sun; it's yer choice."

The two scrawny and shirtless boys looked at each other again, this time their eyes brightening with excitement. They jumped off their wagons and ran to the creek, looking back every couple of yards. The promise of coolness was stronger than the fear of a beating. Hopefully, he hadn't done something wrong, and the slave trader wouldn't find out. He didn't want to get them in trouble.

The slave woman was kneeling on the ground, still as a black onyx statue, shackled next to the little wooden grandstand in the center of town. By the looks of her, she still hadn't had anything to eat or drink. Benji knew of racial prejudice, hated it fervently, but also knew that he was in the eighteenth century and had to live with their customs and mores, no matter how low and wrong they were. Then he saw them: the enticements the slave trader was going to use. The bucket still had water in it, and the ham bone was wrapped in a greasy cloth. He looked around and saw he wasn't the center of attention anymore. It was high noon and too hot for anyone to be out unless he had to be. Or happened to be a slave or an idiot like himself, he thought.

Regardless of its state, it was better for her to have the leaf-mattered water and raggedy ham bone than nothing. Before he started into the dirty and heavy task, he'd take care of her needs, at least as best he could. It wasn't much for refreshment, but if their places were swapped, he'd be glad to have the marginal food and water. He glanced up and saw the boys were now at the creek's edge, splashing each other and having a good time. He ran his hand through the bucket of water and fished out the leaves, threw them on the ground, then tasted the water. He took a second drink then decided that if it was good enough for him, it would be for her, too.

"Here, it isna much, but it's all there is," he said sincerely, giving her a smile of resignation along with the water and hambone. Now what was he going to do with a six foot four black woman?

Benji didn't want to get his shirt sticky and dirty, but loathe taking it off and showing his scarred back even more, so decided to leave it on. The first eight barrels weren't too hard to load. However, the more he worked, the hotter he got. And the hotter he got, the weaker he became. The woman sat and watched him, silently gnawing on her ham bone, occasionally lifting the wooden bucket to her lips to use as a big mug. Every time she lifted it, he got thirstier. Finally, he couldn't resist.

"May I?" he asked as he pointed to the bucket, still half-full of the leaf-enhanced water. All he wanted was a little. He didn't want to take the time to walk to the creek for a drink and doubted the proprietor of the tavern would let him have ale until the wagons were loaded. That was the deal, and he'd abide by it.

She didn't say a word, but put her hands down on her little leather apron. She wouldn't hand it to him, but wouldn't deny him of it, either. He picked it up, toasted her with it, smiled, and said *"Slante!"*

He hadn't meant to drink so much, but realized too late that he had nearly drained the bucket. "I'll get more when I'm done here," he said apologetically.

But she didn't respond. The trader had said she was fresh off the boat. He sighed in resignation. Now what was he going to do with a six foot four black woman who didn't speak English?

ᚷ

"The task is done. Where's my bill of sale?" Benji asked the trader who was now seated in the tavern, polishing off his three-plate dinner.

"Here you go," the man said with a sly grin, handing him a small sheet of paper.

Benji looked it over and saw the man had written out that ten dollars was due as payment for the slave. He set it down on the table and pushed it back to him. If the trader could change the terms of the transaction, then so could he. "I think ye have the wrong document. Ye owe me two dollars fer the extra wagon I loaded. The deal was one wagon loaded fer the one slave. I loaded the second fer the two dollars. Now hand it over," Benji demanded, his huge, sticky and dirty hand outstretched, palm up.

The man looked up at him and gave him a devious grin. His wagons were loaded, and he still had the slave woman. Maybe he'd get more for her in the next town.

Benji turned his palm over and slowly curled his fingers together into a fist, brought it up under the sweaty man's chin, and tapped him gently with the index finger side of his intimidation of muscle and bone. "Ye ken, I can unload those wagons a lot quicker than I loaded them," he purred and smiled just as deviously.

The man pulled his neck back, sucked in a lungful of air in shock, and said, "Oh, wrong document. Here, let me make a fresh one."

Ж

Benji folded the new bill of sale and stuck it in his sporran. He remembered when he had made his enhanced tool belt. He had used a store bought fanny pack as a pattern. He had thought briefly about just buying one of them and bringing it with him through The Trees, but he couldn't find one made without nylon or zippers. And then there was the size. They all looked ridiculously small on his large frame. Between the fabric store and the fur exchange, he had been able to gather all of the materials needed to construct a size proportionate sporran with the added features of separated compartments. Nobody would get into his sporran without him knowing about it, so he had gone ahead and modified the centuries' old design. The slim pockets built into the lining had coins inserted into them that fit snugly between the seams without rattling. Lightweight plastic envelopes were situated into several of the fabric partitions. He used these to hold fishhooks, sewing needles, and a pair of small scissors so they wouldn't poke through. The small pistol was beneath the false bottom, and the Leatherman tool had its own place on top and was easily accessible.

Billy had suggested that he bring antibiotics and pain relievers, too. "Jest in case," he had said in his very accurate Scots accent. "Ye never ken what evils and horrors are out there in the wilds of 18th century North Carolina."

Benji shook his head as he recalled the day that Billy had decided to help him pack. Billy had just returned home from his extended stay at the hospital after the secondary infection he developed from the liver transplant had gone septic. He had nearly died of the infection, and was still weak, but wanted to help. It was the first day that he was really up and about.

Billy tossed him a three pack of condoms, "Here, jest in case."

Benji looked them over and laughed. He tossed them back. Billy's eyes got wide. "Oops, wrong size?" he asked with embarrassment.

"I wouldna ken without tryin' one on, but I really dinna plan on lookin' for a wife when I go back. And, if I do find one who will have me, I dinna want to stop from makin' any bairns. I'm not gettin' any younger, ye ken."

"So *have* you decided on whether you want to come back or not?" Billy asked.

Benji sighed in frustration as he recalled that moment. He didn't know then, and he still didn't know now. Billy made it clear that money was no object, that he would help him find a house and a job, in that order. "You've been through so much," he said. "Just stay here and relax for a few years. You missed a big chunk of your life either being a victim of or chasing after bad guys. How about just taking care of you for a change: do you think you can handle that?"

He snorted. Right. And now he had one more person to look out for: a six foot four black woman who didn't speak English and was apparently very stubborn. Well, he could be stubborn, too, *verra* stubborn.

"Okay, let's go," he said as he unlocked the chain on her ankles and threw the key into the bushes. He had told the trader that he didn't want the lock and chain; that he would leave them for him. He didn't say that he'd leave the key though.

The woman kept her eyes low. If she had heard him, she probably didn't understand him. He sighed in resignation: now what was he in for? He put his hand out to her. "Please," he said softly, not wanting the gathering crowd to hear him beg.

The woman's resolute demeanor was evident by the set of her jaw, but as soon as she heard the word 'please,' her eyes widened in shock. She glanced up as high as his shoulders then brought her knees under herself and stood up straight. She hadn't taken his hand nor looked him in the eye, but had done what he asked. And, done it without a whip or a hambone, he was glad to see.

"Let's go then," he said, his head held high for the gaggle of onlookers to see. The next town should be just a few hours away. He'd get what he needed there. He didn't want to spend any more time in this town, and he was pretty sure she felt the same way—or might if she had any feelings. By the blank look on her face, she didn't care much about anything.

"Weel, it looks like we have a bit of a walk aheid of us, but we should be in the next town before sundown," he told her. "We can get a place to stay and a bit of food there. I would like to thank ye fer the opportunity to make a bit of money. I mean, I only meant to load the wagons fer the meal and drink, but ye made me two dollars, and I appreciate it."

Benji turned back to see her face. It still had the emptiness of a puddle of tar. If there was any emotion behind those eyes, it was well hidden. Yes, it was well hidden, but not absent. He had seen her surprise when he asked her 'please.' He chuckled. It was probably the first time anyone had said that word to her.

He slowed down so she could catch up to him, but she slowed down at the same time. Next, he stopped, but so did she. "Would ye mind walkin' up here beside me; it hurts my neck to keep turnin' around to see if yer all right," he said.

Well, if she understood, she didn't obey. Benji's shoulders sagged in frustration. He had made a trade, not a wager. Maybe that's where he made the mistake. Was it a fair trade, though? He laughed out loud, startling the woman. No, she was too dark to be a 'fair' trade. He had made a good trade, though. At least she was away from the whip, and that was good, *verra* good indeed.

19 The First Supper

The bewilderingly tall black woman and the still taller red haired man ten feet ahead of her were still plodding along the dusty road three hours later: not necessarily further ahead, but definitely further away from the whips and chains and the sleazy slave trader who had been so fond of using them. Evidently, the next town was further away than Benji thought. The sun was going down, and so were his chances of being able to get food and supplies from the general store. Or dry goods store. Or trading post. He couldn't remember what it was called in this era. He had meant to do some historical research of the daily routines and terminologies—sort of a refresher course of life as it was in his youth—but he never found the time. Yes, if there was something his family couldn't grow, hunt, or fabricate, then they'd go into town and see if they could trade or barter for it. But, as he recalled, it was always 'go into town' not 'go to the dry goods store' or 'mercantile' or 'Sears and Roebucks.' He shook his head. He was tired and hungry, and not making any sense, even to himself.

"We can spend the night down here by the creek," Benji announced to his new traveling companion. "I can catch some fish if they're bitin'." Benji bent his head down and slapped the mosquito that had just landed on his neck. "Weel, at least somethin' down here is bitin'." He looked over at the woman as he brought up his head. He didn't see a reaction from her and really hadn't expected one. What he did see was too much skin. He had forgotten that she was practically naked. He had been walking in front of her for the last three hours, and other to turn around and make sure she hadn't run off, he hadn't taken in her full form. All he saw was her face: her glistening, dark skin, almost like high-grade coal, those full, bee-stung lips, and dark, empty eyes.

He didn't know what she had been through to have such a hard demeanor, but if he had been ripped from his family and brought over to a foreign land, made to work as a slave for someone else with only scraps for food to eat, beat whenever the whim hit the man with the whip, then maybe he'd... Oh, wait! That *had* happened to him. He got over it—mostly. Hopefully, she would, too.

"I'll be right back," he called to her as he headed into the brush for a personal comfort break. "Ye can use the bushes over there fer yer business," he said, motioning with his hand toward the tall scrubby growth behind her. "I'll not bother ye. Jest dinna come this way fer a bit," he said, although he knew she wouldn't invade his space. He couldn't get her to walk within ten feet of him, even when he tried.

He took his leisure and made lots of noise when he was ready to come out so she would have time to get herself together. He stretched out his arms and looked around, then froze: she was gone. No, wait; there she was. Evidently, she had made use of the break, too, because first, she was nowhere to be seen, and then suddenly, she was standing like a statue behind the bushes he had directed her to. Well, at least she didn't run away.

"Weel, where would ye run to if ye did decide to bolt," he asked aloud, knowing full well that she didn't speak or understand English. "*¿Habla Español?*" he asked, just to hear someone speak. "Okay, how about *sprechen sie deutsche? Parlez vous Francais? Ching chong chow chow?*" he added in a silly voice, chuckling at his own nonsense.

The blank stare was still there. "Weel, I'm gonna try to catch some fish. If yer feelin' helpful, ye might want to gather some wood fer a fire. Here, I'll get one goin'. Add more to it when it burns low. I mean, ye have to be of some use. I dinna mind helpin' ye out, and yer not my slave, but I'm not yers either. So there!" he added sassily. What difference did it make what he said? At least with her, he didn't need to be guarded with his words.

The site he chose looked like it had been used as a resting place for travelers for a long time. A fire ring was already established and a fallen log pulled next to it for use as a seat. Benji found a few pieces of insect-riddled wood and dragged them to the clearing. "Thanks, Lord," he said as he stomped on the rotted firewood to break it apart, then threw the pieces into the middle of the fire pit. He put together a little tepee of bark shards and fluffy seedpods then reached into his sporran, pulled out the small butane lighter, and lit the kindling cone. The fire was raging in ten seconds flat. He added more pieces of kindling, moving them around to make sure the larger pieces were lit, and would stay burning.

He grabbed his improvised fire poker and held it like a talking stick. "I'd appreciate it if ye'd mind the fire," he said, pointing to the blaze then the additional wood nearby, then dropped the charred stick outside the rock circle. Hopefully, she could figure out what he had said with his exaggerated, improvised sign language.

Benji was big, but he was also very agile. He hopped, skipped, then jumped over the shallow flow of the creek and went upstream where he found a calm, deep pool under a low hanging tree. He looked up and saw a huge spider. "Ugh," he grunted as he batted it away with the long branch he had picked up to use as a fishing rod. Benji hated bugs.

It didn't take long to catch and clean four decent-sized trout. He walked back to the campsite without the hopping or jumping he had employed on the trek in. All of a sudden, he was very tired. The heavy lifting and loading, long walk, and now the new responsibility of taking care of another person, had become emotionally and physically overwhelming.

He was equally relieved and glad to see both the woman and the fire when he got back. She had gathered more wood and stacked it neatly into two piles, larger pieces in one, kindling pieces in the other. He set the fish on a flat rock, then mumbled a mild curse as he remembered: he no longer had a pan to cook with. He'd have to find some greenwood branches to cut down to use as skewers. He sighed in resignation at the delay of his dinner, turned away, and headed back into the copse.

He was only a few steps away when he became aware of the woman moving by the fresh catch. He turned around quickly, half expecting to see her eating the fish raw. But, what he saw was that she had already found green branches, had stripped them with her hands, and was now preparing their meal, skewering the fish onto the sticks.

He waited where he was just a moment longer, trying not to stare, but she was so stunning: regal and composed even though she was considered worth less than two hours of his hard labor. He realized that it didn't make a difference to her whether he looked at, leered at, or ignored her. She was probably used to the stares, and surely would rather have them than the whips or straps.

Benji turned back to the fire. "Thank ye; I appreciate yer help." He could have sworn he saw a reaction: a shoulder shrug maybe, but she hadn't looked up. Then he realized what it was. Earlier today, he had asked her 'please' for probably the first time in her life, and now he had just thanked her. It must be the tone he used when he spoke because he was sure she didn't speak English. Yes, the manner of saying the words 'please' and

114

'thank ye' were the same in every language. Now, if he could just get her to tell him what he should do with her!

"Too bad we're not in the 21st century," he said aloud with true concern for her predicament. "With yer height and build, ye'd be sure to get a college scholarship in basketball. But, ye wouldna ken what basketball is, would ye?" Benji picked up a little rock and tossed it at a boulder at the edge of the clearing. "Two!" he shouted as it hit the stone basket. "Ah, weel, ye were jest born in the wrong century is all. But, ye sure are big," he said then added softly, "and pretty."

Benji didn't have much to do while the fish dinner was grilling. He kicked around a few stones to smooth out a place to sleep for the night, flipped out the camouflaged patterned fabric sheet to use as a tarp, and sat down next to it. It was a parting gift from Peter and was sure to be useful. He fingered the cloth: windproof, waterproof, anti-adhesive, and self-cleaning. The large piece of fabric could also be used as a tent or even a kilt if he got desperate. Of course, he had already used the camouflage aspect of it: he had been asleep under its cover when the thief or thieves had run off with his backpack of goods. They could have easily knifed him in his sleep, but didn't see him. "Thanks again, Lord."

He reconsidered the area he had chosen for sleeping. The area further away from the fire pit looked softer and more comfortable. It definitely had a spongy cushion of grass, but that also meant bugs—fleas, ticks and spiders. If he slept near the fire, the smoke would help keep the mosquitoes at bay. Billy had insisted that he get immunized for malaria, and about twenty other diseases, but he still didn't want to deal with the itch of insect bites.

"Ahem," the woman vocalized loud enough to be heard, but soft enough not to be rude. Benji glanced up and saw that she had pulled the two sticks of fish off the fire and set them on the rock. She was on her knees, head bowed, waiting for him to come eat.

Benji was still sitting cross-legged next to the sheet. He was filthy from loading the barrels of pitch, tired, but didn't want to lie down until he had a bath. Maybe the fish dinner would give him enough energy to make it back to the pool where he had caught the trout. The pond was deep enough that he could submerge his whole body, soak off the grime, and take the weight off his bones. He groaned as he stood up. "Dinner first then a bath," he said aloud in her direction, though not necessarily to her.

"The fish looks mighty fine." He picked up a stick and started pulling the meat from the trout. It did taste great, just the right amount of smoky flavor, moist but not raw, cooked through but not burned. He was halfway finished eating when he noticed she hadn't picked up her food. "Go aheid: that's yers. Ye dinna have to wait fer me to finish," and pointed to the shish kabob dinner, indicating with his finger that it was for her.

The woman blinked, but didn't look up at him. "Ye ken, ye have great peripheral vision. Ye can see me without lookin' at me, I ken ye can. Now, I caught the food and ye cooked it, so go aheid and eat yer share. It's mighty tasty." He started to pick up the spit and hand it to her, but she shuffled backwards on her knees, refusing his offer.

"Okay, I get it. Ye already ate today and I dinna. Okay, here," he said as he pulled off one fish, "I'll take this one and ye can have the other. Ye need to keep up yer strength, too. We have a lot of walkin' to do tomorrow, and I dinna want ye fallin' down and me havin' to pick ye up and carry ye to wherever it is we're goin'. Anyhow, go aheid and eat," he paused then added, "please."

The word please must have won her over again. She nodded a 'thanks' then grabbed the fish like it was going to swim away if she didn't grab it by the tail fin right away. Her fingers deftly pulled the meat away from the bones, which she set down in a neat pile on the rock. When she was done eating everything, including the shrunken eyes, she picked up the little bones and sucked on them again, removing the last bits of protein from them, and then used a big one as a toothpick. "Good idea," Benji said, and copied her dental hygiene example. "I'll save the floss fer later."

Just as Benji had hoped, the meal had given him another burst of energy. Or at least a glimmer of oomph; he was still exhausted. "I'm goin' down to the creek to wash up. Yer welcome to do the same. If ye'd like, I can wash yer back. I have some soap. It looks like there's quite a bit of dirt and leaf matter in yer wounds there." He could tell she didn't understand him even with his gesturing and pointing to her back then moving his hands like he was scrubbing. "Ye should make sure ye get it cleaned up so an infection doesna start in. Ye ken, the redness and fever and pus? Oh, well, ye've been takin' care of yer wounds fer a while there. I guess ye ken how to tend to them yerself."

Ж

Benji stopped at the first water and took off his shirt. He dropped it in a little shallow eddy and put a softball-sized rock on it. "Presoak cycle," he said. He looked back and saw the woman still kneeling by the fire pit, eyes down. "Ach, she wouldna care if I was buck-naked or not," he said aloud. "Ye've probably seen a man in his altogether and yer naked body doesna seem to bother ye." He added even louder, "Even if it does bother me," then chuckled. His voice returned to a softer tone, "I sure hope the cold water does its job. I wouldna want to have her see my manhood in a happy state and think I want to take advantage of her."

Benji set his shoes on a rock then dropped his dirty tan Carhartt work pants. He pulled off his socks and stuffed them through the belt loops to secure them. He set the bundle next to his shirt and put two rocks on it. He'd do the scrubbing on the clothes after he was done doing the same to his skin. "Ach, I canna forget ye, my little gold bar." He ran back up to his little bedding site, picked up his sporran, and retrieved the bar of soap wrapped in a sisal crochet-mesh pocket. A plastic container would have been more efficient for wetness, but less as an exfoliant and scrubber. "And, it's antibacterial, too," he sang softly then realized that he was totally nude and standing fifteen feet away from a young woman. "Excuse me," he said directly to her, "I forgot the soap," then hurried back to the water.

The woman did have great peripheral vision. She had learned to use it well in the last twenty years. She didn't have to flinch when a hand was raised to her, but could lessen its blow by shifting just a little, missing its full impact. She could also tell when a man was getting ready to have his way with her. She could initiate her gag and vomit reflex on demand. Men didn't want to have sex with a woman who was coughing and puking. She grinned as she remembered how she had timed her 'illness' with the man who owned her two—or was that three?—masters ago. His stomach was even weaker than hers reportedly was. When she started getting sick, he started barfing and totally lost the urge. He never bothered her again, although, it was probably one of the reasons he had resold her. Again.

As Benji walked away, she lifted her head and looked hard at him. He had lash scars on his back, too. When he told her how to take care of her wounds, to keep them clean, he was speaking from personal experience. She stood up and watched as he went further up the creek, then was out of sight. She walked over to his clothes and decided that whether it was her duty or not, she'd clean his pants and shirt. The little bag he wore around his middle was too small to carry a change of clothes. It looked like that belly bag and the blotchy green colored cloth, were all that he had. She had next to nothing: just her little leather apron and the cloth on her head, but he didn't have much more. Yes, he helped her when he didn't need to; she could help him, too. She shrugged her shoulder and winced. It still hurt. But, she would help him because he said please and thank you, and didn't look at her 'like that.'

Benji still had the bandana around his neck, which was a good thing. Now he had a washcloth, too. He dipped his whole body into the water and floated on his back, letting his tension dissipate, starting at his neck, working its release down his spine and out his shoulders. He shuddered and his whole body jerked. He realized that while he was relaxing, he had fallen asleep. "Get on with it, man," he said as he climbed to shore. He squatted down and scrubbed the tacky dirt and pitch matrix off of his forearms and neck with the sisal wrapped soap, then employed the sudsy kerchief on his face and other tender spots. "Okay fish, yer jest gonna have to bide with some soapy water," he announced, then jumped into the pool, knees held tucked into his chest in what he called a cannonball. The fish were sure to recover from the shock by morning. For now, he was going to treat himself to another childlike blast into the water. "Yee haw," he shouted as he jumped in one last time.

Benji shook the water off his body like a dog. He kept the hair on his head cropped short. It wasn't the fashion now, but what difference did his unusual hairstyle make? He already stood out because of its bright red color and his giant size. He might as well be comfortable, and in this heat, short hair was much cooler. Besides, he didn't have a comb, or much else. He walked back toward the laundry area and saw the tall woman scrubbing his clothes. Well, maybe he had *too* much—one other person to look after, too much!

Benji heard the lass singing a song, or she was humming with attitude: he couldn't distinguish any words. Duh! She couldn't speak English. But, she did have a nice voice: not shrill, but low and very soothing.

Benji had forgotten to be noisy as he approached. It was his nature to be quiet when moving. "Eek!" she squeaked then looked up to see him ten feet away. She quickly averted her eyes and assumed her servile, head bent, squatted position.

He started to speak then noticed that she was sporting a smirk. She caught herself and returned to her noncommittal stone face. He looked down and remembered that he was naked. "Aye, the water is verra cold," he said as he put his left hand over his privates. He saw her eyes flit up then back down. He looked where she had glanced and realized why she was grinning, or wanting to. "Yes, the hair is red down there, too; even redder still."

She didn't move. He was frustrated at the one-sided conversation, but continued talking just the same: silence was even more aggravating. "And if yer naked, then I can be, too! It's too hot fer clothes, and I do *not* want to put on wet pants, even if I could get them on." He picked up the pants, twisted and squeezed out as much of the water as he could, shook them out, and pulled them back into shape. Before he could get to the shirt, she grabbed it. She put it back in the water, grabbed a fistful of sand, and started rubbing it into the heavily stained spots. "Okay, I'll let ye finish yer task. I thank ye fer volunteerin'. Now, if ye dinna have any objections—and ye dinna seem to object to much of anythin' I do or say—then I'm goin' to bed."

Benji strutted to the area he had designated as his bedroom, his bare butt flashing white against his dark, tanned forearms. With what could be called falling with grace or dropping with attitude, he embraced the cloth-covered ground and fell asleep. The last thought in his head was he hoped she kept the fire smoldering, and that the smoke continued to blow toward him. He had a large buffet exposed to the creekside mosquitoes, and he knew they didn't care to dine in the smoking area.

20 Breakfast of Champions
August 20, 1782

Benji was rudely awakened by a fly making an unauthorized landing in his nostril. He snorted and popped up, wildly smacking the air around him, trying to create a hostile environment for the overpopulation of skin diving, biting pests. When his hand flapping and sputtering were finished, and the flies had left, he remembered where he was: camping outside in the North Carolina woods. He looked down and saw that he had slept naked on the sheet of green, tan, and olive. Why? Right: his camping gear had been stolen and his clothes were wet, drying on a bush just over there and... "Oh, crap," he said under his breath. He had forgotten about *when* he was. Then he saw the naked black woman kneeling by the flat rock next to the fire pit. "Oh, shit!" he said even louder.

He blew out his breath in exasperation. "Now this is a fine mess you've gotten us into, Ollie," he said in a spot on imitation of Stan Laurel. "Yeah, if only this really was an old black and white comedy that I could jest walk away from." He stared over at the woman who was aware that he was awake, but who still wouldn't look at him. "Weel, I guess it is a black and white story. I mean, they dinna get much whiter than me, at least on the belly, and I dinna think I've ever seen anyone as black as ye. It sure is a pretty color, too: kinda like a cup of French roast coffee." He sighed. A cup of coffee would sure be nice right now, but he'd have to settle for using his hands to scoop up creek water for his morning drink.

"Up and at 'em, boys," he said as he rolled over and stood up. Benji also had good peripheral vision and saw that she was stealing glances over at him, and not at his face, either. He looked down and saw that, yes, he had early morning stiffness, just like every other morning. "I told ye the water was cold," he said to her with a grin, covered himself with his hand and wrist, and walked toward the area he had designated as the men's room to relieve himself.

The woman flinched and bent forward, crouched and huddled to protect herself, as he passed by her on his way to the bushes.

"Dinna worry, this isna fer ye," he said as he glanced down at his handful of engorged male member. "It's jest that I have a full bladder and slept verra well. It'll be gone shortly. Or will be shorter shortly," he chuckled.

Benji grabbed his pants off of the bush on the way back and shook them out, making sure ants or hornets or any other critters hadn't taken up residence in them. He put them on then grabbed the shirt, employing the same insect inspection and dislodging method. He left it unbuttoned though. Maybe he could let her use the shirt. It was better than the humiliating scrap of leather she currently was wearing.

Ye'd better not, he argued with himself. Remember 'when' ye are. If ye run around without a shirt, it would be scandalous. A slave without clothes probably jest means her master doesna have much fer money, or that she's fresh off the boat, or maybe she's a field hand and doesna need clothes. It's still summer, after all.

But it's indecent and disgraceful; or should be. The shirt would be better than nothing, even if it only went down to mid-thigh on her. At least her fanny and breasts would be covered.

And how do ye think ye'd be received in the next town, any town, ye jest struttin' in without yer shirt and a slave woman wearin' it? Come on, dinna let yer 21st century ethics ruin yer chances to blend in. Yer here to find yer grandfather and Evie. If ye have to do somethin' distasteful, then do it. It wouldna be the first time.

"Weel, hopefully it will be the last time," he said out loud. His voice startled the woman. He'd been having a conversation in his head and didn't realize that his last resolute words had come out so strongly. "Sorry, I guess it's better when I talk out loud all the time. Ye dinna seem to mind hearin' my thoughts."

Rather than answer—and he knew that she wouldn't—she held out her hand. Her coral pink palm held what looked like a vegetable meatball. She still wouldn't look him in the eyes, but dipped her head and moved her hand toward him, urging him to take the food.

Benji looked over at the impromptu kitchen counter and saw that she had made six of the 'greenballs.' "I'll tell ye what," he said, then started embellishing his words with sign language. "Ye eat one, and then I'll try one. I dinna think ye mean to poison me, but jest to make sure. And I ken ye see me." He picked up one of the 'greenballs' between his thumb and forefinger and held it under her humbled face, moving it back and forth under her nose in encouragement.

121

She lifted her head, stuck her chin out, and opened her mouth, keeping her eyes down. Benji placed the food in her open maw and watched as she chewed carefully, a small smile of enjoyment at the taste creeping in before the blank, unemotional mask came back to retake its residency there.

"Ye ken, ye look verra pretty when ye smile. Okay, here, I'll try one," he said, then picked up a green foodstuff and popped it into his mouth. He chewed cautiously, not knowing whether he was getting mushy or hard fare. As it was, it was chewy and sweet at times. "This almost tastes like sweet and sour chicken," he said, and picked up another one and put it in his mouth. "Here, go aheid, there's plenty." He pointed to the food. "I dinna think I need to be feedin' ye. I appreciate the cookin', but yer a big girl and can eat by yerself. That is, unless ye like it when I feed ye?"

The woman reached over, took one more of the greenballs, and turned away from him, as if to end the conversation. "What, did I say somethin' to offend ye? I mean, yer a good cook and all." Benji took another one and wolfed it down. "What's in this, or do I want to ken?" and pointed to the last one, then opened his hand in a gesture of what is it?

The woman started giggling which surprised him. "What?" he asked insistently. He knew she could tell what he was saying by his tone: no translation required.

In answer, the woman peeled apart the little foodstuff wrapped in what looked to be softened grape or currant leaf. Inside were crushed raspberries and big beetle grubs. Benji gasped then grabbed his mouth, but it was too late to spit out the food. He had already chewed and swallowed three of them. "Weel, I may hate bugs and creepy crawlies, but maybe the best way to get back at them is to eat them. These are mighty tasty, although it might be better if ye dinna show me what's in the food ye prepare next time—even if I ask." He nodded his head, "I think I'd enjoy the meal more if I wasna aware of the ingredients. Here, ye can have the last one." He pointed to the food, not wanting to touch it. "Ye need to keep up yer strength. And ye could use a bit more meat on yer bones, too," he said with a straight face, "even if ye have to eat bugs to do it."

Benji went to the creek, drank his fill of water, and did a thorough tooth brushing with a split twig he had cut just for that purpose. He didn't want any leftovers stuck between his teeth. He headed back up to the campsite and saw the woman shaking out the ground cloth. "Hey, wait," he called. She stopped immediately and dropped her head in submission. He ran up the rise and started thinking out loud. "This will work jest fine fer a dress of sorts fer ye. I mean, it isna as fancy as the sarongs that those Polynesian ladies wear, but it's much better than what ye have now."

The woman was unresponsive. "Duh," he said, "of course ye dinna ken what I'm speaking of. Here, stand like this." He put both arms straight out to his side. She glanced at him, unsure of what he wanted, but certain that she should do what he asked.

He found the corner of the long edge and came close to her, meaning to wrap it around her. She cringed and brought her arms back to her sides and hunched over. "Ah, ticklish are ye?" he laughed, intentionally ignoring her fear of him. "Here, I think ye ken what I meant to do. Here, here," he urged, finally grasping her hand and putting the fabric in it.

She cut her eyes to him then looked down at the fabric, running it through her fingers, making her decision. She would accept clothing from him. At least, she didn't think he wanted to have his way with her in return. He didn't seem to be that sort of man. She wrapped the cloth around her bosom then straightened her posture, suddenly feeling better about herself and her lot.

"Ye look mighty fine," he announced with pride, glad that he had found a solution to the modesty and morals dilemma. He walked around her, looked at her back, and frowned. "The gown willna bother the wounds on yer back, but I think ye should let me help ye wash. Ye have a bit of an infection starting there," he said as he gently touched the skin next to an area that was not only red and swollen, but still had a bit of foreign matter imbedded in it.

She flinched at his touch and resumed her former subservient, head and shoulders bowed position. She was wrong: he did want her body for his pleasure.

Benji could see what she was thinking. "Ye ken, I think yer a lovely lass, but I wouldna take advantage of my position, or whatever it is, and have my way with ye. I mean," he stuttered, "I ken that masters figure that all parts of their slaves are theirs to do what they want with, I mean, I ken the reason the African Americans of my time are so pale is because the masters bred with the slave women. Ye hardly see anyone in America with skin as dark and beautiful as yers."

Benji's talking was working. Even if she didn't know what he was saying, she had figured out that he wasn't trying to have sex with her. "But I'm not yer master, not really. Come on; let's get going. I think we need to get to the next town." He looked around and saw his sporran sitting on the rock by the fire. He kicked apart the residual coals and motioned for her to come with him.

"I ken ye like to walk behind me, but I'd feel better about it if I dinna have to turn around to see ye when we're talkin'." He exaggerated the head-turning-back motion and added a crazy, eye rolling, tongue hanging out the side of his mouth gesture of frustration. "Please; it would help my neck if ye were beside me." He rubbed the back of his neck and gave her sad puppy dog eyes, then stuck out his bottom lip.

She quickly glanced at him and her slight smile returned. She didn't move though.

"Okay, okay," he said with mock exaggerated frustration. "If I have to come back there to walk with ye, I will." He took six steps back—she had been walking closer today than yesterday, he noticed—then put his elbow out as if escorting her. She shook her head almost imperceptively. "Ready, set, go," he said then took off walking, elbow still extended. She was now only two steps behind him. Well, he could live with that. Maybe she'd catch up to him by afternoon.

Benji started talking to her again. It seemed to make her more comfortable, and it definitely relaxed him. When he was talking out loud about inane subjects, he wasn't thinking of his past or what he was going to do with his future.

"Ye ken," he began, "I have that money ye helped me earn. I mean to buy a bit of food, a pot, and a couple of dishes with it, and maybe some cotton fer a dress fer ye. I mean, I dinna mind ye wearin' my bed, but it has lots of other uses, too. I can use it as a tent and its good camouflage, too, fer huntin' or hidin'. I can throw it over me—and ye, too, of course—and we'll jest blend right into the countryside. Ye see, it hides the color of our faces and clothes, makes us hard to see. Hey, did ye ken that in my time, skin color doesna make a difference to people? People of all colors work together, are friends, and even, um, more. I mean they get married..." He paused then started up again. "And slavery was abolished, or will be, in about," Benji started counting on his fingers, "eighty-three years from now, more or less." His excitement was waning as he realized that whether he stayed here and now, or went back to his family in the 21st century, she would still be here as a slave. Suddenly, he didn't feel like talking any more.

Ж

It was only an hour's walk to the edge of the two-tavern town. "Weel, if there're two taverns, then there's bound to be at least one store down the way that has what we need. Let's keep walkin'. And stay close to me. I dinna like the way people are gawkin' at us."

People had indeed come out from the two drinking and eating establishments that were across the dusty street from each other. He was used to being stared at, sort of, but this was different. One person would come out of a bar, then quickly go back in, bringing several more people with him. He felt as if the two of them were the Fourth of July parade and here he'd been caught without the flag.

Out of the corners of his eyes he could see the fingers pointing, the whispering between the men and even a couple of women. A small black boy was sent scurrying down the road, literally kicked in the seat of his pants by the tall, pock-faced man with a pistol stuck in his belt. Almost too late, Benji realized what was wrong besides the gun. Belts weren't commonplace here and now. The man's belt seemed to be solely for the purpose of showing off the fact that he was carrying a gun.

Benji slowed his pace just a little to allow the woman to catch up with him, but she slowed, too. Now was definitely not the time to ask her to *please* do anything. He glanced back and saw that she was back in full blown, cowed and bowed, slave mode. Perhaps it was her survival instinct kicking in. He knew that his was sure on full alert.

They finally arrived at a store with a haphazard array of fabric bolts and various shapes and sizes of pots in the window. Not much for a display, he thought, but it got the message across: he knew what the store sold. He tipped his head in greeting to a woman as she exited the little mercantile emporium. She gasped in shock at his size—that was no surprise—but he saw she wore the look of absolute fear when she saw his traveling companion. And here he thought he was the reason for all the whispers and finger pointing.

The store clerk had the same reaction to the two of them. Benji turned around and saw his new charge had decided that it was her place to stay outside, waiting by the door, not inside with the white folks.

"Good mornin' to ye," Benji said in greeting to the wide-eyed elderly gentleman. "I've come fer some items. And it looks like ye may jest be the man to help me."

Benji spouted off his memorized list of goods. The man quickly, quietly, and efficiently pulled the items off the shelves or out of the barrels. The man never spoke a word until Benji asked him how much it cost. "Well, I'd be smart to tell you twice what its worth and take your money while I can, but I really don't like Mr. Jonathan. You see, he makes us pay him just to do business here in 'his' town. He takes up to half of what all of us make; just how much depends on how's he's feeling and whether he's been lucky at the gaming tables or not. So, let's call this an even dollar. That'll be just that much less that he'll get. Oh, and by the way, he's going to want *her* back, too." He nodded to the woman outside the doorway. "He doesn't like to lose his property, whether it was a fair bet or not."

"I thank ye fer the heads up," Benji said, then noticed the confused look on the man's face. "I mean, thank ye fer the warnin' and have a good day." Benji set the money down, gathered his rucksack of food and dishes, and placed the bolt of blue calico under his arm. He was ready to leave the store then stopped. "Do ye happen to have any candy, like peppermint sticks or lemon drops?" he asked.

The clerk brought out three jars from under the counter. "Penny candy," he said and looked up and out the door at the black female sentinel. She was a slave, but he could also see by the set of her chin that she was guarding her master. "Why don't you take a couple for her," he suggested, "free of charge."

"Weel, I'll do that, but I wanted some peppermints fer me." He ran his tongue around the inside of his mouth. He couldn't taste the meal, but the thought of eating bugs for breakfast was still uneasy in his head. He wanted some peppermint to suck on before the uneasiness hit his stomach.

The man scooped out a few of each kind of candy and placed them on small squares of old newspapers. Benji grabbed one of the mints and popped it in his mouth before the storeowner wrapped up the little parcels. He nodded and smiled at Benji as he gave them to him. "Be careful," he warned, then picked up his feather duster and started dusting the shelves, as if no one was there.

Benji walked out the door and looked up and down the street. He didn't say anything to—or even look directly at—the woman, but he knew she would follow him wherever he went, at least as long as they were near this spooky town. He never went looking for trouble; well, not usually, but it felt as if it had found him today. The eerie feeling, the threat of danger, was as tangible as stickiness on tree sap. He couldn't get out of this town fast enough.

"I say, what're you doin' with my nigger?" a loud and demanding voice boomed from behind him.

Benji's first reaction was to throw a punch. That word always raised the hairs on the back of his neck. He bit down on the peppermint piece in his mouth, glad that he had a focus for the tension he felt throughout his whole body. He stayed his course, though, walking the same pace and in the same direction, not wanting to give the town troublemaker the satisfaction of calling him out.

"Umph!" the woman cried out involuntarily as the rock hit her in the back of the head. She reached for the wound by reflex then pulled back her hand and saw blood. Benji turned to see what had happened and saw a brighter red than what was on her hand. He was livid.

"Say yer sorry and dinna be doin' it again," he said to the man with the pistol in his belt. They hadn't been introduced, but Benji would bet his last dollar that this was the infamous Mr. Jonathan.

"What?" the man asked incredulously. He was obviously shocked by Benji's reaction. "Say I'm sorry to a nigger? *My* nigger?"

Benji turned to the woman and gave her a questioning look as if to ask, 'Are you okay?' She nodded minimally in answer, 'I'll be fine.' He nodded back: 'Wait here.'

"It looks like ye have some mighty bad manners there, mister..." Benji had drawn himself up to his full height and shoulder breadth, an imposing Colossus who was now controlling the conversation by asking the questions.

The man put his hand on his pistol and gave a big, gapped-tooth grin. "I'm Mr. Jonathan, and you have my nigger. I want her back. Now!"

"First off, Mr. Jonathan, I'd appreciate it if ye would not refer to this lass as 'yer nigger.' That's not only an offensive term, but she is not *yers* in any way, shape, or form."

Mr. Jonathan strode toward Benji, his hand still on the pistol butt, his grin of confidence growing. "Oh, yes she is, and I can prove it. Turn around *lass*," he sneered.

The woman didn't move, nor did she look at him. But, she did look to Benji, this time looking him in the eyes with a combination of resolve and hope, not fear. "Ye dinna need to move," he said softly. He turned his attention back to the ill-mannered, gun-stroking town boss and spoke in a controlled, even tone. "I mean to take care of this misunderstanding right now. However, Mr. Jonathan, I think it's best we conduct our business in a more suitable environment. The main street of this fair town is not the place fer discussion of these matters. Now, if ye'll buy us both a drink, we can settle this."

Mr. Jonathan hadn't expected courtesy and sensibility, and it took him completely off guard. "Sure, sure," he said agreeably, "I am a bit thirsty now that you mention it."

Benji had won another round of the head game. He looked at the woman and gave her a nod. "Come on, the man said he'd buy us a drink."

"What? Buy a nigger a drink?" he said in shock. He saw the glare on Benji's face and changed his wording. "Buy *her* a drink? Not for all the tea in England." His rage and anger were back. "No, and no to you, too. We'll get this settled here and now, and with witnesses," he barked.

And, there were plenty of witnesses, too. Benji looked over and saw at least thirty people watching the verbal exchange.

"Everyone here," Mr. Jonathan announced as he surveyed the crowd, giving each one a glare that said, 'Don't you dare cross me,' "knows that I bought this nig, um, *lass* last year. It's kind of hard to miss her, her being a giantess and all. You don't have a problem with the word giantess, do you?" he asked sarcastically.

Benji didn't answer the direct question, but responded with, "Get on with it," crossing his arms in front of his chest in defiance of whatever was coming his way.

"You see, I brand *all* my stock, right down to my wife's little lap dog. And she was no different. See, right there on her right shoulder is my brand. I did it myself," he crowed with pride. "Took all of my men and chains to her wrists and ankles to hold her still enough, but I did it."

Mr. Jonathan started toward the woman. She moved behind Benji for protection just as he uncrossed his arms to guide her behind him. "Ye'll not lay a hand on her again," Benji said. "And she's not yers now, even if she was once. I have a bill of sale right here," and patted his sporran.

Benji could tell by the look of shock then quick recovery that the man couldn't read. That was definitely in his favor. "Here," he said as he opened up the sporran and took out the paper. "This says that I bought one giant female Negro for, well, ye dinna need to ken the high price I paid fer her, and, oh, yes, it says that she can also be identified by an 'X' brand on the right shoulder, and that she also has multiple lash wounds on her back. Here, read it fer yerself," Benji said with mock sincerity as he shoved the paper under the now recalcitrant man's nose.

"Um, no, I broke my reading glasses," he said meekly, then changed his tune, "but I know you're lying; it doesn't say that!"

Benji took the paper and went over to the store clerk who had warned him about the extortionist. "Here, ye can read, right?" The man nodded and let a small grin escape, but quickly got it under control. "Doesna it say that this is the woman I bought, even down to the," Benji winced, "brand?"

The clerk took the genuine bill of sale and tipped his head down as if to read it. He really did read it, too, and saw that the description of the lashes and brands weren't included. He handed it back to Benji. "It's all true folks, every bit of what he said. He bought her fair and square. Sorry, Mr. Jonathan, I think that man who bested you in cards resold her. I mean, you said yourself that she was quite a handful..."

"He didn't best me; he cheated. And you're right; she *was* too much trouble. Well, you can have her," he said to Benji with a sour grapes attitude. "But, if you don't already have a whip, you might want to buy one before you leave town. Tell the blacksmith that you want the 'Jonathan Special.' It's a cat 'o nine tails with little metal tips that adjust a *slave's* attitude right away. There, is *slave* an acceptable word?"

Benji didn't answer with words, but simply turned to leave, confident that the woman was close behind him. "Slave is never acceptable," he said, low enough so no one but she could hear. "The whole concept sucks!"

21 The Name Game

"**W**rongway MacKay, strikes again," Benji huffed in frustration. He wasn't lost, but wasn't where he wanted to be either. At least he had been able to find a decent place to spend the night. This site wasn't as accommodating as their last stop, but it still had access to water.

"Do ye ken where we are?" he asked his charge brightly, hoping to lighten his own dour mood. He knew she didn't understand him and couldn't possibly know where his family lived. "Weel, at least I can ask which is more than ye can do," he said with resignation. "Doesna it bother ye that ye canna understand me?" he asked with eyebrows raised.

She raised her eyebrows in answer to his. He smiled and said, "Weel, at least yer not a bother to me. I like havin' ye around to talk to, even if ye canna talk back. Or willna. I'll wager ye *can* talk. I mean, I heard ye singin' that little bit. I can sing, too. *Happy birthday to you*," he bellowed.

Benji's uninhibited singing brought a full smile to the woman's face. He turned and saw it before she brought it back to stone. "Oh, please, if ye canna do anythin' else, would ye please at least be honest with yer looks? I mean, smile when yer happy or I do somethin' silly that entertains ye, or frown when yer hurt... Weel, I hope the hurtin' part's over. I mean, I promise that I will never, ever strike ye with whip or fist." He shook his head then walked around her to look at her back, shuddering at how anyone could intentionally flail another person's skin until it came apart. "But, I will have to clean yer wounds or ye'll be sick. Come on over to the creek. I have this special soap and I'll use my kerchief for scrubbin'." He bent his head down to look for the bar in his sporran. "And, after we're done, I have a surprise fer ye. Come on," he said and reached for her hand.

She walked to the creek, but didn't take his hand. He squatted down at the water's edge, rinsed out the bandana, then soaped it up. He stood back up and called to her, "Come on now, please dinna be stubborn. It's fer yer own good."

But, the woman was leery. "I'll let ye scrub my back later if I can wash ye now?" He smiled, gestured to his back, and motioned scrubbing, then pointed to her. She tipped her head side to side, walked to a point three feet away from him, and took off the camouflaged cloth that was her sarong.

"No, no, ye can leave it on," he said as he turned and averted his eyes from seeing her nakedness. He kept his head turned and explained, his hands flapping in the air behind him to urge her to get dressed again, "The cloth dries quickly; the water willna bother it."

Benji glanced up and saw that she had figured out what he was saying and was tucking in the cloth. She had wrapped it differently, though, and both of her shoulders were now exposed. He gently applied the suds to the wound and dabbed at the cuts, trying to float the black specks out of the infection. "I think I need to hurt ye a bit to get this cleaned up. I ken I said I hoped the hurtin' part was over, but this really is fer yer own good."

The woman straightened her back, but didn't move away. She hadn't said a word, but he understood her body language: she was telling him to get on with it.

He got as aggressive as he needed, but no more. When he was done, he cupped his hands and poured water over the area to rinse it. "Now hold still; I have some medicine fer ye." He opened his sporran and found the little plastic tube of antibiotic cream. "This should be the ticket," he said, then saw her look at what he had in his hand. "This? Oh, this is to help ye heal. I brought it back with me. We have lots of good medicines where I'm from."

He spread it on her back then pointed to a tree, indicating that they would take a break here. "Ye ken, I've only been *back* to this time fer three days, and I have to tell ye, I dinna recall it bein' so hostile. I mean, I guess we never had to deal with the slave issue back at home. Nobody owned a slave or was a slave. Gamblers and people who take advantage of ye, shoot, they're everywhere, always have been, and probably always will be." He shook his head, then thought out loud, "I wish I could take ye back with me... Hey, what *is* yer name?"

The woman flashed understanding of the question, then returned to her empty look. "Okay, I must apologize, I dinna introduce myself. I am Benjamin Ian Pomeroy MacKay, but ye can call me Benji. See, me Benji and you," he said as he pointed back and forth, waiting for the answer that he was sure wouldn't come. "Tarzan," he crowed and pointed to his chest, "Jane," he said and mocked a thump to her chest. She flinched when his hand got near her. "Benji, um," he said again in a comedic

131

manner, ignoring the shrinking back that she had done, but now only pointing to her, not letting his hand near her body.

"Jane," she said plainly and pointed to herself.

"Weel, I'll be. Ye do talk, and as jest as pretty as ye sing. Jane. I like that name. Where did ye get it?" he asked, knowing full well she wouldn't give him an answer.

But she did. She pointed to him.

"Me? I gave ye the name Jane?"

She grinned and pointed to herself and said proudly, "Jane," then pointed to him and said, "Benji." Her mouth opened as if to say more, then shut quickly, like she had changed her mind about something. But, the slight grin she sported from receiving the gift of her name, remained. Now she was somebody.

22 The Storm

The late afternoon air was so hot and full of moisture that it was hard for him to breathe: the summer heat really was trying to smother him. Benji wanted, needed, had to get cool. True, it was full on daytime, and their location wasn't as secluded as the night before so he couldn't take off all of his clothes, but at least he could remove his boots and socks. He took them off and felt immediate, but short-lived relief. He looked over and saw Jane seated on a fallen log. *Weel, at least she thinks more of herself now: she's not kneelin' on the ground.* He wiped his brow and made his decision: he was going to get comfortable, no matter what.

"Now, if ye dinna mind, and even if ye do, I'm gonna drop my pants. But, dinna worry; it's jest to get cooled down. And, I'll not be exposin' myself, either." He unbuttoned then unzipped his pants, and shimmied them down, stepping on the hems to pull them off all the way. "See, my shirt's plenty long enough to be coverin' my bits and pieces. Lord kens, I wouldna want to embarrass ye or start ye laughin' at me again," he said with exaggerated dramatic flair, his forearm up to his forehead like he was a damsel in distress in an old silent movie.

Her answer was to walk into the creek up to her ankles. Evidently, her feet were hot, too. She looked back toward him and intentionally let a grin escape. Even though she quickly replaced it with her poker face, she had relaxed her guard and let him see it on purpose. He saw it and decided to take it as a show of faith in him as a person.

"Come on, we have one chore to do and then we can chill, I mean sit back and do nothin'."

Benji picked up the bolt of fabric and pulled the leading edge away until he had loosed about three yards. "Watch this," he said as he kept a tight grip on the free end of the cloth. He threw the rest of the bolt up high, out over the water. The calico projectile made a tall, blue arch then dropped into the creek. Benji ran toward the falling fabric display, lily-white legs splashing through the low flow. He tugged on the end still in his fist and pulled the cloth to him, like he was reeling in a big fish. He gathered the azure cotton into a large mass, then pushed and swished it through the water at his feet. He looked back to see her reaction and saw shock.

"Ye see, I need to wash the extra dye out of this and get it preshrunk. I dinna ken what they call it now, but if I dinna do this first, when we make a dress fer ye, and maybe a shirt fer me, it would shrink the first time it got wet. Of course, it might be better if we had some detergent to wash it with, but I dinna think ye brought any along with ye. I mean, if ye did, I dinna want to ken where ye were hidin' it," he said then made a funny face to see if he could get her to smile. It almost worked, he noticed.

He walked up to the long, flat area above the creek, the blue bundle held close. "Come here; I need yer help," he said, and gestured for her to come with him. "Here," he said as he handed her one end of the fabric. She accepted it, but jerked back when his hand touched hers. He moved it aside and let her get a firm grasp of the cloth edge.

"Now, what we're gonna do is play clothes dryer, except that this isna clothing yet." He backed away, feeding the cloth to her while holding the bundle high, not letting the long length of fabric hit the ground. When he had the whole nine yards extended, he called out, "Now hold on tight," and flipped his end up and then down, moving the air under and about the cloth. "See, we're drying the cloth faster this way. And it knocks out most of the wrinkles, too. I dinna think ye brought yer iron either," he joked.

The two of them raised then lowered their banner, Benji singing his favorite early Beatles tunes. He was raising and lowering the yardage gently then suddenly hollered, "Watch out!" and flipped it briskly toward him, like he was snapping a towel, nearly pulling Jane's end out of her hands. He could see her smile release and stay, this time not retreating to the timid corner of her demeanor. She made sure she had a tighter grip on the cloth after that, though.

Fatigue overtook his arms, so he loosely folded up the cloth and took a break. "It may have been that we were doin' work, but when yer with me, it feels like we're playin' a game," he said as he neared her to gather the last yard of cloth.

She could see where he was, even though her head was bowed. She let go as soon as his hand neared hers. Their game time was over. She still needed to be cautious; he was still a man. A nice man, but still a man.

"Jane," he said with a big grin.

She lifted her head, but not all the way up. She wouldn't look him in the eye, but couldn't help but smile when hearing her name.

"Janie," he teased in a singsong voice, "I told ye I had somethin' fer ye." He returned to his normal voice. "I dinna mean to be spoilin' yer dinner, but here." He held his fist out, fingers down, and waited for her to put out hers. She cautiously stuck her hand out, palm up under his, to receive its contents. He opened his hand and said, "The store owner thought ye deserved a treat. I think he kinda liked ye."

Jane's eyes widened when she saw the candy, but when she heard that the store clerk liked her, her chin popped up to look him in the eye, quickly bobbing back down.

"Go aheid and eat it; it's yers," he encouraged, gently touching the back of her hand to guide it up toward her mouth. "It's mighty tasty. Not quite as good fer ye as yer greenballs, but sweet and jest a little sour, like ye," he teased.

Jane brought her head down and palm up, and candy met mouth in the middle. Her back straightened in amazement at the new taste sensation. "It's a lemon drop," Benji explained. "Now, I have a few more, but I'll save them fer later. If ye eat too many, they'll put a knot in yer waim, or worse," he said, and bent over in a parody of a bellyache.

Her eyes cut over to him quickly, and her mouth puckered up as if to spit it out. "No, no," he said, and put his hand in front of her mouth. "That's not what I meant." He put up one finger. "One candy," he held up his index finger several times to enforce his remark, pointed to his mouth, and mimed the bliss of a mouthful of good candy. "Five candies," he put up all five fingers and pretended to stuff his mouth full of mock candies, "ye'll get a bellyache." He bent over and moaned and groaned, then decided to take the act to full tilt, and rolled back and forth on the ground, peeking over to see her reaction.

Her hand was over her mouth as she stifled a full-blown laugh. "Go aheid and laugh; it's good fer yer soul and makes me feel good, too."

Jane dropped her hand and her head at the same time and allowed a hint of a chuckle to escape. He was funny, had protected her, washed her wounds, fed her, even gave her candy, and so far had not tried to touch her body 'that way.' A slight frown darkened her expression: what did he want? She quickly snorted to shoo away the bad thought, then looked at him to see if he had seen her slip of emotional fear.

Benji didn't have to hear any words; he had seen it in her face, the doubt, the concern, about what he wanted from her. "I dinna want anything from ye," he explained as if she could understand. "Weel, except maybe a laugh or to hear ye sing. Ye see, I ken what it's like to be a slave." He sighed, looked around, and saw that they were still alone. There wasn't anything he *had* to do, so he decided to take a break. They had food that was easy to prepare, dry wood, and plenty of water. Maybe it would ease his mind to talk about it, even if it was to a woman who couldn't understand his words. Confession heals the soul or something like that he had heard—somewhere.

He sighed loudly. "I think it was my Grandpa who told me that confession was good fer the soul," he began. "So, that bein' said, get comfortable because I have a lot of confessin' to do and ye," he turned to look her in the face, whether he could see her eyes or not, "are the one who has to listen to it."

Benji kicked back against the tree near the log that she had been sitting on earlier. She sat down on the fallen lumber bench again, politely listened, or so it seemed, as he rambled on about his early life. He told her of the happy times he had in this century, and how he and his mother, father, and sister had to go back 'through the stones' to his parent's time in the 20th century so his sister could have surgery to repair her heart. "The surgery worked," he said as he thumped his chest, "Thump, thump; thump, thump. She was as healthy as could be when they took me."

He turned to look at her. "Would ye please sit down here with me," he asked, and patted the ground an arm's length away. "Please," he repeated with total sincerity. He really needed someone to be close to him, at least in physical proximity. He was suddenly missing his little sister. They had been so close, and losing her had been like losing an arm.

Jane rose from the log and squatted down where he had indicated. He shook his head and said, "Sit like ye would if ye were by yerself, not waitin' to serve a master, because Lord knows, I am *not* yer master."

It was a good thing that Benji wasn't looking at her when he said that. *Not my master—then who are you?* She quickly put her blank façade back on, but did adjust her position so she was sitting on her bottom, turned slightly toward him and leaning forward, her hands on the ground beside her. She looked down, at his hands rather than his face. She really wanted to look into his eyes to see if she could verify that he had a good soul. She could study his hands, though, and still tell much. Yes, they were the hands of a worker. There were scars all over the backs of them, and it looked like he had almost–no, he had–lost the end of his pinkie finger on his right hand. She heard him talking, but didn't listen closely to what he said. She gazed at his white legs that were bent up close to his chest, his arms wrapped around his shins, chin planted on his knees. He was sad, very, very sad.

BANG! CRACK! Suddenly the air broke apart with the sound of thunder. "Quick, get away from the tree," he said as he grabbed her arm to run with him toward the creekside.

Jane was scared and didn't want to leave. She pulled against his grip, trying to return to the shelter of the big tree. "NO!" he screamed, then forced his shoulder into her belly, throwing her over his shoulder just as another shout of thunder and flash of lightning hit, both at the same time.

Jane lifted her head away from his back as he physically hauled her away and saw the tree she thought was her security, was now split in two, a ball of fire burning at the top where the lightning had hit.

"Lightning is attracted to tall things, and that means us, too," he yelled as he set her on her feet. "Lie down, and, oh, shit!"

Now it was hailing. Both of them dropped to the ground, crouched on elbows and knees, their hands over their heads as they tried to keep the marble-sized ice rocks from splitting their skulls. Benji looked around and couldn't see any protection until he saw her sarong. "Take it off," he shouted over the roar of the storm.

The shocked look in her eyes was not because she didn't know what he said, but because she *did* know. Benji pulled her up, pointed to the sarong and grabbed what he hoped was the trailing edge of the camouflage fabric. He jerked it off, spinning her around awkwardly in the process.

She didn't resist when he took off her clothing, but fell back to the ground, sobbing in both shame and terror. Tears were running down her cheeks, afraid of what she was sure would follow. She wanted to scream in anger at herself for trusting him. But, all of her strength and courage were gone. Now she was like all of the other slaves, cowering in the dirt, stripped of clothing and dignity.

Benji grabbed two sticks and pushed them into the sandy soil on either side of her. "Here," he yelled against the wind, and pushed the edge of the storm-buffeted former sarong into her hand, "Hold onto it here, really tight. I'm trying to make a tent to keep the hail from hittin' us."

She did as she was told, not because she was his slave, but because she wanted to. She realized he was building a shelter over her. He was trying to protect her, keep her safe. Now she remembered: he had said the cloth she wore was also a tent, and a means to hide them.

The wind was too strong for his impromptu anchors; it whipped the fabric like a kite away from the large rocks he had set on the edges of the cloth. He shouted to her from outside of the improvised tent, "Use yer feet to hold down the cloth back here, and then hold the front with yer hands."

She looked up from her huddled position and saw what was needed. She stretched out one foot to each corner and held it down, then did the same with her hands and elbows on the front and sides. She bit off the words, "Get in here," but hoped he would. She could see the now plum-sized balls of hail bouncing off his head and shoulders.

Benji ran back to the log bench, grabbed his meager belongings, and then scrambled back to Jane and the impromptu pup tent. He climbed in over her tent securing splayed body, carrying his sporran, rucksack of food and dishes, and the damp bundle of blue cloth held close to his middle. He needed to maneuver around her arms and legs to get a place to lie down in the low-ceilinged, two-poled fort. Gulp. Her naked arms, legs, and back.

Pay attention to the situation, Mac. "Here, let me help," he yelled over the constant cracks of thunder. He took over holding down one side of the tent as she turned away from him to keep the other side from blowing up and away. He held down his side of the tent with his legs and backside as he shoved their worldly possessions under his head like a pillow. She was facing away from him, struggling with her edge of the tent, not touching him, but her nude body only an inch away. "Are ye okay?" he hollered.

Jane nodded, but kept facing the cloth wall. "Are ye sure?" he continued, "Did the hail cut ye?"

She shook her head 'no,' then flinched as another bolt of lightning flared—by the sound of it, hitting the same tree. "Do ye want me to hold ye?" he asked just as loud, but in a gentler tone.

Jane started to shake her head, then froze. She realized too late that she was answering his questions without watching his hand gestures. Her shoulders started heaving with dry sobs she couldn't control. She had fooled everyone for so many years, and now he knew that she could understand his words.

138

"Weel, if I canna hold ye, can ye hold me? I'm scarrit!" Benji declared with just enough levity to stop her crying.

Jane shifted her feet and hands to keep the walls held down, then turned to face him, this time looking directly into his eyes. The lightning flares were slowing down and the crashes of noise weren't as loud: the storm was going away. The hail had stopped, and a steady rainfall had taken its place. Another bright flash without noise and she could see his face. His eyes were as blue as a summer sky, and he had freckles all over his face. She reached up with her free hand and touched the ones on his left cheek, lightly rubbing. "They willna come off," he said softly.

"Angel kisses," she said just as tenderly, then reached around him and thought of her mother as she lay dying, asking to be held. "I'll hold you. Don't be afraid," she said.

Benji bit back his words. He didn't want to be brave. He really was scared. But it wasn't the storm: it was his feelings for her that had him terrified.

Jane held him and sang the song her mother had taught her. She tried to sing it at least once a month, when she got 'the curse,' so she would remember the words. She couldn't tell time passage using the moon. The skies were predictable, but her being able to be outside to see them was not. "Hmm, hmm, hmm," she sang then rubbed his back like she had her mother, letting her tears fall without shame. Holding a person like this felt as good as the lemon drop candy had tasted.

She suddenly pushed him away. "What?" Benji asked, surprised. The frown on her face told him the answer. "Oh, I'm sorry. I dinna do it on purpose. I mean, I told ye I wouldna bother ye that way, and I mean it. I have an oath on my head. Jane, do ye ken what an oath is?" he asked sincerely.

"I'm ignorant, not stupid," she replied with disdain.

"Oh, really? Well, Ignorant, I *am* Stupid," he joked. "No, really, a long time ago, well, more than a couple of years ago anyway, I told God that if He would bless me, then I wouldna have sex with a woman, or anyone else fer that matter," he said as he rolled his eyes, trying to lighten the very serious atmosphere, "unless I was marrit to her. So, since there isna a preacher here, yer safe," he added with a smile.

"So you don't want to have your way with me?" she asked, still unsure of his intentions.

"No, I mean yes, I mean," he stammered. He took a deep breath to try and compose himself, his chest almost pressing against hers unintentionally with the increase in lung capacity. "No, I willna 'have my way' with ye because of my oath. All right?" Jane nodded that she understood, but looked at him like she was waiting for the rest of the answer. "And yes, I would like to 'be' with you. But, that's not the same as 'have my way.' I mean, when I'm from, both people must want it, not jest the one; it isna right otherwise. Oh, crap," he said in realization, "I've been talkin' about.... How much of it do ye believe?"

"Does it make a difference?" she asked. "No one would believe me. I mean, you know what people think of slaves."

"That's not what I asked. How much do *ye* believe?" some of his fear manifesting itself with the squeak of the word 'ye.'

"Did you really mean what you said, that I could go to school there, in your time, college even?"

Benji nodded and bit his bottom lip. She was even more appealing when she spoke.

"And, white folks and Negroes really get along?" she asked as a conditional response.

Benji nodded. "Yes, but we say 'African Americans' or 'Blacks,' and they really do work together, go to school together, get married and have babies together..."

"And, you have a vow on you..." she reminded him.

"Yes, although right now I really wished I dinna," he groaned with his eyes squeezed shut.

"Does that mean that you can't, um, kiss?" she asked bashfully.

Benji's eyes opened wide. "Nope. I can kiss all day and all night and...do you want to kiss me? I mean, I said that I wouldna touch ye, but ye can touch me...or kiss me...or both..."

Jane delayed her answer. She had found the rock anchor for the tent with her foot and set it in place. The wind had died down; it should hold. Benji had noticed her feet moving as she was deciding and had done the same. "So, I can kiss you?" she asked, still a bit unsure if she should even touch a white man, even one who had papers that said he owned her.

"Oh, I sure wish ye would," pled Benji as he arched his back, shut his eyes, and stuck out his lips. "And ye can do it all day and all night..." he mumbled through pursed, anticipating lips.

Jane kept her eyes open as she leaned in for her first voluntary kiss with anyone but her mama. Her eyes shut automatically as her lips touched his. The most wonderful feeling washed down the front of her neck and shoulders, tingling her breasts, then flowing down her belly until it seeped even further down, warming the place between her legs where babies were made. It was like she was wearing a rainbow. She pulled away from the kiss and looked at him again. His face looked like she felt. She might not be able to do it all night and all day, but most likely, hopefully, all night.

The kissing went on long after the thunder was gone. Jane was still naked save her leather apron, and Benji only had on the long shirt that, although it covered the top half of him, it didn't keep his firmness from her. She shifted her pose, trying to avoid being jabbed, but realized that that wasn't going to work. She slid her hand down and gently tried to reposition him through his shirt. She clutched and tried shifting him, but the cloth kept his awkward angle in place. She hummed as she held onto his shoulders and lifted her body up towards his head, allowing some slack in his shirt. She gathered the shirttail in her hand and pulled it up, freeing his stiff cock. She reached down to move it aside and gasped at how hot it was.

"It's full of my boilin' blood," he said softly as he leaned in to kiss her neck. "It feels like it's goin' to explode. I'll keep my vow, but if I run out of here in a hurry, dinna take it personally."

"Um," Jane didn't have any intimate experience with men personally, but she had heard the other slave women talk. She had managed to keep herself from both the masters and other slaves by brute force or cleverness. But, now she wanted to know more, feel more. She was willing to believe some of what the others had told her. At least what she was feeling in her hand felt like what they had said was what made a man happy, and a woman, too, if he used it right. And, she wanted it inside her: it felt like that was where it was supposed to be. "Can I hold it?" she asked. "I mean, will that break your vow?"

Benji stopped kissing her neck and rolled onto his back. He looked down at the obscenely large pole sticking up off of his belly, the anaconda looking for prey. "If ye do, I dinna ken what will happen. I mean, it has a mind of its own about when it, um, goes off."

"Will it hurt if it does?" she asked pensively.

"No, I dinna think so, but it will be a bit wet and sticky."

"Not me; you. Will it hurt you? The other slaves said a man makes a horrible noise when he, um, goes off."

"Ach, no. It feels mighty good when it does. It's nae so fine as when it's ins... No, it willna hurt me," he said, then picked up her free hand and kissed it. "But, ye needna do anythin' ye dinna want to do. I'll survive. A might uncomfortable fer a while, but I'll be fine. Can I kiss on ye some more?"

Jane bent over and kissed him on the lips, pulled back briefly and said, "All night long," then reached down and gently but firmly, wrapped the hand he had kissed around his hot cock, gently pulling the skin around it up then down like the women had told her. Like milking a cow, only slower and firmer, gradually increasing the speed.

"Am I doing it right?" she asked as he gasped.

"Uh, huh," he gasped again, "don't, stop...oh, please...don't...stop..."

23 The Morning After

Benji awoke with a smile that went from his squinty blue eyes all the way down to his long, naked toes. He could feel the sunshine on his face enhancing the warmth he felt, both inside and out. Even before he opened his eyes, he knew it was a beautiful day. It was morning and he was a free man. His first thought was that the passion the night before had only been an adolescent wet dream. His relaxed body, de-stressed for the first time in years, remembered the physical release, all right, but last night's kissing and groping definitely involved another person.

Right now, this other person was five yards away, squatted next to the fire, head bowed, eyes cast down. Since he couldn't see her face, he couldn't tell whether she was happy, embarrassed, angry, or shamed. He crawled out of the crude tent and parked next to Jane, mimicking her squatted position. "Can I kiss ye?" Benji asked pensively.

Jane didn't respond to his question, instead took her fire tending stick, and poked the coals around the Dutch oven. He stood up and walked around her. "Okay, since I ken ye can understand me, and ye obviously dinna care to speak, I'll assume ye jest want to go back to how we used to be. I'll blabber all day about my old life: planes, trains, and automobiles, and how I'm back here to find my way to my grandsire's home. And then ye can keep yer head bowed, walk five steps behind me, feed me greenballs, and laugh at my cock when the cold water makes it shrink up..."

Jane's shoulders were jiggling with her effort to hold back her laughter. "I ken ye were in there somewhere underneath that slave suit they've made ye wear all yer life," Benji said. He added softly, "Ye dinna have to wear it when we're together, at least when it's jest the two of us."

Jane lifted her head and looked him in the eye. "I think it will be safer for both of us if I keep it on, at least during the daytime."

"Oh, Janie," he said and gathered her head into his belly. He let loose, then moved back so he could squat down beside her. "There has to be a way. I mean, fer ye and me to be, well, dammit!" He leaned back and plopped down hard onto his

143

bottom next to her. "I ken I'm no better than ye. There's no reason other than the rules and laws of man that we canna be together."

"The rules and laws of men *in this time*," Jane corrected as she gave him a look of hope.

"Aye, in this time," he agreed. "There may not be much that I cared for *then,* but they dinna have slavery. At least, based on the color of a person's skin," he added, shifting his shoulders in memory of the whips that had crossed his back more than once in his younger days.

An angry voice barked from the edge of the copse, startling them both. "I don't care if you *do* have a piece of paper; I want her back!"

Mr. Jonathan and his pistol had followed them from town.

"And, I *will* get *my* nigger back!" he added. "Come on, men; bring the chains. He won't move as long as I have this pistol pointed at him."

Mr. Jonathan marched up to the unarmed pair and motioned for his mob of vigilantes to follow.

Benji slowly brought his feet under himself to assume a squatted pose as he surveyed his chances of subduing the hesitant horde. He looked over at Jane and saw she was terrified. He gulped as he remembered that a slave would be put to death for touching a white man without his permission. He couldn't expect her to lift a hand in her own defense...or his. He'd have to war alone. And, with the odds he was facing today, it looked like it would be best if he waged it with words.

"What, ye think that ye can jest strut in here and take my property?" Benji accused loudly, "Isna that stealing? I mean, I do have a legal bill of sale here. Dinna ye ken that if ye try to take what is mine, then I'll jest have ye arrested and get her back?"

"Who are you going to tell?" Mr. Jonathan growled back with a sneer. "There aren't any constables or magistrates in this area. *I'm* the only law around here. What I say goes. Come on men; don't be bashful."

Eight men ambled in reluctantly from their secreted positions in the trees, armed with chains, hammers, and a wide range of cutting implements. Benji stood up slowly and dramatically, crossing his arms in front of himself to assume his Titan stance. They'd have to get past him to get to her, and he wanted them to know it.

The posture worked. The men's arms fell slack at their sides, a few of them letting loose and dropping their improvised weapons. Mr. Jonathan turned back and saw the fear in his minion's eyes. "Don't let him scare you, men. There's only one of him. And if he comes at you, he'll get this right between the eyes," he said, as he shook his pistol at Benji and looked at his men.

"That's what ye think," Benji screamed. He lunged forward and rushed him, making sure his shoulder came up under the man's gun arm.

Mr. Jonathan's hand flew skywards with the impact of the full body tackle, and his pistol fired wildly in the air. The mob pulled back from the fracas, afraid that the brawling giant would go after them next.

Benji rolled over and pulled away from his winded, would-be assassin who was now laid out, stunned and gasping on the dusty clearing floor. He stood up and re-evaluated the new situation. He threw a threatening glare at each of the men, intent on intimidating, terrorizing, or both, the motley crew.

Mr. Jonathan regained his breath and shouted desperately from ground level, "Ten dollars to the man who brings me that nigger! And ten more to the man who gets him in chains! Get him! He's gonna be mine!"

Suddenly, eight men with newfound, monetary infused courage were encircling Benji; their scythes, chains, and hammers raised, ready to take him down. "Ye think ye can do it?" Benji taunted. "There hasna been a chain forged that could hold me, ye cowards. Come on, come on little chick, chick, chickies," he chided as he waved his right index finger to one then another in the crowd, as if selecting his next victim. "Who wants to be the first to go down?"

Benji heard an involuntary squeak behind him. He turned his head slightly, and saw that Mr. Jonathan had made use of his distraction with the crowd, and come up behind Jane. He had her captive. His right hand held a knife at her ribs, extracting a slow dribble of blood from his firm pressure. His other hand was kneading her shoulder, as if he was welcoming home a lost dog. "It looks like I just saved myself ten dollars," he crowed. "Go get him, boys. I'll make that fifteen dollars to the man who locks him up!"

The motivation of more money, and their boss's triumph over the slave woman, erased the mob's fears. They paused long enough to look at one another, acknowledging with a shared nod that it was all for one and one for all: they'd split the reward money.

145

Four of the men rushed him at the same time. Benji grabbed the arm of the first one who reached him, a skinny youth broadly swinging a scythe. He quickly twisted the tool out of his hand and grabbed him by his now empty wrists, swinging the boy's body like a hammer throw, shooing the gang away with the flying teen. He let loose of the helpless and stunned youth, then turned him around and kicked him in the butt, knocking him to the edge of the circle, where he stumbled forward to hug the ground, reluctant to get up for more.

Now Benji had a weapon. "It's nae so good as a broadsword," he boasted as he brandished the blade with a showman's flourish, "but I'll wager I can take every one of ye cowards down with it." He challenged the wary vigilantes, pivoting in a tight circle to glare briefly at each man individually.

The now unsure rag tag posse had him surrounded, but he let them know with a glower that it wouldn't be easy if they even *could* take him. He was going to hurt many, if not all of them, in the process.

"Twenty dollars!" Mr. Jonathan yelled to them in encouragement.

The promise of a larger reward to split emboldened the gang. They surged toward Benji in a human wave, their tools of destruction ready to deploy. Benji ducked and missed the first hammer thrown at his head, but the second one came at him just as a chain wrapped around his ankles. The maul hit him in the middle of his back, causing him to lose his balance and stumble forward.

His fall was broken by the broad chest of a greasy man in an apron who was very happy to have his bounty off balance. The growling blacksmith quickly threw a loop of rope over Benji's head, catching him under the nose. Benji ducked and twisted and tucked his neck in, finally able to shake off the noose completely. He grabbed the rope with his left hand and jerked it hard, pulling its owner to him in one, quick movement. Benji flung his right forearm up, and caught his assailant under the chin, snapping the blacksmith's neck with the short, sharp blow. He picked up the fallen hammer, hastily cinching up the head of the maul in the noose. He swung it around his head like the hammer of Thor, growling like a cougar, hoping to discourage any more assaults.

It worked. The men retreated, no longer interested in their attack. Benji saw that the blacksmith—the oily man in the long leather apron—was probably dead. He hadn't meant to kill him, but his forearm reflex must have broken his neck. The angle of the man's head wasn't conducive to breathing, his eyes were fixed with a wide-open, unblinking stare, and his chest was still and silent. Yes, he was definitely dead.

"Now, nobody else need be hurt," said Benji, as he looked each lackey in the eye, counting heads to make sure they were all accounted for. She's mine," he said as he nodded to Jane, still held at knifepoint, "and yer boss man is jest a bit greedy. Dinna let the man be makin' ye do things that arena fair or legal. He may say he's the law, but ye'll have to answer to the Real Man later," he said and nodded toward heaven. "Thou shalt not steal and not bear false witness, either..."

"Don't listen to him," Mr. Jonathan cried out desperately as he saw his gang of wannabe cutthroats start to look like a flock of sheep. "I don't care what he says: I *am* the law around here. Do you want your loans called in right now? I'll take each and every one of your homes and businesses, and you know I can."

Benji, ankles still wrapped in the chain that had caused him to fall, sidled away from the men, turning slightly so he could look the town boss in the eye. "What makes ye think yer shit doesna stink?" Benji asked snidely. *He'd have to play the head game again. At least this man was ill equipped for it and could be intimidated easily.*

"What did you say?" the stunned, dimwitted dictator replied, his hand no longer kneading Jane's shoulder.

"Oh, I'm sorry," said Benji condescendingly, "I forgot, yer mentally challenged. I mean, ye canna read nor write, and yer not much to look at. If it werena for that gun ye show off or the money ye steal, ye'd be no better than a hound dog. I mean, a hound dog canna read, nor write either. At least he can get his own food, though. I'll bet ye dinna even ken how to fish..."

"You're, you're, you're just *stupid!*" Mr. Jonathan screamed in exasperation. He was losing the showdown, and he knew it. But, he also had an ace up his sleeve. "I may not know how to do *some things,*" he admitted boldly, "but I have *yer nigger* and you don't!" He glared at Benji, then pulled his right hand back, and thrust his knife into Jane's side.

Benji flashed lightning hot rage, rushing the brute before he even blinked. Jane quickly spun out of his hold, escaping her captor and allowing her rescuer full access to the man who now held nothing but a knife hasp.

Benji's left fist flew forward and broke Mr. Jonathan's nose, crunching the cartilage up into his eye sockets. As his left hand pulled back, he powered off a right upper cut, catching the

147

fiend squarely under the chin, sending him straight up in the air, landing flat on his back, right at Benji's feet. Benji leaned over the town boss, meaning to pummel his face until it was the consistency of raw sausage, but froze at her words. "Watch out!" Jane screamed.

Benji turned around and saw a hefty man with a huge, ornate cavalry saber rushing toward him. Benji's feet were still tangled up with the chain. He was trapped where he was and without a weapon. He dodged the first thrust of the sword and rolled onto his side, kicking at the mass of iron links wrapped around his ankles, trying to free himself from his twelve-pound prison before the man struck again.

The others in the gang found courage now that Benji was on the ground. They gathered around him like jackals on a downed zebra, cheering on the swordsman, eager for their share of the lion's prey and the bounty. "Argh!" the big man screamed as he thrust anew. Benji's feet came up as one and deflected the blow, knocking his attacker off balance. The assailant was quick on his feet, though, and came back for another assault.

Jane ran towards Benji's saber wielding attacker, and dove in front of his feet, tripping him before he could reach his target: her master, her friend.

The man stumbled sideways, instinctively placing his sword in front of himself to break his fall. In his awkward attempt to stay upright, the swordsman inadvertently skewered the downed Mr. Jonathan.

The town boss was alive, but stunned, flat on his back, the sword straight through his cowardly and portly belly, pinned to the ground.

Benji rolled over and saw the blade that had missed him was now stuck in another. He gulped in shock as he saw the blood spurting out of the fallen man—the manipulative, thieving gambler whose nose he had just broken, the bully who he had wanted to kill for knifing Jane. The brainless brute's body was flailing like a fish out of water. "Take it out of him," Benji yelled to the swordsman. He hated Mr. Jonathan and everything he stood for, but he couldn't stand to see him suffer.

But, the swordsman who had accidentally stabbed the evil town boss didn't obey. He looked down and watched the now trembling body slow in both its blood spurting and thrashing. The body was still alive, though. He shook his head at no one in particular. He couldn't believe that he had just stabbed his own brother-in-law.

Benji, still bound by the tangle of chains around his ankles and unable to stand, crawled on his elbows to Mr. Jonathan. He put his hands around the sword wound, trying to staunch the flow, but he knew it was futile. All of a sudden, he realized that the man under his hands was yelling, screaming the non-words of indescribable agony. "Be still," Benji ordered, then turned to ask the horde, "Willna somebody pull this blasted sword out of him?"

But, nobody was listening to him. Benji changed his focus to the chains around his calves and ankles. After what seemed like an hour, but was more like thirty seconds, he was free and able to stand up. He stood above the body—now silent and only twitching—and put one foot next to the saber, grabbed the ornate hilt, and pulled the weapon from the victim's belly. Only a slight trickle of blood and stinking greenish brown slime came out with it. The body was spent. The vacant, unblinking eyes verified the loss of life.

The stench made Benji turn his head and gag. He paused to compose himself then brought his head back up and saw seven pairs of eyes staring at him. He looked to the side and saw Jane's head bowed, shoulders drooped. He'd have to take care of this situation's damage control right away.

"Weel, I think we have a lot of witnesses here who saw a tragic accident," he said, using the tone of his voice to take command. He walked away from the dead body and looked at the group. "It looks to me like this fine man here was chasin' off a...a...wolf and tripped. The saber went right through Mr. Jonathan here. It was a shame that the wolf got away, but I'm sure that all of ye here will testify that it was jest an accident. And, it looked like Mr. Jonathan had also tripped and fell earlier, landin' on his face, bustin' up his nose, right?"

Benji asked for confirmation with words, but he was actually looking for the real answers in their eyes. "But, but," a small man in the back mumbled, and pointed at Jane.

Benji walked toward the objector who scrambled backwards until he was stopped by an inconveniently placed tree. "Did ye see the lass lay a hand on anyone?" he asked. The man shook his head, but pointed to the place where Jane had dived, tripping the man in order to stop his attack on Benji.

"Oh, ye mean that the lass jumped in front of the wolf to try and keep it from hurtin' Mr. Jonathan? I mean, that's what I saw. How about ye?" Benji asked, then looked at the man with his cold, blue eyes squinted, daring him to deny the fabricated alibi.

"Um," he replied, then bit his lip, shaking his head minimally, not willing to agree.

Benji pulled back his shoulders and tried a different tactic. He took a deep breath. "I was jest wonderin'...now that Mr. Jonathan is deid, who's in charge? I mean, he said he was the law—that he could take yer homes and lands, call in yer notes if the whim hit him. Who's the new man in charge who'll get all yer assets? *Or*," he suggested, "are ye gonna to have a town meetin' and select a real magistrate? I mean, it sounds like a reasonable idea. That is, of course, after a proper burial fer him."

"Yeah, yeah." Murmurs were tossed back and forth among six of the seven, but the accidental assassin stayed mute. He looked back on the men and said, "Grab some blankets off the horses. Let's wrap him up and take him back to town for his funeral." He chuckled, "But first, we'll have an open casket so we can all spit on him. Let's make sure my sister gets first shot. She's earned it."

Benji noticed that there was a new leader in town. But, this new lion who had accidentally taken down the old one seemed to be working with the men, not by intimidation, but by mutual agreement. They might have a chance.

Benji walked up to the new boss man. "I'm sorry fer the loss of the, um, blacksmith there," he said as he nodded to the big man with the face forever frozen in shock. "It was an accident. I was jest meanin' to knock him away. I dinna think I hit him that hard."

The new boss shrugged his shoulders. "No loss there. He pretty much fed Mr. Jonathan's perversions. He even designed the little brand they put on my sister. I'll never forgive either one of them for that. We'll be haulin' him away, too. Sorry to have interrupted your breakfast. I don't mean to be rude, but it might be best if you two left and never came back. I don't think these men will change their stories, but she seems to upset them. I think they're a bit jealous of her size and strength." The brother-in-law looked over at Jane, crouched on the ground, holding her side. "I think you ought to take care of her wound. There seems to be a lot of blood comin' out."

Benji nodded to the man and rushed to Jane's side. "Can ye make it to the creek?" She nodded in answer, both of her lips sucked into her mouth, trying to contain the pain and urge to scream out. "Wait jest a minute and I'll help ye."

Benji dashed to their makeshift tent, grabbed his sporran, and rushed back to her side to help her walk to the water's edge. He glanced back and saw the men dragging the two corpses on improvised blanket sleds, not paying heed to the roughness of the trail caused by the stones and fallen branches. One man used the shovel he had initially bought as a weapon to dig a shallow pit. He was scraping the stinking mess of blood and body fluids into it, doing a quick and efficient job of cleaning up traces of the 'incident.'

"oof," Jane cried as she started to fall, grabbing Benji's arm for support. Tears started flowing, but they weren't from the pain: she hated to show any sign of weakness.

"Hold onto this," Benji said, and handed her the sporran. Jane clutched it with her weakened right hand. Her left arm stayed crossed in front of her body, holding onto the knife wound, trying to keep the blade that was still stuck between her ribs from being jostled or moved.

Benji came around to her left side, squatted down beside her, and put his left arm behind her knees, his right under her shoulder. "I shouldna asked ye to walk," he grunted as he walked with her in his arms over the uneven rocks to the creek.

He set her down carefully and whispered, "Wait," and ran to their site, took the tent down, and bundled up the camouflaged covering. He rushed back to her and opened it out, laying it beside her like a huge tortilla. "Lie on yer good side," he ordered gently. "I'm gonna have to do some doctorin', and I want to wrap what bits of ye that dinna need fixin' with the cloth. Yer getting' chilled, even if it is warm out. Yer in shock, Janie, but I'll take care of ye, aye?"

"aye," she answered softly, and did as he instructed, gingerly scooting onto the soft fabric.

Benji covered as much of her nearly nude body as he could, then washed his hands with the soap. He looked over and saw that the cleanup crew was about ready to leave. He stood up and yelled back to them, "Do any of ye happen to have any whisky?"

The brother-in-law was out of sight, but came into view when he heard the call. "Just a minute," he hollered back. He walked over to the pile of horse blankets that was the funeral shroud of Mr. Jonathan, pulled back the cloths until he exposed the corpse. He opened out the dead man's jacket and took out a silver flask. He quickly threw the blankets back over the frozen, anguished face, and walked towards Benji. "Here, will this do?" He looked over at Jane, all wrapped up with her wound exposed, then at Benji with knife in hand. "It'll burn, but I think she can handle it. You can keep the flask. I doubt anyone else would want it." He nodded in farewell and went back to join the others.

Benji opened his mouth to say 'thank ye,' then thought better of it. "I appreciate it jest the same," he mumbled and headed back to his surgeon's task.

"I said I'd not hurt ye, but it looks like I have to again." He snorted in exasperation then bent down to look closely at the damages. "Good God," he uttered softly. "The blade's still in ye, lass!"

"I know," she said slowly, trying not to whimper. "Take it out, please," she said, this time unable to contain her tears and sobs.

"Ye can cry all ye want and it willna be a sign of weakness. But it would help with the task if ye dinna heave yer chest when ye did. I mean, cry, but try not to sob. I think that's what I mean to say. And I'll be as gentle as I can."

"Just be as quick as you can," she pled, and sniffed back her tears.

The area around the wound was fairly clean. At least, it didn't have dirt or leaves in it like the wounds on her back had. He could see the edge of the blade, but could barely feel it. He opened out his sporran again and dug through it. He took out the antibiotic cream, small scissors, sewing needle, and dental floss. The Leatherman was already opened, large blade out, ready for disinfecting. "I'll need ye, too," he said as he twisted the tool back on itself, revealing the all-purpose pliers. He threaded the needle with the floss then poured whisky over every part of every tool that was to come in contact with her wound, including his hands.

"Here, lift yer head." He held her neck with one hand, the flask with the other. "This should dull the pain a bit. Drink as much as ye can without pukin'." Jane gave him a blank stare. "Without vomitin'."

She nodded and took a cautious sip. She coughed, hurting her side even more. She didn't speak, but shook her head 'no more,' looked up, and closed her eyes. 'Get on with it,' she said without words.

"Lord, help me," he prayed quickly, then bent to his task.

He knew Jane was doing her best to be still, but the pliers on bone made her twitch. "Think a happy thought," he said, then wiped the sweat from his brow on the back of his forearm.

"You," she said softly.

He felt her muscles relax with the single word that described her happy thought. He didn't have time to appreciate it, though. Her relaxed state was what was needed to get to the butt of the blade. He was able to grasp a big bite of the metal with the jaws of the pliers, and pulled ever so slightly to assure his hold. It was secure. He put one hand on Jane's ribcage and pulled out the blade, making sure he extracted it at the same angle it had been thrust.

Jane gulped at the release. It still hurt, but wasn't the excruciating pain it had been. She took several quick shallow breaths, afraid that the old pain would return, then relaxed. "Is that all?" she asked.

"Nae, I have to sew ye up, and then use some of that cream I put on yer back. I dinna want this to get infected. It's gonna hurt again, but I doubt it will be as bad as before. Do ye want to try the whisky again?"

"Um, yes, please," she answered, but didn't move.

"Here." He came around in front of her and lifted the flask to her lips.

She kept her eyes low out of habit, then realized that she didn't have to with him. She looked up and smiled. "Thank you."

"And thank ye fer savin' my life," he said with a huge grin. "And thank ye fer the smile. I hope to be seein' many more of them when yer feelin' better. Now, take as many sips as ye can handle. Ye might want to leave a few, though. It's a might early fer me to be drinkin', but I think I may want to do a little celebratin' tonight. I think we'll be doin' it down the road a bit, though."

24 Camo Castle

"Now, I'm done with the major doctorin', but before ye get too comfortable there, I think we'd better get movin'. The men want us gone, but I dinna think it would be wise fer ye to be travelin' too far with yer wound. I'm sure we can find a place nearby where we willna be seen. I'll get our gear. Try not to go to sleep; I'll be as quick as I can."

Jane nodded that she heard him, then kept nodding to let him know that she would try to stay awake. Suddenly, her head snapped backwards. While she was nodding, she had fallen asleep, awaking with a start. She realized it would be easier to stay alert if she kept her head still and eyes opened. She would rest when he told her she could.

Benji sprinted over to their impromptu kitchen. He used a stick to pull the Dutch oven out of the fire, and pushed the coals apart to die out. He bounded over to the tent site, grabbed the bundled mass of blue calico and the rucksack, scurried back to the pot, and grabbed the handle. "Ouch," he said as he quickly set it back down. He pulled out a short length of the blue cotton and used it as a potholder, grabbing the lidded iron kettle of breakfast cornbread in one hand and the rest of their portable kitchen and pantry in the other.

He was back at her side in less than two minutes, all of their worldly belongings in a two-foot-square pile at his feet. "Do ye think ye can walk across the creek down yonder where it's shallow? If ye canna, I'll carry ye. But, I want to give ye the option. It's a bit slippery, and I dinna want to drop ye if I stumble."

Jane gave a short, shallow chortle, and lifted her head to speak to him with eyes shut. "You hold me up on my weak side and I'll make it." Her head flopped forward then jerked back up to face him, her closed eyes suddenly popping open. "This whisky makes me feel funny. Not ha ha funny, but like my body parts aren't connected to where they're supposed to be."

"Weel, get up while ye still can then," he ordered softly, and reached for her left hand. After three false starts, Jane was standing on both feet, but her camo cloth sarong hadn't come up with her. Benji squatted down quickly and deftly scooped it up, adding it to his bundle of fabric, food, and iron possessions.

"Come on, Janie," he urged. "We'll be jest up the other side of the creek where the road doesna pass."

Despite his best efforts at supporting her, Jane slipped a couple of times. She never lost her footing completely, though. "Ye move like a drunken mountain goat," Benji chided. "It looks like yer gonna be bottom first in the creek, and then yer back up and makin' forward progress. Aye, ye'd make a dandy basketball player, fer sure."

"I'd play basketball or bushel ball or any kind of ball if they'd let me go to college. But, I think I should know how to read firsht," she complained meekly, her words still slurred.

"Ach," Benji replied, "I'll teach ye in no time flat. It's not as if I'm goin' anywhere."

Jane suddenly sobered up—or at least she felt like she had. "Am I going with you?"

Benji felt like he had just been dunked in a pool of ice water. He hadn't thought that far ahead, about how everything he wanted to do would now involve another person. "Uh," he fumbled, then realized he was probably frightening her. He bucked up, put on an iron suit of self-assuredness, and said, "Of course ye are; yer mine arena ye?"

Jane suddenly felt deflated. He thought of her as a possession again. She didn't say anything, but nodded minimally in servitude body language, just in case he was looking.

Benji looked up and saw the humbled posture. "I dinna mean like that!" he squeaked, immediately embarrassed that his voice had cracked. He cleared his throat and repeated his meaning with different words. "I mean, yer mine because I thought ye wanted to be mine. Remember, I said that we could choose who we wanted to 'be' with in my time. I thought ye wanted to 'be' with me. I mean..." he trailed off, not finishing the sentence or even completing the thought as he set foot on solid ground. They were now on the far side of the creek. Last night, he thought that she was fond of him. At least, she was definitely fond of the kissing, and holding onto *that* part of him.

He looked up the rise. The unmarked path to higher ground was a little precarious. "Here," he said changing the subject, glad that the geography had given him the opportunity. "Ye wait here and I'll take these things up there. I dinna want ye climbin' or even walkin' without me to help ye."

Benji practically jumped up the hill, doing his own mountain goat impersonation in scaling the steep bluff. He set down the rucksack and calico, then threw the camouflage cloth over the low tree branches to establish a hunter's blind. They would be invisible to anyone, even someone looking for them, from the trailside of the creek.

Discretion assured, he skidded down the rocky escarpment and landed in front of Jane. He bent over with a deep bow and an arm flourish, and asked, "May I help the lady to her castle?"

Jane shook her head and grinned, not knowing if she wanted to laugh or cry.

"No?" Benji asked. "Are ye sure? I made a grand home jest fer the two of us." He changed to a gentler, sincere tone. "There's no one I'd rather be with, Janie. Ye'll break my heart if ye say no. Please, dinna tell me no..." he said then lifted her left hand and kissed it.

Jane rolled her eyes and let him keep her hand. She gave a quick nod. Yes, she'd let him escort her to the 'castle.' Jane looked up at the camo cloth tent at the top of the rise. They would be resting and healing right next to the creek where murder and mayhem had nearly ended their lives less than an hour earlier. Even if she died from her wound, at least she had found, been close to, someone who treated her like a human being and had made her smile. Yes, if she died today, she could say she had been truly happy at least once, no twice, in her life.

Benji helped Jane up to the improvised, poor person's home with the million-dollar view of the valley. He hadn't chosen the site for that reason. He just wanted someplace close by that wasn't near the road where he was sure they would have been shooed away or worse. No, the strategic observation point was a bonus: unsolicited, but appreciated.

"Before ye travel to the Land of Nod, would ye eat a bit? I'd hate fer ye to get a hangover with yer first taste of whisky. Besides, I have a little pill I'd like ye to swallow. It may take away the pain even more than the whisky."

Jane accepted the chunk of cornbread he had broken off for her. She chewed it gingerly. She wasn't sure what a hangover was, but if it had to do with a queasy stomach and throbbing head, she already had one. She didn't want to ask too many questions. She had already admitted to being ignorant, but didn't want to him to know how little she really knew.

"This is the wee little pill that should make ye feel better all over. Its good fer headaches, backaches, sore shoulders, knifed ribs, stubbed toes, cracked eyelashes...." Benji was looking for a smile, and he got it.

"What kind of *pill* is it?" Jane asked. She had never seen a pill of any sort, but didn't want him to know that.

"It's called Ibuprofen. The ladies really like it fer that time of month. It takes care of the backache and bellyache ye get with the curse...or so I'm told. I've never had that problem, myself," he joked, "I'm a tough one."

Jane started giggling again then stopped. She had to let him know. "I've never seen a *pill* before. How do you use it?"

Benji snorted a quick laugh then realized that he was being rude. "I'm sorry. I dinna mean to be makin' fun of ye. It's jest that *when* I'm from, people take pills all the time. Most times, they're not even needed. Some people think that they make them healthier or smarter. But, sometimes they *are* needed. Some can take away pains, like this one. Some get rid of infections, ye ken, the fever and pus. Some of them are like my Grannie's teas, but easier to take. See, ye jest put this little tablet on the back of yer tongue and drink some water. The medicine in it dissolves—that is, breaks up—in yer belly, and goes all over ye through yer blood to make ye better, or does whatever it's supposed to do." He inhaled deeply, rolled his eyes, and shook his head. "Ye wouldna believe what some pills are fer."

He didn't want to think about the time those men crammed the little blue pills down his throat while he was unconscious. 'We just want to make sure you can perform,' the man with one eyebrow said as he kicked him in the ribs to wake him up. 'It looks like that thing of yours will be the next star on the porn circuit. You play your cards right, kid, stick with me, and you'll have all the dope and pussy you can dream of.'

Benji shook his head again and mumbled, "go away," then looked over at Jane. She looked frightened. She dipped her head to him, looked him in the eye, and asked without words if he was okay.

He was glad she wasn't wearing the slave suit, even if it was daytime. "I'm okay," he answered gently and sincerely. "It's jest that I have some bad memories that steal their way into my heid every once in a while. I have to shake them out." Jane nodded that she understood. "Ye do, too?"

"aye," Jane said softly. "Should I take the pill now?" she asked pensively.

"Here, let me help ye. The first time, it may not want to go down. Open yer mouth and I'll put it way in the back... Here, drink the water as soon as I have my fingers out of yer mouth. And dinna bite me!" he added with levity.

Jane held the canteen with her left hand, tipped her head back, and closed her eyes.

"Now, drink and swallow, drink some more... Ach, ye did brawly, lass," he said when she downed the pill without gagging. "Now, I want to bind yer wound, and then ye need to lie down and rest a bit." Benji found the leading edge of the calico fabric and bit into the selvage, finishing off the small nick with a rip crosswise. He stretched out the piece, looked up at her, and decided he would need to tie two of them together.

"Here, lift yer arms and let me tie this around ye." He brought his arms around her to grab the other end of the blue bandaging material. Gulp. He hadn't thought of her nakedness in the confrontation and ensuing fight earlier. Or in the surgery and the stitching that came later. He still wasn't thinking of her 'that way' when they were crossing streams and scaling creek bluffs. But, now the crises were over, and they were 'home.' He felt stirrings he knew couldn't be satisfied. She needed to heal, and he needed to start thinking of something—anything—else.

He tied off her bandage then patted her gently on her strong shoulder. "Take yer rest and I'll see if I can do some good while yer mendin'. Here, lay yer heid on my shirt." He pulled it off over his head. "I'll need this," he said as he lifted the blue bundle, "fer somethin' else."

Jane rolled over on to her good side and fell asleep with a smile on her face. The pain was already lessened, or at least it wasn't bothering her as much. She had seen him blush at her nakedness. It was nice to know that he still felt that way about her. If she slept for a long time, then it would be closer to nightfall when she awoke. She wanted it to be nighttime. Then she could kiss him all night long again.

Ж

Benji stayed next to the tree, under the cover of the camouflage print cloth. He pulled out about four yards of the blue fabric, ripped it off, and then tore off another piece the same size. He matched the pieces, wrong sides together then pleated them, ready to tailor. He opened his sporran and took out the needle he had sewn Jane's wound with and threaded it with real thread this time. He used the only color he had: tan. He snorted; she probably wouldn't care, although he was sure she'd notice. She was a sharp woman, even if she was uneducated.

Benji sewed a running stitch from one end of the cloth to the other. He turned it over and used his fingers to 'finger press' the seams as his mother called it. He was going to do this right. He was going to make French seams in the Polynesian-style sarong for his African-born friend. He shrugged his shoulders and let himself glow, remembering the horizontal activities of the night before. More than a friend, he sighed. He visualized the two of them, marching down the road—the right road this time—to his Grandpa's house. He had found himself a mate, someone to be his wife...

"Shit," he mumbled. His voice roused, but hadn't wakened Jane. How was he going to marry her here, now? And how was he going to be able to go beyond second, well, third, base with a vow on his head? One way or another, he'd marry her, though. If his Grandpa couldn't figure it out, Grannie was pretty clever, too. Between the three, no four including Jane, they'd solve the matrimonial dilemma. "But first we have to find ye, Grandpa" he said softly.

Ж

Benji heard the soft, unobtrusive cough, just loud enough to rouse him, but not enough to sound insistent: Jane was awake. His back was up against the tree trunk: he had evidently fallen asleep. He looked at her and returned her smile. "If ye only ken how beautiful ye were when ye smiled, ye'd never stop."

"I have to have a reason to smile," she said shyly, then shifted her position, scooting closer to him.

"Why are ye so different?" Benji asked lovingly.

Jane frowned then looked away in shame, turning her hand over, examining it somberly.

"Not yer color. I ken why that is: melanin, plain and simple. We all tend to look like our parents. But, what I mean is, why are ye so different to me? I've been with other women..."

Jane gave him 'the look' when he said 'been.'

"Aye, I'm not proud of that. It wasna right, and that's one reason for the vow. Whenever you're that close, sharing, um, body fluids, ye really do give a part of yerself, yer soul, to the other person that ye can never get back. But with ye, I ken that I'll be givin' willingly, in the right way as yer spouse, and all that I give will be magnified, multiplied, because it's ye."

"Aye," Jane replied somberly, her head still spinning. "I guess that's why I didn't want to give in to the masters or the boss men. I didn't want them to have *that* part of me. I was offered extra food and more clothes if I would *cooperate*. When that didn't work, they'd bring out the strap or whip or switch...whatever was handiest, I guess. But, it didn't work. They never got *that* part of me. But, I made up my mind. I would never do something, anything, if pain or whipping were the motivations. I'd rather die first. I guess...I guess that's why I went with you. I was willing to let that pig whip me to death rather

159

than load those barrels. I know it wasn't that much to do, but he beat me first, even before telling me what he wanted done, just to make a show of me to the men in that town where you found me. He whipped me twice in two days. Of course, he wasn't going to feed me, either. That's when he took that other man's advice about the food and water. Well, I was willing to die of thirst first—I knew I would die of that before starving to death. I've gone long, long times without food, but I could always get water one way or another.

"So, when you gave me the hambone and bucket of water, I took it. If you had laid a hand or a whip on me, though, I wouldn't have. Then, you loaded the wagons so I didn't have to. I didn't know what to think about that. Well, really, I do know. Since I wasn't doing the work, had both food and water, and was sitting on the ground while a white man did the work, I, I thought that I had died." Jane snorted in recall, "Although I did think that heaven would have more to eat than a hambone and a bucket of murky water."

Jane looked back at Benji and grinned, stroking his forehead affectionately. "Then you left and came back. I saw you put the paper in your bag there."

"My sporran," Benji said.

"Sporran, and then you came over to me. I knew you had bought me. But, I didn't know what to expect. I guess I still hoped I was dead and wouldn't have to put up with starving, the mean people, and no one to love or care for."

Benji grinned back at her, "Ye'll always have me. But, yer right: life isna right if ye canna love someone. Even a dog would be good company." Benji realized his gaffe and sputtered, "But, yer much better. I mean, I dinna want ye to think that ye were as good as a dog; yer much better, by far."

Jane put her hand back on his forehead and continued the stroking. "I 'ken' what you mean. I used to have a pet squirrel. My old master had seen me feeding him little bits of my meal. He said he must be giving me too much food if I was giving it away, so he cut what I got in half. Then one day, when he knew I was looking, he put some food down for my pet. Poor little Brownie didn't know better. He was tame. Master let him get close and take a piece of the fancy sweet bread he had put down for him. Then he stomped his head in, crushed him to the ground with his boot, and, and..." Janie made the motion with her hand of squishing and rubbing. She sniffed in recall. "And, then he said there was still a bit of the sweet bread there, that I could have it, and that he'd even let me keep the squirrel to eat."

Jane lifted her head and looked off in the distance. "This might sound horrible to you, but I did eat the bread *and* the squirrel. I cooked his little body over the small fire they allowed us to have. I ate every bit of him: his brains, liver, heart: everything. I made him a part of me at the same time that I made sure his poor little body wouldn't rot and that that evil master couldn't ever touch him again.

Jane started giggling.

"What?" Benji asked, surprised at her sudden change in demeanor.

"Well, not *ever* touch him again. The next morning, I, um, you know," she grunted and he understood. "Well, I did it on a big leaf, and then took it over to his private privy behind the big house. I made sure no one was around, then sneaked in and rubbed it all over the seat. I stayed in the bushes and watched him stumble over to it to do his business. He had the morning headache again—I knew he would. He always had one because he drank so much whisky. His eyes were almost closed. He wasn't looking or paying attention... Well, at least I'm sure he wasn't looking for, you know..."

"Shit! He sat in yer shit?" Benji asked.

Jane was still giggling. "Yes. The squirrel and I both got back at him. He didn't say anything at first because I don't think he knew right away. He came out of there sniffing the air, turning around, looking at the bottom of his shoe to see if he had stepped in, you know..."

"Shit," Benji said laughing heartily. He covered his chuckle, suddenly remembering that they needed to keep a low profile.

"I don't know if he ever figured it out, but it doesn't make a difference. The next week he traded me for a workhorse, one he said he knew would respond to the whip. I never saw him or my mother again."

Benji sat up and held Jane close to him. "I'll promise ye one thing Janie, if, when, we have children, I'll not let anyone take them away, ever, okay"

Jane nodded in response to his graciousness and compassion, then realized what he had said. "We can do that?" she asked.

"Aye, as soon as we're marrit, but not before. Now, if yer feelin' better..."

"Wait," she said with her left hand up. "We can do that?"

"We'll find a way, that is, if ye want me... Me bein' a giant and havin' red hair and all."

"And you'd want me... Me bein' a giant and havin' black skin and all?" she asked incredulously, mimicking his voice.

"Weel, it would be a might easier if yer skin was lighter since we're here, and there are some mighty unfair laws on the books now, but I'd want ye if ye had purple skin and were a wee, bitty thing. It's the person inside of that body who I care fer so deeply." Benji chuckled and looked into her eyes, getting as close to her face as he could without going cross-eyed. "Now I ken what all that talk about findin' a soul mate is all about."

Jane nodded and grinned. She'd never heard the words soul and mate together, but they did describe how she felt about him. He was her other half that she never knew she was missing until he found her. And, he wanted her as much as she wanted him. Benji leaned in a bit further and gave her a gentle kiss. Jane tried to kiss him more passionately, but he pulled back and shook his head, letting her know with a look that she needed to rest and heal.

"It doesn't hurt now," she said coyly, although it did, but not too much. His soft kiss was nice, but now she wanted more: lots more of those delicious kisses that made her tingle all over. "I'm feeling much better," she added, "and it's almost night time."

Benji looked at the sun, low in the sky—it was maybe four o'clock—and then back at her. She knew what time it was. "Ach, I dinna want to chance harmin' ye more. I think I'll jest go to sleep early. We can do some more kissin' tomorrow night. That is, unless ye want to kiss me durin' the daytime? I mean, ye'll probably feel better still after a good night's sleep tonight."

"Well, it hurts only a little bit. Didn't you say that whisky would take away some of the pain?" Benji nodded. "And didn't you want to drink a bit of it tonight? You said you wanted to celebrate?"

"Aye, that does sound like a good idea. It's too early yet fer sleep, and there isna much fer dinner. Aye, I'll sample the brew. I'll see if it's any good. I mean, I'd hate fer ye not to like the taste of whisky because of what he had, I mean..." Benji quit talking, embarrassed about calling up the source of their alcohol—dead man's drink: ugh!

He quickly reached into the rucksack and brought out the flask, pulled out the stopper, and sniffed. "Weel, it dinna burn off my eyebrows with the first whiff, so it canna be too bad." He tipped his head back and took a short nip. "Nae too bad at all," he said, then drank some more.

He looked over at his naked girlfriend. Yes, he thought of her as his girlfriend, his fiancée, and not as a woman whom he had

162

ownership papers for. Owning another person was just too much for him to fathom.

"Would ye like some?" he asked, and held up the silver-trimmed flask.

Jane nodded. If she took a little, he'd probably drink more. She'd take just a little sip, or pretend to. If he drank a lot, then he'd probably start to feel silly like she had. Maybe then, she could get him to start kissing on her. Or maybe touch her. Jane sipped a small amount and handed the container back to him. "It's good," she squeaked. The fire in her throat didn't hurt, but warmed and tickled in a good way.

"Aye, *slante',*" he toasted, and took a long draught.

She looked so fine, lying there on top of the clothes he had sewn for her. She didn't want to wear the sarong yet; she said it was too hot.

Jane slowly wiped her left hand across her upper lip, then moved her finger down her neck, and in between her breasts. She was wiping the sweat away, sort of, but really trying to draw his attention to her body. She knew he wanted her; she could see the evidence. He didn't have on a shirt, but still had on his pants, even though she knew he was hot. She lifted her head to let him know she'd take a bit more of the whisky.

"Here, I dinna want to be takin' all of it," he said. "Share and share alike: that's how we should be, aye?" he asked as he handed it to her.

This time, Jane didn't drink, but only wet her upper lip. She put down the flask and ran her tongue over the liquid that was cool to her lips, but warmed the inside of her throat and belly. She could see Benji shift as he watched her tongue move around her mouth. She did it again, this time causing him to inhale sharply. "Here," she said, and handed it back to him. "Share and share alike, aye?"

He took it, brought it to his mouth, and tilted his head back, drinking more than he should he realized too late. "Aye," he said, and put the stopper back in the bottle. "I think I'd best leave this be, or I willna be able to keep my hands off of ye."

"Are you going to sleep in those pants?" she asked, as she looked down at the bulge in the front of them. "They don't look like they're very comfortable."

"Aye, but I have a better chance of stayin' off of ye if I have them on."

"Will you kiss me?" She could tell the whisky was making her bold, but she didn't care. That must be another part of the drink: she didn't care if what she was doing or saying was right or wrong.

"Aye, I'll kiss ye, but I'll keep my pants on tonight," Benji said, then reached over to kiss her on the lips.

Jane leaned back while he was kissing her, forcing him to lie back with her. The kissing continued, softly at first, and then more insistent. She reached down to touch him through his pants, and he pulled back suddenly. "Ye canna do it; it'll hurt ye."

"Kissing doesn't hurt," she said, then saw the look of admonishment in his eyes. "Okay, I won't touch you, but will you touch me? I mean, kiss me more...here," she said, as she ran her finger from her bottom lip down her chin to her neck, turning her head to expose more area for his attentions.

Benji answered her with unhurried, tender kisses, starting just under her chin, then going lower, slowly descending until he was kissing her across her collarbones. "Lower," she said.

Benji pulled away entirely and stared at her with the question of 'are ye sure?' on his face, but the word, "No," on his lips.

"Please," she asked, then gently put her left hand up as if to guide him to where she wanted him.

Benji took her hand, kissed it, and then let it go. It floated in the air, finally guiding him to her left breast. He had seen them during the day. They were different now. It was still hot, but the nipples were firm and erect from excitement. He couldn't help himself; they were just too perfect, calling to him, wanting his kisses... and she wanted him there.

Jane let out a low moan and he pulled back. "Don't stop," she pled, and put her hand on the back of his head. His tongue rolled around the nipple, causing it to rise even further. Even if he had been cold sober, he couldn't have resisted the sucking. It felt like this was where his mouth belonged, his warm, moist lips wrapped around her firm yet pliable nipple. There was no milk coming from her breast, but he was beginning to feel like he was going to make cream in his pants.

"Oh, oh, oh," she moaned in pleasure. *This feeling was even better than the kissing and grabbing the night before. Was this what it was like for him?*

Benji stopped the suction and pulled his mouth from her breast, afraid that she was groaning in pain. Janie couldn't manage to utter even one word to tell him to continue, but did clasp her hand on the back of his head, urging—no, insisting—that he continue. His tongue went under her nipple and areola, letting them form to the roof of his mouth, swallowing gently to give her the suckling pressure that made her moan in pleasure.

"Uh, don't, stop, oh, please...don't stop," Jane said, then arched her back. "Oh, oh, oh!" she squealed, then held her breath for what seemed like forever. When she finally started breathing again, she grinned and said, "I think *I* just got wet and sticky."

Benji chuckled. "Me, too," he said, "me verra much, too." He smiled lovingly at her, then changed tones. "Now, I want ye to do me a favor. Do ye think ye can do as I ask?" Benji looked at her sternly, like a father telling a child that she had to wear a helmet when she rode her bicycle—it wasn't much fun, but was for her own good.

Jane bit her lip and answered sheepishly, "Yes, sir."

"Not like that!" Benji winced then shook his head. He didn't know if she was teasing him about being submissive or really was feeling like a slave. He'd believe it was the former. "I jest want ye to go to sleep. The both of us need rest. No more kissin' or grabbin' or..." Benji looked over and saw Jane purse her lips and suck; she knew what he was going to say next. "Or that either," he added and rolled his eyes. "But, I'll hold ye. Do ye think ye can stand to sleep with me with jest the cuddlin'? No kissin' or, or...?"

"Aye, but, jest fer tonight," she said in her Benji accent. "Aye?"

"Aye," Benji agreed. He rolled over on his back and laid out his left arm for her to snuggle into. His soul mate.

Ж

Jane was still asleep when Benji awoke at dawn. He shuffled down to the creek and did a hasty personal clean up, then looked back to the site. They'd have to forgo a hot breakfast. "And, I'm sure not gonna eat raw fish," he said under his breath at the sight of a trout, leaping out of the water to catch a flying insect. "Or bugs," he added with a shudder.

He bounded up the bluff and inspected his miniscule legacy. There wasn't anything he could prepare without a fire, and he wasn't going to build one, even a small one. The smoke would be as good as a signal flare to mark their position. He pulled the lid off of the Dutch oven and pulled away a piece of the dried out, overcooked cornbread, and popped it in his mouth. He heard Jane move, and looked toward her.

"This would be mighty fine breakfast fare if we had a pitcher of milk to pour over it. I think it will pass for grits if we use a bit of creek water, though. At least, we have a bowl to put it in. Do ye feel well enough to eat?"

165

Jane nodded her head and started to get up. "No, wait," he said, "I'll take care of breakfast today. If yer feelin' better tonight, I'll let ye take care of supper." He pulled a bowl and spoon out of the sack and grabbed the canteen. He broke off a chunk of the dried cornbread; crumbled it into pieces, then poured the water over it, mashing the concoction with the back of his spoon to make a mush.

"Here, open wide," he teased, as he put a spoonful of corn mush in front of her face. She opened her mouth and accepted the first spoon-feeding she could remember.

The peaceful meal continued wordlessly, Benji feeding her a bite, then taking one himself, until the bowl was empty. "Why didn't you eat when you bought me?" Jane asked after she finished the last bite. "I heard you bargain or trade for all you could eat and drink after the wagons were loaded."

"I looked at the bill of sale," Benji said with a shrug of his shoulder. "It dinna say anythin' about the food or drink that was promised me. I was pretty sure that if I even took a sip of ale, he'd charge me dearly for it. I had a couple of his dollars, and I ken he wanted them back. I wasna gonna give him that opportunity. Besides, that place gave me the creepy crawlies. I wanted to get, to get us, out of there as soon as possible. Creek water and wild berries sounded like better fare than anythin' that came out of *that* place." Benji shuddered as he remembered the incident, then looked at his reward: Jane.

Ж

"Is it okay to kiss in the daylight? I mean, no one can see us if we're hidden behind the cloth, right?" Jane was definitely feeling better today, and she liked being able to speak her mind, too.

"Are ye gonna wear that sarong I made ye?" Benji asked another question rather than answer hers. When he had first showed it to her, she hadn't wanted to wear it. She was afraid she'd bleed on it. Her wound had scabbed over well, and the dressing around her ribs was still clean. All she was wearing was the bandage and her little leather apron...

Jane fingered the sarong then brought the edge of it up to her lips sensuously, briefly touching her lower face, then bringing it down her neck and between her breasts, letting it sit on her lap in invitation. She didn't want to cover up.

"Yer doin' that on purpose," Benji growled in frustration, "I ken ye are. Ye ken I want ye, and that when ye dinna wear clothes, yer naked body gets me excited..." Benji looked down and nodded to his pants, his cock straining at the zipper. "See what ye did?"

"No, not really, but I'd like to," she said softly as she looked at the bulge and licked her lips.

"Yer drivin' me crazy, woman," Benji hissed, remembering almost too late that he still had to be quiet.

He took a break from their conversation and stood up to scan up and down the creek. They were still very much alone. Jane slowly rose and leaned close to him, her bare breast touching him near his elbow. He had left his shirt off, and now he wished, sort of, that he had it back on.

"You told me that we could kiss all day long. I mean, from here we can see for miles, and I can't see anyone. Since we have to wait here and be quiet for another day or two, can't we keep kissing?"

"I, I dinna think I can keep my hands off of ye," Benji whispered in exasperation.

"Your hands can be all over me. Your vow only pertains to that," she said as she nodded and looked down, "right?" Benji nodded in agreement. "And, you let me touch it the night before and it was okay with your vow, right?" Benji nodded again, then kissed her on the forehead.

"And, it's okay if we lie down here in the daytime, right?" she asked, as she led him back to the blue sarong sheet.

Benji answered by allowing her to guide him to their secreted resting spot and assist him in lying down. "Can I take off your pants, then?" she asked demurely. He had been agreeing with everything so far, hopefully he'd continue.

"No!" he answered sternly in a low voice.

Her eyes closed in embarrassment; maybe she had gone too far and been too insistent.

He saw the hurt look on her face, and sighed in resignation. "Ye canna take my pants off because it might hurt ye. But, *I* can take off my pants. *Ye* need to be careful."

"And you said we could be married and have babies?" She was sure that's what he had said, but she wanted to hear it again.

"Aye, but no makin' bairns until we're marrit. But, I dinna think that can happen until I find my grandfather. He'll ken what to do; he always does." Benji tried to sound confident, but he knew he had allowed a small squeak of uncertainty to slip out. He looked over and saw the pain in Jane's face. He could tell it wasn't physical pain, but the pain of frustration. He sighed, turned his back, and took off his pants.

Jane hung her head and closed her eyes, allowing him some privacy, and herself a moment to figure out if she wanted to continue her waking dream of believing that marriage for her really was possible. She knew that getting married was a fantasy. Slaves didn't get married. They were bred—and sometimes allowed to live as family units—but they were never married. Marrying a man, a white man, in this time? Well, dreaming was free. If he could dream it, and maybe even believe it, then she could, too, even if it did sound impossible.

"Janie," Benji called softly as he lay down close to her. "I ken we canna practice makin' the bairns, but can we practice feeding a bairn? Ye did seem to like it, aye?"

"Aye, oh, very much, aye," she replied, happy to be back in her waking dream with her man. "But, can you, um, suck on both sides? This side got a bit jealous last night, I think," she said, and stuck out her right breast.

Benji laid her back. "Okay, but first, I need some kisses. It's still daylight, but unless we make too much noise, no one will know we're here."

"All day and all night then..." Jane cooed.

25 Waiting to heal
August 22, 1782

"Do you think I'll like it?" Jane asked as she stroked his firm member.

Benji gasped at her delicate yet enticing touch, "Lord, I hope so," he said, then put his hand on top of hers, removing it gently so he could think with the big head. "If ye dinna care fer it, then we'll try it a bit differently. I mean, if ye've never been with a man, the first time might be a bit uncomfortable. But I—I mean we—can try a few different positions..." He picked up her cock stroking hand and kissed the back of it, enjoying that part of her body as if it was a sexual organ. He chortled suddenly. It was a sexual organ for them—at least for now.

Benji felt her hand slip out of his, pulling away slowly but decisively. "What's wrong, Janie? Are ye afraid?" and sat up to face her.

Jane shook her head slowly, but didn't answer with words. Instead, she lifted her head and looked into his eyes with shame. "Oh, Janie, did someone take ye against yer will?"

She closed her eyes slowly to answer in the affirmative, then looked back up at him. "I was very young. He took me from Mama and said I needed to come with him for the night. She wanted to stop him, I know she did, but couldn't do anything. She knew what was going to happen. She just cried and cried, and he yelled at her to shut up. He took his riding crop and beat her with it, one hand holding me, the other whipping her, telling her that now she had something to cry about.

"He took me to the big house and had the house maid give me a bath with some sweet smelling soap. It didn't burn like the kind they gave us. Then she put a pretty, soft shift on over my shoulders and covered my hair with a fancy pink cap. She told me that no matter what, that I wasn't to cry. She said he'd be nice to me if I didn't cry, but would beat me and all the house servants if I did."

"I didn't know her, but she knew me. She pulled my bottom lip down and saw that I still had all of my baby teeth. She shook her head and called the master a bad name. I didn't know what the word was, but the way she said it and then spit on the ground afterwards... Well, I knew she hated both him and what he was going to do. She gave me a quick hug and told me to pull myself and all of my thinking inside of here," Jane pointed to her belly button, "and that when I was all the way inside of myself, that Master couldn't hurt me. She hugged me again; this time for a long time, then took me to his room. 'Don't forget, don't cry,' she begged. 'He'll only want you for the one night. When he's done with you, he'll never bring you back to the house.'

"So, I let him do what he wanted. I didn't cry, I didn't smile, and I didn't move except to let him move my body where he wanted it. I pulled myself inside like she said so he couldn't hurt me. Well, not really hurt me, just the inside parts of my body. But, he didn't beat me, and he didn't beat anyone else the next day. The next evening, the cook came out and brought Mama and me a plate of chicken. She said thank you to me for not crying and sorry to my Mama for what had happened to me. And, she was right; he never asked for me again."

Jane finished her story and lifted her head to look into Benji's eyes, the lack of tears as shocking by their absence as the flow should have been. "So, I'm soiled," she said simply.

"No, yer not! Yer *body* was abused, taken advantage of, degraded and defiled, but none of it yer own doin'! Ye told me yerself: ye pulled yerself inside of here," Benji gently touched her belly, causing her to flinch, "and that part, yer soul and spirit, is still jest as pure as the wee lass who was taken from her mother, right?"

"Aye," Jane said, then smiled gently, now feeling better about herself. "I never touched a man or let one touch me until I held you during the storm."

"Weel, I'll never leave ye, so ye can hold me every day fer the rest of our lives, no storm required."

Ж

"Hey there!" called the animated, wiry old man from the far side of the pond. The bespectacled character waved broadly, nearly losing his footing as he did so. "I hear congratulations are in order: two more red-heided Pomeroy men in the world."

Benji was dumbfounded. What *could* he say? He opened his mouth to speak, to tell the man that he wasn't his grandfather, but found that his words were on strike—they wouldn't come out. Rather than chance making the pipping, squeaking noises he was afraid would sneak out if he tried to force them, he waved back at the man, nodding like a little plastic Chihuahua in the back window of a low rider.

The petite, snowy-haired man chose his steps carefully over the river rocks as he neared Benji, arms waving like he had

170

more words to share. He paused when he was six feet away from his goal, placed his hands on his hips, his head and chest bent forward to catch his breath. Air intake assured, the tanned and elated visitor straightened his back and looked up at Benji. His head tilted back a few degrees more and his eyes squinted in puzzlement.

"Did havin' more bairns make ye grow again?" his voice ending in a high squeal. "And why did ye cut yer hair? Oh," he said in answer to his own question, "Yer right; short hair would be a lot cooler."

Benji didn't say anything. He was still in shock. 'More bairns' the man had said.

The genteel wayfarer squinted as he looked down at the ground, then up at Benji again. His eyesight was failing, but this tall man had to be Jody Pomeroy. There couldn't be two men in the world that tall, except maybe Wallace, but the man in front of him had that same, flaming, Scottish red hair and the same squinty blue eyes. "Are ye ailin' there, Colonel Pomeroy?" he asked. "Ye dinna look too good."

Benji gulped and found his throat had relaxed just a little. He chanced speaking and replied, "I'm not ailin', but I'm not Colonel Pomeroy, either. But, can ye tell me how to get to his place? I...I...I'm his grandson," he blurted before he lost his nerve. He bit his lip. Hopefully, he wouldn't embarrass himself or his grandfather by crying. He was finally so close to finding him!

"Oh, oh, of course ye are!" The old man said as realization hit him like a wet washcloth to the face. "Yer his grandson, Benji. Ye have to be," he announced, then backed down in his enthusiasm. "Ye are, arena ye?" he asked, suddenly unsure of himself.

"Aye, I am," Benji replied with relief. "Can ye point me in the direction to his place?"

The wee man was more than happy to lead the way to the promontory where the road revealed itself. "Ye get to the road by travelin' down the other side of this rise. Ye dinna need to go into town; ye get there by goin' the other way. Jest keep headin' down the road until ye see the whirligig on the tower. Jody's kin is an inventor, he said, and there's all sorts of odd bits and pieces scattered high and low."

"Ye said my grandsire had more bairns?" Benji asked, hoping the man would continue the thought. The old man had to be confused because his grandparents were too old to have children of their own. He must be referring to James and Leah.

They had been gone for a year and would have had time to have a child or maybe twins.

"Yes, sirree," the old man crowed. "Yer grandfather said that yer Grannie took some fancy herbs and found herself with child. My wife said she wanted some of them, but I told her we were too old to start all over again. She must have given some to Colonel Pomeroy, your grandpa, too. He's looking better than ever, even after bein' injured. Now, that bein' said, do ye want me to guide ye to their house? I was headed the other direction, but I'd be glad to accompany ye. Hey, where is yer camp? Do ye want me to help ye pack?"

"No, but thank ye jest the same. My camp is jest over there." Benji nodded in an omni-directional manner, not wanting to divulge his site. "I'm not quite ready to travel, so I'll head out tomorrow morning. Thank ye fer the directions. And, Godspeed to ye, and good health to both ye and yer wife."

26 They're Huge!
August 25, 1782

"Grandpa, Grandpa," Jenny screeched as she called out in all directions, trying to find her absent mentor. "There's a man here who looks just like you only bigger. And, he has a Negro woman with him, and she's huge, too!"

I heard the commotion and came outside to see what all the excitement was about. I heard her say the words bigger, huge, and Negro. Well, at least someone taught her some manners along the way; I wouldn't have to teach her not to say the 'n' word. There weren't very many slaves in this area, and we didn't associate with anyone who had them, but what was it that she said?

"See, I told you so," Jenny bragged when I came out to see the giant-sized, red haired man in Carhartt jeans, and the stunning black woman, wrapped in a blue calico sarong, who was nearly as tall as he was. "Where's Grandpa?" Jenny asked excitedly, jumping up and down in place. "He has *got* to see this!"

"I'm sorry," I said to the visitors as Jenny ran off to find Jody. "She gets a little wound up sometimes. We don't get many visitors here. May I help you?"

"Evie?" the ginger giant asked as he stared at my face, trying to place me as someone he knew.

"Benji?" I answered. There could only be one man that tall, that red haired, and with those same, baby blue eyes...except Jody himself. "If you're not Benji, then Jody has a lot of 'splaining to do!" I joked in a Desi Arnaz, Cuban accent.

I walked up to him and shook his hand heartily. "Come in and have a seat," I said, then led the stunned couple up the porch steps. "I'll get some fresh water. I'll bet you're both thirsty."

The two of them appeared to be both overheated and in shock. I'd wait until after they got something to drink for proper introductions. I pointed to the kitchen chairs and table, grabbed the ewer and excused myself, and was headed down the steps to the well when I heard it.

"Eeee haaaaahhh!"

I followed the squealing noise with my eyes and saw that Jenny was on her way back from her scouting mission. The hyperactive, blonde bomber had found her Grandpa, Grannie, and infant uncles and was leading the fast paced parade back to the house. Jody was taking long strides to keep up with her running pace. He held Wee Julian to his shoulder with a wide, one-handed clutch. Sarah was following behind him at a fast clip—half-running—and carrying Raymond in the same snuggled position, but using both hands.

Benji stepped out of the house to watch their enthusiastic approach. He hesitantly walked down the steps and into the yard to meet them, unsure if he was dreaming or awake.

Jody didn't need to be told who the male stranger in his front yard was. He shook his head in astonishment, unbridled tears now flowing down his cheeks. He shifted his infant son to the right side then reached out and grabbed Benji to him, squeezing as hard as he dared with his left arm. Benji reached both arms around his grandfather's back and sobbed, "Yer here, yer still here."

"Aye, I am; and so is yer Grannie." Jody and Benji untangled their arms, but stayed close together, turning around as one to see Sarah rushing towards them, her beaming face streaked with shiny tears.

Benji sighed deeply at the sight of her, his eyes weeping anew. He moved into her, bent his knees, and picked up both Grannie and the bundle of baby she was clutching close to the middle of her chest. "Ye have no idea how happy I am right now," he laughed, crying at the same time with joy.

I watched the greeting and was overcome myself. I looked over and saw my babies contentedly playing 'who's got the rag dog' game in their oversized playpen under the family tree, tugging or biting on a cloth leg or ear of the oversized, remnant stuffed, quilted spaniel. Then I looked back at the porch and saw that someone was left out in this reunion: Benji's traveling companion. The beautiful and statuesque ebony woman was watching the reunion with a reserved smile, her glow reflecting her happiness, even if her reticent posture did not.

"Hi," I said as I approached her. "I take it your Benji's friend?" I asserted and asked at the same time.

She dipped her head briefly in acknowledgment, but didn't look me in the eye.

"Would you like to come in for that water now?" *I didn't wait for an answer, but turned and walked into the house, hoping she would follow me. She did, but only came in as far as the doorway. I poured a cup of water and handed it her.*

"They'll be in shortly," I said to start the conversation. "If I know anything about these men, it's that they'll be in for, shall

174

we say, liquid refreshment soon? And, I don't mean water. Come to think of it, we might want to go to the springhouse right now." I grabbed a basket out of the corner and saluted her with it. "I'll need this for the refreshments. Come on," I said brightly, as I gently touched her elbow in an invitation to follow me.

Jane tensed at the familiar touch of someone she didn't know. She looked down at the smallish, dark haired, perky young woman. The nice lady must have felt her arm jerk away in reflex, but she hadn't responded to it. She acted as if they were good friends, peers at least, and that performing a chore together was normal. Maybe she was like Benji, from the future.

"Evie?" Jane asked tentatively, although she was pretty sure that was her name. If this really was Evie, the time traveling fairy, she wouldn't mind that a slave had been so bold as to speak without being spoken to first.

"Oh, I'm sorry, I didn't introduce myself. Yes, I am Evie, Benji's, um, kin," I explained awkwardly.

I didn't know how much she knew about us, and didn't want to divulge any big secrets to someone I had just met, especially someone who I was sure had been born and raised in the 18th century. I had noticed the array of fresh and old lash scars on her back, and her posture was definitely one of servitude.

"We don't believe in slaves around here," I added softly, as if I was sharing a family secret. I returned to a normal speaking tone as we continued our walk. "You must be a good person or Benji wouldn't have brought you here. Although, I think it was rather rude of him not to introduce you right away."

"I think he was a bit distracted," Jane said in an apologetic tone. "He's been talking about finding his grandfather ever since I met him. Oh, I'm sorry; my name is Jane," she added with a nod of introduction.

"Glad to meet you, Jane," I said and paused in our trek to greet her face to face. Rather than attempt an awkward handshake with my right, basket-holding hand, I patted her on the back with a 'welcome to the family' gesture with my free, left hand. Jane winced at my touch, then sucked in air, stifling a yelp.

"I'm sorry; did I hurt you?" I asked.

"Oh, I'm just a little tender on the right side. I have a wound and it's not completely healed. I'll be fine. Benji tended to it, and I'm sure he did a good job. He did say his Grannie is a healer…" she began, then bit back any more words. Maybe she was speaking too much, she thought. These people were Benji's family, but they might not feel the same as he did. She didn't want to embarrass or shame him.

I noticed Jane biting her lip right after she had spoken. I realized she was between social castes, and even though I had whispered that we didn't believe in slaves, she still didn't know her place. "Are you okay? I mean, you can speak your mind around here. Your opinion is just as valid as anyone else's."

Jane didn't remark on my comment, but did look me in the eye and raised her eyebrows to ask 'Are you sure?' I replied with a grin and a nod. She then gave me a warm smile that said 'Thank you.'

We continued walking to the springhouse in a comfortable silence. When we got to our destination, I made sure I had a good look at her face then asked, "How much did Benji tell you about me?"

Jane grinned. She liked this lady. She was just as open and comfortable as Benji. "I didn't let Benji know that I understood English when we, we first met. He talked a lot about his life and family and I listened. Then I slipped and forgot to play ignorant. He found out that I could understand him without his silly hand language." Jane smiled as she moved her left hand in rapid, nonsense gestures, mimicking the made-up sign language Benji had employed. "I think he was a little *scarrit* when he realized that he had been telling me all about," Jane eyes squinted as she tried to recall the right words, "planes, trains, and automobiles."

I nodded and grinned in acknowledgment that I knew what she was speaking of. "Did he tell you how he got here?" I asked, looking at her for illumination.

"Yes. He said he was born here," Jane replied simply and smiled courteously.

I guess my face showed the discomfort and frustration that I was feeling because Jane added softly, "But he did tell me that he left here and then came back. He said he followed you here from, well, *you know when.* You do know *when* you're from, don't you?"

Jane didn't want to give anything away and was being cautious which I appreciated. Evidently, Benji hadn't planned on telling her his time traveler status. I bet there was a very interesting story about how those two met, but that wasn't important now. What we needed was to bring in the cheese and cold ale for the men.

"Yep, I'm a fairy," I boasted with a smirk of pride. Jane laughed at the remark, or at least how I had said it, and brought her left hand up to cover her chuckling mouth. "What, am I too big to be a fairy?" I asked lightly, grinning at my enchanting new acquaintance.

"No, I don't think so. I mean, I don't know. It's just that I didn't know there were women fairies. I thought Benji was the only one."

"Uh, no," I said somberly. "Although, I suggest you never ask anyone if he or she is a fairy. It's pretty much a secret. There are a few of us here, but not everyone in the family knows about the other ones. My daughter Jenny's too young to know about it. I mean, I could probably tell her and she would accept it and would be fine knowing about it, but I'm afraid she wouldn't keep her mouth shut. Loose lips sink ships and all of that stuff." I saw the confused look and reworded my concern. "I'm afraid she'd tell the wrong person and then someone might think we, I, was a witch or from the devil." I shook my head, recalling both Sarah's close call with witch hunters in Scotland and James and Leah's close call with Dick Short.

"You're too pretty to be a witch," Jane said, then gasped in embarrassment at her familiarity.

"Thank you," I said. "But, I'll bet you're a smart woman and know that looks are deceiving. Pretty is as pretty does, right?"

Jane nodded in answer. Her head felt odd with the movement. Her eyes felt like they were trying to fall out. She brought the back of her hand up to her lips. Yes, she had a fever.

I saw Jane check her temperature by pressing her lips to the back of her hand. I could tell by the momentary shock in her eyes that she had detected a fever. Her wound was probably infected.

"Come on. I'll carry this." I quickly threw a big cheese and as many bottles of ale as I thought I could manage into the basket. "Let's get back to the house. You need rest and water. I want Sarah to look at your owie."

I looked up at her to make sure she had heard me and grinned at the dumbfounded look on her face. "Owie is what I call a wound. You have a fever, don't you?" Jane nodded. "Smart woman, you know to check up on yourself. Hold on to my shoulder. I don't want you to fall down."

Benji looked away from the glowing faces of his grandparents to see Jane and Evie walking toward the house from what must be the springhouse, a small building on the backside of the barn. Evie was carrying a basket, and Jane was a step behind, her hand on Evie's shoulder for support. "Excuse me," he said, "I...I...oh, Lord," he whispered in self-admonishment. How could he have forgotten about Jane?

"Looks like the lad forgot about his lady friend," Jody said to Sarah as he put one arm around her shoulder, guiding her to the house.

"By the look of shame on his face, she's more than just a friend." Sarah looked up to Jody to make sure he knew what she was implying.

Jody's eyes widened in surprise as he realized what she was insinuating. "A slave?" he whispered in disbelief.

Sarah shrugged her shoulders. "Love is colorblind, and he *was* reared in the 20th and," she inhaled deeply as she said the exotic words, "21st centuries. Skin color isn't really much of a consideration in modern times."

"Aye, it may not be *then*, but *now* is where the two of them are today." Jody said dejectedly, "I'm glad to have him here, but if what he feels for her is one tenth of what I feel fer ye, they're gonna have a rough go of it in 1782 North Carolina."

"I'm sure they'll be okay. Just look at what we went through and we turned out fine."

"Ach, finer that fine." Jody swiftly raised Wee Julian in the air, the gesture that always elicited a giggle from him. He smiled and said, "Although, I wouldna choose to do any of the bad parts over again. If I had a choice, I woulda passed on jest about everythin'."

"Passing up helping those in need is not your style, Jody Pomeroy. You'd do it all over again, I'm sure you would."

"Weel, ye would be right if my motivation was to have and keep ye and our family and friends safe. Aye, I'd do it all over again, but," Jody looked up to heaven, "I'm not volunteerin' fer any new tasks, Lord."

"And, our little family keeps getting bigger and bigger, too." Sarah looked over at the tall couple plus Evie, now on the porch. "Benji has himself a woman. Whether she is his *mate* already or not, I could tell by the look on his face when he looked at her, he wants her to be."

"Aye, I think it's *not* though. I dinna think he'd have relations with a woman who wasna his wife. By the looks of the scars on her back, she's a slave and dinna come back here with him. Aye, I'll wager she's from this time."

"Good Lord, Jody!" Sarah exclaimed. "Of course she's from 'now.' Why in the hell would he bring a black woman *back* here to this time?"

Jody shrugged his non-baby laden shoulder at Sarah, then shifted Wee Julian, turning him around to face Mommy. "Here, ye take him back to the house, and I'll catch a couple of chickens fer supper. Or maybe three—Jenny was right. Benji really is huge, and his lady friend isna much smaller."

Ж

Benji bounded up the steps behind Jane and me. "Oh, Janie, I am so sorry I forgot to introduce ye to everyone. They'll all be here in a minute. Can ye forgive me?"

Jane nodded 'yes' then added a weak, "Of course." Her head kept nodding, as if she was falling asleep, but her words were finished. Her neck snapped taut as she came to with a start.

"Benji, go get your Grannie," I said. "I want her to check Jane's wound. She has a fever and probably an infection."

"Yes, ma'am," Benji said. He rushed out the door, and nearly knocked down his baby-laden grandmother as she came up the steps. "Whoa, there," he said as he steadied her. "Evie says she needs ye to look after Jane."

"Sarah, this is Jane," I said in introduction. "She has an owie, and I think it's infected. Do you want her in the surgery?"

"Yes. Here, Benji, take your uncles. Evie, help her get settled on the examination table, please. Glad to meet you, Jane. Come on in here and tell me where your owie is." Sarah smiled at the word owie. She noticed the big woman had grinned when I said it, so repeated it. Jane smiled for her when she said it, too.

"What do I do with them?" Benji asked as he lifted one then the other baby-bearing arm.

"Take them for a walk," Sarah said flatly. "Let them show you around the place. We've only been here a few years, and it's not as nice as our place on The Point, but it has potential."

"Will ye be okay, Janie?" Benji asked as he walked over to her, now seated on the long, tall table.

"She'll be fine," Sarah said, and shooed him then me out the door. The doctor was in and we were out.

Benji did what his Grannie told him: took his uncles for a walk. They were very small—he didn't know how to estimate babies' ages since he hadn't been around too many—but they were old enough to hold up their heads. "Uncles," he said in amazement. He thought his Grannie was too old to have babies, but evidently not. "I guess I'll have to wait to find out yer names. Until then, yer Uncle One and yer Uncle Two." He continued his stroll toward the barn, chatting with the little red headed boys who were enthralled with his voice and face.

179

And then he saw her: the little blond girl who had announced their arrival. "What are ye doing there: looking for gold?" asked Benji, although it was pretty obvious: she was drawing with a pointed stick in the fine, silty dirt.

"I'm making pictures," she said with pride. "See, that's you and her and that's me. Who *are* you? I know you're kin, but am I allowed to know how? Grandpa and Grannie and Mommy and Daddy don't tell me everything because they say I talk too much. But, I just want to know who you two are. Is that okay?"

"I'm Benji. Your Grandpa is my Grandpa, too. My mother—Mona or Ramona—is his daughter." Benji wanted to ask her relationship to Grandpa, but figured that she'd probably tell him in a minute or two. She seemed to bubble over with enthusiasm with whatever she said or did.

"My Daddy is Grandpa's son, and so are Raymond," she pointed to the child in Benji's right arm, "and Wee Julian," and pointed to the left. "Raymond is named after Grandpa's father Raymond, and so is your Mommy. Wee Julian is named after my other Grandpa, Grandpa Julian, but I call him Poppi. The other babies, that's my brothers Judah and Leo, and my little sister Wren—her real name is Danielle—but my, my other kin," she blushed, unsure if she should say more about Scout, her other kin, "gave her that name. Anyway," she said as she took a deep breath to continue the family genealogy, "Those babies call him Poppi, so now I do, too. And Evie is my Mommy and she's Grannie's sister, sort of, not by blood, but they say sister's close enough. They get along real good even if Grannie's her mother-in-law, too. And Leah is my sister, and she and James—that's her husband—live a little ways down that road," she turned to indicate the dusty path that led to an odd shaped abode, "and they have a little girl, Bibb Elizabeth Melbourne," she crowed the name with pride. "She's my niece, and she's *exactly* the same age as my uncles 'cause they were all born on the same day. So, who's the lady who came with you?" she asked, suddenly changing the theme and tone of voice, obviously suspicious of the tall, dark woman.

"She's Jane, my fiancée. That means we're going to get married. Soon, I hope," he added softly, although he knew she could hear him.

"Oh," was her short reply, as if his answer was enough; now let's talk about something else. She picked up a wide, narrow slat of split firewood and wiped through the dirt, erasing her first picture, preparing her earthen slate for a new one. He watched silently as she drew another, very much like the first one, this time adding in what looked like a baby.

"Who's that?" he asked, as he sat down next to her, using his outstretched uncle-toting arms as leverage to sit down on his bottom with a grace that didn't see possible for such a large man burdened with babies.

"That's *your* baby," she announced with pride, then added. "You don't know about him yet, but I still drew him. If I had real paper and coloring sticks—Mommy calls them crayons—then I could draw you better. I could make Jane black, and make your hair and the baby's hair red, and mine yellow, and, and my dress green, and Jane's blue... Hey, are you my uncle or my cousin?" she asked, quickly changing topics again.

"Weel, since yer father and my mother are brother and sister that makes us cousins. But, if yer mother is my great aunt then I guess," Benji counted on his fingers, looked up as he tried to account for the lineage, then huffed in defeat and declared, "that's why it's easier to jest say we're all kin, aye?"

"Aye!" Jenny announced proudly in agreement, then bent back to her drawing, adding a cloud to the imagery's background. "It's kinda hard to tell who everyone is because this stick isn't as good as a pen, and I don't have any paper. Mommy said that paper costs a lot, and that we can't make it, but that her sister-in-law, that's your mother, knew how to make paper. She made some before she left, and we still have a few pieces of it, but they're special. Mommy lets me hold onto one of them sometimes. But, I have to wash my hands *real* good because she doesn't want them to get dirty. They smell good, too, because your mother put flower petals in the mast. I think that's what she called it."

Benji interrupted, "That's mash, not mast. I think I remember how she made it. Do ye want to make some paper?"

"Uh, huh," she chimed, her head bobbing rapidly. "Yes, yes, yes!" Jenny screamed as she sprang up like a jack-in-the-box, continuing to jump up and down. "Can we do it today? Huh, please, please, puh-leeze..."

Benji looked around and didn't see any tasks that needed to be done. Being a guest at Grandpa's was nice, and he hoped he would be allowed to help, but everything appeared to be caught up right now. "I canna see why not. First, I'll have to talk to yer Grannie and see if she has some of the chemicals we need. Then, we have to get some old rags and sawdust, and maybe we can throw in some flower petals, too. But, we dinna do that part until we're almost finished."

"What's chemicals?" Jenny asked, as she picked up a rotted piece of wood, examining its potential as sawdust.

"Well, that's like askin' 'what's food?' Both can be a wide variety of *stuff*. Chemicals can be what ye use to wash clothes, or to spray for bugs, or etch glass. Usually, they're in a solution, but they can be solid, too."

Jenny's eyes widened. "I know how to wash clothes, but I don't know what etch glass is, and why do you want to spray bugs?"

"Poison; ye can spray a poison on bugs so they die, but we dinna want to do that. The bairns might get a hold of it and it would hurt them. Etchin' glass is done with an acid, somethin' that burns even though it's a liquid, like water, but ye canna, or shouldna, drink it. Gee, Jenny, I guess I shoulda paid more attention in school. Science wasna my favorite class, ye ken."

Jenny dusted off her hands on the back of her skirt and reached for her uncle. "Here, I'll take Raymond." Benji handed her the dozing child and stood up, letting her lead the way.

"Now dinna be botherin' Grannie right now. She's busy doctorin' Janie. We have to keep these guys busy. We canna do the paper makin' until later, maybe tomorrow. Fer now, why dinna ye show me where ye keep yer animals."

Benji was glad to have her around for a distraction. With her cheerful chattering, he wasn't dwelling on what would happen with him and Janie now that they were here. It wouldn't be an easy life being married to a black woman in this time—if it was even possible. He'd waited too long to get here to his grandfather to give up right away and go back; that is if he could even find a way to go back to the future. But, he'd waited just as long to find a woman to love and care about. Hopefully, he'd be able to have his wife and life here, too.

Jenny led the way to the little goat shed, holding her Uncle Raymond with finesse, almost as if he were a part of her body. "Shush," she admonished when he started to get fussy. "We have to let your Mommy work. She'll feed you when she's done working on Cousin Jane." She turned her attention back to Benji. "These are my goats. Leah named them Sarah P and Todd. She calls them that because they do whatever they want to do. You can't make them mind you. But, they're nice and follow me wherever I go because I love them, and feed them, and really, they're smarter than a horse and prettier, too. They're still babies, but they'll get lots bigger. Poppi, that's my Grandpa Julian, and José, that's his partner, gave them to me. I'm supposed to take care of them, but they said it's okay if Daddy or

Grandpa, that's Grandpa Jody, help me. They're Angora goats, and when they're older—like maybe next spring—Poppi will help me cut off their hair. José knows how to spin the hair; I mean the wool, into yarn. Mommy knows how to crochet real good, and she showed me how, too. I even made a hat, but it's too hot to wear it now. Hey, are you gonna live here?" Jenny asked, suddenly distracted from her dissertation on the evolution of the cap she had made.

"Aye, I'd like to," Benji said over the squalls of wee Uncle Raymond. "Are ye sure he'll be okay? He looks like he's ready to eat his fist right off his wrist!" He knew the baby was probably fine, but he didn't want to talk about his future housing arrangements with the young lady. His cousin was charming, but the two of them wouldn't be able to solve the dilemma of whether he and Jane would be able to stay here and be married. He'd rather save the emotional investment to spend with his grandparents or the other adults in the family. He was beginning to feel like Wee Raymond: ready to scream in frustration. "I'm gonna take him to Grannie. Ye mind Wee Julian fer me, aye?"

"Okay," Jenny replied brightly, then turned her attention to the quiet twin. "Do you want me to draw a picture of you?" She sat down and prepared a lap for the boy next to her dusty drawing area. "I'll draw you when you're all growed up and a doctor like Grannie."

Benji took long strides to the house, singing a medley of Beatles tunes to Wee Raymond on the way. "They're gonna put me in the movies," he began, then shuddered. "Oops, wrong song, lad. Ye dinna want to be in any movies, at least the kind I was in," he groaned. "Okay, 'Help, I need somebody; help, not just anybody. Help, I need a milky booby to feed my empty belly...help!" Benji improvised as he climbed the steps to the house.

"My uncle," he said again. "Weel, at least I ken where I get my urges from. It seems that age dinna make a difference to either of them. I sure do look like yer Da—too much like him," Benji said to his young uncle. As soon as he stopped talking, though, the little boy started fussing again. "So, how does a man sixty-years-old look so young, and his wife have a baby when she's even older than he is? Weel, Raymond, did he tell ye? Do ye think he'll tell me? Do ye think it matters? Weel, neither do I," he said in resignation. It was a mystery that didn't make a difference to anyone.

Raymond started screaming again, this time Benji's words unable to quiet him. "Time to find yer mama," Benji said as he reluctantly opened the surgery door a crack.

Hopefully, Grannie was done with the doctoring so he could be close to Janie and help her with the healing—or at least feel like he was helping. She hadn't been in his life even a week, but now, being away from her for less than an hour, it felt as if it had been half a lifetime. Yes, he'd move wherever he needed to be with Janie, but as her husband. He'd settle for nothing less. She was worth it. And, by the way the rest of his family had received her, they felt she was family, too.

Ж

"Now, where is your owie?" Sarah asked with a big smile, hoping to get another one in return.

Jane beamed back at her. Sarah was Benji's grandmother and another very nice lady. She was probably a fairy, too, since she was treating her like a person, not a slave. Jane lifted up her right arm and pointed to the site of the wound with her left hand. "Do you want me to take this off?" she asked, referring to her sarong.

"Well, it would make the examination much, much easier," Sarah joked, then offered her a hand to help her stand.

Jane stood up and Sarah followed her height with her eyes. "How tall *are* you?" she asked in awe before she could think.

Jane put her left hand on top of her head then pulled it straight out in front of herself. "So big," she joked. "Taller than most men, but not Benji. He's this much taller than me," she said, and indicated a three-inch span with her index finger and thumb. She began unwrapping her sarong, but kept it close to her belly to hide her lower body. She was used to wearing clothes now and was beginning to feel bashful.

Sarah removed the ribcage bandage made from the same cloth as Jane's Polynesian-style dress. "Good Lord," she gasped at the sight of the vicious gash sewn together neatly with what appeared to be dental floss. "What happened here?"

"I was stabbed in the ribs, and the knife blade broke off in me. Benji pulled it out with his *Leatherman*," she said, making sure she said the word correctly. "He cleaned it out and put on some *antibiotic* and stitched it with *tooth floss*."

"Dental floss," Sarah corrected. "He did a fine job, but by the looks of this, part of the blade is still in there. That's why it's swelled up and infected. The body is rejecting the foreign matter." Sarah saw the confused look on her patient's face and

184

clarified, "I'm going to have to open it up and get the fragment out. It's going to hurt, but we have to do it now or you'll never get better, or maybe even worse."

Jane's eyes opened wide at 'even worse' then nodded and said, "Yes, please, go ahead and do what you need to do. But, um, do you have any *Ibuprofen*?"

"Yes, as a matter of fact, I do. Wait, you know what Ibuprofen is?" Sarah asked, dumbfounded.

"Benji brought some with him," Jane said. "Can I lie down for this? My head feels too heavy."

"Yes, lie down on your left side and get comfortable. I'll scrub you up, and then take out his stitches. But first, I'll give you a couple of Ibuprofen. I'll let it start working before I start poking around."

Sarah brought Jane a couple of the little brown pills and a cup of water. Jane carefully put them at the back of her tongue, then hurriedly gulped down the water, grateful that they went down on the first try and that she hadn't gagged. She smiled. She was glad she knew what a pill was and how to take one. Even though she could tolerate pain, she didn't like it.

Jane settled onto the long, elevated table next to the window, while Sarah assembled the tools she would need onto a tray. The healer then went to her basin and scrubbed her hands for what Jane thought was long enough to wash off the skin. She finally finished and came back to the table, skin intact, and put a clean cloth along each side of the wound.

"Now, try to relax. I don't have anything to numb you," Sarah said, watching her patient to make sure she understood. Jane's face went blank at the word 'numb.' "Deaden or completely stop the pain; I don't have anything like ice or Lidocaine or... The Ibuprofen will help, but won't stop this from hurting. Please, don't move. Try to think of a happy thought," she added.

Jane's body went limp as her feelings of peace and security relaxed her. Her happy thought was Benji, and he was outside, visiting his Grandfather. And, his Grannie was in here, taking care of her wound, treating her like a white woman. A rich, white woman, she corrected. "Is this good enough?" Jane asked, very comfortable with her many happy thoughts.

"You're doing fantastic," Sarah praised, as she dabbed some of Leah's antibacterial soap on a square of clean cloth. "We'll get this done as soon as possible. I'm sure everyone wants to meet Benji's, um, Benji's friend."

Jane was a model patient. "Now I want you to take a couple of slow, deep breaths. You've been helping me out by breathing shallowly, but I want you to tank up with oxygen." Sarah saw the confused look on Jane's face and said, "Just breathe for me. I'm not ready to probe yet, but it's going to be uncomfortable when I do. Once I find all the fragments, I can sew you back up. Then you shouldn't have any more problems."

Jane did the breathing as instructed while Sarah swabbed her with the Betadine solution. "Okay, this is the most uncomfortable part. Hold very, very still and no more deep breaths, okay?"

"Okay," Jane whispered and sunk into the hard bed.

After several minutes of probing, pulling, and producing sharp pains for her patient, Sarah grasped the shard and pronounced, 'Got it!" She flushed the site with a antiseptic solution, blotted away the excess blood and pus, then said, "Now all I have to do is to sew you back together." She grabbed the sterile suture and bent to the task. "shit," she whispered just as she was ready for the first stitch.

"What's wrong?" Jane asked softly, trying not to show with her voice the fear she felt.

"I'm leaking; leaking milk," Sarah said in frustration, looking down at the wet spots on the front of her blouse. "It's time to feed one baby, at least, but he'll just have to wait until I'm done here."

Just then, Benji came to the door, peeking into the room with a squalling baby on his shoulder. "Ye did say this is my uncle, aye? I mean," he said, not waiting for her answer, "I think yer son is hungry, and I'm not equipped to feed him."

Sarah took a deep breath of annoyance, not knowing whether to scold her grandson—couldn't he see she was busy— or should she suggest he ask Evie if she could play wet nurse.

"Can I hold him?" Jane asked.

"You can't move," Sarah said sternly, then saw the sadness on Jane's face. "But, if Benji will put him next to you, and you don't move, then yes, he can lie down with you. But, if either one of you moves while I'm stitching, then you, young man," she said in mock scolding of Benji, "need to take him for another walk until I'm done here, okay?"

"Yes, Grannie," Benji said obediently, and walked up to his prone and slightly bloody fiancée. He gently lay Wee Raymond down alongside her, then took a step back to admire the sight. She looked so right with a baby lying next to her.

The infant boy immediately hushed at seeing the strange new face, forgetting to resume his crying. Instead, he grinned, cooed, and patted her chest, knocking at the sterile drape Sarah had around her work area. Jane's left arm was crooked up next to her body. She moved her hand out from under her chin and was able to hold onto his little fist with her long fingers. "He's very handsome."

"He likes you," Sarah said as she appraised her new situation. "Are you going to be able to control him with that one hand?"

"Aye," Jane said, totally relaxed at the proximity of the red haired baby boy. "Is this what Benji looked like when he was a baby?"

"Very much so," Sarah said. "Benji, why don't you see if your grandfather needs some help?"

"Yes, ma'am. I willna be far," he said to Jane, then walked out the door backwards, a big smile on his face at the sight of her holding a baby.

"Now, just a little more pain, and then you're home free," Sarah said to Jane.

Jane didn't move a muscle other than the ones that focused her eyes. She peered up at Sarah, asking her wordlessly what she meant. "Oh, 'home free' is a phrase where I'm from. It means were out of the woods, no longer in danger..." Sarah babbled, finally deciding it was better to shut up then continue the awkward definition.

Sarah felt a miniscule twitch from Jane, but other than that, both she and Wee Raymond were quiet and content. Jane hummed a little song to the baby and both of them—all three of them counting Sarah—were soothed by it.

"Did he fall asleep?" Sarah asked as she piled all of the surgical tools onto the tray table. She took them to the sink; she'd clean them later.

"No, he's awake. I don't think he was too hungry; I think he just wanted to suck. Can I move now?"

Sarah was back to washing her hands again. "Yes, you can move, but don't sit up too quickly. I don't want you passing out, that is, fainting."

Jane stuck her finger into Wee Raymond's mouth and broke the suction. A little bit of bluish white fluid slobbered out as she did. She quickly wiped it away, trying to mask her shock at seeing it: mother's milk! She grasped him with her good left hand and brought him up over the left shoulder, rubbing his back with her pinky.

"Suck!" Sarah squawked as she realized what Jane had said. "He'd do that? I mean, Leah and Evie have nursed him for me a few times; he's comfortable with them, but you didn't just have a baby, did you?"

Jane shook her head quickly. "No, I've never had a baby. I'm sorry; I didn't think I was doing anything wrong." Jane sniffed and bit her bottom lip. She was only trying to help calm him. And besides, it felt so good.

"No, no, you didn't do anything wrong," Sarah soothed. She thought for a moment, then added, "Well, I guess you've already been acknowledged as one of the family by the youngest member. If you don't mind me asking, what is your relationship to Benji?"

Benji stepped forward. He hadn't spoken, and wasn't sure if Grannie knew that he had come back into the room, but now he could lay claim to her. "She's my fiancée. We're to be marrit as soon as I, or ye, or Grandpa, or someone, anyone, can figure out *how*. And," Benji added with a comical full body twitch, "the sooner the better."

Benji felt a firm hand clasp him on his shoulder. "See, what did I tell ye?" Jody said to Sarah, "I told ye he'd wait. Now," he added with a sour tone, "we'll have to figure out how to get it done right."

"Excuse me," I said as I walked into the now crowded surgery. "I think we have more family showing up. Leah, James, and Bibby just arrived. You have more kin to meet! So, Benji, after you do the meet and greet, would you help your grandfather pluck those chickens? Yer long fingers have to be good fer somethin' besides pickin' yer nose, aye?" I mocked.

"Come on, lad. A few introductions then we can leave the ladies be. We'll go out and do the women's work of pluckin' chickens while they chatter," Jody said as he herded Benji through the door. "Uh, I dinna need to give ye the talk about the facts of life, as Evie calls them, do I?" Jody asked with a mix of mirth and apprehension once they were out of earshot of the others.

"Ach, no," Benji began, then changed his mind as soon as the first words had escaped his lips. "My father did have a talk with me a long, long time ago. Now, which parts go together?" he asked in jest, then burst into laughter, smacking his grandfather on the back. "But, he never did tell me how ye make a bairn..." he continued with a grin.

James had just finished unhitching the horse when he saw the two men heading to the barn. He walked up to join them, very curious about the man who looked like Jody on steroids.

Leah and a squalling Bibby were already out of the wagon and on their way to the house. Jody paused and introduced his grandson to the pair.

"Oh, so *yer* Leah!" Benji exclaimed. "Ye sure look like yer mother. Ye ken, I missed ye by this much," he said, as he put his thumb and index finger apart by a scant quarter of an inch. "I meant to come back with ye last year. But, I'm sure it was meant to be that we dinna travel together. I met, and got to be good friends with, yer brother-in-law, Billy, and his mother—Bibb the First, would that be? Ye did say this was Wee Bibb?" He stroked the fussy, bald-headed, little girl under her chin. The child thrashed her head side to side in frustration, trying to decide if she wanted to be tickled and cajoled by the nice man, or scream because she was in a poopy diaper.

"Yes, this is Bibb Elizabeth Melbourne, and she is in desperate need of a clean clout. So, if you'll excuse us, I'm sure we'll get a chance to talk more later. But!" she said before he could turn to leave, "how are they: Bibb and Billy?"

"Last I saw them, Bibb, Billy, *and* Peter were all doing fine," he said, making sure she understood that Peter and Billy were still a happy couple. "And no cancer," he added, realizing that that was probably what she had been referring to.

"Great, glad to hear it," she said over the now screaming baby Bibby. "Later, dude," she called back familiarly over her shoulder. He seemed like a very nice man.

Ж

"Mom, where can I put her down to change her?" Leah asked when she walked into the kitchen, forgetting even to say hello to her mother. "She's a mess and could use a butt bath if you have any water warmed already. Oh, hi," Leah said in surprise when she saw Sarah and an unknown, very exotic looking woman come in from the surgery.

"Jane, this is my eldest daughter, Leah. Leah, this is Jane, Benji's fiancée. Benji's your sister-in-law Mona's oldest son, or only son. I don't know if she had any more or not. Oh, and Jane knows about me," I explained, referring to my status as a woman from a future time.

Jane would probably figure out on her own that Leah also wasn't from 'now' after talking to her for about ten seconds. This was my hint to her that she didn't need to be subservient around her either.

189

"Glad to meet you, Jane. And, this is my stinky butt daughter, Bibb Elizabeth Melbourne. Her father is out there with Jody and Benji. I just barely met him, but," Leah shook her head, "we've sure heard all about him. I don't think there's an antic or caper that boy ever did that we haven't heard about at least three times. Of course, he's a man now, but he sure had a colorful first five or six years living near Grannie and Grandpa. Mom, a little help here, please."

I brought a pan of warm water, a rag, and a clean clout and held Bibby Liz's legs while Leah did the dirty work. Leah wrapped the clout through her daughter's legs then secured it with a shiny diaper pin with a pink plastic duck-shaped cap. I looked up and saw Jane's eyes blink in shock at the colorful apparatus. "Real handy little items," I explained, then let the subject drop.

"How old is she?" Jane asked, as she admired my granddaughter.

"She's the same age as her uncles. They were all born within an hour of each other. Now that was a *very* busy day," I said, bobbing my head in recall. "At least, she's easy to tell apart from them, with or without the diaper," I said as I rubbed her bald-head. "Yep, she'll have dark hair when she finally gets it. Just like her mother, me, and my mother before me."

I watched as Jane lifted up her head and looked out the door. She was watching Benji talk with Jenny, my blondie. "That's Jenny, my adopted daughter. My other children are under the tree, tearing apart their dog." I saw her eyes open wide at the remark. Those big, dark orbs didn't make a sound, but they sure said a lot. "It's a toy dog; a rag stuffed doll that they don't ever seem to tire of. Yes, I really did break the mold with those three: all red headed."

"Three—at the same time?" Jane asked.

"Yup, I'm a tough old broad," I said, then looked over at Leah. "Tougher and older than I look," I added with a squint that said, 'Just believe it; don't question it, okay?'

"I still say you're pretty," Jane answered with a blush that, although I couldn't see in her skin, I could tell by her demeanor.

"So, what brings you and Benji here?" Leah asked without preamble as she settled back on the chaise, legs up and breast bared, to feed her voracious little vixen.

"Benji wanted to see his Grandpa," Jane answered, "and…I…um, came along with him," she finished, looking back and forth in embarrassment.

I spared her a detailed explanation by announcing, "I'm sure Benji will tell us the whole story at dinner or whenever he's ready. I'm going to feed my little ones first, so anyone up to it, grab a baby, a biscuit, and I'll bring the noodles."

Jane helped me feed my three. I could see her fascination with their hair. "It's not common. I mean, red hair in white people is unpredictable unless both parents have red hair. If that's the case, their children will positively have red hair. Were you born in Africa?" I asked.

"I think so," she replied. "I know that my mother said I was a very small child when she came over on the boat. I didn't have any teeth yet. They let her keep me because I didn't need to eat food. She was suckling me. They said they wanted her to keep the milk coming. Um, wet nurses," she said as a question, as if she wasn't sure of the polite term, "were at a premium. I kept her milk coming in so I could stay with her. She was always feeding someone else's child," she said reflectively.

"I just asked because if you never had a white parent, you probably won't have any red haired children with Benji, although, depending on whether there is a white parent in your children's spouses, you might have red headed grandchildren. I'm not an expert, but that's what I remember from school. It has to do with recessive genes, and, by the way, are you right-handed or left-handed?"

Jane looked down, turning over first one hand and then the other, confused at the question. Duh! She probably didn't know how to write—how rude of me. "Um, when you pick up a spoon or fork to eat with, which hand do you use?"

Jane reached down and picked up a twig with her left hand, and held it like a spoon. She set it back down and picked it up with her right hand. "It feels better with this hand. I know I throw with the left hand," she grinned in recollection of her hidden assaults with rotten eggs when she was younger.

"Well, then there's a good chance you and Benji will have left-handed children. That's another recessive gene that kind of pops up, but it's not as predictable as red hair. And, they'll probably have brown eyes, but I think he'll like that. You have beautiful, expressive eyes."

Jane had never felt better. Benji wasn't here—he was still visiting with other family members—but the women were so kind. "So, where's their father?" Jane asked me, trying to, and succeeding at, overcoming her shyness.

"He's in town, but he should be back any time now. He's Jody's son and Sarah's stepson, but we don't use that four letter word *step* around here." I saw the confused look on her face when I said 'four letter word.' "You see, we're all related, by blood, choice, or marriage around here. And, you will be, too. It's just easier to say kin. I mean, Sarah's my sister, sort of, and Wallace is Jody's son, but his biological mother died when he was one week old. Maybe later on, my husband, Wallace, will bring his," I whispered the word, "step," then continued, "father, Julian, here. He reared Wallace. Now that my husband's a father too, Julian and Jody are both considered the grandfathers to our children; no distinction is needed or desired as to whose blood goes through whose body."

"So, Sarah is your sister, sort of, and Leah is your daughter, and those are your babies, and Jenny is adopted, and Benji is your..." she asked by not finishing the sentence.

"He's my nephew which means that you'll be my niece. And that little blond bullet over there, bending his ear, is his cousin, your cousin. I'll bet you never thought you'd have a blond cousin, did you?" I laughed.

"I never thought I'd ever have any cousin, or a husband," she said, then started to waver, even though she was seated.

"Here, drink more water, and hand me that baby. You need to lie down."

"Oh, I'm fine," Jane replied, although she did pass Judah to me and leaned back against the tree.

"Drink," I said as I gave her my cup. Her eyes flashed fear at taking a drink from my vessel. "What, do you think I have cooties?" I asked. "The only germs I have are good germs, here," I insisted.

Jane took a long drink then handed back the empty cup. "I still think I'm dreaming, but I don't want to wake up. I like this," she moved her left hand around to indicate everything around her, "and these nice people. Is it always like this?"

"Uh, no, sometimes it gets scary," I said as I recalled the incident the year before with Captain Asshole MacLeod, knives, threats, and assorted mayhem and bullets. "We've been through some very rough and dangerous times, and I agree that this, my dear, is as good as it gets. Good food, good company, a healthy family, nice weather...gee, pinch me; I think I'm dreaming, too," I said with a laugh.

Just then, James, Benji, and Jody walked up to join the ladies and babies. "Are ye sure they're my uncles?" Benji asked as he bent over to pick up Raymond. "They look a wee small? And how old are ye now, Grandpa? Ye look to be about my age. Grannie, yer lookin' mighty fine for an elderly lady."

192

"My wife, yer Grannie, is not an elderly lady, she's, she's..." Jody fumbled for words that didn't sound harsh to describe his mate. He certainly wasn't going to explain in mixed company that their dosing a year earlier with the Fountain of Youth tonic had not only rewound their biological clocks, it had brought Sarah out of menopause, acted as a fertility drug, and allowed her to have a perfect pregnancy and deliver twins at just over sixty years of chronological age.

"How about an older woman?" I suggested. "Being older is fine, but being elderly sounds gray and wrinkled. And Sarah, you are definitely not wrinkled, and the gray just highlights your brown hair. Although," I said as I reached over and moved the tips of my fingers through the curls around her ears, "I don't see much for gray hairs."

Sarah looked a little embarrassed at the revelation in front of her grandson that her gray hairs had disappeared. "It must be the henna and egg wash I used last time I shampooed my hair. I must have used too much henna."

"Um, yeah," I fumbled, "that must be what it is. And I hear that the henna won't wash out, that you'll have to wait for it to grow out. I guess you're *stuck* with it for a while."

I looked over and saw the men were in different states of eye rolling. Jody was relieved that the topic was over, James was enchanted with his mother-in-law's babbling and quick recovery, and Benji just wanted to talk about something other than women's hair care.

"Excuse me; I think I'm needed, um, somewhere else, I mean, elsewhere." I nodded to each of the men, picked up my skirts and walked as fast as I could without running to get away from there. Next time I'd shut up and just nod. At least if I dipped my head, my feet wouldn't find their way into my mouth!

27 Back Home with Grandpa

I hid my embarrassment in the kitchen, which was a good place for me to be: dinner wasn't going to cook itself. Leah was tending to Bibby, Jenny was watching her little brothers and sister, and Jody was in charge of his young sons. Sarah had come inside to clean up her tools or whatever after performing the minor surgery, and Benji and Janie were taking care of each other. Everyone was basking in the joy of family and peace. All that was needed was a big dinner to make it a perfect day. That was going to be my job.

James had followed me inside, carrying the three plucked and cleaned chickens for our supper. "Well, since there are enough caregivers out there for all the babies and wounded, I figured I'd volunteer for KP duty. Do you need any potatoes peeled, corn husked, ale brewed?" he joked.

"Ale," I said, "I probably didn't bring in enough, but how about some snacks to go with it? Got any ideas?"

"I'm on it, and I'll bring back a little something special, too," he said, then headed out the door.

I grabbed three good-sized onions and a couple of garlic bulbs. I trimmed and peeled, then stuffed them into the heavily buttered and salted birds. I had three clay pots, one moderately chipped, but still serviceable, so employed them all. I scrubbed a dozen potatoes and threw them in a basket. I had baked bread the day before and held back a couple of loaves from the men, planning to make French toast. Well, it looked like we wouldn't be having that for tomorrow's brunch—sourdough pancakes would be fine—but I had the bread for dinner. I could glaze a couple dozen carrots in Jenny's maple syrup and bring out a rum-soaked fruitcake for dessert. I couldn't have accomplished a finer Thanksgiving dinner if I had worked on it all day.

Jenny popped up at my side at just the right time. Sometimes I think she has the sight, too. She and Leah both seem to anticipate my needs, even before I have them. "Daddy already has the fire going outside," she informed me, then asked, "Can I poke the potatoes into the ashes, huh? I know I was supposed to clean them out today, but I thought we still might need them for baking, so I left them for just one more day. But, I promise I'll clean them out tomorrow, okay?"

"Yes, you may set the potatoes in, and yes, tomorrow will be fine, but let's put the clay pots in first. And leave room for the Dutch oven. I used some of your maple syrup for glazed carrots. It's a good thing we can cook outside. I don't think I could fit this many pots and potatoes in the hearth."

Jenny helped me ferry the food to the cook fire while the rest of the family visited. I shrugged off their offers of help. I had all I needed with Jenny, and then I let her go, too.

She sat next to her Grannie, both of them looking like spectators at a ping pong match, watching Benji speak, and then their eyes bouncing back to observe Jody's reply.

It was uncanny how much those two men resembled each other. It's a good thing Benji's hair was short and his clothes were different, or we wouldn't be able to tell them apart from a distance. Benji was at least four inches taller than his grandfather, but proportionately, they were built the same, and even moved the same. Both of them had the same regal bearing and walked with long, confident strides, as if they knew where they were going, and you'd be wise to follow them. Yup, they were both natural leaders.

I went back inside one more time to clean up my mess and heard James pull up with the promised snacks. He came in the doorway with a couple of crocheted sacks of what looked like small potatoes set on top of a basket filled with bottles of ale. "Will these do?"

"What do you have there?" I asked as I helped him unload. I opened the sack and grinned. "Salted peanuts? Salted in the shell peanuts and cold brewskies? I'd better hide one of the bags or everyone will fill up on these and won't have room for dinner."

James set a couple of linen dishcloths on top of the bottles then used the ewer to douse them with water. "These were already chilled, but this will help keep them that way. I haven't quite got the refrigerator to the point where it can freeze water, but I'm working on it. I really miss having ice cream, especially on a day like today."

"What d'ya mean?" I drawled, "We have ice cream here in the 18th century." James gave me the 'what you talkin' about, Willis?' look, and I continued. "But, only in the winter." We both laughed at that one. "Ice cream in the summer, though," I sighed longingly as I took out a bottle of ale for him, then grabbed one for myself. I saluted him with the brew, said, "Cheers," and then chugged down almost half the bottle at once. "Yes, ice cream would be nice, but having a cold beer is good, too. Although, I think we're going to have to work on a recipe for root beer or sarsaparilla for the young ones. This isn't fair to them."

"I already beat you to it," James said. He moved aside a couple of bottles. There were three half pint bottles sealed with the same little latch top caps. "I put some root beer in here for Jenny. Um, I hope you don't mind that I didn't bring enough for the wee three. I thought they were too young for soda."

"You're right there, although I might take out one of these and mix it half and half with milk for a treat for them. I just remembered doing that when I was young." I shook my head and explained, "I just flashed another memory: a poor man's root beer float. Hmm, another unrequested, but friendly memory pops back in."

"Does it bother you," James asked gently, "not remembering?"

"Actually, no, it doesn't. I have such a good life now, and what had to be the best part of my past life, Leah, is here. I hate to say that you can't miss what you can't remember, but it's true. I didn't miss Leah until she wound up as my nurse at the hospital last year and I realized that she was, had to be, my daughter. I didn't miss you because, even though I had found that business card of yours in my backpack, I didn't remember who you were. Hell, I didn't even know that I knew you."

"Well, we had only met briefly that one time. You had a whole lifetime—hers at least—with her, and less than an hour with me."

James gave me a slight grin of discomfort, letting me know that he wanted to change the awkward subject. "So, now that Benji's here to help with the harvesting and everything else, it looks like I might be able to spend more time with my, ahem, inventions."

I looked down my nose at James and shook my head in admonishment. "Okay, okay," he clarified, "I'll be able to spend more time on my re-creations. Is that better?"

"Yes, my number one son-in-law. Let's see, the chickens and potatoes are baking, carrots are glazing, I think I've scrounged enough plates and bowls for everyone, and gee, we're set." I stuck my head out the door and called to my family outside, "Why don't you bring it inside? I want to hear the latest gossip, too. And I think those babies need a nap out of the weather."

I set out the peanuts and poured more water over the towels covering the bottles. It wasn't as good as an electric refrigerator, but evaporative cooling was all we had at our place.

Sarah and I already envied the solar hot water heater and ceiling fans James had put in their house, and were eager for him to build them for our homes, too.

The men, women, children, and babies all filed through the door, bits of their stories still floating in the air. "And then I found out I had to wait one more year!" Benji declared.

I gave Benji a bottle of ale and let him continue. He toasted us with the homebrew, took a long draught, and set it down on the kitchen table. I wasn't sure, but I think his revelations about his challenges getting back *home* were making him feel like a part of the family again, and not just a visitor. His whole demeanor had brightened with his story telling. I set down a bowl of the peanuts for him to munch on while he continued his soliloquy, and we waited for our dinner to finish baking.

"I took on all types of jobs to keep me fed and sometimes housed. Ye see, I can operate pretty much anythin' that has wheels, wings, or tracks," Benji boasted. "Although, when it comes to flyin' those Super Cubs, I have to take out the front seat. They arena made for anyone over five foot seven, or so it seems. Bein' a foot over height made fer cramped quarters even with the front seat removed. And of course, I couldna take anythin' other than my lunch with me because I was right close to maximum load with my clothes on. And I sure wasna gonna fly naked!" Benji paused then amended his statement. "I wouldna minded *flyin'* without my clothes, it's jest that I wouldna thought it proper to leave the plane without them."

"Ye flew a cub, a super cub? What kind of cubs fly, bear cubs?" Jody asked in total sincerity.

"No, no, it's jest a name they gave to a wee bit of an airplane that can take off and land in short areas. Its verra good fer sites with lots of trees or next to creeks. I've landed and taken off from little sand bars no longer than, than from here to the barn." Benji saw the confusion on his grandfather's face. "I'll tell ye what; I'll build ye a little model out o' pieces of scrap wood. It's much easier to see how one of these things flies than to explain drag and lift and air pressure coefficients."

I watched Jane as Benji spoke of modern technologies. She didn't seem shocked which surprised me. Then I remembered what she had said. He talked to her about planes, trains, and automobiles when he didn't know she could understand English.

It was a good thing Jenny had fallen asleep with her siblings. She knew about her brother James and his inventions.

He had all sorts of ideas and incorporated several of them in his modernistic home. His fancy venting kept their home relatively cool in the summer, and he had even fashioned a solar water heater. But, it was his story of his trip to America that could have been trouble. He had covered his slip of the tongue about his nine hour 'flight' from England by saying it was a dream; that he had dreamt he could fly over the water to America in a coach that sailed through the air rather than in a ship that took a month or more to cross the sea. She had accepted it as a good idea, and incorporated it into some of her tales she used to entertain Judah, Leo, and Wren.

Well, at least I thought Jenny was asleep. She walked up quietly beside Benji as he was speaking about his days building roads with Caterpillars. "They're really called Caterpillars, but we always referred to them as Cats. And, we who ran them were called Cat skinners," he said.

"Eww, that's awful," Jenny said, suddenly making herself known to Benji the entertainer. "You didn't really skin a cat, did you?"

"No, no," he explained, then thought fast, picking her up and setting her on his lap to buy more time to fabricate a cover story. "Ye see, we had tools—great big, huge tools—that we used to build roads. We called them Cats. And when a man, or woman, used the big tools, they were called Cat skinners. No animals were hurt or killed in the making of the roads using Caterpillar equipment," Benji added in a monotone as a comedic disclaimer. Of course, only James, Leah, and I laughed at his mockery of the movie industry, but we howled.

"Uh, oh," I said as I realized we had awaken the two youngest red heads. "I'm sorry," I apologized to Sarah. She was snuggled into Jody and nearly asleep. Or so I thought. I realized that she was actually in a deep sleep when she snorted then nodded, a sweet smile crossing her face. I may have inadvertently awakened the babies, but she could use a bit more rest, at least enough so she could finish her pleasant dream.

"Here, let me," Benji offered. "Jenny, do ye want to go with me while my uncles show me some more of the property?"

Jenny sat up straight—she was still on his lap—and nodded briskly. "I want to show you something special," she said in a voice so soft that only he could hear, or so she hoped. It was still a secret.

Benji and I looked at Jane. I could see that she was still in pain. Before he could ask her if she wanted to go—and I knew she probably *wanted* to go—I ran interference. "Janie, I think you might want to stay here and rest a bit before supper. You can take a nap in the surgery or lie down over here," I said, nodding to the cramped little corner where Jenny had been lying with the still slumbering Pomeroy-Hart toddlers.

"The surgery will be fine. Thank you," she said with her mouth, her eyes adding, 'thank you very much; I'm beat!'

Jody gently laid Sarah's head down, allowing her to finish her nap on the floor. "I think I'll jest go out to the garden and check on the traps I set. That raccoon is smarter than I am at getting out of one."

Wallace piped in, "I didn't know you got trapped? I didn't think it was big enough for you?"

Jody groaned at the joke and James spoke up, "How about if I look at it? I saw a humane trap for foxes once. I might be able to adapt yours."

"Come on, men," Jody said softly, "let's see if three big men can figure out how to catch one verra intelligent raccoon. And if we canna figure it out, we'll send fer ye, Leah."

Leah grinned at the compliment. "I'll hold down the fort while you're gone. Actually, I think I'll claim a spot on your bed, if you don't mind."

Jody pulled his neck back in mock indignation. *"Mi casa es su casa, mija.* Anything I have is yers. Help yerself."

28 Hey, There!

Jenny and Benji took their uncles for another walk, babbling idly as they meandered around the grounds. Ten minutes into their getting acquainted trek, Benji spotted six riders approaching at a fast clip, a cloud of dust kicking up and blowing ahead of the horde. "Come on Jenny; let's take our uncles into the house. They dinna need to be breathin' in the dirt," he said with concern. But, it wasn't the air quality that had him worried. There were too many people on horseback and riding in too fast to be bringing good news. "Here, on second thought, give him to me; I'll take them both in. Run ahead and tell yer Grandpa and Da that we have visitors."

Jenny passed Raymond to him then sprinted toward the house, screaming, "Grandpa! Daddy!" at the top of her lungs. If they were within a quarter of a mile, they'd hear her.

Ж

Benji entered the house and handed one uncle to me, one to Leah, and nodded his head as he counted babies to make sure that my three and Leah's were all here. "What's wrong?" I asked seeing his dour expression. He hadn't said a word, which was my first clue that something was amiss; he was always chatting. His lack of humor and furrowed brow were the other indicators.

"I have this itchin', crawlin' feelin' that somethin's wrong with these men comin' this way. How about ye, Leah?" he asked as he looked her way; he knew she had 'the sight.'

She had perceived the ill will, too. The uneasy look on her face was unmistakable: danger was imminent. "Um, do you have a gun?" she asked nervously, glancing at the door, looking for her little sister Jenny. "Mom, does Wallace carry his gun? I know James does; he never leaves home without his equalizer. These men are armed and emotional, Benji, so don't be bashful about showing off what you have."

Benji patted his sporran in answer to the gun question. He opened it, pulled the contents from the top section, and set them on the sideboard. Then he lifted out the false bottom and took out the revolver, flipped out the chamber, made sure it was loaded, peered down the barrel checking for obstructions, popped the chamber back in position, and set the gun into his

200

waistband. "And Jenny's with her Da and Grandpa," he said, making sure we knew she was safe.

"Carhartts?" Leah asked, suddenly realizing that the pants he was wearing weren't era correct.

"Aye, yer the first one to say anythin' about them. If anyone else noticed, they dinna mention it. Come to think of it, do ye have any extra knives around here?" he asked as he put his thumb in the self-fabric loop on the outside of his thigh. "I think I'll dress up a bit. A little intimidation goes a long way, aye?"

"Oh, yeah," I said dryly, and grabbed the butcher knife out of the block, eyeing the carving fork, finally deciding he could take that, too. "Here, let them know you're not afraid to carve 'em up," I joked, then laughed nervously.

I didn't have a gun, didn't really feel comfortable with one, and wasn't very hot on the idea of stabbing anyone either. But then again, with so many male kin around who could, would, and had taken care of me and my children, I didn't feel the need to be armed.

Jane walked in quietly from the surgery, not saying a word, but very aware of the tension. Benji could see the fear in her eyes that mirrored his own. "Janie, ye stay inside with the other women and the children. And dinna come out here unless *I* call ye; no one else, aye?" Benji commanded stressing the word I.

"Aye," Jane answered meekly, sniffing back a tear.

Benji took two long steps over to her and gave her a hard kiss on the mouth. "It'll be okay, I promise," he said, and held her firmly by the shoulders. He turned back to look at Sarah, Leah, and me, making sure we had our end under control. We all nodded in silent answer. He forced a smile, then went out the door to investigate the gathering of riders.

Jane stood petrified. Her eyes followed Benji's exit, then looked to me for direction. At first, I couldn't understand why, and then realized that I was the first one here who had shown her friendship, treating her as a peer as we shared the chore of fetching refreshments, moments after she had arrived.

Jane was idle—without a chore to perform—and in a new environment. The person she cared about most had just left to face a possible mob. Leah, Sarah, and I were all in our element and had our hands full with children and household responsibilities.

"Can you sew?" I asked, hoping to distract her from the brewing commotion outside and the uneasiness inside. She nodded that she could. "Great, I could use a hand with some of this mending." I saw the concerned—hell, terrified—look on her

201

face, and told her, "Don't worry, the men can handle anything that comes their way. We won't be thinking about what's going on out there if we keep busy…"

I was interrupted by the 'pop' of a musket firing.

"What the fu…?" Leah screeched as she bolted to the window to look for the source of the boom. "It's okay. Some idiot either missed or just fired in the air, I guess." At least, I don't see anyone on the ground or grabbing his shoulder," she said with a raised eyebrow to me.

Leah had been my recovery room nurse last year when I had been shot in the shoulder with a musket ball, then sent back for a one-day hospital trip to the 21st century, courtesy of Master Simon. It was a lame joke and didn't even get a groan out of me. "Get away from the window," I said brusquely, "and shush. I want to hear what's going on."

I pulled the door ajar and Sarah, Leah, and I gathered next to it, making sure we were out of sight. I looked back and saw Jane had practically become one with the back wall, a large, *bas relief*, black-fleshed and blue calico clad clump of wallpaper. "Good idea," I whispered to her. "Better yet, sit on the floor in case they get close and look in a window."

I paused to think about what I was going to say next— which didn't happen all the time, thinking first, that is. I made up my mind and decided to pose the delicate question anyway. "You're not an escaped slave, are you?"

Jane shook her head rapidly. "Benji has papers for me," she said meekly. She shut her eyes tight in embarrassment and admitted uneasily, "He owns me."

"Yeah, well, he may have papers that say that, but I'll bet you a million bucks—even if I don't have it—that he does *not* feel like he owns you." I ended my remark with a snort, "Hmph!"

Jane could tell I meant what I said and nodded that I was right. At least, that was what Benji had told her even before he knew she could understand him. Even before they had kissed, he hadn't felt like he could, or should, 'own' another person. It was the others out there who were the problem.

Ж

The group, all six of them white males, came to a halt in front of Jody and Benji, the two tall red headed guardians, their arms crossed in front of their chests in a united attitude of defiance. If Wallace and James were aware of the situation, they were keeping a low profile.

The wind was coming toward us, so we could hear the confrontation. The fat man with the sweaty tri-corner hat smashed too far onto his head yipped more than barked his words. "Hey, there!" His squeaky voice tried to sound tough, but failed almost comically.

He paused, and waited for the other horses to settle down, then started again. "We've come to take her back." He shifted in his saddle, pushed the toes of his boots down into the stirrups, so he was actually standing up, trying to appear taller than he was. "The boss's brother was killed by her, so she's to be burned at the stake," he shouted in his off-key soprano voice.

"There's no one here who doesna belong here," Jody said, shoulders back, eyes squinted, as he studied the men, assessing their hunger for battle. It looked like Mr. Tinny-voice was in charge. Right now, words were the only weapons being used. The young man at the back of the group had dropped his musket to the ground, causing it to discharge. He hadn't meant to fire, so that shot didn't count. The lad was terrified and looked like he was about to piss his pants, either in fear, or in shame at his gaffe. Either way, he, too, was a threat because he would instinctively follow his leader, like a hungry cat after a rat through a burning briar patch. But, Jody knew these men were also joined together by a cause. Whether it was a righteous one or not, didn't make a difference. They were a mounted, armed mob, fueled by a passionate pip-squeak of a man. Jody knew he would have to take him down a few notches. But first, he'd hear him out and let the joker supply him with intimidation ammunition.

"We know she's here. The old man down the road said that he sent him," the mashed-hatted leader pointed to Benji with his chin, "to your place, Pomeroy. He told us he called himself your grandson. The old man said he saw him leave with the Negress." The man changed from his accusing voice to a snide, belittling tone and added, "Holding her hand."

"Like I said, there's no one here who doesna belong. Now, I'd appreciate it if ye'd leave jest as fast as ye came in," Jody said with confidence and poise, hoping that there wouldn't be any more gunfire, intentional or otherwise.

"Oh, she's here all right, and she's a witch. I wasn't there, but she hexed Samuel—that's Mr. Jonathan's brother-in-law—making him stab him, his own sister's husband! We have witnesses! And she's a thief, too. She stole the silver whiskey flask right out of the dead man's jacket!" the ringleader shouted, his voice getting louder and higher pitched with each accusation.

Benji stepped forward and addressed the petite prattler, ignoring all the others. "Weel, if ye arena a witness, then where are they? Ye see, I *was* there and I saw it all. The lass never laid a hand on anyone. It was me on the ground who Samuel was goin' fer. If he hadna tripped and fallen over his own big feet, Mr. Jonathan would still be alive today."

Benji was supposedly explaining the scenario to the vigilantes, but was really using the revelation to relate what had happened to his grandfather. "So, if there had been a problem with her, if she was guilty of anythin', the witnesses would have said so before they left. No, since there's nothin' but hearsay on yer part about poor Mr. Jonathan's accident, I suggest ye all leave." Benji slowly stepped back to stand next to his grandfather, spreading his shoulders wide to make sure the men saw his pistol, and realized that there were two very large men and one shiny gun they would have to overcome to get to the house.

"And I don't think that pointing that gun at them will do you any good," James said, as he came out from the trees in front of and to the side of the riders. "Right, Wallace," he said loudly, announcing his father-in-law's presence to the trigger-happy horde.

Both Wallace and James had seen the man readying his shot. The vigilante had used the younger man beside him to hide his waist high aim at Benji. When he heard James's warning, he lay his pistol down across his lap, but kept the smug look on his face. He wasn't going to give up his weapon—he'd just put it on hold until a more opportune moment arose.

"Now I dinna think it very neighborly of ye to come to my house, armed to the teeth with pistols and muskets, accusin' my guest of murder and witchcraft. So, I'm askin' ye nicely now: turn around, go home, and if there's any truth to yer story, we can have a trial. But, it willna be without every one of the witnesses who were there and the magistrate to hear the story. Now, good day to all of ye and farewell," Jody said graciously, but with the tone that his dismissal of them was not up for discussion.

Vernon was tired of hearing the banter. He wanted his boss's murderess now. It had been a long time since he had a chance to use his whip, and his hands were yearning for the feel of its hilt, the wrist action of flicking the cat-o-nine tails, the tremor that passed up the strands when they impacted skin, breaking up and splaying bits of bloody flesh with each lash. If he shot from where he was, he was bound to hit one of the two big red headed men. Sure, there'd be a melee, but then he and the rest of the men could go right up to the house and find her. He had seen someone at the window, heard women talk and a baby cry. Yes, they were probably hiding that tall, murdering slave in the house with the women and babies.

"If you raise that gun again, I'll shoot first and ask questions later. Do I make myself clear?" James announced to the man who had lifted his pistol again, this time a scant four inches off of his lap.

Vernon set his gun down gently, cut his eyes to his brother, the swiftly lifted the pistol, and pulled the trigger.

Bang, pop: the two sounds were almost simultaneous.

James fired his pistol. He had seen the twitch and eye signal. He knew the man was going to shoot, to try to hit either Jody or Benji. He probably didn't care which one as long as he created chaos. Hopefully, he hadn't waited too long.

Benji and Jody ran for cover in opposite directions at the shots. Benji ran to the goat shed, his pistol drawn to cover his grandfather's hasty retreat to the backside of the outhouse.

Vernon had fallen forward, and now slumped over the horse's bloody mane. His eyes were frozen, forever wide in shock at what he had last seen while alive; his own throat blown apart, the red fluid spurting out, his lust for another's blood causing him to lose his own.

The horse reared at the loss of his rider's control and the shift in weight. Hal grabbed for the reins to subdue the high-strung steed as his brother's corpse dangled from one side, the lifeless foot caught in the stirrup. The horse continued to rear up and dance around Vernon's slack body, trying to rid itself of the awkward encumbrance, the smell of fresh blood like a hot poker up his nose. Hal finally jumped off his ride to free his fallen brother's boot from the stirrup, to release the corpse tether, allowing the body to fall to the ground. Now Hal's horse caught the scent of carnage and backed away frantically, pulling the reins out of his hand. All at once, both horses were gone, running back in the direction from where they had come, getting as far away from the smell of blood and death as their long legs and riderless backs could take them.

Hal stood petrified in the midst of the unplanned calamity, slowly turning his head side to side. This wasn't how it was supposed to happen.

"Now, I dinna want any more blood to be shed. Jest take the man's body and get out of here." Jody called out from behind his privy citadel. "If ye have a valid claim, send someone— unarmed mind ye—with a notice of when the magistrate wants the trial to be held. We'll do this the right way, aye?"

205

"Get him up on your horse," squeaked the squatty leader to the young misfiring rider, instructing him to load Vernon, the dead would-be assassin, onto his horse. "And you double up with him," he said, and pointed from Hal to the other slim built vigilante. He looked around to make sure his orders were being followed, then allowed himself the indignity of wiping his brow. He was sweating profusely with fear, partially blinded by the drops in his eyes. "We'll deal with you later, Pomeroy. And your grandson, too, if he even is one."

"I'll be sendin' ye a bill fer the cleanup of the mess ye made here today," Jody said as he walked out bravely and pointed to the bloody area on the ground. "And dinna be comin' back here without papers from the magistrate, or yer the one who'll be in court."

Benji walked up and stood next to his grandfather, watching the pathetic posse ride away, the two double-ridered hoses struggling to keep up with Master Toad's swift retreating pace.

"Dinna ye think the magistrate might side with them, I mean, that he might be swayed a bit with them sayin' a slave killed a man?" Benji asked softly before James and Wallace joined them.

"No, no chance of that, lad," he said with a chuckle. "Ye see, as of last week, I'm the new magistrate. Those idiots jest dinna ken it yet."

Jody looked over and saw that Wallace and James had paused in their short trek to join them. James was bent over at the waist, his hands on his knees, Wallace standing mute beside him a respectful six feet away.

"Are ye ailin' there, lad?" Jody asked as he rushed over to him.

"Oh, God," James said, then threw up. He wiped his mouth then kicked dirt into his mess. He looked up at his mentor and shook his head in embarrassment. "I didn't think I'd ever have to shoot a human being and now I've killed two in one year. The first one, I'm ashamed to say, didn't bother me. He really, really deserved it, and would have been dead in a few days anyhow, but him," James paused and shook his head and looked over at the bloody area where the man had fallen.

"Weel, if it was to be him, me, or Benji, then I'm glad it was him," Jody said simply. "He was a bad man and was killin' fer sport. Ye were killin' to protect yer kin. I canna say that there's a more honorable way to take a life. It was to protect yer own, aye?"

"Aye," James replied then looked over at both Benji and Jody in shock, suddenly realizing there was more to the incident. "Did he hit either one of you?" he asked in embarrassment. "I could have sworn he had a chance to get his shot off. I didn't want to wait until the last moment, but...but...I thought I had, did."

Benji reached over with his right hand and pulled his shirt from away his left arm. "He ventilated my shirt a bit, but no harm done. Janie can fix it fer me. Oh, shit, I mean, excuse me." He nodded quickly to the men. "I'll bet she's scarrit sh.." he started to say, then shut up quickly.

"Yes, I'll bet she's scared shitless," James finished for him. "I'll be there in a sec. I want to clean up a bit before I greet the ladies. Can you help me here a bit, Jody?"

Wallace picked up on the subtle hint that James wanted to speak with Jody alone. He had noticed long ago that there seemed to be an odd bond between the two men. Leah had told him that James had been reared by Marty Melbourne—the man he thought was his grandfather. The two were very close despite the age difference.

It wasn't until just a few days before Leah and James left their own time that James had found out that his grandfather, Marty—at that time missing and presumed to be in the 18th century—was really his biological father.

Last year James traveled back to 1782 with Leah. They caught up with Marty the day they arrived. James was only able to have one day with his dear grandfather—his newly acknowledged father—when the patriarch made the difficult decision to leave James and return to the 21st century. James told him that his newly discovered biological mother, Bibb Stephens—the woman Marty should have married—had cancer. James knew it was the right thing for his father to do: make up some of the time lost with the woman he loved, but hadn't spent enough time with.

James was still pained, though. Evidently, he still had an empty spot in his soul that only an older man—one more experienced in the horrors of the world—could fill. Legally, he was James's stepfather, but biologically, was a few years younger. He understood, and didn't begrudge his son-in-law feeling more comfortable with the grandfather persona.

"What do ye need help with there, Wee James," Jody asked when the others had left. He only called him that name when they were alone or with family. He did it because he got a smile from James every time he said it. James was the shortest man in the family at six foot even.

James gave Jody the grin he knew the man was expecting by calling him 'wee.' "How do you do it? And how long does it take?" James asked weakly.

Jody cocked his head and asked without words, 'please explain?'

James elaborated, "How do you get that look, those looks, out of your head. That first one: when he's shot and realizes that he's death waiting to be fulfilled, and then that blank stare when you see that his spirit is gone."

"Aye, there are two moments when a man dies. It's only when yer up close when takin' a man's life, as ye were today, that ye see both of them. The first time is the soul separatin' from the body, not really wantin' to leave—that's the shocked look ye see, the one with the blink. But, it's the second face that's jest as bad. That's when the soul is gone and only the shell remains. That's why it stays with ye: it's frozen, like a portrait carved into yer brain where ye canna run from it. Ye see that face in yer heid and part of ye believes that it willna ever leave. It never really does, but with a good life, it doesna come to haunt ye as much. It may help if ye realize that the body that stays is jest a hull, like a walnut picked clean and left behind. The rest is either one place or the other. And in this case, I would suspect he's havin' to answer fer his bad intents. He was sure to wind up with the devil sooner or later. Ye jest sent him on his way a bit earlier, and kept him from doin' more harm to others, with yer clean shot. It's not much to brag about—and I ken ye wouldna—but the man dinna suffer, and neither did Benji, Janie, or me because of what ye did today. If it helps, when that man's face comes to try and haunt ye—and it will—think of the three of us who are here, now, because ye did the right thing. And fer yer own sake, pray that the Lord has mercy on the man's soul. Ye canna be damnin' him more than he already has been, aye?"

"Aye," James said. "Would you make an excuse for me not coming back to the house right away? I want to go home for a bit. It may sound—no, you probably understand this—I want to, need to, be by myself. And I want to take a bath and scrub this horrible feeling off of me."

"It willna scrub off, but the washin' does help. That and the solitude and prayers to the Lord, askin' to help repair yer soul. What ye did today wasna a sin, but it wasna an easy task either. I'm verra glad ye did it and so is my grandson. Dinna take too long. I'm sure yer wife wants ye to be with her and the bairn. And that's another part that will help the healin': bein' close to yer wife." Jody moved his shoulders uneasily, trying to decide how to word it.

"Do you mean being intimate with her?" James asked softly.

Jody nodded. "Aye, it will help, and I'm sure Leah would want to help ye with the healin'. That's what she does."

"All right. I won't be too long then. At least, now I have something to look forward to. Thanks for everything," James said, then bowed his head to take his leave.

"Oh, 'tis me that should be thankin' ye!" Jody said and planted a hearty pat on the distressed man's shoulder. "Take care now," he added and returned the farewell nod. He headed back to his own home, his wife, and the rest of his family who were safe today because of the reluctant warrior.

29 Make room

"Sarah, do ye think ye can let Jane sleep in the surgery tonight? Benji can have the barn," Jody announced when he came into the house, totally ignoring the topic of the shooting death that had just occurred. He didn't want to talk about the altercation right away. That could wait. The women had probably seen more than they wanted to anyhow. The bad men were gone and his family plus one were safe. Right now, that was all that was important.

Before Sarah could answer him, Benji protested weakly, knowing full well that what Grandpa said was how it was going to be. "But we've been sleeping together on the road for the last week. We'll be fine," he said, just in case the arrangements hadn't been finalized.

"Ye willna be sleepin' with a woman unless yer marrit to her. Ye'll be apart as long as there's at least one room and a barn or a shed or the open sky to separate the two of ye into. Leah," he called to change the subject and address his concerned granddaughter, "James will be along soon. He wanted to clean up a bit. Now, where is that bald-headed great-granddaughter of mine?"

"Jane has her. She was being fussy again—Bibby, not Jane—so she took her into the surgery. I don't know what it is about that woman, but she starts singing, and the child is enthralled. Can you hear her?" Leah asked then looked toward the closed door of the surgery.

Ж

Jane walked slowly around the small room addition, trying to soothe the baby cradled in her arms, singing her mama's love song to her. Little Bibby's mother—Leah was her name—had just fed her, but the baby acted as if she was still hungry. Maybe she just wanted to suck, too. Jane had never wet-nursed a baby before—intentionally, at least—but she felt something strange when Wee Raymond had suckled her. His tiny mouth pulling on her didn't feel the same as when Benji kissed and sucked and licked. And then there was that bluish white fluid the baby had in his mouth when she pulled him away. She'd seen it in the corner of babies' mouths before when her mother wet-nursed them. Could she have milk? She'd never had a baby, but maybe that didn't make a difference with people. She enjoyed the sucking—too much if that was possible. Just thinking about it made her feel warm and moist in the junction between her torso and her legs, and made her nipples tingle.

She looked down at little bald-headed Bibby snuggled in her arms, gnawing her fist in hunger, and sympathized with the child's frustration. She had felt that discomfort many times in her life, too: the belly that didn't have enough food in it to be satisfied. At least she could let the child suck. It would feel good to her, and the baby; well, maybe, just maybe, if she really had milk in her breasts, then she would be able to feed the child.

It could be that she was like her mama that way. She was the only baby her mother had birthed, but Mama nursed other babies for years, sometimes even when she hadn't had one sucking on her for months. Maybe the milk was a gift like singing. Mama had told her that her voice was a present from God. Her mother could sing and nurse other people's babies. Maybe she had received both gifts, too. Jane loosened her sarong, bared her right breast, and offered it to Bibb, continuing her song of joy to the bright-eyed little girl.

Wee Bibby rubbed her nose back and forth on Jane's nipple, making it rise in response. As soon as she felt its firmness, she opened her mouth and started sucking, getting a taste of the sustenance that she had not been getting for the last few days.

Jane felt it; the same feeling she had the moment after Wee Raymond had latched onto her. It was a warm, comforting flush of relief. Her milk had let down, she knew it had; just as it did with cows and goats. When she milked the farm animals, only a small amount of milk came out when she first pulled and squeezed on their teats. Then, all of a sudden, the milk would let down and flow by itself. That must be what was happening to her. She put her finger in Bibby's mouth to release the suction and pulled the nipple out to check. Milk sprayed out from at least twenty points and onto the baby's face. Jane gawked at seeing her suspicion confirmed. Wee Bibby didn't wait to be proffered it again, but bounced her mouth back onto its target, latching onto the nipple, stimulating the flow with a gentle but insistent tug, swallowing the milk and sucking gently to keep it flowing, not relaxing lest its source be removed again.

Jane's shock disappeared quickly as her gentle song of grace resumed, a little more grateful for the added blessing she had just discovered. The rocking chair in the corner was empty. Normally she would never think of sitting on a white person's furniture, but these people were her new family. Her mother would let her sit in her chair if she was tired; Sarah probably would, too. She pulled the rocker away from the wall with her foot and sat in the chair that, just like all the others, was too small for her. Her legs were too long for the seat, but her bottom wasn't too wide. She lifted her heels as she sat back in the chair, rocking the both of them to sleep.

Ж

Evie and Leah continued dinner preparations for the extended family while Jody and Wallace played chess. Wee Raymond had fallen asleep on his father's shoulder during the game. "See, if ye hadna taken so long to move yer man, he'd still be awake," Jody said. "Yer little brother weel be walkin' and talkin' before we're finished with this game."

Sarah went into the surgery to nurse Wee Julian. Maybe she could get him down to sleep early, too. The surgery was the one place she was sure to get some quiet time. She also wanted to check on Jane and Bibby; the singing had stopped. The odd couple was asleep in her rocking chair—baby Bibby's lax mouth hanging away from Jane's milky breast.

"oh kay," Sarah whispered and walked over to the straight backed chair in the corner, selecting it as her nursing chair. She got Wee Julian to start feeding, and then moved her upper body back and forth in the stationery seat, as if it were a rocker. The movement was to soothe and relax her as much as it was for him. Between the pseudo rocking chair and his gentle sucking, Sarah found her inner peace and clarity of mind.

She had never taken obstetrics classes in medical school. All she knew about babies was from her own real life experience, but she was pretty sure that a woman had to have a baby before getting milk. But then again, that's just what she thought, not what she knew to be fact. If Jane's oxytocin hormones had been triggered by suckling, then they could have responded to the call for milk without the need of a pregnancy. Or maybe she had a miscarriage... No, the way she shook her head at the suggestion she had a baby was not how a woman who had just lost a child would have reacted. And, by the way Benji was so anxious to be married, he hadn't had sex with her yet. But, Benji was his grandfather's child and may have been getting familiar with her in other ways, ways that may have involved stimulating Jane's lactating hormones.

Oh, well. Jane and the baby looked to be at peace. She'd have to have a quiet talk with Leah when she was done feeding Wee Julian, though. If Leah had just fed her daughter and she

212

was still fussy, and then Jane fed her again and satisfied her enough that she had fallen asleep, it would seem that there was something amiss with Leah's milk. Or she was pregnant again.

Sarah fed Wee Julian until he was asleep then sneaked out of the room to put him down in his bed, letting the two dozing females stay zonked out in her rocking chair. She really didn't want Jane to know that she knew her secret—yet.

"Jody, may I have a word with you?" she asked the frowning chess master.

"Aye, might as weel. I'm not doin' any good here. Oh, Raymond, I'll put him to bed," he offered as he stood up and took one more look at the chessboard, trying a different view to get a new perspective on the stagnant game. He followed Sarah to the corner, set his son next to his sleeping brother, and asked, "What's on yer mind?"

"How's James doing?" she asked softly.

"Nae too good; I told him all the ways I kent to recover from takin' a man's life, and he's takin' it to heart. It would be nice, mind ye, if he and Leah could spend some time alone together. I love wee Bibby, but she sure has been fussy. Is it too early fer the teethin'?"

"Yes and no," Sarah answered. "I think Leah might be pregnant..."

Sarah saw Jody's eyes widen as he asked her the silent question, 'what about you?' "No, I'm fine. I'm taking precautions. I think she's relying on nursing alone to be her birth control. I don't think it's working, though. She's nurses Bibby, but says the child's always hungry. It happens with babies during a growth spurt—eating more frequently to bring in more milk—but I don't think that's the case here. She also has the first trimester fatigue syndrome going on. I wouldn't know for sure without checking her, and even then, it might be too soon to tell. But, Jane, um, has milk and she just fed Bibby. Do you hear her crying?"

"Bibby or Jane," Jody asked, and then realized he had unintentionally made a joke. "Oh, I see... Or I dinna see. Did she jest have a bairn?"

"No, I don't think she needed to. She evidently had other stimulation." Sarah cocked her head and grinned. "Hey, he's your grandson, aye?"

Jody shook his head, trying to keep the visual representation of what had apparently occurred on at least one occasion from slipping in. "So, it willna make a difference if Leah has Bibby with her tonight; her milk isna good anyway. And that

213

means," Jody's face brightened, "that maybe she can help Wee James heal in the other way." His head kept nodding in acceptance of Sarah's undeclared plan. "Janie can spend the night here, in the surgery, away from our randy grandson, and keep Wee Bibby fed and happy."

"Sounds like it's a good plan for everyone all around," Sarah said with self-assurance.

"Except fer Benji. He'll have no one but the goats fer company, but I'm sure he'll be fine." Jody sighed deeply as he remembered the other dilemma: finding a way for Benji and Jane to marry. "We'll talk about the other problem at dinner. Maybe someone will have an idea of how the two of them can get marrit and stay here." He shook his head in sadness. "But I dinna ken how it could be possible."

Ж

James Melbourne stomped up the steps to announce his arrival, walking through the door with feigned self-confidence, his hair still wet from his prolonged bath. The sunny day and his roof mounted solar water heater had assured him of plenty of hot water. He had soaked in his custom-built wooden tub for nearly an hour, at least until the water got cold. He couldn't scrub enough, so didn't even try—at least not too long. Jody had been right, though. Soaking in the water had helped, although he did feel guilty for using all of the available hot water. They'd just have to heat water at the hearth for the baby's bath tonight. He sighed then grimaced. It would be nice if he could get the other part of the cure Jody had suggested. But, that probably wouldn't happen.

Bibby had been fussy for the last week and was now sleeping with them in their bed. Leah was tired from taking care of her day and night. Just one good night's sleep would help. A thorough romping would be better still, although he'd settle for another one of their late night sneaky pokes. He grinned in recall. At least, Leah didn't protest if he took the initiative, and Bibby didn't seem to mind the bumping around her mother got while she nursed. Maybe the two of them could leave the baby with Jane and Benji for an hour or so. A little privacy, unrestricted, uninhibited... Oops, change the subject before you get too wound up, Melbourne!

"Weel, look what the wind blew in," Jody said when he saw James enter. Leah sauntered over to him, snuggled into his chest, and looked up at him like he was her hero. She pulled back and sighed in appreciation of her brave man, then moved in for another full body hug.

214

"Where is everyone?" James asked, although it was obvious that the only two missing were Jane and Bibby. Jenny was sitting in the corner with her little brothers and sister, telling them a story about giant flying birds with people inside them, using her hands and exaggerated facial gestures to accentuate the strange sounds of her monsters and heroes. I was finishing the gravy for the chicken and baked potatoes, and Wallace was setting the table.

"Looks like ye have a babysitter fer the night if ye'd like," Jody said with a twinkle in his eye. "Yer Bibby and her Aunt Janie have a real good arrangement goin' on there. Janie sings to her and Bibby puts her to sleep. They'll be out when they wake. Leave them be fer a bit."

"Well, I guess it's good that she's sleeping, although I would rather Bibby slept all night rather than all day," Leah said, her face furrowed in frown. "I'm up feeding her every couple of hours, as it is."

"We got it covered," Sarah said, looking quickly at Jody then back to me. "I think we have enough wet nurses around here to cover her for one night. How about everyone goes and washes up, then we'll have Jody say grace? Benji, would you see if your fiancée is ready to wake up?"

Benji didn't have to be asked twice. He was up and almost running before the end of the request.

I looked at Sarah to see if she was going to let me know what was going on, but saw that she was doing her best to busy herself, putting on an unneeded apron. She must be stressed. I've never seen her try to wear two of them at the same time. She'd either tell me later, or I'd find out about it myself. Either way, a thanksgiving meal was being set out, and I needed to help Jenny wash up the youngest of the Pomeroy-Hart clan.

Ж

Jane was fast asleep, baby Bibby at her breast, both of them totally relaxed, mouths hanging open. "Janie, are ye awake?" Benji asked softly.

Jane started at her name. The momentary panic she felt being caught asleep was quickly replaced by a smile of contentment. It was Benji calling her, calling her by the name he had given her. "Oh, I see ye got a little nap there. Are ye hungry? We have a fine chicken dinner, and all we're missin' is ye and little bit here," Benji said.

Jane suddenly remembered the baby she had been nursing. She scooted the rousing baby over her shoulder, effectively covering her bared breast with the child's body.

Benji was all smiles at seeing her, and she was happy to reflect them back to him. "I'll be in there shortly," she said, and looked toward the door, asking him subtly to go back without her.

Benji left quietly and Jane got up. She set the baby down on the surgery table and rewrapped her sarong. It didn't look like Benji had seen that she had been nursing, or at least allowing the baby to suck on her breast. She wanted to keep her blessing of having milk a secret for now.

"Come on, sweet child," she said to Bibby as she lifted her up over her shoulder, "there's nothing wrong with feeding and caring for you, so I won't feel bad about it. But, I'll bet your Mommy and Daddy miss you."

Bibby replied with, 'braat,' a healthy, dry burp, and almost a giggle then nuzzled her face into her cousin's shoulder. She was full, warm, happy, and ready for Daddy's snuggles.

Ж

I saw Sarah stare at Benji as he came out of the surgery. She was definitely looking for a reaction from him. I followed her line of sight and didn't see anything except the overly perky tall man coming over to the table to pick up his cousin Wren and attempt to carry on a conversation with the one-year-old. If he had seen anything unusual in there, he was keeping it a secret, and wearing his poker face. Oh, well, it must not be important, at least not yet.

30 The teen years

We all gathered together at the small kitchen table. It was time to eat our Thanksgiving meal. "We thank ye Lord fer the food, the friends, and family. Thank ye fer keepin' us safe today and fer the new member to our family. Bless us, O Lord, and gives us Yer strength and wisdom in all that we do; in Jesus name; Amen." Jody looked up from the blessing he had just invoked and smiled at his family: safe again, at least for now. "Okay, eat hearty everyone, there's plenty fer tonight and we dinna need to save any fer tomorrow. *Mangia!*"

"That means 'let's eat' in Italian!" Jenny declared although everyone but maybe Jane and Benji knew it. "And Grannie said I don't have to use a fork or knife when I'm eating chicken, but I have to make sure that I use a napkin. I put some extra ones out in case anyone's hands get too messy and hey, I wanted that piece," she carped as Leah took a drumstick.

"Don't worry about it—Grandpa and I fixed three chickens. That means there are how many drumsticks, Jenny?" Wallace asked.

"Six!" she announced with pride. "And, if Leah and I both eat one, that means there are four more drumsticks for everyone else."

"And lots of other pieces, but if ye dinna stop talkin' and start eatin', ye'll miss out on yer fair share," Jody admonished then passed the plate to Benji.

"Ooh, a nice juicy breast," Benji said as he stuck his fork into the golden roasted piece of meat, "my favorite part."

Sarah and Jody snorted at the same time then turned to look at each other. "I'm sorry," Sarah said at the same time Jody said, "Excuse me, something went down the wrong way," as lame explanations for their guttural responses to Benji's preference for breasts.

Benji shrugged with a sheepish grin. His slightly off color joke was made for the wrong audience. To apologize for it would draw more attention to it, so he decided to drop the subject. He took a big bite. "Mighty fine fare here, mighty fine," he praised as he chewed the chicken that tasted just like Mom used to cook, more than happy that he didn't have to eat grubs wrapped in grape leaves anymore.

After dinner I nursed my babies then put them down on a quilt covered pallet in the corner, letting Jenny snuggle up to them so they would settle down and hopefully go to sleep. Leah sat as close to James as humanly possible with clothes on as he cuddled Bibby to his chest, his gratefulness to be alive and have his family with him evident in his Mona Lisa smile of peace and contentment. Jane took Sarah's advice and went to the surgery to lie down. The rest of us paired off and found chairs, stools, or fat quilts to settle onto to get comfortable for an after dinner conversation with my nephew, Benji, the great big time traveling fairy.

"Ye see, I was, had been, a prisoner of Sept—that is Atholl MacLeod the Seventh—since I was nigh on twelve-years-old. He came to me at school, tellin' me that my mother was in trouble, and needed my help. Hmph! I was so gullible. Imagine, someone askin' a child fer help rather than goin' to my father or a police officer."

"Weel, at first he and his gang called me their hostage. They were gonna make a lot of money when my parents paid the ransom. Months later, when they couldn't get anybody to give them what they wanted, they called me a prisoner. Hmph. Prisoner woulda been a step up; I was more a slave than anythin'. They sold me to anyone to do anythin' from cleanin' out shitters, I mean privies, to shovelin' coal or other, um, stuff. And they werena verra nice to me either; not that I was verra nice to them. But, no matter what they did, I still wouldna tell them where they were or what was in them, The Letters, that is." He shifted his position on the hard stool, then sighed. "They thought I was deid."

"Who," I asked, "your parents or the men who held you prisoner?"

Benji didn't answer my question, but continued with his narrative. "The bad men werena too smart and were sendin' their ransom notes to the wrong place. Ye see, I wasna too cooperative in givin' them the right address, and they relied on the postal system to get the letters delivered. Sept could read and write and made sure I wrote the notes jest like he said. I had only seen him write his name, and it was all scribbled, like he had held the pen in his mouth. So, rather than writin' the notes himself and them bein' illegible, he had me take down his words then he'd read them and make sure I wrote what he told me."

Benji wriggled his shoulders like his shirt was too tight. "Although I wished I had known he could read before I wrote the first note for him. He took a switch to me and laid me open fer writin' 'It's been a hard day's night and I've been workin' like a dog' instead of his request fer gold and gems fer my safe return."

Benji snorted then continued his story. "We dinna have any gold or gems. My parents werena rich. They had to work like everyone else. And if there *had* been any extra money anywhere..."

Benji looked toward Jody and I could swear he gave him a 'look,' then continued.

"I certainly dinna want it to go to the man who stole me, beat me, and threatened my family!"

"But, you said they thought you were dead: who? Everyone?" I asked again.

"Oh, weel, like I said, Sept could read, so I made sure I wrote the right words after the second whippin'. I was mad about the first one and wouldna do what he said no matter how much he... Weel," Benji sucked in his bottom lip, "I stopped bein' so pig heided and realized that since the letters werena goin' to the right place anyway, I would go aheid and put down the words like he said. I musta written six letters, each one a couple of weeks apart. I told him that it took a long time to get the letters delivered by post there in Scotland. It sounded logical to me and since he saw that I believed it, he did, too. He dinna tell me where we were, but I figured by the accent of the men, we were in England, not too far from London, maybe Soho district.

"Weel, after a few months and no answers, he and his boys packed me up and we all heided fer Scotland. He figured if he mailed a letter nearby, it would get to my parents sooner. He waited day after day fer the ransom of gold and jewels that was never delivered.

"We were stayin' at an old abandoned brewhouse there in Angus. It was winter and he was tired of feedin' me since he couldna hire me out: there wasna any work fer anyone. I wasna makin' him any money so he decided he'd jest take that letter to Garden Hall himself, leave me locked up there at the brewhouse, outta sight. He dinna want to chance me runnin' away, um, again.

"Of course, when he tried to find the address of Garden Hall where the letters were sent, he had a wee bit of a problem. He found out that there wasna such a house number, or even road... I wasna there, but I'm sure he was *verra* mad! He found a tavern, of course, and asked where this Garden Hall place was. The locals realized he was confused and set him right; told him exactly where Barden Hall was."

"Um, dead?" I hinted again, hoping to get him back on track.

"Oh, yeah," he said, and laughed out loud. "That Sept wasna too bright, and not careful about what went out, the mail, I mean. Ye see, I was able to post a letter jest after I found out that the man was wantin' to ransom me." He shrugged in embarrassment. "Weel, it seemed like a good idea at the time and maybe it was wise in the end. I'm sure it caused a lot of anguish over the years, though. Ye see, I, um, sent a note to the newspaper, the one I kent my parents read, sayin' that a young lad, identified as one Benjamin MacKay by a witness who wished to remain anonymous, had fallen into the smelter at Lochaber and was incinerated, leavin' nothin' but ashes behind. I was hopin' they'd publish it, maybe even verify that I was gone, ye ken, askin' my family when they had last seen me. Ye see, while I was with Sept, I never saw any newspapers around, never heard a TV or radio, so I was pretty sure he dinna keep up with current events."

"TV and radio are like watching or listening to books or newspapers; well, kinda," I explained or rather reminded Jody and Wallace. "Sorry for the interruption. Please continue."

"So, I was hopin' my family wouldna be vulnerable to Sept or his cousins. I was pretty sure they never got any of the ransom notes. If they thought I was dead, they wouldna be scourin' the countryside lookin' for me. But, whether I was missin' or kidnapped, I still dinna want them askin' around about me. So, I had to make sure they believed I was deid."

"But, dinna ye ken the pain and anguish ye musta put yer parents through? They thought ye were deid? If ye let the ransom note get delivered to them, at least they coulda found out where ye were and got ye back. I'm sure yer father coulda found a way to pay the note." Jody was twitching with discomfort, identifying with his daughter and her family's pain at the loss of her only son.

"But, they were gonna to kill me as soon as they had the gold and gems. That's what he said, 'yer jest a way to get the treasure. When we have it, yer...' and then he," Benji took his index finger and mimed slitting his throat. "Ye'd be too much trouble to hang, and cuttin' yer throat is a bit messy, but weel make sure we're not wearin' our good clothes when we do it,' he said. And I dinna have a reason to doubt him. I'm pretty sure that if he or the others got close enough to my mother, they'd try to get her, too. They had this unnatural hatred of red heided people."

"Or jest my kin," Jody said. "Ye see, Sept, as ye call him, is Atholl Grant MacLeod the Seventh. His ancestor, Atholl the first or," Jody dipped his head as he said the name softly, "Captain Asshole," then returned to his normal stature and voice, "was a verra bad man. He tried to kill yer Grannie and Auntie Evie there and do even worse to yer cousin Jenny. And he did quite a few other bad deeds that we needna speak of. But, ye see, it was my testimony that got him sentenced to hang. As it turned out, he escaped and it was yer cousin James here who shot him, killed him, before he did harm to another of my family, yer," Jody closed his eyes and counted on his fingers, "Yer second cousin once removed or, weel, your mother's cousin's son. The lad Wee Ian is still alive because of James here and his fancy gun."

"So yer sayin' that these MacLeods I've been dealin' with since I was twelve years old were causing, are causing, will cause, problems because of what went on here, in what, 1782?" Benji asked in disbelief.

"Well, it actually started in 1781 when these guys were only about six weeks old," I said, pointing to the penned in trio plus one who were now asleep. "And I have the scar to prove that he tried to kill me. I mean the," I whispered the name, "Asshole," then resumed my normal voice tone, "shot me in cold blood. And he kicked your Grandpa in the head, threatened your Grannie with a knife, killed Jenny's biological brothers, and threatened even worse than that to poor Jenny herself..."

Jenny popped in, suddenly awake and involved in the conversation, "But Daddy whooped the tar out of him. And then he and Grandpa Jody made sure that after he was caught, he got a fair trial, huh, Daddy?"

"I thought you were asleep," Wallace said with a mix of embarrassment and agitation. He looked over at his nephew Benji and admitted, "I'm not proud of the, um, thrashing, but he had just shot, and I thought killed, Evie, my fiancée at the time. But it all turned out okay, right?" he asked Jenny.

Jenny nodded her head, sucked in and chewed on her bottom lip, but didn't say anything. I could see she was remembering her 'other brothers,' Clyde and Clayton, who Captain Asshole had killed. Rather than call attention to it, Wallace opened his arms and Jenny crawled right in—right where she belonged. She rubbed her head under her daddy's chin, then tipped her head back and gave him a kiss on the neck. "I sure love you, Daddy," she said, and nestled back into him, at peace again.

My quiet son-in-law James cleared his throat and looked around. It had quieted with Jenny's appearance, but it was obvious that he wanted to say something. "Yes?" Jody, Benji, and I asked at the same time.

"I think I should tell you, oh shoot, it doesn't really make a difference now, but," James looked over at Jenny and decided to continue the thought. "My father told me that *I* was the treasure; that the letters referring to a treasure were just to make sure that someone came back to save Ian Kincaid so that his heir, me, would be born." James finished his report with his eyes on Jenny, his future great-grandmother. She wasn't paying attention to what was being said, but was running her finger around the button on Wallace's shirt.

"But, but?" I asked as I saw him look at Jenny. *He shook his head quickly, and I took his cue to shut up. I'd probably, hopefully, hear about it later.*

"Weel, that's a relief, in a way. The treasure was a person, not gold or jewels. Hmm. It's a good thing they dinna ken. I dinna think they woulda been too pleased if ye were given up as the ransom," Benji joked, then slapped his knee. "If ye'll excuse me, I think I need to go see a man about a horse."

"A horse?" Jenny brightened up. "Are we getting a 'nother horse?"

Jody looked up at Benji, now standing in the doorway. Jody didn't say anything, but knew he was missing something.

"Um, I think he just wants to go make sure one didn't fall down the privy," I explained lamely, and then whispered to Jenny, "I think he needs to go pee."

"Oh," she said with a big round 'O' mouth, looked down in embarrassment, and hid in her daddy's chest.

"But, if I find a *'nother* horse wanderin' about, I'll make sure I give her to ye, okay?" Benji said to try and ease her embarrassment.

"Okay!" she said brightly and popped away from Wallace's pectoral comfort zone. "But if she's been down in the privy, I'd appreciate it if you washed her in the creek before giving her to me," she added, head nodding with excitement at the prospect of getting her own horse, even an imaginary one.

"Aye, I'll be sure to do it—that is if I find one...," he said with a grin and a nod in farewell as he headed to the wooden-seated personal comfort station.

31 He'll clean ye up

Jody remained mute as Benji finished the tale about his youth and how he had let—no, made sure—that his parents believed he was dead. He watched Sarah during Benji's revelation; he could see that she was as torn up inside as he was. He had to talk to him about it, but not in front of the others. An hour passed; "Let's walk," he said softly to his grandson, taking advantage of the break in the other family members' after dinner conversations with the garrulous and congenial fellow.

Benji was taken aback at the sudden change in tone of the party that his grandfather's request had caused. He looked over at Janie and saw that she, Evie, and Leah were all making a fuss over the cute, petite ribbon that Jenny had affixed in Bibby's hair, or lack of it. She had tied a bow and fastened it to the very top of the little girl's bald head with a dab of honey. Jenny was holding one-year-old Wren's hands, making sure the little big aunt didn't pull the blue adornment off of her niece's nearly fuzzless head. Wallace and James had gravitated to the window, both on them holding one of Wren's brothers. It appeared that they were discussing the next building they planned to construct; the movements of their arms and hands indicating roof slopes and intersecting room additions. The Pomeroy-Hart boys were enjoying the security of their man jungle gyms, climbing over their family's shoulders then retreating, batting at each other, slapping hands and giggling in glee. No, the general mood of the family wasn't dour; it was just his and his grandfather's.

The patriarch and his giant heir walked quietly onto the porch. Jody took a deep breath, turned and looked back into the house, and watched Sarah join the other women in their adoration of Bibby's hairless coif. She looked back and saw her husband, tried to smile at him, but only managed a half grimace. She knew he had a difficult discussion to undertake. If Benji were anything like Jody, convinced that what he had done was right, there would be loud words tossed around. Jody frowned back at her and realized that his persuasive conversation might wind up becoming a confrontation with loud, angry voices. Yes, he had better get further away from the rest of the family than the porch. This wasn't going to be easy. No doubt, an ego or two would be bruised.

"Let's check out the goats," Jody suggested, his hand heavy on Benji's shoulder to guide him. "Ye sure got big there, lad," he said as he patted him gently. Hopefully, these weren't the last kind words he'd share with him this evening.

"What? Ye dinna have that ornery old spotted sow anymore?" Benji asked in jest. He knew that when he was a child, Grandpa and Grannie had a huge sow that seemed to be indestructible. It wasn't what he wanted to talk about, but he was fairly sure that speaking of long dead pigs was better than discussing what he feared his grandfather had ushered him outside for.

"Why'd ye do it, lad?" Jody asked somberly.

"Come here?" Benji answered brightly, "To see ye and Grannie, and maybe even a few of those cousins of mine. I dinna ken if they'd be here or not. Last I heard, Angus and family were in New Bern. But, I was hopin' that maybe they took a bit of a vacation—that is a trip, out here to see ye and Grannie—and I'd get to see them, too. I decided to come even though I wasna verra sure of where to find ye, jest a general location," he joked then deadpanned, "North Carolina." He added a hearty laugh. "I had a bit of trouble findin' ye but..."

Benji finally stopped his inane banter. He thought it was a good ploy, but he knew Grandpa was a smart man and could see through anything, even if his chatter was only a dodge and meant to be transparent. "What do ye wish to speak of?" Benji asked soberly, hoping the words he would hear wouldn't hurt too much.

Jody tried to hold back his anger, but the passion was too strong to be held in check by reason. "Dinna ye ken that it jest about kilt yer parents to think ye deid?" he asked, his voice gruff and harsh, in spite of his effort at self-control.

"It was the only way to keep them safe!" Benji snapped back. "We were all a target, it wasn't jest me. I was jest the pawn to draw them out. If my folks had come forward with the ransom or The Letters, they'd be deid, jest as sure as ye and I are standin' here!"

"Dinna take too lightly yer mother and father and their skills," Jody argued. "I'm sure they'd find a way to get the Fool's Gold." Benji shook his head and Jody knew. "Ye never told anyone where the gold and jewels were, did ye?" he asked.

"Nae," Benji answered. "It's still there for what good it does anyone. But ye see, the MacLeods wanted me and my family

224

deid jest as much as they wanted the treasure. They were, are, vile, sharp, and resourceful."

"Aye, that may be, but I'd wager yer parents coulda found a way to turn over the kidnappers to the authorities. Kidnappin' is still against the law, aye?" Jody asked.

"Aye, but I dinna ken all the men involved. There were others Sept and his cousins spoke of. It was..."

"Letters?" Jody asked, suddenly realizing it wasn't just money and revenge the MacLeods were after. "What are these 'letters' ye and James and Leah have been talkin' about?"

"It seems they believed there was a map or directions to a treasure in the letters that were kept by our family. I think that James's family had valuable letters, too, because he was runnin' into the same problem as me. Maybe the MacLeods thought they were the same ones; I dinna ken and never cared to ask. I kent ye and Grannie wrote letters. They were, are, the biggest treasure of all fer my family. I remember waitin' fer Saturday nights. Da would bring out the box and we would all cuddle up on the couch and he'd read one. Or rather, he'd recite one. We had heard them all. Da and Mom used to read jest one a month, but after they'd been through them all the first time, it became a family tradition: sittin' on the couch with our cocoa or cider, listenin' to Da read the letters."

Benji grinned in recall. "I blushed every time he told about the antics ye recalled about me when I was a wee 'un. Aye, I turned red, but I was so happy that ye were so proud of me. I hope I havena disappointed ye with the deception I had to do. I really dinna do it to be mean, but to protect my family. Da and Mom could take care of themselves, but what if they went after wee Becky?" he asked, his eyes begging for forgiveness.

Jody didn't speak: he wasn't ready to pardon him for the deception, at least yet. There also seemed to be more that he wasn't being told.

Benji sighed deeply and spit it out. "I'm alive, but so are they because of what I did. Ye dinna ken that MacLeod family. They were, are, will be, insane. They'd never give up tryin' to find the treasure. That's reason enough to stay away from my family, but," he said sadly, shaking his head in self-disgust, "I canna go back—ever. I've disgraced them."

"How's that, lad?" Jody asked gently. This wasn't a simple case of telling his grandson to go back to his parents. Evidently, there was more involved in this, and his grandson needed counseling, not chastising. "Certainly there's nothin' so

225

horrid that yer family couldna forgive ye. I mean, ye havena kilt anyone who dinna deserve it, have ye?"

Benji's eyes widened in shock and distaste. "No!" he exclaimed, then slipped back into his morose mood. "It's worse than that and I dinna care to speak of it," he said with distaste. Benji realized as soon as the words were out of his mouth, how harshly he had spoken. "I'm sorry. That was rude and uncalled fer. Its jest, it...it...well, it's humiliatin' is what it is"

Jody shook his head. "That's what family is fer: to turn to when there's no one else. We're here to support ye, forgive ye if need be, but always accept ye jest as ye are, perfect or full of bad deeds in yer past."

"Well, can ye keep this to yerself? I mean, not even tell Grannie?" Benji asked softly. Maybe confessing to his grandfather would help at least a little.

Jody inhaled deeply. This was a big request. But whatever it was that Benji was going to tell him was so hideous—at least, to him—that he had let his family continue to believe he was dead rather than admit to it. "Okay, until ye tell Grannie yerself or tell me that I can tell her, I'll not share yer secret." Big commitments sometimes meant big sacrifices.

"Weel, ye've heard about movies from Grannie and Mom and...ye do ken what movies are, aye?"

Jody nodded. "A bit like a play, but also like a picture on the wall; it's a story told, but the picture moves and talks."

Benji nodded and bit his bottom lip. "Except sometimes they dinna tell a story, but jest show, um, private acts: like those that are enjoyed by a husband and a wife when they're alone and feelin' full of love and..." Benji looked at his grandfather to see if he knew what he was talking about.

"Ye mean performin' sexual intercourse?" Jody asked. If that wasn't what his grandson was talking about, he didn't want to know. Or maybe he did. The boy—man he reminded himself—was quite conflicted.

Benji nodded again, but didn't speak. Jody did, though. Now he was curious as well as shocked. "Do ye mean they have movin' pictures of people copulatin'?"

Benji kept nodding and was back to biting his lip again. He glanced up. "And I, I..."

"And ye watched them?" Jody asked, trying to help his grandson set the revelation free.

"That's not it," he said. He had watched some, but that wasn't his problem. Benji looked up, saw the confused look on his grandfather's face, and could tell the man wouldn't be able to figure it out without further explanation. The morals of the 18th century—at least as far his grandfather's life was concerned—evidently weren't as depraved as what he had lived with.

"So if ye dinna watch them, then..." Jody was truly was searching for words, but was clueless.

"I was *in* one," Benji blurted out, and then burst into tears. "I dinna want to be; refused them politely at first, but they wouldna hear anythin' of it. They did everythin' they could to get me to cooperate, offered me money and, and lots of other *stuff.*" Benji wiped the tears from his face with the back of his hand, omitting the part of the story where he was offered drugs and more sex for participating.

"They used a machine to render me unconscious. While I was down, they bound me with straps that cut into my wrists. They asked me again when I woke up. When I still refused, they whipped me 'til their arms wore out and, and," Benji sighed, not knowing how to explain a taser, then decided to bypass the instrument's details.

Benji straightened his back, hoping that the physical movement of trying to show some spine would actually help him relate his confession. He shook his head side to side and decided he would have to tell the story as a narrative and try to take his personal feelings out of the chronicle.

"They beat me with rubber hoses; soft sticks that wouldna leave bruises, but I still wouldna do it. So, they used a machine that paralyzed me so I couldna move, but was aware of everything bein' said and done around me. They took a handful of these pills..." Benji shook his head, trying to disassociate himself, but the disgust was creeping back in, backing up like vomit in his mouth. "They have these pills fer men that canna, canna get an erection." Benji glanced over at his grandfather to see if he understood. Jody frowned with uncertainty, so Benji elaborated with common dialog. "They have wee tablets that can make a man's cock hard, whether he wants it to be or nae." He grunted with disgust. "One pill is enough to, um, serve the purpose, but these men wanted to make sure I could, could *perform,* so crammed a whole fistful of these down my throat, nearly chokin' me to death in the process.

"Weel, the pills worked," Benji continued dejectedly. "Whether I felt kindly to the lass or nae dinna make a difference. But, I dinna want to do it and she was, weel, she dinna care about anythin'. It was like she was drunk, but without the slobberin'. They gave her bad drugs and had her wantin' more. She dinna ken right from wrong; just wanted more of the drugs. She'd agree to do anythin' to get what she needed—nae, not needed—wanted. She dinna need them, but thought she did."

Benji shook his head again. He had to continue what he had started, no matter how awkward or difficult it had become. "I told them again that I wouldna do it after I was recovered from the taser, that is the paralyzer, and my mouth would work again. Since they had either stripped or cut off all my clothes, they could see that the pills had, um, done their job, and even if I wasna willin', I was able. They even put a gun to my head, but I still wouldna do it.

"Ye see, I had…hmm, other incidents, encounters, whatever, in the past when I was younger, much younger, that made me decide to, to…" Benji blurted out with exasperation, "Well, anyway, I had vowed not to *be* with a woman unless I was marrit to her. I was gonna keep that vow, even if I had to die keepin' it. When they saw I was not to be persuaded with pain, or even my own death, they turned the gun, that is, the pistol, on the lass. If she saw it, she dinna realize what they meant to do, either because she thought it was part of the *movie* or because she was so drugged up."

Benji found the nerve to look into his grandfather's face. His grandfather wasn't judgmental in the least, but was stone-faced, waiting for his little four-year-old grandson in the grown up man's body to finish his horror story. Jody nodded his head and let him know that he could proceed with the tale: he was following the sequence of events and understood the strange words and concepts of the 21st century.

"Grandpa, it wasna jest the pistol. They had a whole box full of tools, a brace bit with electric power, punches, awls, hammers," Benji shook his head, beginning to feel light headed, but continuing the movement, just the same. The story was incredible to him, and he was there and knew it was true. "They were going to punch holes in her body, everywhere, until she was deid, and film it, that is, make a movie of it! They were gonna kill her a little bit at a time and make money from showin' it to other people if I dinna," Benji snorted, then said, "have relations with her."

"So ye saved her life doin' somethin' that was against yer wishes, yer vow?" Jody asked, although he knew that was what he had just heard.

"Aye," Benji said with closed eyes, relieved that he had been able to finish his confession.

"I gave up a part of me to keep yer Grannie safe, to save her life, and weel, keep other parts pure, before yer mother was born. Ye wouldna be in this room with me if I hadna done somethin' so vile and disgusting to me that it still makes me ill to think about it. But, no matter how horrid it was," Jody shuddered as he recalled being cut, beaten, and sodomized by two soldiers nearly forty years earlier, "I still have yer Grannie, four children, many, many grandchildren, and even a great-granddaughter, because of my sacrifice. It really isna my business, but the lass, was she harmed?"

"Nae, she was fine last I saw her. They tried to make her do more, um, sinful deeds in order to get the drugs. But I did a bit of an intervention there. Ye see, they dinna have that taser, the paralyzer, handy, and I broke the arm of the man who was gettin' ready to shoot the drugs into her body. Ye do ken what an injection is, aye?"

"Aye," Jody said, as he rolled his eyes. Sarah had given him injections on several different occasions in their life together. Even though each time was to save him from dying from either an infection or blood loss, he would chance recovering on his own rather than get another needle poked into him.

"I broke the man's wrist, the wrist of the man holdin' the drugs. I told him if I ever caught him givin' drugs to *anyone* ever again, I'd break his neck. Weel, I think he believed me. At least, I scared him so bad—or maybe it was from the pain of the broken arm—that he pissed himself. When he did that, I'm sure he lost the respect of his minions. I took the lass with me and left that place, his lackeys runnin' all over each other, tryin' to get away from me."

"The lass..." Jody prompted.

"I took care of her fer three days and made sure the drugs were out of her system. I told her to go home and get back to her family; that they would take care of her." Benji saw the look in Jody's eyes, the wide-eyed look that meant he was getting ready to tell him to do the same thing. "But, I agreed with her that family wasna always the best place to go, dependin' on the circumstances. So, I gave her a note to go see the constable in the next town over. He wouldna ken of her past with drugs or the other, um, stuff she'd been doin'. The police, as we call them, are pretty well connected. I mean, a police officer may not be able to help her, but he could contact an agency—that is a group of knowledgeable people—who *could* help her."

"Weel, at least it was one lass and not two men," Jody said flatly. He sighed deeply and saw that maybe it was time to share some of his pain. "Come here and let me hold ye like I did

229

when ye were a wee lad and scarrit of the thunder and lightnin'."
Jody reached over and Benji cuddled into his arms like their
sizes were of no importance because emotionally, they really
didn't matter.

Benji started sobbing into his grandfather's shoulder.
Jody kissed him on the top of the head and started his revelation.
"Believe it or not, I ken how it is because of the, um, sacrifices I
made, too. Ye made a gift of yer body, not to the man who made
the movin' picture, but to the lass who ye saved from the drugs
or bein' kilt or whatever. Ye see, I had to trade my body to save
yer grannie's, but I had to give it to two men. It was me or her,"
Jody shook his head and shuddered with recall. "But, she still
loved me and I'm grateful. It isna easy to give up that part of your
body under duress. It's supposed to be given in love, not taken
against yer will."

"How did ye get over it," Benji asked as he sat up, feeling
better for crying in Grandpa's arms like a young child.

"At first, it's minute by minute, then hour by hour until,
weel, until ye brought it up, I hadna thought of that, um, time fer
nearly a year. But, ye canna take yerself away from yer parents.
If ye have a way to get back to them, weel, I'll miss ye, we all will,
but..."

Jody was without words. He had lost Sarah for 20 years,
and then she had returned. It had been awkward at first. He
couldn't, hadn't dared, tell her what he had done while she was
gone. She found out about it, and then all hell broke loose. The
two of them got over it, but this wouldn't be the same for his
grandson. Benji was the man-child returning to his parents, the
prodigal son. And then he had the words to share.

"Ye do remember yer Bible, aye?" he asked.

Benji shrugged his shoulder. "There werena many
churches where I was, and I wasna allowed out by myself. After I
got away, I dinna feel worthy of being in the house of the Lord. I
do remember a lot from when I was younger, about what is right
and wrong, the Ten Commandments, and most of the Lord's
Prayer." He shook his head. "Nae, I havena seen a Bible since I
was at home and a lad."

"Two things I have to share with ye. Jesus said, 'Come to
Me as ye are.' That means even if ye have a lot of sin, come to
Him and He'll clean ye up. And ye need to read the story in the
Bible of the prodigal son. It's about a lad who leaves and, even
though he does some bad deeds, the father is glad to have him
back. He even kills the fatted calf and has a big party in the young
man's honor. Of course, the Bible says it better than I can. I have

a wee Bible I can give ye. It should fit in yer sporran and ye can read a bit every day. It will feed yer soul and, from what ye tell me, it's been starved fer quite a few years."

32 Don't Tell My Mother
August 26, 1782

"Do you ever reread the letters you've written to Mona and Gregg?" I asked. "I mean, I looked back at what I wrote last year and I sounded sappy, but I left it the way I had written it. I mean, those *were* my real feelings at the time..."

"I know what you mean, and that's why Jody and I agreed not to reread ours. Once they're folded and in the box, they're off limits. They belong to our heirs at that point, not us."

"So what are you going to say about Benji coming back?" *I had heard the raised voices the night before. You definitely didn't want to get between those two red headed giants when they disagreed. Theirs were the only two opinions that mattered, and arbitration or anyone else's suggestions weren't even a consideration.*

"I was *asked* not to say anything. Benji doesn't want Jody or me to write anything in our letters to his parents about him being here. I guess he's afraid that those MacLeods will get our letters and will use them against his mother. It doesn't make any sense to me. If I could just tell them that Benji was here, safe, and not to worry about him: that he was alive and didn't die in a smelter accident when he was just a child..." Sarah put her head in her hands and started sobbing. "I can't imagine the grief she must be going through; believing that her son is dead..."

"Sort of like when you thought that Jody had died in the war?" I asked. "You went on though, didn't you? You had to let it go, as best you could, and raise Mona, I mean rear Mona, to be a good person. You had a full life even, with his loss."

"No, I didn't," Sarah said with a heap of hostility in her voice.

I didn't take her attitude personally. I could tell she was reliving her past life, or bits of it, in the 20th century. I stayed mum, and let her continue.

"I never got over the loss of him, never felt complete again until I was back here, in his arms, in the 18th century. If I had found out earlier..."

"Well, what would you have done? Would you have left Mona with Fl.., with your first husband?"

I gulped as I realized that I knew the name of her first husband was Floyd—and for no known reason why. She had never mentioned his name that I was aware of. I only knew his name because I had read about him and her and everyone else in her family in Lisa Sinclaire's 'Lost' novels. I spoke quickly in what I hoped was a good cover story.

"Would you have come back, traveled through the stones with her as an infant or small child, and subject her to the intense pain?"

"Did I tell you how much it hurt?" Sarah asked. "And how did you know that I didn't find out about Jody until much later?"

"Shit, I mean, shoot, I don't know," I said then bent over to take the lid off the Dutch oven to check on the bread, hoping that I would be able to continue this line of conversation without revealing my inside source. I already knew more about her, Jody, and their personal *history* than I felt comfortable with. I wasn't lying when I said, 'I don't know'—I didn't remember which book it was in.

"Well, the pain was indescribably horrific, all three times, and I know it hurt Mona and Gregg the first time they came through; they told me. Since they went back the same way, through the stones, I think they had to endure it again. I'm just glad there are other ways—or at least one other way—to travel that doesn't cause you to feel like your liver is coming out your nose and your hipbones through your ears."

"And you did that *three* times?"

"The first time was an accident. The second time was for my unborn child, Mona, to make sure I had modern medical help for delivery. The last time was to come back to be with Jody. I could do it for love, but there is no way I would have done it for anything, even anyone, else."

"Well, *you* can't write about Benji, but have no fear, you have a sneaky sister. Let's just leave it at that, okay? I mean, I wouldn't want to tell you anything you would have to keep from Jody. You can keep your word that you won't write about Benji being here to his mother or father, okay? Now, the bread is ready, but the crock is empty. Would you go out to the springhouse and bring in some more butter and another wedge of cheese? Oh, and don't hurry," I added with a grin.

Sarah sniffed, wiped away her tears, and let a smile of hope escape. "Did I ever tell you that you were my favorite sister?"

"Nope, but if you're saying it now, back at ya, sis. Oh, and you might want to see if you can scare up a little jam, too." I looked up at the cupboard where Sarah kept her writing supplies and the dishes. "I'll set the table," I volunteered, "and do anything else that needs doing."

"I'd appreciate it. I'll be back in *a while*," she added with a nod and a wink, and took her leave, humming brightly as she closed the door behind her.

I opened up the cedar chest in the corner and pulled out my 21st century jacket from the back corner. I dug into the front pocket and found it: my ballpoint pen. I kept it stashed along with the zippered coat to keep questions from my middle daughter down to a minimum. Jenny was just a little too perceptive at times.

Writing with the ballpoint pen was faster by far than the dip, stroke, stroke, dip of the quill and inkwell. I absconded with a piece of Sarah's precious homemade paper—an odd shaped remnant of the batch of paper made by Mona when she lived here with her parents and Benji was a baby.

I hastily wrote out:

Mona, Gregg: Benji will disappear, but he's fine. He's here with his Grandpa and Grannie. Do NOT look for him or you will endanger him and yourselves. Take care of each other, Evie (your sister-in-law).

"There, that ought to do it," I said softly. I folded the note and stuffed it inside the second to the last epistle that Sarah and Jody had written. This way, the script wasn't obvious. The steady flow of ink made by the ball point pen made the format look glaringly different, but now it was enclosed inside another letter. If Jody did happen to go through the folded letters, he wouldn't see it. And, since Sarah said Jody didn't reread his letters, mine was as safe as if it was inside a double sealed envelope. Integrity is such a wonderful concept, and I hoped I wasn't compromising mine with the little deception. Nah, probably not, since I didn't feel guilty about it.

33 Bust of buddies

"Are you sure it's okay with James?" Jane asked cautiously.

Leah nodded her head and answered, "If Benji's chosen you, you're family. I mean, you are going to be married just as soon as Sarah or Jody or *someone* figures out how to do it legally, right?"

Jane felt her face warm suddenly with the glow of happiness, "Aye," she replied with a new emotion for her—family pride. "But, I hope it doesn't take too long. I'm sorry; I shouldn't have said that. What I mean is that you just met me and I haven't even spoken to your husband. Are you *sure* he won't mind?"

"Here, take Bibby Liz and we'll all go have a chat. If you don't feel like he wants you to keep our daughter for the night, to keep her here in the same house with her grandparents—which just happens to be a four minute run up the hill from her mother and father—*then* I'll cancel my much needed night's rest and, um, quality time..." Leah subconsciously twitched with anticipation, then shuddered as she quickly composed herself and continued, "With my husband, all right? Come on. Meet my husband, James Ignatius Melbourne, although I suggest you just call him James."

Leah handed her daughter over to her new kin. Bibby was all too eager to be held and reached out for Jane. Her infant eyesight wasn't the best, but this dark-skinned, milk-sweet smelling companion was welcome to hold her anytime. She wasn't hungry, but knew that dinner was close by when this warm person was holding her. She stuck her fist in front of her nose and sighed as she nestled into a comfortable position.

Jane followed obediently behind Leah, a little bashful at being given such a wonderful and honorific trust by these people she had just met. Family, she reminded herself. These people were her family of a different color, but still family. Leah looked back and gave her a 'look' to tell her to catch up with her. Jane nodded and widened her pace so she was walking beside her kin.

Family. Kin. How wonderful to have them she thought as the tears welled up. This moistness wasn't from grit or sawdust in her eyes, and there wasn't any pain or sadness involved. Happy tears: she'd never had them before that she could recall.

Yes, she had experienced many new wonderful emotions these past few days spent with Benji. These happy tears falling right now, the warm flush and joy of nursing a baby, and the other kind of joy—the wetness and tingling between her thighs when Benji kissed her all over. And she was going to having even more exciting feelings as soon as she and Benji could be married. A momentary fear stopped her smooth smile of peace. What if they couldn't be married and he couldn't *be* with her? She shook her head and put that horrible thought back in the dark place in her mind where she buried all of her other bad memories and fears. "Not today," she said softly to herself, "hopefully, not ever."

Ж

"Jane, this is my husband James. James, Jane," Leah said in an abbreviated introduction. "Jane has *volunteered*," Leah grinned and shot both of them a wink at the word, "to watch Bibby Liz for us so we can be alone tonight. Is it okay with you, dear?" Leah asked, her eyelashes fluttering away provocatively at her now wide-eyed mate.

"That would be awesome!" James exclaimed, suddenly embarrassed at how unguarded his response had been. "Janie, I, we, would both *verra* much appreciate it." James face suddenly fell as he remembered that Bibby would have to be nursed.

Leah had sensed his indecision based on their child's nutritional needs and answered his unspoken concern. "Between Mom and Sarah, there are plenty of wet nurses around," she said. "It's just you and me tonight, dear. Do you think we can manage?"

"Just you and me? I'll just time-trip back a year and remember how it used to be," he purred as he slid his hand around Leah's waist. "Just like the good old days. When do we start?"

34 A New Discovery

"Okay, let's play the 'what I miss most' game," Leah suggested as the moon peaked through the window.

"What I miss is not having to kill people," James said sourly. He saw Leah's face fall, then quickly amended his answer. "Other than friends and family I'll never see again, there's nothing I miss. I just wish there was a way to have everyone here at the same time. But, I want to stay here, now, even if I have to get rid of a mongrel every now and then to keep the rest of my family safe."

"It could have been just as bad in 2013," Leah suggested.

James snorted. "No, worse. The creeps would have had semi-automatic weapons and fast cars; drive-by shootings where I, we, couldn't protect ourselves."

"And they'd get off more than one shot..."

"Yeah, well I guess the odds were tipped in our favor there. I didn't have to shoot more than once, but it was a comfort to know that if several of them had started shooting, Wallace and I had enough rounds to take care of every one of them without having to stop and reload."

"Well, we're safe and healthy here," Leah sighed, "and mostly happy," she added with an eye roll, referring to the earlier deadly row. "You know I love you, dear, and I'd follow you to the ends of the earth."

"Well, I don't think you'll have to follow too far, sweetheart; I'm not planning on going anywhere, now or ever. And I don't even want to think about what kind of event or power could separate us." James sighed deeply. "I just hope the memory from today fades quickly."

"Do you think you'll ever get over it?" Leah asked cautiously as she snuggled into his chest.

James was trying to hide his uneasiness, but even if his wife wasn't psychic, she would have picked up on the flashes of terror that riddled his whole presence. He tried to keep a calm demeanor, but couldn't stop frowning. He tried to swallow the glowers as soon as he realized they were there, but they were dark and dirty and left a smear of a grimace on his face that wouldn't go away. No amount of soap or scrubbing could remove the memory of having to kill a man to save another. Only time and a bright, healthy life with a loving family could help it fade. And tonight he had his wife's attentions all to himself. Let the fading begin!

"I doubt that I'll ever forget, but Jody did say that this," James grabbed a handful of pubic mound and skirt and continued his report on suggested therapy to feel better, "was the best cure for me. But, do you think *you* can handle it? I mean, since we don't have Bibby Liz here tonight, I won't have competition, and you won't have distractions. I might just wear this beautiful, fuzzy field of pleasure down to a bald patch."

"Yes, and I might wear this," she grabbed a fistful of his man parts through his trousers and whispered, "down to a nubbin..."

The couple walked awkwardly toward their bed, both of them clutching the other in the lower regions. "Well, you may wear it down for a half hour at a time, but give it a break for another half hour or so, and we'll see. I'd like to see if we can set a personal best!"

Leah let loose and turned around to pull down the shade over the window. "I was going to do a little strip tease for you, but I hear voices over at Mom's. I think the men are taking a walk. At least Benji and Jody were. I don't want to perform for anyone but you, sweetheart."

"Well, go ahead and get started. I'll just have to watch the show in Braille," James said, as he unbuttoned his pants.

"Are you sure?" Leah asked as she worked her shoulders out of her shirt suggestively. "I mean, is there anything else I could do to make you feel better? I mean, to help you forget?"

Leah pushed her skirt down then looked over at her now naked husband in the dim glow of candlelight. She cleared her throat as inspiration hit. "Ahem, so you just took a long, hot bath," she said rather than asked and urged James over to the bed, gently shoving him so he fell backwards into its downy softness. She knew it to be true: he had told her when he apologized for using all of the hot water.

James wondered why she had asked for a whole second and a half. He didn't even have a chance to answer when he realized why she had made the comment. "Uh," he squealed when he felt her warm mouth on his semi-erect organ. "Uh, yeah, bath and, um, that'll definitely get the fire go, go, going," he stuttered as she nibbled in between kissing and licking.

James let Leah take him to the edge, then stopped her, putting his hand on her forehead, gently urging her away. "Now, you," he said.

Leah wiped her slobbery mouth and grinned. "Oh, no you don't. I didn't get a bath today and I stink."

"What, do you think I want to kiss and lick soap? No, seasoned Mama is just right, trust me. And if it isn't, you'll never know because I won't tell." He urged her to the top of the bed, grabbed a pillow, and placed it under her fanny. "Bottoms up!" he said, then made a comedic nosedive to her crotch.

Leah couldn't help but giggle at their antics, then a lightning flash of memory from the afternoon's horror burst in. She had peeked out at exactly the wrong time and seen James fire his pistol. Her eyes had zipped from the noise of the shot to the sound of impact, the young man's chest exploding as she watched, then back to see the white pallor of her husband's face. It was as if James's spirit had left his body because the trauma was too much for it. A brief split second later, his soul was back, but very contorted and malformed. Leah thrashed her head to move the images away; now was not the time. They both needed oblivion, not recall or reevaluation of the incident.

James nuzzled his nose where he hoped another part of his anatomy would be soon. For now, her scent was heavenly, although a bit sweeter than normal. He brought his right hand up and patted her swollen vulva. They hadn't been involved yet, but she was already puffy. He reached his hand to touch her dark, curly pubic hairs, pretending to play with them, but actually checking her in a clinical way. When she had first found out she was pregnant with Bibby, she had him feel the ever so gradual swelling of her uterus. He touched her pubic bone then slowly moved up toward her belly button, enjoying the sensation of her hair then her skin as he felt for the telltale firm womb under his fingers. Just as he had followed its increase in size along with her during her pregnancy, he had also been privy to feeling the womb shrink back to the new normal size during the few weeks after delivery. Leah was the nurse, not him, but she loved to share her knowledge. "After all, it's your body, too," she would tell him.

James brought his other hand around and stroked her belly as he moved his kissing upward toward her navel, crawling and kissing his way to her chest. "Mine for tonight?" he asked, although he knew they were. Evie and Sarah had volunteered to nurse Bibby so the two of them could be alone. He would have full access to her swollen breasts.

239

"I'm all yours, aft to stern, top to bottom, inside and out! Oh, my!" she exclaimed as he accepted the invitation boldly. "You do *not* feel like a baby when you do that!"

James was sure now. He had tasted Leah's milk before. No wonder their daughter was being fussy. Mommy's milk tasted 'thin,' almost watery, instead of the usual honey sweet sustenance. Her womb was growing again, and the entrance to it had changed, too. "I sure love you, woman," he said, and dove into a long, passionate, tongue thrusting kiss, clutching her to him as he rolled over so she was on top of him.

"Wow, what got into you?" Leah squeaked as she came up for air, "and is there any more?" she laughed.

The two of them shared the best kiss of the year, then progressed to what both of them hoped was the first of many finales for the evening. The joining felt almost like, no, better than the first time. The two of them now knew what each one liked; the little grabs and clutches that tonight were unrestricted by a baby in the bed or need for sleep. Even if the day had been long for both of them, they would be able to sleep late, assured that other family members would take care of their daughter and their critters. The two of them shared their moment of ecstasy and sighed in unison as they snuggled into each other's arms for a nap.

James woke with a start. "Again," he asked, although he already knew the answer: she had planted the question in his head.

"I thought you'd never ask." She grabbed him by the buttocks and pulled him on top of her. She didn't know when she'd get another unrestricted opportunity like this. She'd take him as many times as he'd let her. One more whoopee for both of them, then they could nap until sun up. Then they'd greet the day like they used to BB: before Bibby.

Ж

Wallace and I were lying in bed, looking up at the ceiling, silently reflecting on the day's events, but neither one of us wanting to talk about it yet. "I wonder what they're doing over there?" Wallace asked, a sly grin spreading across his face.

"Uh, I think you know what they're doing and I do, too. She is my daughter, you know," I reminded him with a chuckle. "Um, I mean, I don't know what I mean by that. Part of me doesn't want to know that she has sex, and part of me is proud that she is so, um, frisky." I said almost as a question.

"Oh, I'm sure James is glad that she's so, so healthy," Wallace said, not quite sure of what I meant when I said frisky.

240

"They're a happy couple, and I'm sure glad they decided to stay here. James is a bright young man."

Wallace and I both snorted a laugh when he said young. Chronologically, James was older than Wallace, although by the calendar, Wallace had him beat by well over 200 years. "He's brought with him so many new ideas and has the talent to take common, everyday items here and make them into time saving or comfort devices. I can't wait until we can fabricate and install a hot water heater here for us."

I leaned over and pulled my husband close to me, glad that we were safe. "I'm sure glad we all got through that mess this afternoon unscathed. And I, uh, think Leah might be pregnant again."

Wallace's eyes widened, asking a question that I didn't have his hoped for answer to. "But, I think she's the only one due next year," I added glumly.

"Well, we'll just see what we can do about that! This family never seems to have babies one at a time," Wallace said, and wiggled his belly against mine. "But, it might be easier on you if I only planted one seed. But, let's plant a lot, just in case, to make sure at least one finds fertile ground."

35 Getting reacquainted

Benji wrapped a thin strip of rag spirally around another long, thin piece of charred hardwood branch. He set it next to the others then took out his Leatherman and began sharpening the end of one of the charcoal sticks. He was making several of them for Jenny to use for her drawings.

"Did ye bring one of those knife tools along with ye?" Jody asked, although it was obvious that he had: it was in his hand and he was using it as he spoke.

"Nope," Benji said flatly, almost rudely. He looked up and saw his grandfather's shocked reaction. "I brought two of them," he said with a smile and handed the multi-tool he held to Jody. "I dinna ken what to get ye. I meant to bring ye a better gift, but this was all I could think of."

"This is a nice gift," Jody said as he turned the Leatherman over in his hand then pulled out the little pair of scissors. "A nice one, but not the best one ye could have brought." Jody kept his head down. He sighed deeply then looked Benji in the eye. "The best one was ye. Ye canna ken how much I've missed ye."

Benji sniffed in acknowledgment that he understood. His voice was stuck between his heart and his throat again, and he knew better than to try and use it. The squeaks that came out when he felt this way were embarrassing, even if he knew that his grandfather understood. He reached into his sporran and took out the second Leatherman, opened out the long blade, holding it up to the light to look for non-existent nicks or gouges so he could pause to compose himself. "Weel, if it's only half as much as I've missed ye, then I ken," he said and swallowed hard, glad that he was able to finish the compliment without breaking up.

Jody picked up one of the fabric covered charcoal sticks and joined in the pencil making. "Ye ken, I've been thinkin' about yer dilemma, with gettin' marrit to sweet Janie." He sighed in resignation. "But, bar movin' to another colony or to Indian country, I dinna see how it can be done. I mean, ye could stay here and we could maybe kidnap a priest and hold his feet to a fire until he promised to perform the ceremony..."

"It doesna have to be a priest. I mean, ye ken my father was a Protestant and it would be jest fine if it was a preacher. I dinna think it makes a difference to Janie. I never asked her preference, but I ken she believes in the Lord. Do ye ken of any Protestant ministers in the area?"

"Aye, but I dinna think it would make a difference. And then there's the other consideration. Is she a slave? I mean, if she's been freed, she has to be gone or she can be enslaved again by, weel, jest about anyone who lays claim to her."

"No, she's not free: I *own* her. I loaded some barrels in exchange fer her. I dinna mean to come here and be a slave owner but," Benji looked over at his mentor, "ye ken how it is when ye do somethin' that isna logical, but ye do it because ye ken here," he said as he patted his chest, "that it *is* the right thing to do?"

"Aye," Jody chuckled, "I've been in that position more times than I can count." He touched the thumb on his left hand to his fingers one at a time, then moved to his right hand and gave up his mock counting with a shrug. "And done deeds I kent werena in my best interest here," he said as he pointed to his right temple, "but couldna deny here," and pointed to his heart. "I would say that ye have the..." Jody shook his head as he tried to find the right word. "I dinna ken if it is a curse or a gift, but it's certainly a responsibility: to look after the needs of others."

"Weel, I dinna ken if its a hereditary trait or nae, but from what I recall of the tales my mother told me when I was younger, ye've been the leader and protector fer people since, weel, fer a long time."

"Aye, a verra long time. It may not be welcome—the burden that is—but I thank the Lord that He made me strong enough to take on the tasks," Jody said humbly.

"And seein' ye in action earlier, I'd say we were all blessed that ye arena bashful in standin' up to the greater numbers," Benji said.

Jody shrugged his shoulder, grinned modestly, and then tried to bring the conversation back to their original dilemma. "I think this one will be harder to sort out: how do we get ye and yer lass marrit?" He shook his head and said, "I'm sorry, son. I've talked to Mr. Morris, the former magistrate, and he said that a white man and a Negro canna be marrit, at least if they want to live here in North Carolina. Now, since ye have papers on her, he said that most people turn a blind eye to, um, relations between a master and a slave."

243

"Hmph!" Benji snorted loudly. He looked up and knew that he was just delivering the news; Grandpa didn't like what he was saying any more than he liked hearing it. Benji shut his eyes and shook his head, trying to rid himself of the image of being a slave master having *his way* with a slave, his beloved Janie.

He felt his grandfather's heavy hand on his shoulder. "I dinna think there's a way ye can stay here and be marrit to her. Maybe if ye moved to another colony or further west still... Or ye could live with the Indians. They dinna seem to care about the color of a person's skin as long as he's not stealin' his land or goods. But, I ken ye want to be marrit; I dinna ken where ye can do that, at least anywhere near here."

"What ye arena sayin' is louder than what ye are tellin' me. That I need to go back," Benji said glumly. He chuckled, "Aye, I need to go back to the future."

"I love ye nearly as much as I do yer grannie, but if what ye feel fer Janie is like what I feel fer yer grannie," Jody shook his head in amazement, "well, I'm glad I got to see ye again. I can take ye to The Trees yer talkin' about whenever yer ready. We had to go there to pick up Evie when she came back last year. Now, do ye still have yer coin?"

"Aye, I managed to keep it. I think if the two of us hold each other tight, it will work fer both of us. I ken there are a few more of those coins here in the family, but I'll not ask fer one fer her. If somethin' happened and James and Leah had to leave in a hurry, they'd need one fer wee Bibby. Aye, I'm glad I got to see ye and Grannie again, and meet my uncles, Evie, my cousins and weel, everyone here. And if I hadna come, I never would have met my Janie."

36 How auld are ye?

"How auld are ye, lad? Jody asked as he pushed the fresh pile of straw out of the wagon.

"Weel, I had to get used to a new birthdate, so April first, April Fool's Day, 1980 is on my driver's license, that's a certificate for operating... Anyway, I'm 34 years old. Why'd ye ask?"

"Accordin' to when ye were born, that is April first, 1767; ye should only be 15 years old. What happened to the other 19 years?"

"They werena verra pleasant so I erased them, scrubbed them from my life. Hmm, yer right, though. I never thought about that," Benji said, his jovial attitude suddenly becoming serious and concerned.

"I think I may have an explanation," James said, as he walked up to join the two. "Sorry, I couldn't help but overhear. You see, Leah and I came here using the movie of her mother as our focus. You do remember that little smartphone Evie had; the one you stuck in your sporran after the little red light came on?"

"Aye, and Leah said it made a movie of me and Sarah and Evie, and that ye saw what we looked like, and ye used it to concentrate on when ye came through The Trees with the wee Greek coin," Jody said to make sure that was what James was referring to.

"Yes," James said, "and it didn't make a difference what year it was, we were going to see her. And yes, we both consciously left out her pregnant condition as our focus. If we hadn't, we would have been here before the babies were born and she came to the hospital and saw Leah. But, I'm getting ahead of myself. We, at least I know I didn't, focus on a year; it was a person. The Trees are only part of the time ticket. Hmph. I've always heard that the brain, the mind, is a very powerful tool but that we don't know how to use it. Evidently, The Trees are an amplifier of sorts. I know they're on a magnetic ley line, too. Shoot, I don't need to know how it all works. I'm just glad that it wasn't painful and that we got here unscathed."

"Aye," Benji said, "and I used the same video, I mean movie, as my focus to get here to ye and Evie. I already ken what ye looked like. Actually, it was pretty scary; almost like lookin' in a mirror. But, if ye'd like, I can leave and come back in another 19 years?" Benji joked.

"Nae, ye have it wrong: ye'd have to come 19 years earlier from yer time to be here today at the age ye should be. But, I'm healthier now than then. And I rather like talkin' to an adult rather than a teenager, although I woulda urged ye to change a few decisions ye made," Jody said with eyes narrowed in mild admonishment. "Yer here now, but I'm afraid yer gonna have to go back. Yer sure ye want to do it tomorrow?" Jody asked, hoping that he'd visit longer.

"Aye, I canna think of a reason to stay another day in a time where she's a slave. I woulda been gone already, but I'm a bit selfish. I wanted to see ye and Grannie jest a little longer. And now I ken I have two uncles," Benji said, stopping his sentence in mid thought before he added, 'and I can tell my mother she has twin brothers.' Time traveling 232 years forward was a cinch: reconnecting with his parents wasn't going to be so easy.

37 Really Scarrit
18th and 21st centuries

"Hold onto my elbow with this hand and keep a grip on the coin with the other," Benji said as he patted her right hand. "This is where we'll walk through tomorrow morning. Remember to concentrate on the image of Billy. Do ye think ye have a good picture of him in yer heid?"

Jane nodded then looked over at him. "I'm a bit scarrit," she said in a Scots accent. "Would ye hold me one last time before we go?"

"Aye, ye were rememberin' me being scarrit in the tent, werena ye?" he asked.

"Aye," she nodded once and smiled nervously as she recalled, "but, I don't think you were as *scarrit* as I was that day. I didn't know *what* you were going to do to me after you found out I could understand English."

"Me? I thought *ye'd* want to stone me or burn me at the stake after tellin' ye that I was from yer future. I mean, dinna ye think I was a witch or somethin'?"

"No," she said as she shook her head slowly, "just a *verra* big fairy. But, whether you were a man or a fairy, I wouldn't have hurt you, even if you weren't my master. I, um, kinda liked you, um, from that first day when you did the loading for me, and gave me food and water."

"Weel, I'd like to think that ye'd do the same fer me if the situation was reversed," Benji said.

Jane didn't reply to his comment. He looked over to see if he had missed her reply or if she had only nodded an affirmation. But, she hadn't done either. He could tell by the puzzled look on her face that she didn't understand the concept. He reworded his statement, hoping for clarity. "If it was *me* who was the slave, and ye were the white man, then *ye* woulda helped me out." Jane still looked confused. "If ye saw another slave who needed food, drink, and a hand, ye'd help her or him if ye could."

"Of course," she answered, as if he had completely changed his assumption. Suddenly, she realized what he had suggested. "Oh, you mean, like you and I are the same?"

"We've both been slaves and we're both gonna be free as soon as we're through these trees. So, do ye think ye can handle it?" He grinned, turned toward her, and held her face in his hands.

"I learn pretty fast, or so I've been told. I think I can learn to be free. At least, I'd like to try." Jane's face fell suddenly. "You're not leaving me alone, are you? I mean, if I don't know what to do, you'll be there, right?"

"Jest try to get rid of me..." Benji kidded. Jane looked even more panicked at his joke. He held her close to comfort her, and explained, "One of the first things we're goin' to do is get married, legally, okay? That is, if ye still want me after ye see how fancy the world is in the 21st century. Ye may not want anythin' to do with me after ye see how many good lookin' men are out there; schools to go to, jobs to have..."

"Jest try and get rid of me," Jane replied dryly.

Benji burst out laughin', the tears of mirth rising in his eyes. "Weel, if there's nothin' else I've given ye, ye did get my sense of humor."

Ж

The next morning was chilly, the air calm. The ground was still damp from the brief summer rain that had fallen during the night. The combination of the cool, early false start at autumn and warm, damp soil had dressed their site in low, diaphanous fields of ground fog. Jane had been awake for at least an hour. She really didn't have any fond memories of her life, so leaving the 18th century was fine with her. Actually, other than Benji and his kin, the only pleasant recollections she had were incomplete, shattered images of her mama. She couldn't remember what her face looked like completely, just her sad eyes filled with hope that life would be better for her daughter than it had been for her. She couldn't remember her features, but she *could* still hear her voice in her head, "Don't be mean, don't let anyone make you mean," she said. "You're a smart, gentle person, so don't let any man or woman beat you into a stone.' Yes, Jane was sure that she wouldn't miss anything about this place except for Benji's family.

Benji stirred next to her. She instinctively moved in closer to him, enjoying the comfort of *spoonin'* as he called it. She felt his hand move from being draped over her waist to touching her gently on the shoulder, sliding his hand down her arm then over the outside line of her hip. "Are ye ready, Janie?" he asked softly.

She answered with a nod then turned toward him, "Verra much so."

"Me, too. Let's get on with it then."

The two of them continued their slow-paced walk even after the gentle breeze—a magnetic vortex James had theorized—had ceased. "We're here, I think." Benji reached across his chest and patted Jane's hand that had a vise grip on his arm.

"It doesn't look like we went anywhere except through the trees," she said, trying to hide the sound of disappointment. She saw Benji's distressed frown and quickly added, "And I concentrated on Billy, really, I did!"

"Weel, if ye did, and everything else was right, then we're here in the 21st century."

Jane suddenly dropped into a squatted position on the ground, covered her ears, and then ducked her whole head into her lap and knees, a low moan of fear escaping from her hunched over form.

"What's wrong?" Benji looked around for rattlesnakes, then he realized what it was. The noises of 21st century civilization—still familiar to him, but alien to her—were surrounding them. There was a highway nearby and, although it wasn't visible, the ascending and descending roars of the traffic probably sounded like a hoard of wild animals attacking then retreating then coming back again, constantly changing directions.

"It's okay, I promise," Benji said and reached for her hand to help her to her feet. "There's nothin' here, no person, no animal, no, no nothin'," he faltered, "that will harm ye while I'm here, okay?" He wanted to make sure she knew that she had her protector literally at hand. "I ken this world, remember? What yer afraid of is what ye dinna ken. Yer a smart woman; ye'll learn about this verra fast, I'm sure. Now, a great metal carriage without horses will come here to take us to where we'll be stayin'. I'm not sure where that will be, but I can jest about promise ye that the accommodations will be grander than anythin' either one of has seen in the last month." Benji swatted at a buzzing fly, "And a lot less buggy."

He reached into his sporran and took out the smartphone. "James said this would still work: somethin' about payin' fer lifetime phone service and a solar charger. Oh, here it is," he said, as he pointed with his index finger to the photo icon of Billy. "See, I jest touch this picture and *voila!*"

Benji held the phone to his ear, a fabricated smile of hope displayed for Jane's benefit. The phone started ringing and both his confidence level and the sincerity of the grin grew.

"James?" squeaked the voice on the other end of the line.

"Nae, its Benji. James let me have his phone. He stayed back with Grandpa and the others, but do ye think ye can come to The Trees? I need a ride. Oh, and make sure ye bring the truck. I brought a friend and I dinna think all three of us will fit in that sweet blue 'Vette of yers."

"Uh, okay. I mean, no, I mean...Oh, shit...I mean, shoot. I'll be there, but not in the truck, but I promise that the rig will be big enough to hold at least two people your size and me," Billy said, biting off the words, 'and anyone else I decide to bring along, like your son.'

38 Busted

It wasn't Billy's classic pickup truck that pulled in, but it was a Dodge. Benji held Janie close to him as they walked up to the golden chariot pulling in under the huge realty for sale billboard with the SOLD sign slapped across it. Billy stepped out of the Grand Caravan, leaving the driver's door open as he ran into Benji's one outstretched arm. "It looks like you found someone, eh?" Billy sang as he walked up to the newly arrived travelers.

"Aye, I did. Ye were right about waitin' on the Lord. I assure ye I wasna lookin', but when I saw her, it couldna been any plainer than, than that sign up there," Benji said as he pointed to the 8' tall letters S-O-L-D. "This is Jane, my fiancée. Janie, this is Billy, my friend, and as ye can probably see, Wee James's brother."

Jane nodded and squeaked, "Pleased to meet you," and dipped her head.

"Oh, no you don't, girlfriend," Billy teased as he grinned and shook his shoulders. "If you're his fiancée, then you're family. Gimme a hug, sweetie," Billy said, as he reached around the giantess's waist and gave her a 'welcome to the family' squeeze.

Jane didn't know what to do, but let him clutch her close, rocking her side to side with excitement in a familiarity that she wasn't used to nor expecting. He finally let go and said, "Now you, too," and reached around for a brother-in-law welcome back. "I never thought I'd see you again," he exclaimed, not even trying to contain his excitement. "So, you got to see Evie?" Billy turned to Jane and explained, "Evie is my brother's mother-in-law. I guess we're kin now, kind of..." Billy's jubilant enthusiasm suddenly slowed down. "Oh, and I'm a father now," he said with reserved pride and a wince. "We had a baby."

Benji looked up from his conversation and shared hug with Billy, and saw Jane walking toward the open door of the van. She wasn't the least bit intimidated by the metal goliath. She had heard the baby's cry and was climbing through the portal to the source of noise.

"She's really from the 18th century?" Billy asked softly.

Benji nodded and said, "She was a slave. I, um, bought her, sort of. At least I traded some hard labor fer her. That's why I came back. We couldna be man and wife back there. This was, is, the only place for us. And it looks like she's adaptin' pretty fast. I thought she'd be terrified of cars. She climbed right into the belly of the beast; or is this 'the Beastess?'" Benji asked jovially. Billy had called his Dodge truck 'the Beast.'

"It's just the family rig. I went ahead and sold the 'Vette. Peter fell in love with the Prius, so he's driving Leah's old car, but you knew that. This is big enough for the baby's car seat and all the diapers and formula he goes through. We take it on visits to the park, and we've even been camping with it twice already," Billy said, then asked nervously, "and are you sure she's okay in there? I mean, she's never even seen a car."

"Aye, but she *has* seen a baby. They must be fine since I canna hear either one of them cryin'," Benji joked, as they walked toward the van.

"Are you all right in there?" Billy asked, then pushed the button on his keyring to open up the side door.

Jane yelped, but didn't scream at the sudden noise and movement. "He's beautiful, but he was hungry," she said as she patted the baby's head, his face pressed to her chest.

"You can do that?" Billy and Benji chorused at the same time, both of their voices an octave higher than normal with the shock of seeing her nursing the baby.

"I mean, did you just have a baby?" Billy asked, his eyes wide with shock.

Benji added, "I dinna think ye could get milk all at once like that. I mean, I ken how it is with other mammals."

"My mother was the same way. They'd give her a baby to feed after the master's wife decided that it wasn't proper for her to put her breast in the baby's mouth. Her own baby!" she added with a scolding tone. "It took a day or two, but she got milk even though she hadn't had a baby since I was born."

"Yes," Billy said slowly, "but he seems to be getting sustenance and you two just met..."

Jane looked down at the baby's head, but didn't speak.

"Ahem, ahem," Benji cleared his throat. "I think I may have, how shall I say, primed her a bit in the past few days... I mean, I have a vow on my head and I canna, um, have relations until I'm marrit, but there are other things I'll allow myself to do," he said bashfully, then added a provocative double eyebrow pop at the end.

252

Jane didn't say a word, but looked up at Benji with a pained frown. "Is he hurtin' ye?" he asked. "I mean, Billy, did ye happen to bring a bottle fer the lad?"

Billy reached in the van and grabbed the diaper bag, pulling everything out of it, looking for the formula. "Shoot, no, I forgot. I just packed us up as fast as I could and got right out here."

"He isn't hurting me," Jane said softly. He wasn't causing her pain, but she was definitely feeling bad. She put her finger in between her nipple and the baby's mouth to break the suction, then lifted him up to be burped. Billy saw her exposed naked breast and turned back in embarrassment. Jane saw that her bareness made him uncomfortable. A slight smile crept onto her face as she covered up. She might just like this time where her body was her own...

"I said, what's his name?" Benji asked for the second time. Billy had returned to his uneasy posture. "And am I keepin' ye from yer work?"

"No, I mean his name is Billy Burke Melbourne, Jr. and you aren't keeping me from work. I'm on family leave for a year," he added with a sigh.

Jane looked at Billy, then Benji, then back at the baby who was now nursing on her other breast. Benji couldn't see why the mood was so dour, so ignored it and asked, "So where's Peter? Ye told me that *we* had a baby. Now, yer not gonna tell me that Peter birthed this here lad? I mean, medical science canna changed that much so soon!" he said brightly.

"No, no; Peter is now a manager and works out of town about two weeks out of four." Billy said somberly, then sighed and started again. "That's why I'm the stay at home parent. But Mom helps, too. We all live in the big house you helped build. She's doing fine, by the way—no more cancer. She may not have been able to be a fulltime mother, but she's definitely a hands-on Grandma!" Billy bragged, then took a deep breath and fell back into sad mode.

Benji finally asked, "Am I missin' somethin' here?" but got no reply. "Okay," he said in resignation and decided to change the subject. "So what do ye call this fine red heided lad: Billy Junior, Wee Billy, BB..." Benji trailed off in his suggestions, waiting for an answer.

Billy had never planned for this scenario. "I'm his father on the birth certificate, but I wasn't the biological, well, you know. We call him Mac after the, um," Billy faltered, then didn't say a word, but looked at the ground, kicking a stone in frustration at not being able to handle the situation.

"Sperm donor?" Benji asked, then laughed. No one else was laughing, though. He looked at Jane who looked back at him, then down at the baby who was now asleep on her chest.

"Oh, shit," Benji whispered. "Dinna tell me that it was MacKay..." he practically begged.

"She came to me with a note you had written a few months before. She needed help, but I wasn't going to give her what she was asking for!" Billy said sharply, referring to her wanting an abortion.

The worst was over, he hoped. Benji now knew he was a father. But one look at Jane's face, and Billy saw that there was much more to this. "You said that you and Jane couldn't, um, get together, um, well, hell! You said you wouldn't have sex with her because you had a vow on your head. So what was that all about? And just so you're clear on this," Billy said, his bashfulness suddenly overridden with indignity, "I'm not asking for me, but for her. She can see that he's your son, can't you?"

Jane bit her bottom lip and nodded.

Benji took a deep breath then snorted, frustrated, embarrassed, and exasperated, all at the same time. "Life is sometimes about sacrifices," he said cautiously, hoping he would be able to explain his side of the story so they'd understand. "I took a vow as a young man. I vowed that I wouldna have relations with a woman until I was marrit. And I meant to stand by it. I'd give up that special pleasure—well, save it—if He'd spare me. Now, ye see this?" Benji said, and raised his right pinkie finger with the tip at the first knuckle missing. "This was a small price to pay fer savin' a man's right hand. I was given a choice and took it. I had a rough life, but I always managed to get by with jest about everythin' intact," he held up and wiggled his pinkie again. "But I had to make a choice for Autumn. I couldna jest give up the end of a finger. The man who held her said that I had to have..." Benji shook his head, trying to erase the image of the scrawny, drugged out young girl and the box of weapons that was beside the film producer's desk. "I would have to have *sex* with her or she would be the star in a snuff film."

Benji turned to his fiancée. "Janie, remember I told ye about the movin' pictures they put together so other people can *see* stories. They call it a film or a movie, and they're of jest about everythin' there is in life: people, animals, goin' fishin', war, happy times, sad times... Weel, sometimes they make the pictures of people havin' relations, sexual intercourse. Now, I can see that bein' a source of entertainment if everybody's havin' a good time and doin' it of their own free will; then that might be fine. But, I dinna *want* to do it, and neither did the lass, not really. They were keepin' her, her, well, she had some bad medicine she was wantin', desirin', somethin' fierce. She'd do, did, anythin' to get it. But, I dinna want to do it! I let them beat me rather than break my vow. I wasna goin' to, to, weel, I jest refused to *do it*. They finally realized that I meant it. I guess the man's arm wore out before my back did. So, they had to find another way to get me to cooperate.

"They do some horrid things here, Janie; jest as bad as in yer time." Benji looked at Jane first then Billy, desperately trying to get them to understand, practically in tears as he told them, "They said that they were gonna *kill* her and film it, make a movie of it! He showed me the box of knives, hammers, screwdrivers, and power drills, tellin' me how they would poke her full of holes unless I... Well, ye get the idea."

Benji was finished with his story. Emotional fatigue had completely overwhelmed him, and tears were now dribbling down his cheeks. He looked up at both of them for forgiveness, "I dinna ken where to look, but I'm sure that somewhere in the Bible there's some sort of special dispensation fer breakin' a vow in order to save someone's life, isna there?"

Billy looked at him, a small smile of forgiveness and compassion overtaking his hard-featured scowl of anger and indignation. "I'm sure there is, and if there isn't, then we're just not looking hard enough. I mean, what that man meant for evil turned out for good. What you did for Autumn afterwards, keeping her from drugs, saved her. She stayed clean." Billy turned to Jane and said, "That means that she didn't need or want to use that bad medicine anymore. And she had a great, perfect pregnancy. But there were complications with the delivery, and she died the same day he was born. She did get to hold him, though. She even signed the birth certificate and gave him his name. He was only six hours old when she started bleeding real bad. They couldn't stop it and then," Billy gulped and started crying, his chest heaving as he sobbed, "then, then she was gone."

Benji approached Billy hesitantly and put his arm around the man's now shaking shoulders, pulling him close for an encouraging, brotherly hug. "I'm sorry fer yer loss, but happy fer yer gain. I mean, ye did get to keep the son, right?"

Billy sniffed back some tears and wiped his face with the shoulder of his shirt, keeping his face low. "I hope I do. I mean, I don't want to let him go, and I don't want to fight you for him. Legally, he's mine, but if you wanted to challenge it, you could request a blood test. Then there'd be the lawyers, and they'd want to know where you were for the last year and ..." Billy looked up to see if Benji realized how sincere he was about keeping his son, even if he was not his biologically.

"Can I be his godfather?" Benji asked as his reply to Billy's feared custody issue. "And I kinda like the nickname. Makes me proud, even if I dinna make him on purpose. Janie, are ye okay? I mean, when I said that we couldna, you ken, have relations, it wasna because it was ye. If we can get the paperwork done today, we can be marrit by tonight. That is, if ye still want me."

Jane nodded her head in acceptance of his proposal, but looked down at the sleeping baby, and then at Billy. "You give him milk out of a bottle? I mean, all the time?" she asked pensively.

"Well, these ducts won't work for that!" Billy said as he looked down at his own chest, puffing it out just a little. He saw the yearning look on her face, and toned the levity down a couple of notches to lighthearted. "Why, are you volunteering?" he asked hopefully. He really did care for Benji like a brother, and would love for him and his bride to stay with him and his little non-traditional family.

Jane looked at Benji for his okay before answering. Benji saw 'the look' of desire, but reticence to answer, her slave upbringing still undercutting her self-assurance about making a decision. "How much room do ye have left in that house ye share with Peter and yer mother? And do ye think ye have room fer a handyman and a wet nurse?"

39 A Great Day for a Wedding

"Here, let me put him in his car seat," Billy said to Jane as he reached in to take his son from her. She carefully unclenched the boy's fist from her sarong and let Billy have his child. "You go ahead and sit here and Benji, do you want to buckle her in and tell her a little about what to expect? I don't know what you've told her about cars and such."

"Weel, this here is a seat belt," Benji said, as he pulled the nylon strap across her chest and clicked it into the latch. "Ye see, these cars go so fast that if they happen to make a mistake or the car aheid of them stops too quickly, and there's..." Benji saw the terror flash in Jane's eyes. He changed his approach. "It's the law," he said simply. "And fer the bairns, it keeps them still. Is yer owie okay?" he asked, grinning as he adjusted the diagonal belt across her.

"Aye, it's fine," she answered. She paused for a moment then looked up. "How fast do we go?" she asked anxiously, suddenly remembering some of the stories Benji had told her about racing cars.

"Faster than a burp, but slower than a sneeze," he replied comically then issued a fake sneeze.

"Bless you," said Billy, happy that the mood had brightened. "And, after I get a few questions answered, I can make some phone calls, and we can get your wedding set up for this evening. Unless, of course, you want to have some, ahem, friends and family fly in from overseas..."

"Ye dinna call anyone, did ye?" Benji asked, his voice squeaking like a scared little boy. He realized the fear he had inadvertently shown and added with a stern bravado, "I mean, ye did say ye wouldna talk to anyone overseas, aye?"

"No, I told you I wouldn't, and I haven't. I just thought you might want to invite them to the biggest event of your life!" Billy said sternly, then literally bit his lip.

Billy huffed in resignation when Benji didn't reply. Not even the multiuse comment of 'hmph!' had boomed through the big man's angry chest.

Benji continued to stare straight ahead, obviously still irritated at the reference to a *verboten* subject. Billy tried again. He didn't want to anger his friend; it hadn't been his intent. "But

I understand completely if you want to have a small, *verra* private ceremony. I mean, it's just as legal, and whenever you decide to, to…" Billy stuttered.

'*Think fast man,*' *Billy scolded himself.* '*Sweet Janie speaks English and knows something is going on, but probably doesn't know he has a family, and he evidently doesn't want her to know, at least yet.*'

"Just let me know when you want to have a big reception. Peter and I had a small wedding, and James and Leah did, too. I guess you're right," he admitted sincerely, hoping his honest feelings were evident in his voice, "small weddings are better at keeping the stress down, aye?"

"Aye," Benji agreed flatly, hoping the subject was closed. He turned around and looked to see how Janie was reacting to the conversation. He groaned softly as he realized that he had forgotten to ask her for her opinion. "Did ye want a grand wedding, or will a small affair be okay with ye?" he asked gently.

Janie gazed at the little red headed baby who looked so much like the twins, Wee Julian and Raymond. She responded to his question with a shrug of her left, unrestricted by seatbelt, shoulder, and shook her head minimally, letting him know that she didn't care either way. She could feel the atmosphere of contention between Benji and his friend—kin she remembered—and she didn't want to add to it with how big or small she felt a wedding *affair* should be.

The sound of the engine starting caused her to twitch; she had successfully swallowed the yelp she had feared would escape. Her eyes opened wide with wonder at the smooth movement of the car over the ground, crunching the gravel noisily beneath them. This was nothing like a wagon ride. She turned her gaze away from the baby, looked out the window, and gasped. "How fast?" she asked again.

"Ye ken how long it took us to get from our *castle* by the river to my Granddad's place?" he asked. Janie nodded her head, focusing her eyes wide with awe on his face to keep from getting dizzy watching the trees whizzing past. "Weel, in this *automobile* we coulda made the trip in less than an hour."

Benji didn't think her eyes could have gotten any wider, but they did. "Of course, that would be if had paved roads. We also have other, um, *automobiles* in different configurations that can go over rough terrain."

Benji shifted in his seat, turning around as far as he could to face her. "Janie, I have lots to show ye, but I really would like to do it as yer husband. If we have a small ceremony, we can do it soon. I dinna want to wait fer ye to be my wife. I dinna want to chance ye changin' yer mind about me," he pled sincerely, then added a grin, hoping to get one from her in return.

"Jest try and get rid of me," she said, and relaxed, just a little, into the comfortable seat. "I'd stay with you, married or not, but I really would like to be *marrit*," a big grin appearing with the word marrit.

The baby nursing earlier was comforting, had felt great, but only reminded her that there were more pleasures she and Benji would be able to share: but only if they were legally married. "How long do we have to wait?" she asked timidly, hoping that she could be heard over the roar of the road moving away from under them.

Billy answered, "We'll be home—your new home, too—in about twenty minutes. I'll make a few calls, call in a few favors, get Mom to take you shopping for a dress, and send Benji to get something a little less ragged," he finished dryly, putting his finger through the hole in Benji's shirt sleeve. "Bullet?" he asked.

"Musket ball," Benji replied with a shrug. "No good guys were hurt. James is a good shot," he added, in a tone that said, 'Not now; I'll tell you about it later.'

"How are you doing back there, Janie?" Billy asked, then added. "It's okay if I call you Janie, isn't it?"

Jane nodded her head then realized that he couldn't see her. But he could; she looked up and saw his reflection smiling at her in the little mirror in the middle of the big window in front of him and Benji. "You just seem like a Janie to me—tough, but real sweet, too, aye?"

Jane blushed as Benji answered for her, "Aye, verra much aye," then reddened a bit himself as he realized that he was thinking of her sweet kisses. "How much longer?" he asked to change the subject and settle down the excitement that was starting to stir in his pants.

"Are we there yet? Are we there yet?" Billy chanted in a childlike voice. "Gee, Benji, I didn't think I'd hear that until Mac was bigger."

Billy squinted in emotional pain at the remark. He still wasn't sure that this was going to work, Benji the biological father so close to his son. Surely, there would be feelings that would start to grow, at least on Benji's part.

"Aye, he's sure to be a talker. I mean, it isna like ye arena. Lads do tend to take after their sires, aye?" Benji said, then patted Billy on the shoulder, letting him know with the words and the touch that he wasn't going to lay claim to the boy.

Billy sniffed back the tears of relief at the acknowledgment. "Aye," he replied sweetly, "but they're also influenced by friends," he added, and patted Benji on the thigh.

"Friends fer life and more," Benji said, as he put his large hand on top of Billy's. "If I'm his godfather, then that means yer my godbrother, if there is such a title. I'll be there fer anythin' ye need, but I willna take him from ye, I promise. He's *yer* son."

Billy sniffed again, nodded in appreciation, swallowed the lump in his throat, and then found the profound words to wrap up the awkward conversation, boldly proclaiming as he pulled into the driveway, "We're home!"

"Looks like that lawn finally filled in," Benji said, his voice cracking slightly as he tried to override the tears he had just gulped. He wasn't sure if they were tears of joy from the cataclysmic discovery that he had a child, or sadness at the sudden, abysmal loss of him, his firstborn child, just a few seconds later. He exited the car, pushing down the sweet and bitter bile gurgling in his throat, and concentrated on getting Jane extracted from her mysteriously twisted seatbelt. Yes, he had missed the first few months of his biological son's life, but he would be there for him as a godfather. And, God willing, he'd be there for the births of the many children he and Janie would have together.

"Are you sure you're okay?" Billy asked, as he shifted Mac to his other hip, allowing his free arm to gently guide Benji's open side toward the house, not that he needed the help.

Benji clutched Janie tighter to him with his other arm and planted a firm kiss on the side of her brow. "Of course, I am; I'm getting' marrit today!" he crowed, realizing halfway through the feigned glee that it had become genuine. "Will ye be my best man?" he asked Billy. "I mean, ye are my brother now, aye?"

"Aye," Billy replied brightly. "And, if you care to get acquainted with your godson, I'll just slip inside and make a few phone calls. You know where everything is. Just go ahead and take the guest room and get your bags..." Billy paused in his banter and took a step back, looking anew at Benji and his fiancée. "You don't have anything to unpack, do you?"

"Not unless ye want us to run around in our birthday suits," Benji joked. He glanced over at Jane and saw the confused look on her face. "Birthday suits are what yer born with: no clothes. I dinna think he wants us to take our leave naked," he whispered.

"No," Jane said, as she shook her head. "This may not be much, but I think I like wearing clothes now."

Jane smiled sweetly at Billy when she noticed that what she had said, didn't make any sense to him. "Benji made this for me," she said, and fingered the edge of her blue calico drape. "The," she groaned the word, "*master* I had before Benji didn't think I deserved to wear clothes. He thought I should earn them. However," she took a deep cleansing breath and divulged reluctantly, "I wouldn't do what he wanted me to do, so I decided I'd rather run around in nothing but a scrap of leather than..."

Billy held his hand up with the gesture to stop. "I get it. However, I think you deserve a proper wedding dress. White maybe?"

Jane inhaled as if to speak, but didn't know what to say. "Of course," Benji answered for her. "She's pure and earned it. Now, wasna there a women's side to that big and tall clothin' store that ye took me to?"

"Yes, and as soon as my dear mother gets back from the hospital, I'll have her escort Miss Janie to the boutique."

"Bibb is okay, isna she? I mean, ye said there was no more cancer..." Benji asked fearfully.

"Oh, she's fine. She just went to check on one of our girls. April went into preterm labor, so they put her on some sort of drip..."

Billy realized that Jane didn't know what he was talking about. "Janie, my mother, Bibb—you'll meet her when she gets back—has a home here for women who are pregnant and don't, um, have a man or a family to take care of them." Billy bit his lip as he thought about whether to tell her that this place was a safe and sane alternative to women getting abortions. He shook his head, realizing that she didn't need to know about the culturally accepted, but hideous practice of birth control. "So, we become our own family here. April, one of my sisters as I call them, started to have her baby early. We now have medicines, good medicines, that can get *dripped* into the woman's body so the baby can stay inside of the mother and grow until he or she is big enough to be born."

Billy didn't have to ask if she understood: he could tell she did. "When the bedrest doesn't work, you have special teas that help the womb be still?" she asked to make sure she did understand.

"Exactly! Now Benji, are you familiar with modern diapers?" Billy asked, as he showed Benji into the brightly painted nursery, the walls covered with photographs of lions, elephants, and other wild critters alongside their pastel animated characterizations. "Oh, and here are the wipes and the trash. Now, I really do have to make those phone calls or you'll have to wait another day."

Benji took his non-baby laden hand and comically shoved Billy out the door. "If I canna figure it out, Janie can. Now out, out!"

"Wait! I need Janie for just a minute, and then she'll be right back. Come on, dear. Let's go to my office," Billy said, his arm out to accept hers.

Jane looked shyly at Billy, then grinned at Benji, and put her hand on his chatty new brother's arm. She wasn't used to touching people, but he was family, just like James and Leah, Jody and Sarah, Evie, Wallace, Jenny, and all those babies. She would be happy to have more kin.

Jane walked arm in arm with Billy down the hall to his wood paneled office, the walls adorned with a series of strange, colorful pictures. Billy saw her confused look. "Those are ultrasound pictures of Mac before he was born. They can take pictures of the babies, even before they come out, now. And that's his birth mother, Autumn. She was a wonderful person, my first sister." Billy sniffed back the unexpected tears. "She would have stayed with us here to help the other sisters if she had lived. She liked Benji, but she wasn't his fiancée or girlfriend. She was just someone whose life he saved by giving his body. But Janie, he didn't give her his soul. I can tell by the look in his eyes when he sees you that you're the only one he wants. And, from what I know of him from when he was here before, there has *never* been anyone else in his life. You, my dear, are getting a pure man. He deserves to wear white at his wedding, too."

"Yes, I'm glad he saved her," Jane said sincerely. "and I'm glad she gave you her child, but I'm confused. Benji said something about a Peter and having a baby and..." She didn't know how to finish her question, but by the uneasy look on Billy's face, he understood.

He shrugged his shoulders, both of them this time, and explained as simply as he could. "God made us all different, inside and out. He made you black on the outside and me gay on the inside. Benji likes you because you're a woman. You like him because he's a man. I don't like women *that way*, but I do like men, one in particular. Peter is my husband, although we call it 'partner for life' in some areas of this country. Just like people didn't think you were a complete, normal human being worthy of being married in your time, I've had the same problem here because I'm not the same as some of the people who make, or made, the laws. There are bigots still, Janie, it's just they hide behind their holy books and old ways. They say that Peter and I are less than they are, that we're sick," Billy added a circular finger movement around his ear indicating 'cuckoo,' "but I'm just the same as you and Benji and everyone else.

"It's getting better all the time, though. Janie, some people may still shun you or be rude to you because of your dark skin color, but you can walk into any restaurant—that's a tavern—in this town, and they'll serve you food just like a white person. It took a long time for that to change. It was only fifty years or so ago that a few black men sat at a lunch counter, tavern, right here in Greensboro, refusing to leave until they were served a meal. They were brave men and won the right to eat alongside of white folks and did it without anyone being hurt, without wars or lynching or... Janie, you're free here in this time. Both you and I are still going to have to deal with mean people who think they're better than you and me because we're not the same as them, but we really are."

"You mean we're the same, but different?"

"We're all people, and we're all different, but God made us that way on purpose. He does *not* make mistakes. He wants us all to get along. So, sometimes we have to put up with the rudeness, cruel words, and hopefully nothing else, but we can't let it make us mean."

Jane nodded then her tears started to fall. "I know; that's what my mama told me: You have a kind heart; don't let them make you mean." Jane wiped her tears on the back of her hand and asked, "Does this mean that you're my brother now?"

"Real soon, sweetie, real soon. Now, where were you born?" he asked.

"Africa, I think," she replied uncertainly, "but I don't know where. Benji said it's a big place."

"Yes, it is, but no worries. Okay, when," he shook his head, realizing that a birth year would be of no use. He couldn't write down a year like 1762. "Um, do you know how old you are?"

"No, but I've, um, been a woman for," Jane tapped her fingers on her thumb on one hand and then started on the other, "for nine years."

"Cool; that means you're about twenty years old, or close enough. Do you know what season, I mean was it summer or winter or..." Billy saw the confused look on her face turn into embarrassment. "How about a springtime birthday, say April 25th, and 1983?"

Jane looked back and forth. "Um, what year is it now?" she asked innocently.

"Twenty thirteen, that is, the year of our Lord two thousand and thirteen… Oh, shit, sit down!" he ordered when he saw her reel. He pushed the spare chair toward her. "Put your head between your knees and good girl," he said; she knew what to do.

Jane composed herself, took a deep breath, and then sat up cautiously. "I never thought about the number of the year before. I was just going forward in time to a good life, where the color of my skin didn't matter, and Benji and I could get married. I, I'm sorry."

"Well, I think I have enough information to get you some documentation. I already know about Benji. You see, he was born in the 18th century, too, and I had to help him get both a driver's and a contractor's license when he was here last year. Hey, I'll bet you're hungry. There's a basket of fruit on the table to tide you over until I can make a proper meal. Just give me twenty minutes in here, a half hour, tops."

Benji and his little charge arrived at Billy's doorway just as Jane was ready to leave. "Hungry?" he asked, ready to lead her to the kitchen. He had heard about the snack bowl offer. "We have a few fruits here that I dinna think ye've ever tasted. How about ye, little man," he asked baby Mac. "Are ye old enough fer fruit?"

"You can mash some banana for him," Billy hollered, as he stuck his head out the door, "Oh, sorry about that, mate," he said to the man on the phone. "I just got a new babysitter, and he doesn't know what Mac can eat. Now, remember when…"

"It looks like Billy is workin' on yer papers," Benji said.

"Papers?" Jane squeaked, too horrified to say any more.

"Oh, no, no, no, NO!" Benji exclaimed. "Not ownership papers: a birth certificate so we can wed. I ken it seems crazy," he said, as he rolled his head around, eliciting a giggle from both Mac and Janie, "but they want a paper sayin' that yer alive. I mean, I suppose they have their reasons, but it's obvious that yer not a child and are old enough to wed. Yer sure big enough," he joked, happy to hear her laugh again. "Lord, I dinna think I'll ever tire of hearin' ye happy," he said as he placed his free hand on her cheek.

"Well, as long as you're nearby, I'm sure I'll be happy and stay happy. Now, what's this?" Jane asked, pointing at, but afraid to touch the yellow claw-like configuration in the middle of the wooden bowl.

"Bananas: they're good fer ye and good tastin', too. Here, take," Benji inhaled deeply as he voiced the baby boy's name for the first time, "Mac," then continued, "and I'll get a bowl and some eatin' utensils."

Jane sat down with Mac. Benji brought the dinnerware to the table, pulled off a banana, showed it to her, and then waved it in front of the boy's face, laughing with the child as he grabbed at the elusive golden fare. "Ye like these, aye?"

Mac answered with more giggles, hand waving, and straining against Jane's arms, his tiny fingers reaching for the food.

"Ye see, this is how yer supposed to peel a banana," Benji said, as he illustrated the task. "Ye pull it apart here, not where it was attached to at the bunch. At least, that's how my monkey friend showed me. Ooh, ooh, aah, ahh." Benji added a monkey face and scratching under his armpits to his ape impersonation, and they all giggled and chortled.

"Janie, I really dinna plan on havin' a baby first," he apologized, suddenly somber, "but I couldna give up the chance to be in his life now that I've met him. I hope ye dinna mind…"

"Jest try and take him away from me," she said with a smile. She put both arms around her charge and rocked him back and forth, and placed a kiss on the top of his fuzzy head. "From what Evie said, this will be the only way we'll get a blue-eyed, red headed child. Godson," she asked, "what *is* a godson?"

"It means I'll be there to take care of him should anything go wrong with his parents, and even if they're still alive and healthy, I'll be a part of his family. Almost like a…a…a," Benji struggled for a word or description. He didn't know if she knew the word 'substitute,' and didn't want to embarrass her if she didn't.

"Like your grandfather? He wasn't your father, but you still loved him, and he was special to you." Jane broke off a piece of the banana, took the fork from the table and mashed the pale fruit into the bowl, smiling sheepishly when she saw that she had found the right analogy. Benji was speechless, but nodded his head in agreement.

"Here you go, Mac; try this," she said, offering the mashed fruit.

"Now you," Benji said. He held the peeled banana near her face, offering her a taste. "A kinder, more gentle and forgiving woman I've never met." He snorted and said, "And I had to travel 230 years and fight a dozen men to get ye! But, ye were worth it. I hope I never disappoint ye again."

Any more mushy talk was interrupted by a clamoring at the front door. It sounded as if someone couldn't quite get the door open. Benji bounced up and opened it, then grabbed the cloth bag of groceries as it fell out of Bibb's overloaded arms.

"Benji!" she squealed. She dropped the rest of her bags and grabbed him around the waist. She backed away and scolded mockingly, "Come down here for a proper hug, you big galoot."

Benji squatted down, let her wrap her arms around his neck, and then stood up and spun her around, eliciting childlike giggles out of the gray-haired lady. Mac heard his grandmother laughing and joined the chorus, shrieking with excitement. Jane stood up and walked into the living room to bring the boy to the reunion, but stood against the wall, still unsure of what was happening.

Benji spied the pair by the doorway and stopped the grandma carousel, setting the ecstatic lady down, but not letting go of her until he was sure she was steady on her feet. "Bibb, this is my fiancée, Jane. Janie, this is Billy and Wee James's mother, Bibb."

"Fiancée?" Bibb squeaked, "You found someone in the 18th century to marry?" she asked, and then realized she wasn't being guarded about the time frame. "Well, she knows when she's from, and if she's made it this far, I'm sure she'll be fine."

Bibb looked back and forth from Benji to Jane, then realized that Jane was holding Benji's biological son. She didn't have to ask with her lips—the question was on her face.

Benji lowered his eyes in shame, and this time it was Jane to the rescue. "Billy asked if we would stay on here to help with the building and, um, taking care of Benji's *godson*. It's fine with us, but we want to make sure it's agreeable to you, too."

"Of course, it is, sweetie," Bibb said, then scurried over to hug both Jane and Mac. "And you sure got a tall one," she called back to Benji as she hugged the odd couple. "And a pretty one, too," she said softly to Jane alone.

"Mom! You're back!" Billy said, as he came into the room. "And you've met the happy couple... I know you just got home, but after freshening up a bit and getting a bite to eat, would you take Janie here shopping? She needs a wedding dress and a...a..." Billy shook his head as he remembered his mother knew what was going on. "Both she and Benji need clothes. All they have are the clothes on their backs. Now, I'll stay here and make the rest of the arrangements for the ceremony. By the way, they're getting married here tonight. I'll keep Mac while you do the shopping. Benji can pick out his own clothes, but Janie needs a personal dresser. I can't do it since I have a full agenda with getting a birth certificate, a wedding license, arranging for…well, everything else." Billy paused before continuing, holding up one finger, as if he had just had a brain storm and needed to sort something out.

"I picked you two up, at, um," Billy looked down at his watch and asked, "what? eight-thirty?"

Benji looked at Jane. They both had a blank look on their face. They didn't know, and neither of them paid attention to clocks or hours of the day.

"Fine; I'll just say Janie first became *acquainted* with Mac at eight-thirty. So, Mom, try and be back by eleven-thirty…" Billy saw the look on her face, then grinned his all-knowing smile. "Mac wants her back for lunch. You can finish your shopping after that." Billy added a double eyebrow pop and smile to Jane, but didn't elaborate to his mother about Jane's new status as his son's wet nurse. For right now, it was on a need to know basis.

"Oh, and here," Billy said as he handed an envelope to Benji. "Mom will treat for the wedding dress and trousseau, but I'm sponsoring the groom. You might want to buy a few work shirts and jeans while you're at it. After your honeymoon, I'll let you get started on phase two of *Bibb's Place*: parenting, and nutrition. Here," Billy said, as he grabbed a plastic bag out of the cupboard, "have some beef jerky for the road. We can eat a real meal later. Eleven-thirty, right Mom?"

Bibb took out her smartphone and did a couple of slides and taps. "The alarm is set. Here, give me a couple of those granola bars. I don't need to be tearing out any crowns with that stuff. Come on you two. We'll let Billy work his magic while you two freshen up. It looks like you brought most of the dusty road home with you."

Ж

As soon as the three were out the door, Billy was back on the phone, watching Mac chew on his set of colorful plastic keys, bouncing up and down in his doughnut shaped scooter/walker. "Michael, Michael Callahan? Yes, you don't know me, but we have a friend in common: Benji MacKay. Yes, yes, he's doing fine. As a matter of fact, he's getting married tonight. Well, I'm kind of his brother now, and he asked me to keep the wedding small. I'm not supposed to invite anyone to the ceremony, but I have a free hand in getting everything else set up. Yes, that's why I'm calling; I need a hair stylist. Hmm, maybe for him, but definitely for his fiancée. Oh, and feel free to bring your family with you. Here's the address…

"Forever Flowers? Yes, how many roses do you have? Hmm, I guess we'll need to bring other varieties into play here, too. How fast can you set up a wedding? It's a smallish room— twenty by thirty—but there will only be, say, ten people in the wedding party. Give it your best shot. Is Steve still the owner? Good. Make sure you tell him that this is for Billy Burke. Yeah, well, I'm glad to hear it. I hope everything works out for them. Make sure you're here by six and done by seven. Okay. Hey, do you know a baker who can put together a five star cake by the same time? Really? He's doing that now? And catering, too? Do you have his number? Great, thanks.

"Carlos the caterer, how the hell are you? What, you can't tell? This is Billy, Billy Burke. See, I told you you'd like that job. And none of the old family found you there, right? Well, they won't be looking in this circle now that you're out. Hey, my godbrother is getting married tonight. I know it's pretty short notice, but could you do a special dinner for say, ten people? The ceremony is at seven and should be over by seven fifteen. Yes, you and your partner can come. I understand, and I doubt the bride and groom care if they know you or not. I know, I know; weddings are special, and there just aren't enough of them anymore. Hey, do you know anyone who takes pictures? He does? Well, ain't that somethin'? See, he was already invited, and now he has another reason to be here. Hopefully, he won't let the crying get in the way of getting some great shots. Oh, but the bride is a little bashful, so if I ask him to stop, he won't get offended, will he? Great. Being sensitive is so underrated. Okay, see you about six so you can set up. Bye, now.

"Let's see, Mac," Billy said, seeking counseling from his five-month-old son, "we got the dress, caterer, photos, flowers, and cake taken care of. What else is there? You're right, the honeymoon! Do you think they'll want to stay downtown or take a cruise?" Mac babbled in response then bent to chew on his keys again. "Right, they'll want to stay close to home. Okay, let's go fix up the crafts room again. You can help me put everything back in the totes. Again. I don't know why Mom thinks she can ever do any of that beading or whatever..."

40 Showertime

"Um, before we leave, I'd like to use the privy, and at least wash my face," Jane asked Benji shyly. She had seen trees outside, but hadn't noticed an outhouse.

Benji snorted and chuckled briefly, then answered, "Oh, darlin', ye have no idea what awaits you. Bibb, do ye have a big bed sheet or long length of fabric we can use for another sarong for my Dorothy Lamour here? I think we both need a quick shower before gracin' the stores with our *eau d' road* aroma."

Bibb grinned as she realized what Benji was up to: introducing his fiancée to modern day plumbing and a shower. "Use my bathroom and I'll set out something for her. I have an old pair of coveralls you left here you can wear shopping. I think you'll have to go shirtless unless I can find an oversized t-shirt in the girls' clothes. One of my ladies was big to start with and insisted on wearing men's t-shirts for comfort. Take as much time as you need, but try and keep it under an hour. The hot water heater only has a sixty-five gallon tank."

Benji dipped his head, said thanks to Bibb, and then held out his arm to Jane. "This is probably the best part of modern times," he crowed, "and what I missed the most: inside plumbing."

Benji led the way to Bibb's room. He knew his way around; he had built and helped design the house himself. He had talked Bibb into putting in the fanciest Jacuzzi tub and shower combination available, embellishing the stock design with twin shower heads and ports for air-drying the bather with warm, forced air.

"Now, here is the privy. We call it the toilet or john or potty or crapper or..." Benji saw the wide-eyed look and realized he was giving too many names to the simple, human waste conveyance. "Potty will work; everyone kens what a potty is. So, ye jest sit on here, do yer business, and when yer done, wipe yer, um, weel, whatever needs wipin', ye wipe with this." He pulled out the leading edge on the roll of toilet paper. "Ye just pull out as much as ye need, tear it off, wipe, and put it in the commode, I mean the potty, and then push down this handle."

Benji tore off a foot-long length of tissue, dropped it in the toilet bowl, and flushed. Jane's head popped back in shock at the sudden rush of fresh water into the standing bowl of water, and then its rapid disappearance. "It washes yer waste out to either a holdin' tank or to a main tank in the city. We have a septic system—that is a private holdin' tank. The wastes get pumped out once or twice a year and taken away so it can get cleaned up and used, I mean, they do somethin' with it. All ye have to do is flush; someone else down the line will take care of the wastewater. I'll wait out here and when yer done, come out and I'll show ye the shower."

Benji closed the door then ran down the hall, used the other toilet, and was back just a little too late: Jane was already standing outside the bathroom door with a confused look on her face. "Everything came out okay, dinna it? I mean, ye figured it out, dinna ye?" Benji asked.

"Aye, it's just that it seems like such a waste. And how does paper get so soft? Do all people wipe their bottoms with soft paper, or are Bibb and Billy so rich that they can afford to use it instead of leaves or cobs?"

Benji grinned and held back the laugh that most likely would have embarrassed his naïve young fiancée. "Even the poorest of people here have toilet paper, although there are still many who use the old-fashioned outside privies. But, those people usually live in very remote areas. Towns and cities tend to keep the plumbin' inside. Now, are ye ready fer a shower? I'd introduce ye to the Jacuzzi, but we're in a bit of a hurry. I wouldna want ye to rush *that* experience."

"Shower, like in rain shower?" Jane knew they were getting cleaned up to go shopping, but it wasn't cloudy and didn't look like it was going to rain.

"Aye, it's like a rain shower, but ye can control the temperature of the water and how fast it's movin'." Benji led her to the shower, reached in, turned the handle, and flipped the switch so water came out of both showerheads. "But, unless yer feelin' too bashful, I think ye ought to take off yer clothes before we step inside."

Just then, there was a gentle knock at the bedroom door. "I set out some clothes for you," Bibb called through the door. "They're not very fancy, but will keep you decent enough to go shopping."

Benji held up one finger to Janie to tell her to wait. He bounded over to the door, opened it up just enough to grab the pile of fresh cotton, and said, "Thanks," to the happy lady walking away.

"You're very welcome. And *thank you* for coming back," Bibb said as she looked back over her shoulder, doing her best to not be intrusive, leaving the two young lovers to what she was sure would be a very private moment.

Bibb was truly glad to have the perpetually cheerful and multitalented big galoot back in her life. And by the contented smile he had on his face when she first saw him with his biological son, she was pretty sure he wouldn't be laying claim to the boy, but would let her, Billy, and Peter rear little Mac. He evidently understood and embraced the concept of being a godfather. And that was good for everyone. Besides, with the passion and lust he had in his eyes when he gazed at his fiancée, it wouldn't be long and they would have a child of their own.

"We got clean clothes," Benji announced, and set the neatly folded linen and used clothing on the foot of the bed. "Now," he said softly as he walked toward the shower, pulling his shirt off over his head as he neared her, "like I said, this is probably the best part of life here."

Benji tossed his shirt on the floor then bent over to take off his boots and socks. He stood up to unfasten his pants and saw that Jane had already joined the strip club, her blue wrap on top of the dirty clothes pile. Gulp. Benji felt a surprised blush of embarrassment cover him from forehead to belly button. Jane was more naked than he had ever seen her. She had removed both her travel-dirtied sarong and her leather apron: that insulting little scrap of animal hide that was the only clothing she wore when he had first seen her. Even with all of the passionate kissing and groping they had shared, he had still never seen her without it.

"Are you okay?" Jane asked, as she saw his color change from white to red in a hurry. She placed her hand on his forehead to check for a fever. "You don't feel feverish..."

"Aye, I'm fine, um, actually finer than fine. I've jest never seen ye totally naked." He paused, then looked up at the strip of blue calico wrapped around the old rag that was always on her hair. "Weel, I guess yer *still* not totally naked." He reached up with the intent of unbinding the cloth, but stopped halfway up, his hand frozen in the air between them. The look of absolute horror on her face was totally unexpected. "What's wrong?" he asked, and pulled his hand back in shame at invading her personal space.

"I, I don't want you to see my hair," she replied in humiliation. She didn't want him to view her rat's nest of braids and tucks of wiry hair, but was also embarrassed that she was

271

being so guarded with the man who she would be sharing her most intimate parts with before the end of the day. "Maybe later," she offered in compromise.

'Maybe never,' she thought. Her mother had asked her never to cut her hair, had said that a woman's hair was her beauty and glory, and shouldn't be shared with just anyone. The only person who had touched her hair, other than herself, was her mother. She cherished those special moments when her mother would run the little homemade pick through her hair, separating the tresses section by section then re-braiding them, wrapping them close to her head, binding them with a rag torn from the dress she had worn on the boat trip from Africa. It was all that was left of her mother's heritage. It was skimpy now, and quite threadbare, but just as dear as ever. She had discarded the ugly brown rag that had covered her legacy cloth, the one she wore when Benji 'bought' her, and replaced it with fabric that matched her sarong. Sarah had put a new bandage on her ribs that first day when she cleaned and re-stitched her wound. She said she didn't need the improvised cloth bandage that Benji had employed. Jane had asked for, and was given, the blue calico bandage. Sarah even washed it for her and suggested that she use it as a new hair covering. Jane hadn't told her that was what she wanted it for, but was pleased that Sarah had suggested it.

"It will complement your pretty dress," she said. "You look beautiful in blue." Jane shook her head gently and smiled in recall at being called beautiful by another woman, the only person besides her mother and Benji who had described her as such.

"Are ye cold?" Benji asked as he saw Jane shake her head and shiver slightly. "It's nice and comfy in here," he said as he pulled back the shower door in invitation.

"Comfy?" That was another word she had never heard. There were so many new words to learn, she thought in momentary panic. She grinned and relaxed. At least she had a translator who wouldn't shame her with her ignorance.

"Comfortable," Benji clarified. "Here, I'll go first." He stepped into the gentle mist. "The pre-wash cycle," he explained as he shut his eyes and addressed the warm water flow. He took a deep breath as the soothing wetness washed away the first layer of dust and filth, then gasped. Jane was standing behind him, her body pressed close to his in either fear or passion. He relaxed his pose and turned to face her, his wet body slipping around against hers that was still dry. "There're two shower heads here, so we can both get wet. Can I wash yer back fer ye?"

272

"I think I owe you one, remember?" Jane replied coyly. The warm water did feel very nice, but his body, wet and slippery, and so close to hers, felt even better.

"Aye, I said I'd let ye wash my back if I could wash yers. But, I dinna ken ye could understand me back then. But either way, I'll let ye wash my back and, um, jest about any other parts ye think might need cleanin'," he added softly, hoping that she'd take the hint, and that she hadn't heard his squeak of anticipation.

"I would have understood your hand talk with or without the words. You said some other words, too. *Ching chong chow chow* and *spracken zee doitch*? How many languages do you speak besides the hand talk and English?" Jane asked, as she slipped her hand down the side of his face to his collarbones.

"Weel, I speak a bit of about six or eight—at least enough of those to get me into or out of trouble, dependin' on the situation. I kind of made up the sign language, the hand talk, though. I was pretty desperate to speak with ye. I'm really glad ye speak English, although I woulda made the effort to learn whatever African dialect ye spoke." Benji handed her a washcloth, loaded up with liquid soap, and turned away from her so she could begin scrubbing.

"I don't speak Afrikaans, just the words to the song my mother gave me. You remember that song, the one I sang the night I first held you?" She started washing his shoulders, marveling at the old whip scars on his back. He must have at least twenty, she thought, as many as she had fingers and toes.

"Aye, I remember the song verra well, although I dinna think to listen to what the words were. I was a little distracted." Benji ended his sentence on a high note. Jane's soapy washcloth had dropped down lower, and he hadn't been expecting it.

"Here," Jane said, handing him the cloth, "I think it would be better if you washed your, um, other parts."

"They're all yers, darlin'," Benji cooed, then turned to give her a slippery-faced kiss. He pulled back and ran his hand over his stubbly beard. "But, I think I'll use Bibb's razor and smooth up my face a bit. Here," he said, as he rinsed out the washcloth and soaped it anew, "I'll let ye wash yer, um, private parts while I shave. I dinna think I could stop if I started helpin' ye there. I still want to wait until we're marrit, even if it is only a few hours away."

"Okay," Jane replied, trying to hide the dejection she felt.

"Hey," Benji said as he stopped his in-shower barbering, "we'll have lots more shower times together, I promise. I'd stay in here until the hot water ran out and all of this nice slippery soap was gone, but we have to go buy ye a weddin' dress and me somethin' proper to wear so we can be marrit. Do ye think ye can wait, say, six or eight more hours?"

Jane snorted and laughed. "I've waited my whole life for something I didn't think was possible. I'd be willing to wait another, twenty," she said the number as a question, "years."

"Twenty? Is that how old ye are?"

"That's what Billy thinks. At least, that's what he's going to put on my, um, papers," she said, unable to hide the tone of sadness.

"That's a birth certificate, and everyone now has to have one. He had to build one fer me, too, because I was born in the 18th century, jest like ye. Now, remember, we're the same..."

Jane looked down at his happy male member and started giggling, but didn't say a word. "Weel, that part isna the same," Benji explained, "and I'm glad it isna since I have feelin's fer ye. But, even if we both had one, it would be fine. Ye did ken that Billy's mate is another man, right?"

Jane nodded that she knew and added, "And it doesn't make a difference because even though we're all different, we're all the same, right?"

"Right, now turn around and let me scrub yer back so we can get out of here, and ye can discover what most women like to do most: go shopping!"

Jane turned around, then reached back and grabbed Benji familiarly, eliciting a squeal from him. "I don't think I'll like shopping more than this!" she exclaimed then giggled. "Only six or eight more hours, right?"

"Right, oh so verra right," Benji crooned.

Ж

"Now," Benji instructed after he made sure they had turned around in the shower spray three times to get all the soap removed, "not many places have this special touch: air dryer on demand." Benji turned the dial to low, and a warm, dry wind blew out from six ports built into the shower walls.

"It feels like you caught a summer wind and brought it inside," Jane sighed as she turned around slowly, letting the breeze caress her skin.

"And if yer a bit cold and have a lot of hair to dry, ye jest switch it to high." Benji pointed to the letters on the faceplate. "Off, low, high." He flipped the knob around in illustration.

"That's what those marks mean: off, low, and high?"

"Aye, yer a fast learner. I'll wager I have ye readin' in no time," he smiled, remembering the wager he had made to bring her into his life.

"Just don't wager *me*," Jane said with a glint in her eye. "I don't want there to be any chance that you'll lose me in a bet."

"No chance of that, darlin'. Now, let's see what kind of dress Bibb left ye. Weel, look at this," Benji said, as he lifted up a long length of red, pink, and white patterned fabric with finished edges. "It isna a bed sheet, but it's wider than yard goods. Hmm, weel, whatever it is, I think ye can use it as a sarong. Here, hold it here and jest turn around."

Jane held the fabric under her armpit and pivoted in place, allowing Benji to dress her. "Now how come yer lettin' me do this? Ye ken how to dress yerself. Ye can wrap it even better than I can."

"Aye," she replied coyly, "but I like it when you dress me. Do you want me to dress you?"

"No, I mean, yes," he said, finally adding a frustrated, "I mean no!" He saw the hurt look on her face and explained. "Yes, I want ye to dress me, but no, not now. We need to go shoppin' so ye can come back and feed," he sighed deeply, and said softly, "Wee Mac."

"Okay, but don't sound so sad about it. I like feeding Mac, and you should be happy that he's in our life, okay?" Jane admonished.

"Aye, and I promise ye, we'll have as many babies as we can make. Jest dinna think that I love ye any less because of him, okay?"

Jane shook her head in amazement. "I could only love you more because of him, not less.

Ж

"Looking good, you two!" Billy crowed when the freshly washed and dressed couple came out of his mother's bedroom. "Now, Benji, you need to come with me. You're in isolation from the bride until the wedding. Mom, bring Mac in to see his nanny. It is okay if we call you his nanny, isn't it?" Billy asked Jane, totally ignoring Benji in the discussion.

Jane looked to Benji, trying to get his reaction to the question. She didn't know how she felt—she didn't know what a nanny was. "Did you say mammy?" she asked, although she was pretty sure she heard the strange new name of nanny.

"Nope, nanny. That's a caregiver of a young child. Mammy tends to bring to mind a black female slave who wet nursed babies and also took care of her master's children. You

275

may be black and female and have milk, but no one here is your master. *Capisce*?" Billy asked.

Jane giggled, she knew that word: Jenny had taught it to her. "*Capisce*," she answered. Not having a master felt good, but having a family, a baby to feed, and a wonderful man to love who would soon be her husband, felt even better.

"Weel, Nanny Janie, can I have a little kiss before Billy sends me off to God only kens where while he prepares ye fer our weddin'?" Benji walked up to Jane and held both of her bare shoulders in his big hands. "Please say yes," he requested, his bottom lip poked out like a pouting three year old.

Jane answered him by placing her hands on top of his, tiptoed in, and gave him a long, but discreet kiss in front of her soon to be kin. "I hope that lasts you. If it doesn't, just sneak in for another. I know you can move without being heard."

"I'm sure he can," Billy interrupted, "but I don't think he's learned how to be invisible yet. He's got a tent to set up outside after he gets done clothes shopping."

Benji grinned when he heard Billy say he didn't think he knew how to be invisible. He'd keep the secret of wearing a dunbonnet, a brown hooded sweatshirt, and assuming a beaten man demeanor, as the trick to being non-descript and essentially invisible. "A tent? Aye, I can set up a tent in no time," he boasted. "It'll take more than that to keep me busy fer the rest of the day."

"Then you can set up the tables and chairs and decorations and, if that doesn't take all your time—and I'm sure that it won't—don't forget to get a nap. It's been a long day for you already, and I think you'll want to be rested up for tonight." Billy looked and Benji and gave his version of the double eyebrow pop.

Benji laughed out loud, maybe a little too loud, when he saw Billy's impersonation of him. "Aye, I'll do as I'm asked, and even try to take a little nap."

Benji quickly changed his tone and attitude, and was firm with his instructions to Billy and Bibb. "Now, remember, be gentle with my wee wife-to-be. She's not familiar with the words and traditions, um, around here. She's still a foreigner in many ways."

Bibb moved in close to Jane and put her arm through hers at the same time Billy made the same movement on the other side. They looked at each other, a little surprised, but both very happy that they had thought of the same gesture of support for their new kin. "Foreigner or not, she's still our family," Bibb boasted. "And Billy's twice as compassionate as I am, if that's even possible. You have the rest of your life to take care of her. Trust us with the next few hours, okay?"

Benji hung his head down in embarrassment. Of course, they would be gentle with her. It was just hard to be away from her now that he had found her. He nodded in agreement, then felt Bibb's arm in his. "She'll be fine. I won't let any harm come to her. She's family."

41 The Girls Go Shopping

Bibb ushered Jane down the hall then through the side door into the garage. "I keep my car in here so it stays cool in the summer and warm in the winter. You rode here in Billy's van. Mine is a different shaped means of transportation, but rides on four wheels and has seats inside, very much like his. It's not as big as his rig, but you'll fit just fine. If Benji can ride in it, and he has, so can you. Plus, some of my girls are pretty big just before they deliver. I got this so they'd be as comfortable as possible for rides to the doctor or hospital."

Jane looked closely at the exterior of the shiny, white carriage, letting her hand briefly touch the smooth, glossy surface. She looked down at the tires, "These wheels sure look different than wagon wheels," she said. "And I think you'll have to show me how to open this door. The door was already opened when I got in Billy's *rig*," Jane said as she stressed the word, hoping that she had said it correctly.

"There are different door latches on different rigs and cars, but they all use the same basic grab and pull technique. See, reach your fingers under here and pull. It unlatches the locking mechanism as you pull it open." Bibb pointed out the gear, latch, and cog metal works on the inside of the opened door. "You just pull the door closed, here, once you're in and seated. The latch engages automatically when its shut.

"I'm a chatty person normally," Bibb said, then saw the confused look on Jane's face, so explained. "Chatty means talks a lot: its short for chatterbox. I'll tell you what; you just keep giving me that blank look," Jane automatically flashed that same 'blank look' at the new, unknown word. "Yes, that's the look. When I see you do that, I'll make sure I give you an alternate, I mean another word that means the same thing. See, we already found a way to help you learn and understand new words. Benji told me you're a very bright..." Jane flashed her confused look and Bibb reworded her statement, "I mean, you're a very smart woman and learn quickly."

Jane smiled at her compliment and said a soft, "thank you." She changed her focus to the seatbelt on her right. "Can you show me how to put this on?"

"That's a seatbelt and is a safety precaution. But don't worry about the safety part; we use it because it's the law. A cop," Bibb saw the look and chose another noun, "an officer of the law, sheriff, magistrate," Jane finally nodded that she understood, so Bibb continued, "will drive up behind me and flash his lights... Gee, this is tougher than I thought. Jane, you're going to have to trust me and just let me babble about everything. You don't have to understand everything that's going on, just know that no one in this family will ever steer you wrong. Just pretend you're in a dream and suddenly have been transported to a different country, that there are some words you understand, but the others will reveal themselves after you've spent some time here."

"That's how I already feel except it's more like I died and went to heaven, and I'm surrounded by angels. Honestly, there is nothing bad here that I've seen. Everything is grander than any dream I've ever had."

"Oops, there's one thing we have to do before we leave," Bibb said as she looked down. "Just wait here in the car for a minute." She reached across and showed Jane how to latch the seatbelt. "I'll be right back. I have to find you some shoes."

Jane looked at the wheel in front of the seat next to her. She had seen Billy turn the wheel and noticed that the carriage moved in the same direction at the same time. The wheel ring steered the rig just like pulling the reins on a team of horses. She lifted her bum up and sat back down. She had never sat in a seat so lush and comfortable. She shook her head as she realized that she had never even seen a chair so lofty and sleek, even in any of her master's homes. Yes, she couldn't imagine that heaven could be more magnificent than this.

"Here you go, Janie; try these on." Bibb pulled the passenger door open and bent over to put a sandal on Jane's foot.

Jane turned toward the door to make the task easier for her new friend. She inhaled deeply at the shock of having her feet tended to by an elderly white woman. Bibb looked up and guessed correctly at the reason for the shocked gasp. "Kind of nice having someone tending to your needs, isn't it?" she asked.

Jane answered, "I'll let you know when the shock goes away. I mean, right now I don't know what to think. I've never had anyone touch my feet except to whip them for being bad."

Bibb took the left foot that Jane offered for the other sandal. She tipped the toes back and saw the old scars on her soles. "Whoa! Why'd they do that?" she asked before thinking.

"They said that I could still work while sitting down, and that the raw feet would keep me from running away again. They took me from my mother and I tried to find her. They caught up with me after only half a day. I, um, was kind of obvious: a lone black girl running through the woods without anyone else nearby. My new master was mad because he had to pay to get me back. He whipped my feet until they were bloody, and then put me in chains, too. At least, he put me to work in the kitchen, plucking chickens, and peeling potatoes and carrots. He thought it was punishment, but I was still able to sneak a carrot or two when no one was looking. The house slaves were happy to get the help, so didn't tell on me. They said to make sure I didn't tend to my feet so they wouldn't heal, and I could stay with them for a while longer. Otherwise, as soon as my feet were better, I'd be in the fields. I couldn't help but take care of my feet, though. I didn't want to lose them and be crippled. But, the bosses didn't put me in the fields; they put me working with the blacksmith. I guess I was big enough that they didn't care if I was female or male. At least, I learned a trade, sort of, and the other slaves didn't bother me. You see, I had a hammer, and even though I never used it on anyone, I started the rumor that I had, um, killed two men who tried to have their way with me. A good story meant I didn't have to be mean."

"Very clever," Bibb said. "Now let's go shopping, twenty-first century style!"

Ж

"Wow, where'd you get that? That is awesome. Is it tribal? How much did you have to pay for it, or did you have a friend do it for you?"

Jane turned around to see who was talking. It sounded as if someone was speaking to her, but the young woman standing next to her wasn't making any sense. "Were you speaking to me?"

"Yeah, your back, the cuts: those are totally awesome. See, I did these myself, but I've never seen them on a back before. It looks so awesome," she repeated, then held out her arms for Jane to see. The young woman with the shaved head and multiple piercings in her ears had slash marks across her left forearm in a very precise pattern. The right arm had a similar pattern, but without the symmetry. "I did these myself. I'm right-handed, so this side came out kinda sloppy. Did it hurt when you had it done?" the gaga girl asked, eager to hear about the process of self-mutilation and marking.

"Yes, they hurt, but no, I don't think you should have it *done*," Jane answered.

"But, it looks so awesome!" the smooth-pated girl with the limited vocabulary repeated.

"It would be better—and wouldn't hurt—if you just painted the stripes on your body," Jane suggested. "At least that way you can change the designs whenever you felt like it. I can't change these, but I wish I could. Your back, your skin, is beautiful. You should be happy with it."

Jane knew she was talking bluntly, and probably too much, to this unknown girl. She had skin much lighter than hers, but most definitely had Negro heritage; she could even be a long distance cousin of hers. She smiled as she realized their common ancestry. "It's what's inside that's pretty," she said with compassion to the teenager, "the outside is just a shell, okay?"

The young girl looked up at the very tall and very black woman who was giving her a facts of life lecture as if she was her grandmother. "Hmph," she replied, "if you don't wanna tell me where to get it done, just say so," then turned away, disgusted at being deprived of finding out where to get the fancy body work done.

Ж

"Are you okay?" Bibb asked. She had noticed that Jane looked overwhelmed with her new surroundings. She had been handling it well until now. She looked almost terrified.

"I don't know," answered Jane pensively. "I mean, I feel okay," Jane put the back of her hand to her lips. "I don't have a fever, and the greens we had for lunch didn't upset my stomach, but, um..."

"Yes, go ahead," urged Bibb. It was obvious that her new charge was reluctant to divulge her problem.

"I keep hearing noises. They're pleasant enough, and sometimes I even hear people singing, but I can't see anyone, well, you know, doing the singing."

"Oh, sweetheart, there's nothing wrong. We have music just about everywhere here and now. I mean, they broadcast it in the stores and restaurants and..." Bibb saw 'the look' and took another approach. "Honey, just know that man has found out how to capture sounds and even moving images, that means moving pictures."

Jane nodded, said, "Movies," grimacing slightly as she recalled Benji's experience making a movie.

"Yes, movies, but music can also be broadcast, that is spread over the air or through wires, to just about anywhere and

281

everywhere. You see all those young people? I'm sure you've seen many of them today with the cords..." Bibb saw 'the look' and reworded he explanation. "You saw the string going into the people's ears? Well, they have a wee box on the other end that sends the noises from the little boxes right into their ears so others don't have to be bothered by the sounds. You see, not everyone likes the same kind of music. The cords keep the music confined to one person."

Jane nodded that she understood. So many things were different. She thought that the colored strings were a form of jewelry. "Aye, Benji told me about movies and watching them on a screen, but he forgot to tell me about music."

Ж

Bibb thanked the clerk for her help, and accepted the receipt and oversized bag full of clothing. "Are you ready to go home?"

"Um, yes," Jane replied hesitantly. "But how did you pay for the clothes? Or do they just give them to you here?"

"No, they're not free, and we don't trade or barter much here now. You see, money doesn't change hands as much as it used to. See this," Bibb held up the embossed blue plastic rectangle, "this is kind of like a bank..."

Bibb saw 'the look' and realized that bank was an unknown word or concept for her. "This is like a money bag or purse." Jane nodded that she understood, but the frown of disbelief stayed. "See this little brown stripe." Bibb pointed to the magnetic strip on the back of the debit card. "This is like a ledger, a book of accounts that keeps information about how much money I have and how much I'm spending."

Jane's eyes widened. She understood, mostly, but the technology was almost too fantastic for her to accept. She breathed deeply, smiled, and said, "I don't have to understand it or know how it's done. You see, even though I don't know how the sun shines or the wind blows, I can accept that it does. So that's called a *money card*?" she asked, hoping that she had the right word.

"Debit card or you can say credit card. I'll get you and Benji one tomorrow or whenever you're up to it after your honeymoon."

"Honeymoon?"

"That's your private, special time alone with your husband after you're married."

"Oh..." Jane blushed as she realized that was the time when she could share all of her body parts. A smile of pride quickly took the place of her bashfulness. "When I'm a wife: Benji's wife."

Ж

Later, back at the house...

"It looks like Mac is ready to get up from his nap. Would you go bring him in? He's down the hall on the right; just follow the noise. Oh, and feel free to change his diaper before you bring him out," Bibb said, then added a short chortle and a discreet grin. She'd give Benji a little one on one time with his godson, even if it was just to change a wet diaper. She was sure he wouldn't mind, and he'd probably appreciate the opportunity. He had to be curious about the boy, even if he was being very respectful of the awkward parental situation.

"Aye, I think I can manage," Benji replied with the same sly grin. He knew that Bibb was giving him the chance to be alone with Mac. He opened the door and saw his little charge smiling and reaching up for him. His eyes suddenly and unexpectedly filled with tears when he heard the boy's babbles turn into words, "Da Da, Da Da."

"No, I'm not yer Da." He wept as he picked up the boy and held him close. "Billy's yer Da, but I'm still close, and I love ye verra much. I'm yer godfather and we'll jest have to find a special name fer me."

"Da's okay with me if it's okay with Billy," Peter said. Benji hadn't heard him walk in, and Peter knew it. "I mean, we already decided that I was going to be Papa and he was going to be Daddy, so Da is okay with me. Welcome back, Benji. Are you going to stay a little longer this time?" Peter asked sincerely. He really liked the man who he had adored as both a superstar wrestler idol and a brother/cousin figure.

"Aye, it looks like I'm back as yer contractor and maintenance man," Benji answered, then leaned in and hugged Peter to him with his non-baby laden arm. "Oh, and I dinna come back alone. I have a fiancée. Billy's in there dollin' her up right now," he said with pride, then bent down and quickly changed the baby's wet diaper. "These sure are convenient," he said, as he pulled the little Velcro closures shut.

"Really? A fiancée and she's going to stay here, too? I mean," Peter babbled, as he realized his faux pas, "of course, she's going to stay here if you are and she's going to be your wife. When are you getting married?"

Benji looked down at the non-existent watch on his wrist. "In about four or five hours, dependin' on how long Billy takes with gettin' everythin' set up." Mac reached out and grabbed a fistful of Benji's nose, "and after this wee little fiend gets fed. Come on, I'll introduce ye to the most beautiful, kindest woman in the world...weel, at least as far as I'm concerned. Yer mother-in-law is pretty special, too."

"Yes, Bibb is one in a million, but I'll bet your wife-to-be is a bit younger than she is."

Benji coughed back a laugh: Jane was nearly 200 years older than Bibb by the calendar. "Aye, Janie's only twenty," he managed to say after his minor coughing fit and laugh swallowing. "Now," he said, as he tipped his head toward the door, "get ready to be dazzled!"

Benji tapped on the office door and asked, "Can we come in fer jest a bit? Mac is ready fer his nanny, and I have someone else fer Janie to meet."

"There's my little boy; come to Daddy." Billy's eyes were only for his son.

He looked up and saw him. "Peter! When did you get here? Hey, Mac," he said, his nose nearly pasted to his son's, "why didn't you tell me that Papa was coming home today? Were you trying to keep it a secret? You know you're not supposed to keep secrets in this family," he said in a teasing manner, then blushed. Peter still didn't know about the time traveling that was rampant with his family and best friends. Well, it was more than a secret; it was a special legacy only to be shared when it was pertinent or absolutely necessary.

"Oh, and by the way," Peter said. He came in close to give Billy a quick kiss on the cheek, then hugged him and Mac at the same time, "Mac named Benji. He calls him Da."

Billy looked over at Benji, then back to Peter. Both of the men made identical shoulder shrugs of acknowledgement. "Okay," Billy agreed, then looked over at Jane to see her reaction.

Jane grinned and nodded. "He looks like a Da to me," she agreed. "Now, why don't you come over here to Nanny Janie and we'll sit a while." Jane took the very eager and hungry boy and sat in the rocking chair, her back turned away from the rest of the family.

"Where's the bottle?" Peter asked, confused at how this new person whom he hadn't even been introduced to yet could feed his son without formula.

"I'm sorry I dinna introduce ye. Peter, this is Jane, my fiancée. Janie, this is Peter Anthony, Mac's papa and Billy's partner or husband or, weel, they're marrit," Benji said, more than slightly embarrassed about not knowing the politically correct word to use. "Oh," Benji added, glad to have the opportunity to change the subject, "Janie's his nanny. She has super powers, and doesna need a bottle to feed him. Or rather, she has the most beautiful set of bionic bottles in the world, but ye'll jest have to take my word fer it. At least, Mac sure likes them."

Peter looked at Billy, then Bibb, then Benji for an answer, finally craning his neck to try and see what was going on with his son and the very tall and beautiful black woman who Benji claimed was his fiancée. Billy came up close to Peter and put his arms around him, distracting him from his staring, and giving him a more adequate welcome home hug. "Hey, we're all gifted in different ways. Besides mother's milk is better for Mac, and like Benji said, it sure comes in beautiful containers. Have you ever seen such an attractive smile on a bottle of formula?" Billy teased.

"No, you sure got that right. Welcome to the family, Jane. Is there anything I can do to help?" Peter asked Billy, discretely avoiding the topic of the real aspects of Jane's anatomy his partner was referring to.

Billy's answer was interrupted by the doorbell. He didn't know who it could be, but did know it had to be one of the people he had called to help with the wedding. "Yes, dear," Billy said in answer to Peter's offer of assistance, "Benji got a late start and hasn't had a chance to go shopping for his wedding outfit yet. Would you take him? I was going to do it, but I have my hands full here. You have a great sense of style and he, um, well, I think he got short changed in that department." Billy looked down at Benji's work overalls and hand me down tee shirt, then up at how tall he was. "Even if he did get the lion's share of a lot more." He nudged Benji and smiled at him. "Go, go, go, you two. I have lots to do and you, big boy, will just be in the way until the heavy lifting and moving tasks come up. You can set up the tent later."

Peter saw and heeded Billy's eye movements to take Benji out the back door. Evidently, his partner didn't want him to see who was arriving at the front entrance. He didn't want to admit it, but he still had a bit of a crush on the 'The Flying Scotsman,' the wrestler persona Benji had portrayed in his younger years. "Come on, Benji," he said as he hooked his hand into his hero's elbow, "why don't you tell me where you've been in the last, gee, it hasn't even been a year yet, but it seems like you've been gone a century, at least!"

Benji laughed heartily, then looked back to see if Billy, Bibb, and Janie had heard the sharply dressed man's remark. They had, and were all smirking back belly laughs. "Weel, Peter, it seems like I've been gone at least two hundred years," he said with a wink back at Bibb and Billy. "I'll tell ye a bit about it on the way into town. Now, jest dinna tell me that we're goin' be ridin' in that bitty purple car of yours..."

Peter held up his key ring. "Nope, I think we'll take the family rig. I doubt I could fit all of the new clothes I plan on buying you into the Prius with or without you along."

42 Pre-nuptial Preparations

Billy answered the door and saw two people he had never met before. "Hi, I'm Michael Callahan and this is my wife, Alisha, but you'd probably know me as Wee Michael," the youthful-looking man said with a grin.

"Oh, so you are," Billy said. "Welcome to my home. Oh, and this is now Benji's home, too, and the home of his fiancée. They just got in from, um, out of town. They're starting from scratch, so my partner Peter just took Benji shopping to get his trousseau. I know you want to see him, but you're his surprise present or guest or whatever. I knew he'd want to see you, but he told me not to invite anyone. He did agree to having the immediate family members and of course, caterers, photographers, and..." Billy looked over at the tall, caramel-colored woman who Wee Michael had introduced as his wife, "I'm throwing in the hair-stylist and his family. Are these lovely little girls yours?" he asked, although by the look of the two clinging to Daddy's legs, they had to be.

"Yes, this is Beatrice and this is Chandra. They're five and three. And this is," Wee Michael patted his wife's bulging belly, "is baby 'D.' We don't know yet if we're having a son or another daughter, but we're working our way down the alphabet." Wee Michael tiptoed up and gave his tall, very pregnant wife a kiss on the cheek. "At least until we reach the letter 'L' and catch up to 'M' for Michael."

Alisha rubbed her lower back in obvious discomfort. "I'm not too sure about that anymore. Lately I've been thinking about adopting a few cats and puppies to fill in some of the letters. I don't think I can handle eight more pregnancies. Now, where is the queen for the day?"

"I'll bring her in, in just a moment. Let me show you to the beauty salon," Billy said, "and there's a bathroom just across the hall from it," he added with a wink. "You see, we know all about pregnant ladies here. This is a home for pregnant mothers. If they can't be with their own families during their pregnancies, we bring them here and give them care, comfort, and career training. Beats the heh, heck," Billy caught himself before he finished the word 'hell,' "beats the heck out of the alternatives." He grimaced. He could tell by the shared look and nods that

Alisha and Wee Michael knew he was speaking of abortions, and felt the same way he did.

"So, this must be part of your career training, then," Wee Michael said as he pointed to the salon chair, rollaway cart with hairstyling accruements, and adaptive sink. "Just a moment, please, before we get started. Girls, do you need to use the restroom? It looks like it's time for another potty stop for Mommy." Both girls buried their faces into their father's thighs, then turned aside in tandem, curious about the new man Daddy was talking to.

"I'll be right back," Billy said, allowing Alisha a few minutes for her break, "I'll bring Janie, or Jane, in here. She's taking care of my son, right now. Make yourself comfortable. There's yogurt, juice, and milk in the little frig, and fresh fruit and granola bars in the cabinet. We have to keep these girls and their babies healthy!"

"Thanks," Wee Michael said, then turned his attention to his daughters. "Remember I told you about my good friend, the red-haired giant?" he cajoled. "Well, we're going to meet him later, but first Mr. Billy is bringing in the woman he's going to marry. Your mommy and I get to fix her hair for her wedding. You do remember what weddings are, don't you?"

Beatrice pulled away from her daddy's thigh and bragged, "That's when two people who love each other make it a law that means they can be together forever and ever, and nobody can break them apart. Just like you and Mommy, huh?"

"Yeah, huh?" echoed Chandra, eager to emulate her big sister.

"Right!" chorused Michael, and Alisha, who had just come in.

"When was the last time you saw Benji?" Alisha asked, as she settled herself gingerly into the oversized salon chair.

"The last time you saw him, too; when he was on his way to Alaska. Beatrice was only about three or four months old. If he's been back very long, he never called. But you know Benji: he was probably busy helping somebody or chasing down some bad guys. I don't think that man has a mean bone in his body."

Ж

Billy walked in and saw Jane with Mac over her shoulder, gently rubbing his back to get a burp out of him. "Are you and my son ready to meet one of Benji's old friends?"

"Blarp!" Mac let loose a giant burp.

"I think so. He's fine, and so am I, but can I ask you a question? I know I'm ignorant, but, but..."

Billy interrupted to save Jane from stumbling over more words. "Janie, ask me about anything and everything. You may not believe this, but I'm fascinated by what I think you'll ask me. I take so much of everyday life for granted. If we were swapped around, and I was back in your old time, I'd be confused to be sure, but I'd manage. I can't imagine, though, what it would be like if I was thrust two hundred and thirty years into the future. You're a mighty brave woman to trust us like this."

"I was just going to ask about Mac's clout. I don't know how to change it or where the clean ones are. I really appreciate how nice you and your mother are to me, and Peter, too. He seems like a very nice man. When I saw you hug and kiss him, it didn't seem wrong like I thought it would."

Jane hung her head down in embarrassment, suddenly aware of how blunt she had just been. She had grown up guarded with her thoughts and miserly with the few words she uttered to those who knew she could speak English. Now she was a regular magpie with her chattering.

Billy neared her and put one arm around her waist. "You're not used to talking very much, are you?" he asked softly, looking up into her face. Jane shook her head, not wanting to speak any more less she say the wrong words. Again.

"I told you how it was with Peter and me, and I'm glad you said what you did. I don't think you can ever say anything *wrong* to me. I want to know you better, and if you can't, or won't, speak your mind, how will I know who you are, and why Benji fell in love with you? Now, we'll have lots of time to talk about that later, but right now, I have an old friend of Benji's and his family in the other room. They're a surprise for him. He doesn't know they're here, so don't say anything to him, please. They're actually here in a professional capacity, that is, they're doing their job. I thought I'd have them come over and give you a makeover before the wedding. I'll bet you've never had a facial or manicure, have you?"

Jane shook her head, still leery of speaking. She didn't know what makeovers, manicures, or facials were.

Billy looked up at the tangle of torn calico cloth binding Jane's hair. He started to make a comment about getting a new hairstyle, too, but bit off his words. This time he was the one wary of saying too much. He knew she and Benji had just showered, but her hair and the headband looked the same as when she arrived. He'd let the professionals deal with that issue.

"Come on; I want you to meet someone who's known Benji much longer than I have."

Billy held Jane's arm close to him as he escorted her to the beauty salon room, patting her hand as they neared the open door. "Janie, this is Wee Michael and his wife, Alisha, and their two daughters, Beatrice, and Chandra. Everybody, this is Janie, soon to be Mrs. Benjamin MacKay."

Jane turned her head in horror at hearing the last two names.

"Benji, Mrs. Benji," Billy amended, then nodded to Jane that it was okay; don't worry about the names. Evidently, she didn't know his real name.

"Wow!" Alisha and Wee Michael said softly at the same time then looked at each other in amazement at their common reaction.

"He won't get out of line with you around," Wee Michael said, then winked at his wife.

Jane didn't know what that remark meant, so just smiled. That seemed to be the best reaction to have when she didn't know what she was supposed to say or do. At least she didn't appear stupid when she did that.

"You don't mind if the girls stay in here while we work, do you?" Alisha asked. "They've been with us whenever and wherever we've worked since before they were born."

"They're yours?" Jane asked. She shook her head in embarrassment. Of course, they were—they were just introduced as such.

"What, can't you tell," teased Wee Michael. He picked up Chandra and held her face close to his. "See, she has my blue eyes," he bragged.

Jane could see that the girls were of mixed heritage. They both had light brown skin and very curly hair; not kinky like hers. But, Chandra had blue eyes like her white father. Evie had told her that although Benji had blue eyes, they probably wouldn't have blue-eyed children because she didn't have blue-eyed ancestors. The girls' mother, Alisha, had light brown skin, so probably had a white parent, or grandparent at least, who had blue eyes.

"Her eyes are beautiful, just like the rest of her, and so is her sister." Jane resisted the urge to touch the girl's hair, but did bring her hand up near Chandra's. "Their hair; I wish mine was like that."

Alisha reached up and patted her own coif, partially covered with a scarf. "We can make yours just like theirs. Michael did mine, but the girls' hair is naturally that way. Chemicals can take over for genetics nowadays. He's concocted

290

his own formula that won't burn or stink. I only need a touch up every four months or so, to keep mine like this. Would you like him to fix yours?"

Jane didn't know what to answer, so said nothing, hoping that Alisha wouldn't think she was being rude, but only trying to make a decision. She glanced down at the girls, stretched out on the floor on their bellies, looking at a book filled with colorful pictures. Jane had never seen paper so bright and exotic. She looked back up at Michael, unsure if she should let a man who wasn't her husband touch her hair.

Wee Michael saw the indecision in her face. He tried not to stare at the length of calico tied around her head, bulging with the hair wrapped underneath. He really wanted to help her have the hair she obviously wanted, but could tell that she was reluctant to have him, or anyone, work on it.

"You know, Benji used to let me brush his hair," he said. "He had the longest, most beautiful, red hair I had ever seen, or seen since. He said he wouldn't cut it until he was free. You see, he had been a prisoner, captive, hostage, whatever you want to call it, since he was about twelve. He said that as long as he was a slave, he wouldn't cut it or let anyone else cut it either. He left it long for a few weeks after he broke us out of that prison compound, too—just in case we were found. We happened upon a camp of homeless folks and lived with them for a while. Unfortunately, the bedding they let us share was full of lice. Well, rather than fight the little fiends, he let me cut the hair. I told him I wanted to save it because it was so pretty, but he said he wanted to burn it. Man, did it stink! But, all burnt hair stinks, not just the lice-ridden kind. He said it was the stink of bondage flying away."

Wee Michael finished his story with a smile. "I haven't seen Benji in about five years. Is his hair long or short?" he asked, hoping that relating some of his personal history of Benji and his hair would warm up the relationship with the timid giantess.

"He keeps it short," she answered. "He said its cooler and besides, he didn't have a comb." Jane looked at Alisha's hair, then at the soft, lighter brown curls of the little girls. She knew what they had said, but decided to ask anyway. "You make pretty curls out of wiry hair all the time?"

"Here, touch mine," Alisha offered, "then touch theirs. You can't tell the difference. And the chemicals didn't make my hair fall out. See," she said as she took off her turban, "still thick enough that I have to bind it to keep it from flying all over the place. I keep it covered when I'm working, but let it down when we're at home. Michael loves my hair," she said with a smirk, and a wink at her husband.

Jane took Alisha up on her offer and touched her coif, then asked the girls, "May I touch your hair?" Her envy was overriding her shyness; their soft curls were so beautiful.

The two girls looked at each other and smiled in agreement. They both liked this tall, gentle woman. She wasn't loud and pushy like some of the other people who came into their parent's salon. They both got up from the floor and their book reading. Beatrice turned away from Jane and presented her hair for examination "Don't you want to touch it?" she asked.

"I did; it's very nice," Jane replied as she moved her hand back from the butterfly light stroke.

"Can I feel yours?" Beatrice asked, looking up at the tall lady.

Jane squatted down next to her, then reached up and untied the knot in her cotton cloth head covering. She was in a different time and different place. The old rules she had lived by that pertained to her and her mother didn't apply to her here and now. She was not a slave; these were friends and almost family, and this little girl was just asking to be treated the same as Jane had treated her.

"You got a lot of hair," Beatrice remarked as she peered at the thick braid. "Is it all yours, or do you have a weave?"

Jane didn't know what a weave was, but did know that it was all her own hair. "It's all mine," she answered with self-assurance. "I've never cut it. When I was a little girl, my mother braided it, wrapped it close around my head, and covered it with this cloth. It was from Africa, like she was." Jane gulped as she realized that she might have just told the little girl too much.

"Your mother was from Africa?" Beatrice asked, as she tapped the individual colors in the frayed rag, as if counting the hues. "My great-great-great-great-great grandma was from Africa, too. Maybe we're cousins."

"Maybe," Jane answered with a relaxed smile, "maybe."

"So, are you sure you want Michael to fix your hair like mine? I mean, you have so much hair, he could do braids or dreadlocks or just about anything with it. Even if he relaxes the hair, he can still braid it later. But, I don't think he can make it tighter again. At least, no one's ever asked to go back the other way, but he could probably figure it out. He's pretty sharp that way."

"No, I don't think I'd want to go back to this," Jane said, "if I had this," and gently touched Beatrice's hair again.

"Well, I'm just glad I brought extra product," Wee Michael said. He reached up and began untwisting the wrapped and tucked braids. "You really do have a lot of hair here. If you're ready Janie, just sit here. I'll get started on the hair, and my wife can start with the pedicure."

Alisha saw the blank look on Jane's face and remembered the warning Billy had given Michael: she was new to this way of life and was unfamiliar with many words. "We want to pretty you up from head to foot for your wedding. Not that you're not already pretty, it's just that you should have others attend to you on your day. I've got some herbs and salts that will make your feet feel like they're brand new. I'll give them a great massage, too, with some sweet smelling oils and creams. Then I can do the same to your hands." Alisha picked up Jane's hand and marveled at it. "You have the longest fingers I have ever seen on a woman. I'll bet you could span an octave and a half on a piano, maybe two."

Jane tried to smile to cover her ignorance about what octaves were and how she could cross them, but the look was more of a grimace. Alisha saw the embarrassment she had inadvertently caused. "Maybe you'd like basketball better?" she asked.

"Benji said I'd be great at it, but we haven't had a chance for him to teach me yet. Do you need me to do anything?" she asked.

"Well, first, sit up so I can wrap this towel and cape around you, then you can lean back and let your neck rest on the edge of the sink. After that, all you need to do is relax. I've had ladies, and gentlemen, too, fall asleep while they're getting the full treatment. You might as well get a nap. I'm sure you'll want to be well rested for your wedding," Michael said.

"And your wedding night, too," Alisha whispered coyly. "Michael said Benji's been waiting for someone special for a long time, and you're obviously the one."

"You're sure getting a good man as a husband," Michael added. "He's the greatest man I know, and I don't mean just in size. He was a leader and protector for many of us when we were in that slave camp. Did he ever tell you any of the stories?"

Jane's neck and shoulder's tensed at the word slave. Her head was laid back over the rim of the sink, but she still managed to shake it slightly to let her hairdresser know that he hadn't.

Michael felt her tense at the subject of Benji's past life. "I'm sorry, I'll let him tell you about it. I just want you to take it easy and let us treat you like a queen. Do you think you can handle that?" he asked, stroking her temples the same way he did for his wife when she had a headache or had just had a rough day.

"I'll try," she said, then remembered what both Sarah and Benji had told her to do when she was tense: find your happy thought. She thought of her fiancé and his family, both in the past, and those she had met only a couple of hours ago. She sighed deeply, letting her tension flow out with her exhale. The man she was letting touch her hair was a longtime friend of Benji and had a wife with Negro heritage. Even if Alisha was lighter skinned than she was, she had married a white man and had children with him. They seemed very happy, and their daughters were beautiful and well behaved. Benji had told her the truth when he said that skin color didn't matter in this time. She sighed again and settled into an even deeper level of relaxation. "You said it was okay to fall asleep?" she asked, suddenly very tired now that she was snuggled in the warmth of her own little cocoon of contentment.

"It'll make the time until your wedding go faster if you do. I'll just tap you on the shoulder when I need you to sit up or move. You don't even have to wake up all the way."

Michael sighed at his own peace. He was glad Benji had a good woman in his life and had given up on his crazy scheme about going back in time to see his grandfather. He loved the man, even if he was a little cuckoo.

43 Amy

The Callahan clan's royal treatment was completed. Jane looked like a new person with her softly curled tresses cascading over her shoulders, down her back, nearly to her knees. She was a sparkling beauty in her yellow floral print sundress. Her freshly buffed fingernails pushed the hair behind her ears, but the bride-to-be was still the quiet and timid former slave on the inside.

Bibb decided the insecure woman needed distraction before going back inside the house. Billy's energy level was so high that she could swear it was contagious, spilling over to everyone within twenty feet of him, whether walls were involved or not. She didn't want to go into town again; the shopping trip earlier had shown that it would be best to ease Jane slowly—very slowly—into modern civilization. Instead, she took her new kin on a tour of the grounds, showing her the small orchard and vegetable gardens.

"This is where the old out buildings were that we used for storage. Before that, they were, um, slave quarters. Benji helped knock them down so we could build our new house and clear an area for the garden." Bibb chuckled and said, "You know, he knew what those run down shacks used to be. It was doubtful that they were in much better shape two hundred years ago. He's not a violent man by any means, but the grin that he was sporting—that means wearing—when he drove that tractor over them, smashing down the old walls that still had the iron loops for chains, well, he really enjoyed it. He told me that he had a personal grudge against slavery and would tell me about it 'one of these days.' We had a bonfire that night to get rid of the wood. You should have seen him glow."

"Yes," Jane said, "he told me how proud he was of you, that you had sold your business to your employees so you could start a new, um, treasure?"

"I think you mean venture, dear," Bibb said.

"Oh, yes, a new venture where you could help women in trouble. He said you were like a mother to him."

Jane didn't know if she should speak freely, then remembered she wasn't who she used to be. She reached up and touched her new hairdo. She wasn't a slave who bound her hair anymore. And, she had clothes that were given to her as a gift, not for doing nasty deeds. Yes, she could speak her mind now.

"I'm not sure, but I think his mother and father are dead. He never talks about them, and I don't bring it up. I'm sure he'll tell me about them when he feels like it. They must have been wonderful people, though, to have such a great son."

Bibb cleared her throat and forcibly swallowed the words that tried to come forth, the words she knew were not hers to share with Jane.

"Excuse me," Bibb said as she coughed, stalling for time, trying to find the words she should use rather than revealing that Benji's family was alive and well in Scotland. She took a deep breath and said, "Well, one thing for sure about his parents, at least one of them was tall."

Just then, a short, very pregnant blond woman with Down syndrome walked up to them, saving Bibb from hunting for further honest, but non-revealing comments about the MacKays. "Janie, I'd like to introduce you to one of my girls. Janie, this is Amy. Amy, this is Janie. Janie's getting married here this afternoon," Bibb said as she affectionately placed her arm around the petite young woman's shoulders.

"You sure are tall," said Amy as she gazed up, her head tipped back, jaw relaxed in uninhibited amazement. "I'll bet you can get the apples right off the top of the trees without a ladder, huh?" Amy realized that she had just been introduced to a new person, and should use her manners. "Pleased to meet you, Janie," she said in a halting, determined speech, then quickly looked to Bibb to make sure she had said the right words.

"I'm pleased to meet you, too, Amy." Jane smiled at the young woman, then gave a quick double nod to Bibb to let her know that she really was happy to become acquainted with this very straightforward and honest person. "Can you come to my wedding?" she asked, then gulped. She looked at Bibb, eyes half-closed, ashamed that she had asked Amy before making sure that it was okay with her and Billy.

Amy blushed slightly, then looked to her surrogate mother to see if it was all right with her. Bibb nodded that it was okay, then Amy replied to Jane, "Yes, thank you; I'd like that."

"Janie, if it's okay with you, can all of my girls come to the wedding? We don't have much to do around here except light housework, schooling, and doctor's appointments. I know Billy's planning a big to do and I'm sure all the girls would like to come. Right now, there are only four sisters here. I guess I should have asked you sooner."

"And can I be the flower girl?" Amy asked excitedly, then looked embarrassed at interrupting. "Sorry," she apologized with head bowed down. "It was your turn to speak."

"I don't know what a flower girl is," Jane said gently, "but if that means you would be in the, um, ceremony with me, I'd like that very much."

Amy looked up at her with a smile that brightened the whole outdoors. "That means my baby can come, too. I'm having a baby girl, and Billy and Peter's friends, they live just down there," she said, and pointed to a cluster of large homes down the road, "are going to be the mommies. I'll be living almost right next door and can come over and see the baby girl whenever I want. I'm going to be her aunt. And nobody's going to take me away from here, huh?" Amy asked, and turned to Bibb for confirmation, evidently not for the first time.

"That's right." Bibb said, and gave her young charge a quick, one-armed hug. "Jane, I'm adopting Amy, and she'll be my helper forever and ever, or until she decides she wants to live somewhere else. But right now, Amy, we have to go inside. Janie is Mac's new nanny and she needs to spend some time with him. We'll see you later this afternoon. Are you in charge of watering the garden today?"

"Yes, ma'am, and I made sure the scarecrow's hat stayed on. The crows took it off, so I got some tape from Billy to make sure it didn't come off again." She pointed with pride at her resourcefulness. "Billy said the corn is almost ready, and that's why the crows are here. But, I'll go back and make sure the hat is still on. Bye, bye, Mom and Janie," she said. She excitedly waved farewell to the two women, then turned and walked away, a definite purpose in her stride, eager to shoo the crows away from the small garden area.

Bibb chuckled when she looked in the direction of the cornfield. "Quite a resourceful young woman. That's what we call electrical tape, and it's for a totally different purpose. But, she made it work."

Jane didn't know the words electrical or tape, but did know what a scarecrow was. She smiled when she saw the straw-stuffed clothes and burlap bag on a pole with black ribbon wound all around the head and hat. It was even spookier than a plain scarecrow and was certain to frighten the crows away.

"Is she okay?" Jane asked, watching Amy waddle away. There was something odd about the her, but she didn't know what it was. She could see Amy was both very small and very pregnant, maybe too small to carry a baby.

"Amy's different," Bibb explained as the two of them walked back to the house. "She has what's called Down syndrome. She is, um, for lack of a better way to say it, special." Bibb knew that Jane didn't know about chromosomes or genetic anomalies. "She has limited intelligence. She'll never be what most people refer to as smart. She's also shorter, has a weaker heart, but has an overabundance of love, if that's even possible. Her parents didn't want her because she was different, and put her in a group home when she was ten. That's like an orphanage. Do you know what that is?" Jane nodded, so she continued. "There was a man who worked at the home. He, um, took her away and um," Bibb stalled. She didn't know how to explain what happened.

Jane said, "He had his way with her without her permission?" she asked.

Bibb shook her head no and shuddered at the thought of someone raping her little Amy. "No, the man wasn't, um, smart, either. I think he fell in love with her. He was caught kissing Amy and was fired." Bibb saw Jane gasp in shock at the word. "I mean he lost his job; they told him he couldn't work at the home anymore because he had kissed her.

"He and Amy liked each other a lot. She told me she was sad when he had to leave. But, he didn't stay away. He came back one night after everyone was in bed. He may not have been smart, but he *was* clever and knew how to sneak Amy away without being seen. He wasn't mean to her; I think he really loved her, but he shouldn't have taken her away.

"Amy had been gone, missing, from the home for four months when I found her. The first time I saw her was at the grocery store, frustrated and crying. Her man friend hadn't come home for a week and she was hungry. She didn't know what happened to him, but did know that the store had food. She walked right up to the produce department and started eating the apples in the boxes, putting back a pear after taking a bite because she didn't like it. I saw she was unintentionally causing a ruckus and attracting a crowd. I didn't know what was going on, but could see she needed an advocate."

Bibb saw 'the look' and clarified, "She needed a protector. I told the man at the store that I was sorry about what happened, and that I'd pay for the food. I filled my shopping bag with the kind of apples she liked and sort of lied; I told her she was supposed to come home with me.

"I brought her back here and let Billy do his job. You see, he's a policeman, a problem solver, kind of like a magistrate, only

298

better." Bibb grinned with parental pride. "He found out that she had gone missing from the group home and that the man who had taken her, used to live there, too. No one knew he had moved her into his little apartment with him, that he'd been taking care of her."

Bibb winced, recalling that horrid day when she had to tell Amy that Oscar wasn't coming back. "Billy found out her friend had been killed in an accident the week before I found her. She didn't know where he went and was afraid when he didn't return. When she ran out of food, she went to the store to eat."

She looked up at Jane, saw her sadness, and was glad that she had left out the rest of the horror. It was an automobile accident, a pedestrian hit and run, that had struck down Oscar. Jane didn't need to know of the many hazards of modern day life on her first day here.

"I contacted the group home she had lived in. They said they'd be happy to have her back. They loved her. She was a part of their family, and they all missed her. I kind of hated to hear that because I really had grown fond of her in those three days she was here with us. I didn't want to see her leave. I made sure I told them that I thought she was pregnant and that she should go see a doctor right away. She didn't appear to be sick, but definitely had morning sickness. They told me not to worry about it. They'd get her an abortion and then have her sterilized so it wouldn't happen again."

Bibb saw Jane's blank look and decided to tell her about the dirty little secret that happened behind closed doors. "Amy was pregnant," Bibb said and saw Jane nod her head that she understood that part of the story. "And they wanted to cut the baby out of her and make it so she could never have a baby again."

Jane's eyes widened and jaw dropped as she gasped with horror. "Yes, it's a terrible thing to do, and I wouldn't let them near her after that. I went to court and convinced the judge that Amy was better off living with me than in the home; that I could and would take care of her and the child she carried. He agreed, so now she'll legally be my daughter next month." Bibb glowed with pride as she revealed the abbreviated version of having her first daughter.

"Will she be okay?" Jane asked. "I mean, she's so small."

"Oh, she's big enough inside. We just have to make sure she doesn't overexert herself, I mean, that she doesn't work too hard. She's a good helper, so I give her small jobs to do. The baby is fine, too. The doctors now have tools so they can look inside the womb without cutting into the mother. That's why we know she's having a daughter. The baby won't be like her: she doesn't have Down syndrome. And even if she did, the ladies down the way wouldn't care. They've taken Amy under their wing and love her almost as much as we do. They've offered to have her stay with them, but I think Janetta and Mary need to have time alone to bond with their adopted daughter first. Amy will be in the baby's life as much as they like, but only as an aunt. It will be another non-traditional family for sure, but certainly not one lacking in love."

44 The Wedding

"Okay, okay, everyone; can I get your attention here for just a minute? I didn't realize you'd all get here at exactly the same time."

Billy was overwhelmed with floral and catering crews, but grateful that it looked like the wedding event of the mixed centuries was going to come together on time. And that Benji hadn't discovered the presence of his surprise guests, Wee Michael and family.

"Caterers, this way, please. Hey, Carlos, nice to see you again. After the wedding, maybe we'll get a chance to chat. Right now, the tables are in there and the kitchen is this way. If you need more refrigerator space, there's a spare one in the garage. You're Tom, the photographer, right? Of course, you are; not many people carry around a tripod as a keychain!"

Bibb saw the parade of vans pull up to the house and knew that the proceedings were getting underway. "Janie, why don't you come inside to Mac's room? I want you to be surprised with the, um, party that Billy's putting together. I'm sure Benji's being isolated, too. I'll bring Mac to you, and he can show you his toys. And remember: don't let Benji know that Wee Michael and his family are here."

Bibb and Jane walked down the hall, shoulder to elbow. Jane was mute and stunned that someone, anyone, was throwing her a party. She snorted aloud as she realized the ultimate shock: the celebration was because she was getting married. She pinched herself and sucked in a squeal before it escaped. Yes, she was awake, and this miracle really was happening.

"Look what I found," Bibb said when she saw that Benji and Mac were already in the room. "Now, Mac, I want you to keep these two, your godparents, inside your room. Your Daddy is putting together a party for them. They're getting married, and we'll have lots of food and flowers and people and..."

Bibb saw Benji's happiness fade at the word *people* so clarified, changing to a serious tone as she addressed the big, fearful man. "Billy is having some friends who do this sort of thing—put together parties and such—take care of the arrangements. He asked them to stay for the ceremony. The 'I

301

do's' won't take too long, so there really wasn't any reason for them to leave then come right back…"

Benji held up his hand, letting Bibb know that she didn't need to explain further. "I'm sorry. I hope I dinna come across as rude. He *is* jest invitin' people who are helpin' with the, the weddin', though, right?" he asked, his voice ending with a squeak of insecurity.

"Well, I also invited the girls who live here, but no, there aren't any, ahem, out of town guests flying in on the Concorde," Bibb said, then rolled her eyes.

"A Concorde is a verra big and fast plane," Benji explained to Jane. "I told ye about airplanes, aye?"

"Aye, but I thought you flew in them, not on them," she said.

"Weel, technically yer in a plane, but I think they say *on* because yer *on board.*"

"Maybe Benji will take you on a trip *in* an airplane after, after a while," Bibb said, then blushed as she realized that she was subconsciously trying to get Benji back to Scotland to see his family and show off his new wife. She shook her head minimally, admonishing herself for being such a busybody. He'd get to it in his own time. Hopefully.

Ж

Billy popped his head into Mac's room. "Okay, Janie, you go with Mom, and she'll help you into your dress. Benji, you can't see your bride in her dress until you're in front of the preacher. You did put your suit in my room, right?" Billy asked.

"Weel, I put the clothes I plan on wearin' in there. Where do I go once I'm all spruced up?"

"Peter will come get you. Now, go get ready. And don't forget to shave…and I don't care if you already shaved today, I want you to look your best. I hired a photographer, too."

Benji rolled his eyes and sighed in resignation. "Do I get a kiss first?"

"Well, if you insist," Billy said jokingly, then tiptoed up and bussed him on the cheek.

Everybody laughed at Benji's blush, then he joined them in the guffaws. "Weel, this'll be the last kiss I get from my fiancée because she's going to be my wife in just a wee bit."

Benji walked up slowly to Jane. "I never thought I'd find anyone to share my life with, but when ye finally let me look into yer eyes, I kent ye were mine. This is yer last chance. Do ye still want to marrit me?"

302

"Verra much so," Jane answered, then gave him a reserved kiss, chagrined that they were kissing in front of others. "And you?"

"Aye, more than anythin' I can think of." He gathered her close, picked her up, and lifted her off the ground, giving her a more adequate kiss, swinging her side to side before he put her feet back on the ground. "Now, jest dinna change yer mind; it'd break my heart and everythin' else, too, if ye did."

Ж

"Well you sure cleaned up well. What happened to your jacket?" Billy asked.

Peter answered for Benji. "He refused to buy one. He said that even if he could find one that fit—which we couldn't by the way—that it'd be a waste of money since he'd only wear it for the one day."

"Nae, I said fer the five minutes or so," Benji corrected.

"Five minutes, ten minutes, it doesn't matter. There was nothing we could find that was worthy of the occasion, and the shirt was so nice that I hated to see it covered up. And well, you said it best, he sure cleaned up well." Peter tugged the open collar to one side, pulling it into alignment, and smoothed out the slight wrinkles across the shoulders. "You look like you belong in a pirate movie with that shirt. Shoot, you look like you belong in the 18th century, not the 21st. Either way, you're the sexiest groom I've seen today!"

"Here, here," Billy said in agreement as he elbowed Benji in the ribs and winked at his mother. "I'll agree to that on both counts!"

"Okay, Billy, where's the groom?" asked the young man in jeans and a sports coat as he walked into the room. "Oh, this must be him. Benji, I'm Jake, the preacher. What's your full name, and are you sure you want to do this? I mean, this is your last chance to stay single," he joked, then playfully punched the tall groom-to-be in the arm.

"Benjamin Ian Pomeroy MacKay, and I've never wanted anythin' more in my life. Is she ready? I mean, where do we go, and are we ready? Oh, did I jest ask that? I'm a little nervous. I've never been marrit before."

"Well, I do marriages right the first time, so you'll never have to do this over again. I performed the ceremony for Billy's brother a little over a year ago. By the way, how are James and Leah doing?" Jake asked Billy.

"I saw them jest last week," Benji answered, not giving Billy the chance to find an excuse for or to lie about their whereabouts. "They have a wee daughter, Bibb Elizabeth, named after family." Benji winked at Bibb. He hadn't had the chance to tell her that she had another grandchild, her first granddaughter. "Bibby Liz has big, beautiful hazel eyes and jest about the baldest heid ye ever saw on a bairn. She's the same age as Billy and Peter's boy, Mac. Sorry, I dinna get a picture of her. Ye'll jest have to believe me when I tell ye she's the prettiest, wee lass ye ever did see."

Bibb sniffed back the tears that had sprung up when she heard she had a granddaughter. Bibby Liz was back in the 18th century. She'd never see her. But, her heir in the past had good parents, and would be loved and safe, as long as they were alive.

"Ahem," announced Bibb to both clear her throat and get the men's attention. "We have a beautiful bride waiting patiently in my room for the man in charge to tell her it's time to be wed. Now, if you'll all take your places, she's allowed me to have the honor of escorting her down the aisle. A bit untraditional to be sure, but that seems to work for this family!"

Jake took Benji's left arm as Billy took his right. Peter looked around, feeling left out of the proceedings. "Come on, son," Bibb said as she held out her elbow. "You can escort me to the bride and take charge of our little Frodo."

"Mac's going to be the ring bearer?" he asked. "Isn't he too small?"

"Well, the ring's in a case, so he can't put it in his mouth, or at least swallow it. I have a ring for her that was Marty's. Dang, he sure chose a bad time to go to Australia for his research! Anyhow, I had Janie close her eyes while I tried it on her. She knows, sort of, that she's getting a ring, but doesn't know what it looks like. It fits her like Cinderella's slipper, just like it was made for her."

Ж

Bibb knocked softly on the bedroom door. "Are you decent?" she asked.

"Excuse me?" Jane answered as she opened the door to let her in, balancing Mac on her wedding dress-covered hip as Amy stood attentively behind her.

"My, my; you are more than decent, Janie, you're stunning. You have the most beautiful hair I have ever seen," Peter said as his hand air glided above her long, soft curled tresses. Peter turned his attention to the eager young pregnant woman beside her. "I see you already have your roses, Amy. My, my, you look beautiful, too."

304

Amy blushed, then nodded, "Thank you; you're beautiful, too."

"Thank you," Peter said, then gave her a short, courteous bow. "Oh, and here, Janie; I'll trade you my son for the bouquet. He's gorgeous, I know, but the bride is supposed to carry flowers down the aisle, not little boys."

Jane handed Mac to Peter, then stepped back. "Is it time yet?" she asked, her left hand nervously twisting one of her newly formed ringlets around her index finger.

Peter and Bibb looked up at her head at the same time. "Just one more thing, dear; here, sit down." Bibb patted the end of the bed, then went to her dresser. She pulled open the top drawer and took out the tissue wrapped package. "This is the same veil Leah wore when she married James. I'm sure she'd want you to wear it, too." She sighed deeply. "Too bad her daughter, Bibby Liz," she sighed the name and paused in reflection, "too bad she won't be able to wear it when she gets married. We'll keep it in the family, though, so your daughters, or son's fiancées, can wear it, too."

Bibb arranged the simple yet delicate veil on Jane's head, gently guiding the lacy edges so they framed her face, flowed over her shoulders, and then down her back.

The bride blushed with pride at the thought of being a wife and mother, of having children who she and Benji would be able to rear as married parents. It was more than she had ever hoped for.

"Okay; *now* it's showtime, Janie." Bibb patted her on the back in reassurance. "Peter, will you escort the ring bearer and flower girl ahead of us?"

Peter carried Mac in his left arm, and Amy held onto his right elbow as they walked down the hall. "Come on, little Frodo. This may not be a ring of power, but it's still special." He added softly, "I do believe this is the one that Grandpa Marty said had something to do with Australian fairies. Can you believe that, fairies down under? Yeah, well, neither can I."

Ж

"Billy," Jake whispered from the doorway, "what's the bride's name?"

"Janie, no, it's actually Jane," he said, then sucked in a huge lungful of air as he pronounced a possible fib—maybe an out and out lie. "She only uses the first name of Jane. It's traditional where she's from, only one name. Janie is what family calls her." He winched then added, "But, she'll take Benji's last name when they're married, so don't worry about it."

305

"Sounds good to me; Benji has enough names for the both of them."

Benji looked at Billy then Jake. "Is it time yet?" he asked anxiously, trying to keep his voice even.

Billy turned around and looked down the hall. His mother was standing beside a very nervous bride, patting her hand and whispering assurances up to her. It must have worked because a wave of calm washed over Jane, a smile of confidence taking the place of the nervous facial twitches. Peter was two feet away, trying to wrest the ring box away from Mac who had decided that the carved hardwood box was a better teething ring than his plastic keys. Peter looked up and saw Billy smile at him. "We're ready," he mouthed, as he nodded to Mac and the ladies.

"Let the wedding begin," Billy announced to Jake, then smiled at Benji. "It's been a long time coming, aye?"

"Aye," Benji squeaked, then swallowed hard and said in a lower tone, "Verra much aye."

Jake pointed to Tom, the photographer, who took the cue, and flipped the switch on the oversized boom box. Bagpipes and the tune of The Highland Wedding filled the air.

"Come on," Billy said to Benji, tugging gently at the suddenly terrorized man's elbow. "This is the first step to your glorious future as a husband and then, in about a year or less, a father. Don't be scarrit; jest put one foot in front of the other," he added in a lighthearted, Scot's accent.

Benji looked down at his big feet in the brand new Wellington work boots and said, "Ye heard what the man said, one foot in front of the other." He put one foot out, took a deep breath, and moved forward. "First step: husband. Second step: make the bairns. I think I can handle that."

"I ken ye can handle that," Billy said. He held onto Benji's elbow, and they made their way to Jake in their step pause, step pause, ritualistic walk down the aisle. They arrived at Jake and stopped. Billy patted Benji's arm, then walked around him, turning Benji around to face his bride who was now making her way up the same rose petal strewn pathway.

Bibb looked very small and pale next to the tall, dark bride, but her pride was obvious. She couldn't have been more radiant if this was her own biological daughter she was escorting to the groom and the preacher. The tears of joy were streaming down her face, unrestrained by hankies or the back of a hand. The glistening only made her simple aqua suit more elegant.

They came to a stop at the men. Bibb patted Jane's hand, then picked it up and placed it in Benji's open, widespread palm.

Benji placed his other warm hand on top of hers, and sighed. "Mine," he whispered to her alone. Jane didn't say a word with her mouth, but looked up into his eyes and gave a minimal nod in agreement, a smile of peace enhancing her already glowing beauty.

Jake cleared his throat to get everyone's attention. He held up a very small Bible for everyone to see. "We are gathered here today to join this man, Benjamin Ian Pomeroy MacKay, and this woman, Jane, a true lady who is so awesome that she didn't even need a maiden name, in wedded matrimony, in the eyes of God, and all of these witnesses. The groom has let me use his family Bible here, and we'll record this special date in it for their future generations to share. Now Benji, as your friends and family know you, do you take this woman, Janie, to be your lawfully wedded wife, to have and to hold, to cherish and protect, in good times and bad, in sickness and in health, in prosperity and poverty, from this day until forever and ever; death will not break you two apart?"

Benji took a deep breath and concentrated his whole being on making sure his words didn't squeak out. "I. Do!" he said emphatically and with an artificially lowered voice. He had overdone his anti-squeaking effort and gone an octave too low. He snorted a quick giggle, then lifted his left shoulder in slight embarrassment, but didn't say anything, not wanting to bring more attention to his overcorrection.

Jake nodded, and proceeded. "Jane, Janie to your closest friends and family, do you take this fine, young man, Benji, to be your lawfully wedded husband, to have and to hold, to cherish and support, in good times and bad, in sickness and in health, in prosperity and poverty, from this day until forever and ever; death will not break you two apart?"

"I do," Jane said, "and I'll protect him, too, if he needs it." She blushed at her own remark, then looked to Benji. "He asked if you'd protect me, but didn't ask me to protect you. I'll do it if you need me to," she looked to Jake, then Bibb and Billy. "Really, I would, I will."

"I'm sorry, Janie," Jake said, "I should have put that in your vows, too. Thanks for the correction. Now, that being said, if anyone here sees any reason why these two should not be married, tough stuff: they're married! The husband may now kiss his wife, Janie MacKay, the lovely lady who now has two names."

Benji put one hand on each side of Jane's face and bent forward to kiss her. She looked up at him and said, "You can have my smiles and everything else now."

He paused before kissing her and said, "And you can have my name and everything else now, including my children." He leaned forward and gave her his first kiss as her husband.

"The ring, the ring! Jake, you forgot about the ring!" Peter said as he rushed forward, pulling the slobbery ring box out of Mac's mouth, wiping it on his shirt. Mac squealed with excitement as he wriggled in his papa's arms, trying to make a getaway to Nanny Janie.

Benji pulled back and said, "Aye, Mrs. MacKay, I dinna have a chance to pick out a ring, but my dear Bibb said she had one that was jest right fer ye. It has a story behind it, so it's even more special than if it was brand new. And it almost has yer initials in it: JIM. Either someone put in one too many letters fer yer name or not quite the right ones fer mine, but either way, it's a gift from the Melbourne family to you, to us. Thank ye, Bibb, and to Marty, too, wherever he may be."

Bibb nodded, looked down, and mumbled softly, "or whenever."

45 The Reception

Benji placed the ring on Jane's finger then bent forward, bringing her hand to his lips, kissing the iridescent opal gently. "I ken that I'm only supposed to have one kiss, but can I have another one, here?" Benji asked playfully, pointing to his pouty bottom lip.

Jane glanced from side to side and saw that everyone was rapt, waiting for her to give him that second kiss. "Anythin' ye ask," she said, then kissed him again, melting in the completeness that she felt as part of something bigger and better than she ever thought possible: a married couple.

Benji's put his hand behind her head to pull her closer to him. "Yer hair!" he exclaimed as he pulled back from the kiss. "What happened to it? And when?"

"Um, it was like this when we were in Mac's room. Don't you like it?" she asked in momentary panic, remembering that Alisha had said that she didn't know if she could return the now loosely curled hair back to its former wiry condition. She'd only had the long, soft hair for a couple of hours, but really didn't want to go back to wearing it twisted, braided, and wrapped under a cloth bound around her head.

Benji saw her frown of uncertainty, then decided he'd better confess. "I'm sorry I dinna notice it earlier. I think I was a bit distracted with..." He saw her mouth twitch, trying to decide whether it was appropriate to smile or not at his embarrassment. "Aye, now *that* I remember seein': yer smile. Yer eyes and yer smile are the same as before. Nae, they're even brighter and prettier if that's even possible. I'm sorry I dinna notice yer new hairstyle earlier. It seems to fit ye, if that makes any sense. How'd ye do it?"

"Oh," Jane grinned broadly, then looked at Billy to make sure it was okay to let her hairdresser, Benji's surprise guest, be known. Billy nodded, then stood aside and revealed Wee Michael. "I didn't change my hair," Jane said coyly. "I got a *makeover* from some verra nice people."

"Michael?" Benji squeaked when he saw his longtime friend walk toward him. "Wee Michael and Alisha? Of course, yer Alisha. And is that Wee Beatrice? And who is this lovely little bit? Aye, she must be yers, Michael; she looks jest like ye."

Jane stepped back to allow Wee Michael and his family access to Benji's opened arms. Chandra wasn't sure about the group hug and pulled away, seeking refuge behind the bride's wide skirt. The three year old reached up, took one of Jane's hands, and then raised her other arm, asking wordlessly to be held. Jane picked her up and whispered, "Do you want to meet the red-haired giant? He's a very nice man and he's my husband now." Chandra pulled her head away from Jane's hair, nodded her head, 'yes,' and then buried her face back into the downy coif. "Benji, this is Chandra. Chandra, this is my husband, Benji."

"Weel, Chandra, it's a pleasure to meet ye. Now, I have it on good authority that there's lots of tasty food in the other room, jest waitin' fer us to come eat it. There's even a cake and probably some food that's good fer ye, too. But," he said, as he looked up at Jane, beaming with pride at his wife, "the cake is the most important part. It's traditional fer the bride and groom to eat a bite or two, to signify a long and happy marriage."

"Ahem," Alisha cleared her throat and looked at Benji to get his attention. "The sharing of your first piece of cake is to show unity. The sweetness of it is to ensure a harmonious relationship. And the flour the cake is made of, the wheat, is symbolic of," Alisha patted her very pregnant belly, "fertility. Come on everyone, Carlos has prepared a grand feast with a beautiful three-tiered white cake for dessert. And you men can catch up on old times after the honeymoon. I think these two belong together, not you two," she said as she nudged Wee Michael away from Benji, then extracted Chandra from Jane's arms. "Thanks for being here for him," she said softly to Jane.

"Well," Jane said meekly, "I'm sure glad he was there for me. I don't know where I'd be without him." She shook her head as she thought back to that time—only a week ago—when he had rescued her from the slaver and more flogging, when she had decided that she'd rather die than be beaten again for no reason. "I'm *verra* glad."

46 Finally

"**O**kay, okay, thank you everyone for coming, getting everything set up, *and then* cleaned up so quickly. I think we'll pass on the traditional partying until the wee hours and getting drunk, though. I don't think anyone here cared that we substituted fresh juices for the fermented kind. Now, the ladies in waiting and young girls waiting to be ladies," Billy said with a wink at Beatrice and Chandra, "need their rest. And I'm sure the bride and groom are a bit tired, too. They came a long, long way to get here today." Billy winked at Benji and Janie at his reference to the long *time* they had spanned.

"Aye," Benji said as he faked a yawn and stretched his arms wide behind Jane, "I think I could do with a little shut eye."

Jane gulped. She didn't want to go to sleep, but certainly didn't want to tell anyone what she *did* want to do. Billy looked at her and gave one more of his winks. "However, I think the groom has one more duty to perform before he can get his shut eye tonight."

Benji blushed, then hung his head, trying to hide the red glow he knew was radiating. "It's okay, Benji," Wee Michael said. "I think everyone knows what comes next, and it's okay because you're married now. So, how long did you have to wait for her, I mean, how long were you engaged?"

"Weel, I've waited practically my whole life and—dependin' on how ye figure it—it's either been a long, long engagement or a verra short one. But, it doesna really matter. Whether it was two days, two weeks, or two centuries, she was worth waitin' fer. Come on, Mrs. MacKay; let's wish everyone a good night."

Hearty handshakes, hugs, and kisses on cheeks were shared to such a great extent that almost no one noticed when Benji and Jane slipped away from the laughter and squeezes. Bibb, however, did. She caught up to the couple as they walked outside for a breath of fresh air before leaving the party area. "Janie, I went ahead and put Mac to bed. I hope you don't mind and that you won't get too uncomfortable," she said then looked at Jane's breasts.

"Oh, the milk. Will he be okay? I mean, did you give him a bottle?"

"Yes, he's fine, and he sleeps through the night now, so don't worry about him. I just thought I'd tell you so you wouldn't be concerned. He'll be happy to see you in the morning, I'm sure."

Jane pressed her upper arms in close to her chest and felt the fullness of her breasts. "I'll be happy to see him, too." Jane bent down and gave Bibb a kiss on the cheek. "You're such a wonderful person. I'll always love and miss my mother, but you sure help fill the empty spot that I've had for so many years."

"Oh, well, I'm glad I could be here for you," Bibb said, blushing with pride. "You two go ahead and have a good evening. I left your new clothes in my bedroom, for tonight at least. The room is bigger and has an attached bathroom. If you need anything, well, I'm sure you have everything you need in each other."

"Ye have that right!" Benji said. He grabbed Janie by the waist and gave her another kiss. "And there's plenty more where that came from! Good night and thanks again, for everything," he said, then gulped her name, "Bibb," suddenly missing his mother.

Billy was right: he should have waited a few days and invited his parents to the wedding. He still missed both of them, nearly as much now as when he was a teenager. He had lived without them for most of his life. But, they were the ones who had been there for him since the beginning. They had nurtured, counseled, and tried to prepare him for life; their stubborn son who always believed he was right, no matter what the facts said. He thought he had done the right thing, letting them believe that he was dead, but maybe, just maybe, he was wrong. But, he couldn't change the past. He snorted. Now wasn't the time to reflect on what he should or should not have done. He looked down at his boots in shame; he had probably spoiled the mood. One foot in front of the other, Billy had said. He looked over at Janie. Her smile had faded. She could see his sadness and certainly didn't know what it was from.

"I'm sorry, Janie. I jest had somethin' botherin' me and weel, it'll wait." He smiled as he looked at the bedroom door in front of him. "Now, earlier we had the traditional Scottish wedding song played fer our party, and now I need to—rather I want to—perform another Scottish rite. Ye did ken my family is from Scotland, aye?"

"No, I don't know anything about Scotland. Is it near Africa?"

"Nae, but I'll give ye a geography lesson later. I'll show ye where we are now, North Carolina, and how far away

Scotland and Africa are from here. But fer now, we have somethin' more important to do."

Benji squatted down and put his right hand under Jane's knees, his left arm around her back and under her armpit. "This is where I carry ye over the threshold. Ye see, the old superstition said there were evil spirits livin' in the threshold of a home, and the husband was to protect his wife by carryin' her across it."

Jane snuggled into his neck, then gave him a quick kiss on the cheek. "I remember, sort of, the first time you carried me this way. You were protecting me, for sure. They weren't evil spirits, but evil men you were keeping me away from then. And, I like this much better than the way you carried me the first time."

"What first time?" he asked as he cuddled her closer, rocking her side to side, not wanting to set her down.

"When the lightning struck that tree we were under. You tossed me over your shoulder, then threw me on the ground, and took off my dress and…"

Benji sighed. "Aye, but I was savin' ye, or tryin' to."

Jane rubbed her nose into Benji's ear then whispered, "You did. And it all turned out fine."

"Aye, finer than fine. But, I'm gonna have to set ye down. I canna kiss ye and hold ye like this at the same time."

Benji let her legs slip out of his arms, but kept her upper body close. "Now that we're here in the room," he whispered, then stopped. He was suddenly tongue-tied and embarrassed. The intimacy had been so much easier in the wilds. He felt constrained in Bibb's bedroom, where she and Marty must have…

"Would you help me?" Jane asked, hoping to divert him from his brooding. She could see Benji was afraid of what came next. She'd seen him like this before. But, now he didn't have the excuse that they weren't married to keep from doing more than kissing and holding and stroking. He didn't reply to her request for help, so she added, "please?"

"Aye." His mood lifted as he remembered asking her 'please' that first day they met. Jane had turned around so he could help her undress. "Let's see. Now why do ye think they put these zippers on the back of the dress? Dinna they ken that it's nearly impossible fer the bride to get out of by herself?"

"I don't think the bride is *supposed* to get out of it by herself." Jane pulled her shoulders in, and let the dress drop to the floor.

"Wha, what's that?" Benji squeaked.

Jane stepped out of the pile of wedding dress. "Bibb said that I needed proper undergarments. Don't you like them." She turned slowly in place, showing off the lacy panties and deep plunged bra.

"Good Lord, yes!" he said in a very American accent. He gulped and tried to compose himself. "I like them verra much," he said, now sounding like himself, "but I like what's in them even more."

"Did you get new undergarments, too?" she asked, hoping that he'd start taking off his clothes.

"Uh, huh." He untucked his shirt and pulled it off over his head. "But, I dinna get a bra, just..." He unzipped his pants, scooted them down, then realized that he still had his boots on. He sat down clumsily on the floor and pulled off one boot, the sock coming off with it. He tugged and pulled at the other boot, but it wouldn't budge, his awkward pose with pants half on and half off restricting his effort.

"Here." Jane turned around and bent over, presenting her lacy backside to his face. She grabbed the boot firmly and yanked, getting it off easily. "They're new boots, aye?"

"Aye," Benji said in embarrassment, then accepted her hand to stand up. He inhaled deeply and shoved the pants down further, stepping on the hems to pull them off all the way. "Peter said you'd like them."

"They're okay," Janie said, commenting on the leopard print briefs, "but I like what's in them better." She walked up to her new husband and put her hand on the bulge that was trying to escape the elastic waistband. "They're soft..."

"Aye, but what's in them..."

"Is jest right," Janie said seductively. "We don't have to wait for anything else, do we?" she asked as she continued her briefs brushing.

"Weel, it would be better, I'm sure, if ye were out of these," Benji said and gently moved the bra strap off her shoulder with one hand, reaching around her with the other, slipping it into the back of her panties, caressing her bottom, pulling her firmly to him.

"Would you help...?" Janie didn't have to finish her request for assistance in removing the awkward breast container; his hands were already there. "Bibb said it's what women wear, but it couldn't have been a woman who designed this one. The closures are in the back and hard to reach."

Benji began kissing his bride's neck, then came up and kissed her mouth thoroughly, unhooking her bra with one hand, his disrobing skills from his old days as a young gigolo returning. He quickly swallowed that unwelcome hint of a memory and concentrated on the feel of her mouth, so right with his tongue inside, her body rubbing up against his. Gulp. Her hand was inside his skivvies now, her hand wrapped around his eager cock.

She pulled back from their wet kiss. "Mine?" she asked as she gave it a quick, firm squeeze.

"Mmm, hmm," Benji grunted lustily, then lead her awkwardly to the bed. Suddenly, he didn't care who had been in the bed and whether or not anyone or anything had ever made love in it. This was *their* bed tonight. Mr. and Mrs. Benji MacKay were going to consummate their marriage right now, whether there was a bed under their intertwined bodies or they were conjoined on a leaf littered forest floor.

He pushed his briefs down his hips and felt Jane's hands take over, continuing the strip, pulling them down past his knees to his ankles. He stepped out of them then looked at her, clad only in lacy panties. He shook his head in amazement. She looked nothing like the woman who had arrived with him earlier today, even less like the onyx statue he had seen at the slaver's sale. She had metamorphosed into a grand and glorious butterfly, too fantastic for words. "May I?" he asked as he put his hands on the outside of her panties.

"Oh, I wish you would," she moaned, eager to be one with him.

Benji slid them down, his nose in her belly as he proceeded to her feet. She held onto the back of his head as she stepped out of her panties, part of her wanting him to continue the kissing that was getting closer and closer to her female parts, the other part wanting to hold his man part that felt so right in her hand. And, she was sure it would feel so right inside her, too.

Benji stood up halfway, stopping his belly kissing to hold her full breasts. "I did hear Bibb say that Mac had a bottle tonight..." The tone of his voice asked the rest of his question without saying the words.

"Aye, they're yours for tonight—yours again. Oh, please, though, let's lie down..."

The two naked bodies lay on the bed, her legs thrashing in ecstasy as Benji suckled his favorite part, and Jane received her virginal climaxes. "Now?" Benji asked, as he scooted up to be face to face.

"Oh, aye, now, please." She knew she sounded as if she was begging, but she didn't care.

315

Benji rolled on top of her, one elbow supporting his weight as he felt for his target. He slid his thumb up to make sure she was moist and ready. He brought it back down, intentionally tickling her clit. "Ooh!" she squealed. "Wha, what's that?"

"Jest the beginnin', darlin', jest the beginnin'." He gently eased his way in, using considerable self-control to keep from pushing in all at once.

"Whoa, whoa, whoa," Janie moaned.

"Am I hurtin' ye?" he asked, stopping in mid-stroke, afraid that he was hurting her.

"Whoa, as in this is good, great, greatest! Don't stop. If it hurts, you and everyone else in this house will probably know, but, ah, that's it..."

Ж

"I think I'm going to like this too much," Jane said after they finished their second round of lovemaking.

"I dinna think that's possible." He noticed her frown of confusion and explained. "Ye see, I like it too much, too. And since we're marrit and can *be* together, weel, jest about anytime we want..."

He paused and gave his glowing bride another passionate kiss, not feeling rushed to finish the act. "Now, see what ye went and did?" He rolled onto his back and showed her the result of their late night smooching.

"Aye, and now I know how to take care of it, jest about anytime we want." She purred as she rolled over on top of him. "How about if we give your elbows and shoulders a rest? I think this will still work with me on top. At least, I'd like to try and see."

"Ye can try anything ye want darlin'; I'm all yers, inside and out, but especially here, inside." Benji thumped his heart. "Thank ye fer comin' back with me."

"And thank you for bringing me. I would have stayed with you as your slave at your Grandpa's farm with him and his family, but Bibb and Billy and your family here, are nice, too."

Benji winced at the word family. He didn't try to hide his emotions around Janie. Or hadn't yet. He'd have to rethink that decision.

Jane saw his grimace, but misread it. "Maybe we've made more family tonight," she said, then giggled. "But, just in case we haven't, let's see if my being on top helps. I don't think it could hurt."

Benji sighed in appreciation at her mood brightening words. "Aye, and if it does, weel jest try another position."

47 Return to Barden Hall
November 1, 2014

"You have family?" Jane asked. She didn't know whether to be happy that they were alive, or angry that he hadn't told her, but she was definitely shocked at the news. "I thought you were all alone, that they died years ago."

Benji shook his head in shame. "I was kidnapped, stolen from them, when I was a lad. I let it be kent that I was deid so they wouldna try to find me. Some verra bad men woulda kilt them if they tried to get me back. Aye, my parents are still alive, but dinna ken that I am."

"Benji, you need to go see your family. I care for you deeply. You know how much I love you, but I would give you up if I could see my mother just one more time. I can't say that I'd do that for my father because I never knew him. That's a whole different kind of hurt. But you, and only you, can mend this. Once they're dead, you can't let them know how much you loved them."

"Aye, yer right, Janie. I've missed too much time with them already and there isna a reason to delay seein' them. All the bad guys are in prison, last I heard. Besides, I have someone fer them to meet. I couldna keep ye from them. I mean, I ken I dinna own ye, but ye are my greatest treasure."

Ж

"Bibb, I havena said anythin' to Billy yet, but do ye think it would be okay if we left fer a few days? I mean, the lad, can he go back to the bottle while I take my wife to meet my family in Scotland?"

"Of course; he'll be fine. That's all he had for the first four and a half months. He might get a bit fussy, but I don't think it will be because of the milk or formula. I think he's fond of Janie. We all are. Just make sure you both come back, at least for a while. It's your life to do as you both see fit, but know that you'll always have a place in our home and in our hearts."

Ж

Benji was apprehensive about coming out to the house unannounced. He should have called ahead. All he had told her

317

on the phone was that he'd try to get to Scotland 'one of these days.' And now he was almost there.

He could have kicked Billy for making the call two days ago, and then just handing him the phone. Hell, he didn't even know who he was talking to! How could he have known, or even suspected, that it was his sister on the other end? He hadn't seen her in five years or talked to her or anyone else in the family for over twenty.

"I knew you weren't dead!" she squealed through the phone line. "Mom and Dad knew it, too. But, they still wouldn't look for you. All they would say was that there was a good reason, a *verra* good reason, for it. They promised me over and over again that one day you'd come back; come back when we'd least expect it. Well, they were sure right! Then again, they usually are. But, don't tell them I said that: I don't want them to get swelled heads."

He let her babble on for a few minutes. The tears were flowing down his face and throat. He tried to answer her questions, but she was pretty sharp and picked up on his inability to speak. When she told him that she was married and had two children, it was too much for him to fathom. He felt rude when he told her that he had to go. He didn't want to admit to her, or even to himself, that he couldn't handle it. She was gracious about it, but made him promise to come see her and her family at Barden Hall sometime. "You do remember how to get home, don't you?"

"Um, hmm," he mumbled, then listened to her tell him that she loved him. There was a long pause as she waited for him to respond, but he was in shock. He went ahead and pushed the end button on the phone rather than make her wait for the words he couldn't cough up. He wished with all his heart that he could take back that moment, but that was impossible. Hmph! He could go back 230 years, but couldn't reverse time one minute. But, he would do what was second best: he'd go to tell her in person.

Ж

"This is where I grew up," he told Jane as they drove down the dirt road from the main highway. "I mean, not all the time. I was born there in North Carolina near where my Grandpa and Grannie lived. We came back to Scotland when I was six and lived here until I was kidnapped at twelve. But those were six great years," he said, trying to hide his fear of meeting his sister and his past.

318

Jane reached over and patted his leg in reassurance. She could see he was frightened. "Weel, I try to not hide anythin' from ye, but, aye, I am slightly scarrit," Benji admitted.

Jane chuckled and asked, "Slightly?"

"Aye, slightly," he said, then amended his statement, "slightly terrified."

"They're your family and they love you. Be glad you have them to go back to," she said, then added softly, "and that you know who they are."

"Aye, I'm sorry I'm actin' like such a ninny. I ken ye miss yer mother and ye dinna ken if ye ever had any brothers or sisters, but now ye have my family, back in North Carolina both in the now and then times, and also here in Barden Hall. And *voila*! We're here," he announced with a newfound confidence.

"This is a verra old property. It's been in the family fer centuries." He pointed to the remnants of the long, white rock wall, eager to share his family's heritage. "That's part of the garden wall. The property once had grand flower gardens. That's all that's left of it. It was old when my Grandpa Jody was born here. The house was fairly new when he was born. Two centuries later, when I was a wee lad, my parents returned to live here. They added or upgraded plumbing and electricity. I guess ye woulda been more comfortable without the changes, aye?"

Jane exhaled and said, "Aye," and did her best not to show the fear she felt—she was going to meet the sister he cherished and her family.

Benji parked the rental car next to the black Mercedes minivan. He looked at the house and noticed the change in shadows as the kitchen door opened behind the screen door. There was a two-second pause, then the screen door burst open, and a dark haired female spitfire dashed out.

"Benji!" Becky screamed as she shot past the bushes, an ecstatic running back racing toward her fraternal goalpost, a young child rather than a football clutched close to her shoulder.

Benji didn't know how either of them would react when they first saw each other. Would they be shy and uncomfortable in each other's presence? Would she be mad that he hadn't called earlier, or even worse, would she be aloof?

He grinned from the bottom of his size 16 boots to the top of his short cropped red hair when he saw her flying toward him, totally uninhibited, squealing with a high pitched, irrepressible excitement. Becky jumped up into his open arms. He lifted her and the now squalling baby, holding them close, swinging them around until he was dizzy. He stopped the twirling, but didn't want to let go. "You're back, you're back," she kept repeating as she painted kisses all over his cheek, ears, and neck, her tears mixing with his.

He finally set her down when he realized that the baby probably needed tending to. "Yours?" he asked, although he knew he had to be. She had told him on the phone that she was married and had two children.

"This is Jim. Jim, this is your Uncle Benji," she said as she introduced her six-month-old son to his uncle, multitasking by wiping her face on her shoulder. The boy had settled down now that his mother's squealing had stopped. "I know, I know; there're already so many 'J' names in the family, but since he was his father's first son, I felt like I should honor him... Oh, I'm sorry," she apologized to the woman standing ten feet away, next to the rental car. "I was distracted, I mean, you must be Jane."

Jane didn't know how to react and looked to Benji for direction. Evidently, he was as stunned as she was. "How did you ken her name," Benji asked. "Did Billy tell ye?" Billy had promised not to tell anyone about anything. Dialing his sister and handing him the phone was not breaking the promise but *was* a sneaky and very clever way around it.

Becky's attention was drawn to a screeching noise behind the house. "Here," she said as she thrust the child with the curly dark hair into her brother's arms. "I'll be right back." She turned away and ran toward the strangled animal sounding squeal. "Bibb Elizabeth Melbourne, you put down that squirrel, right now!"

Benji's arms went slack in shock at hearing the name, inadvertently dropping the baby. "Oops," he said, as he caught the bundle of boy slipping past his belly. Little Jim started laughing—evidently he thought they were playing a game. "Ye like that, do ye?" Benji recreated the same movement, this time on purpose. "Come on, lad," he said to the bright-eyed boy, "let's go meet yer Aunt Janie."

Benji carried the cheerful boy child over to his pensive wife. "Here, meet yer nephew, Jim." He turned the child around in his arms to face her. The baby stuck his hand out to reach for his aunt just as Benji moved in to close the gap between the three of them. The boy's hand touched her nose gently, then suddenly grabbed a fistful of face, his tiny thumb shoved up her nostril, fingers clutching to get a better hold. Benji put his index finger in the middle of the grasp, trying to break apart the boy's fist before Jane was scratched. Young Jim protested and started wailing in distress at his uncle's attempt, holding on even tighter.

"Okay, okay; I'll let yer Aunt Janie free herself," he said, as he handed the child to her, still attached fist to nose.

As soon as Benji let go, Jim released the nose grip and buried his head into Janie's neck, taking that same grasping fist, and shoving its thumb into his mouth. He looked sheepishly over at his uncle, then up at his new companion, patting her shoulder with his free hand. He wanted to be held by a woman.

"Ach, a ladies' man already, aye?"

As if in answer, Jim smiled around the thumb stuck in his mouth, drool slipping past his chin onto his shirt, and buried his head back into Jane's neck.

"Bibb Elizabeth Melbourne, meet your Uncle Benji and his wife, Jane," Becky said to her daughter, who appeared to be four or five.

"I told you they were coming," she said to her mother, then turned to greet the two visitors. "Glad to meet you," she said with perfect poise. "And it's about time!" she added with unbridled frustration. "I've been hearin' about you all my life!"

"Ye have?" Benji asked, totally baffled. He looked to Jane, then Becky, and then back to the little girl. "And yer name's Bibb? Bibb Elizabeth Melbourne?"

"Yes, sir, and it's not Vivian either. It's a good name, and I *like* it," she bragged. "I'm named after my great-great-great-great, oh, shoot; I keep forgetting how many greats, but there're lots of them. She was born in America, but we still love her. My Mommy was born in America, too."

"I was, too," Benji said. "And that's where I've been fer a long time. I'm sorry I dinna get to meet ye sooner..."

"That's okay," young Bibby said soothingly, "you're here today, and that's better than having to wait until tomorrow. Were you born in America, too?" she asked Jane.

"No, I was born somewhere in Africa, but I don't remember where. I was about his age when I moved to America, though," she said as she hoisted her curly haired nephew.

Bibby neared Jane cautiously, clearing her throat to get the tall lady's attention. "I got you a present," she said boldly, then added softly, "Mama said you probably wouldn't want it, but I said you would. She made me promise to tell you that," Bibby sighed and recited the words dispassionately, "you don't have to take it if you don't want it." Bibby finished her oral presentation, ending it with her mother's mandated escape clause and a smile of confidence. She was sure that Aunt Janie would like her gift.

Jane didn't know if she was supposed to ask for the present or just be patient and wait for it to be given to her. She still wasn't used to speaking with people. As a slave, she was supposed to be quiet around the masters and all white folk. But, she had been shy with the other slaves, too. Most of them were afraid of her because of her size, and shunned her even though she had never— or would even think to ever—hurt anyone. She hadn't been close to anyone, black or white, after she was separated from her mother. She had moved from one owner to another more times than she could count. The only memories she had of those years were bad ones that she hadn't been able to bury, although she never did quit trying to get rid of them.

"Well, aren't you going to ask me what it is?" asked Bibby as she performed a little hop, step, hop, shuffle, trying to contain her excitement.

Jane squatted down so she was at Bibby's eye level. "Okay, what is it?" Receiving gifts was still new to her.

Bibby turned around and picked up the cardboard shoebox behind her. She had wrapped it in the colorful Sunday comics section of the newspaper and poked holes in the shape of a heart in the top cover. "Here, you can just lift the lid off. I didn't want her to suffocate. You can use this for her home until we get her a bigger cage. I call her a *her*, but she might be a boy. I don't know how to tell on squirrels, just dogs, and since I don't see a penis, it must be a girl."

"Bibb Elizabeth!" screeched Becky at her daughter's frankness about gender checking an animal.

"Well, I can't see a penis, and if it's a boy, then his balls are real small, so small that I can't see them. Daddy told me how to check."

"She's beautiful," Jane said as she held the pale little squirrel with the pink ribbon leash close to her chest. "Thank you," she said as the tears welled up in her eyes.

"You don't have to keep it," Becky explained, once again giving her an opportunity to back out of keeping the squirrel. "We have lots of them around here, but this is the only white one I've seen. *She* just happened to be a little too slow for our little Miss Safari Hunter. Bibby wouldn't name her. She said that you got that honor. But, you really don't..." Becky stopped talking when she saw the huge black woman bonding with the itty-bitty white squirrel.

"I had one when I was about your age," she told Bibby. "But she wasn't white on the front like this one. Their tails look just the same, though. Or will; this one is pretty young."

"See, Mom; I told you she had one before!" Bibby boasted, then stuck out her chest in pride.

"How did you know?" Jane asked as she stroked her new pet that had decided that her neck was a great nesting site.

"I know lots of stuff!" Bibby said, once again with pride. "But, I'm not supposed to talk about it, except with family," she added softly. "But, Jane is family, huh?" she asked her mother boldly.

"Aye, she's family," Becky said, leading the way back into the house. Her big brother had found himself a sweet wife. Maybe now the two of them would stick around.

Ж

"Do you want to see your picture?" the pert little pixie asked with a newfound burst of energy. "I drew it last week. Nobody knew who it was, but I told them that it was my Uncle Benji and his wife. I also told Mommy that you were coming here, both of you," she said as she grabbed her Uncle Benji's hand. "Come on," she called back to Jane when she saw that she wasn't following them. She waved her hand in a 'come hither' movement. "It looks just like you."

Benji grinned as he walked through the front door. It was a habit, one born of safety, that he automatically dipped his head as he walked into a room. He noticed that the doorway was tall enough that he didn't have to do more than nod. He could probably walk through it upright if he wasn't wearing boots. He paused inside the hallway, waiting for Jane and baby Jim to join him.

"It's in here," Bibby called impatiently from the living room. "See, it looks just like you, huh?"

Benji led Jane and her little charge into the room. He remembered the stairs, the slash marks from the second Uprising when Grandpa Jody was a young man over 250 years ago. The smells were familiar, too. The furniture had changed, though, as had the picture on the mantle. Jane and Benji gasped at the same time. 'Uncle Benji and Aunt Jane by Jenny Pomeroy-Hart, August, 1782' was printed at the bottom of the framed charcoal drawing of a happy couple, one tall man with short red ochre colored hair and one black-skinned woman in a blue sarong, both of them wearing oversized smiles.

"It looks jest like the picture Jenny drew for me before we left," Benji said to Jane. "She wanted to give it to me, but I told

323

her I kent what I looked like, and I wouldna leave yer side, so," he paused in his revelation to his now expanding audience, "I told Jenny to keep it to remember us by. I told her we were takin' a long, long trip, and I probably would never see her again."

"Uh, huh," Bibby said. "And she told me to draw a picture just like it for you, so you'd have it here. See, I even wrote her name. I spelled it right, huh?"

"Aye, ye did." Benji looked to his sister who was now in the doorway. He gave her a questioning look, hoping she would add some insight on how her precocious daughter had managed to produce the miraculous artifact.

"Bibby is smart beyond her years and she, um, evidently has 'the sight.' My husband's great, great—oh, we don't even count how many times over—grandmother had 'the sight', too. Her name was Leah Melbourne..."

Kerplunk. Benji had fainted, falling backwards to the floor. He was saved from cracking his skull on the hearth by his quick thinking wife, her one arm clutching the baby at her hip, the other, supporting his shoulders.

"Water?" Jane called, hoping that someone would get some for her. She didn't know where the water was in this house and didn't want to leave her fainted husband's side.

"Here," Becky said as she gave her the cup, exchanging it for baby Jim. "Oh, and here, wet this and put it on the back of his neck if you can reach it. Otherwise, slap it on his forehead." Becky had pulled a handkerchief out of her pocket and handed it to her new sister-in-law. "I'm glad *you* were there to catch him, because he sure got big!"

"Aye, weel, the bigger they are, the harder they fall...oof!" The now awake Benji groaned as he struggled to sit upright. He used the wet cloth to try and wipe the embarrassment off his face. Finally, feeling more composed, he asked, "Ye say that Leah is yer husband's ancestor?"

"And my children's. Big Jim is from Australia. We met on a school excursion ten years ago. We did the long distance romance for a while and then I went Down Under for a year. I really didn't like the heat, and he said he'd give Scotland a try. I'm really glad he liked it because we've been here ever since. Mom and Dad moved to Edinburgh, but they come out every couple of weeks or so. Dad can't keep his hands off the kids, and Mom is always trying to either update or restore something around here."

"My daddy got a picture like this from his great-great—shoot, I don't remember how many greats—Grandma Jenny. She married Mommy's first cousin's son, but we're not supposed to talk about it because no one would believe us, but it's true."

"Your father doesn't have any picture like that!" Becky exclaimed with frustration at her imaginative daughter.

"Yes, he does," asserted Bibby. "He just hasn't found it yet. But he will. I *know* he will. Hmph!" she added in mild defiance.

Becky rolled her eyes in defeat at her daughter's insistent attitude.

"I take it that this happens all the time?" asked Benji, still seated on the floor, cradled by his equally intrigued wife.

"Yes, if she tells you something, you'd better believe it, or at least prepare for it, because it's going to come to pass. I think I'm going to have to home school this one. I don't want to think what would happen if she started spouting her little *revelations* around the other students. Plus, I doubt she'd learn much if she knew the answers before the questions were even written!"

"I can read already, huh, Mommy?" Bibby interjected.

"Yes, dear, you can read and do your numbers, but that doesn't mean you're better than anyone else, right?"

"I know, I know," Bibby said in exasperation, as if she had heard the lecture eight times too many already, and then recited dryly, "We are all special, and everyone has gifts. It's just that we don't always know what our gifts are when we're young, and sometimes people never do find out what they are." Bibby suddenly brightened up. "Can I teach you to read, Aunt Janie? It is okay if I call you Aunt Janie instead of Aunt Jane, right?"

Becky sputtered at her daughter's impudence, but Benji held up his hand for her to hold off with her scolding. He wanted to see what would happen without their interference.

"Aunt Janie is fine, and I would love for you to teach me. "Do you know that you remind me of someone?"

"Who?" Bibby asked, although she was only being polite; she already knew the answer.

"You don't look like Jenny Pomeroy-Hart, and you're a lot younger than she was when we left, but you have her, her..." Jane couldn't think of the word to use and was spared embarrassment by Benji.

"Ye have yer Grandma Jenny's spunk," Benji said. "And ye ken who she is, aye?"

"Oh, yes sir! Mom used to think that she was my imaginary friend, but now she knows she's a real person, huh, Mom?"

"Yes, dear. I believe everything you tell me, *now*. But remember, I won't believe *anything* you ever tell me again if you lie to me even one time, right?"

Bibby nodded, then went to the side drawer in the rolltop desk. She pulled out a tattered box that held a partial set of pastels. "See, I got these from the white elephant sale at church. They really didn't have any white elephants, just a bunch of stuff from people's attics and garages. Jenny's going to get some of these, too, from Poppi, but not until Christmas. But, she has some black sticks with cloth around them and a piece of an old clay pot. That's how she colored your hair. But, she did that after you left. She didn't have any blue crayons. I just did it by myself because I knew the dress was blue. But, the picture she drew for you was only gray, huh? "

"Aye, it's true. Did ye ken that I made the charcoal sticks fer yer Grandma Jenny so she could draw that picture? Her daddy, Grannie's brother, yer Uncle Wallace, must have found her the red clay to use fer the color of my hair."

Bibb Elizabeth nodded then changed subjects. She was eager to find out about her new kin. She could 'see' many things, but could tell that her uncle was undecided about where he was going to live. "Are you going to move to Barden Hall? We got lots of room here," she practically begged. "I was trying to build you a house in the back. Mommy said my tree house was too small, so I was trying to make it bigger. But, I don't think I can make it *that* big. You're real tall...and so are you. You're even taller than Nana, my Grannie. I only have one Grannie and one Grandpa, though, because Daddy's parents are both dead. And I have a Great-Grannie and Great-Grandpa, but I can't see them. They're far, far away, but we have letters that they wrote to us. We get to read them once in a while, but Grandpa doesn't really read them. He holds onto the paper and tells us what they say. He's read them so many times, he has them memorized. Nana cries when he reads them sometimes, but she says they're happy tears. They're gonna be here soon, too—Nana and Grandpa, not Great-Grannie and Great-Grandpa."

Becky had been mute during her daughter's rambling conversation. She'd get her chance to talk to her brother later. Right now, she was enjoying the initial bonding her daughter was having with her one and only uncle. "What?" she suddenly blurted, as she realized what Bibby Liz had just said. "Your grandparents are on holiday. They were supposed to leave for Greece yesterday morning."

326

"Unh, unh," the four-year-old wonder proclaimed. "I called them and told them that Uncle Benji and Aunt Janie were gonna be here today, about noon. They said, 'thank you,' and that they would try to be on time, but not early. They wanted *me* to get a chance to meet my new kin first," she bragged.

"How did you ken yesterday that we were gonna be here today?" Benji asked.

"I *kent* two days ago," she said. "I know things early, but I'm not supposed to talk about it to anybody except family. But, you're family, so I can tell you."

"Okay," Benji said slowly. "I can see that you're definitely Leah's descendent. I mean, the dark, thick hair and hazel eyes were a tell, but the second sight is a dead giveaway. I mean, what can ye tell me about us?" he asked as he stretched tall and put his arm around his new wife.

Bibby cocked her head and said, "You're gonna have six children... I think."

"Oh, ye dinna ken?" Benji teased.

"Oh, I know about the six for sure. It's just that there's one more, but he doesn't look like the others. I mean he's real white and has red hair, but he's kinda yours and kinda not..."

Benji jumped right in and explained, "That's my godson, Mac. He's mine as if he were born to me, even if he doesna have my name. He's a brawly lad, though, not even a year old. As a matter of fact, he's about the same age as yer brother..." Benji paused for effect, then added, "and he has the same last name! Now how's that fer coincidence. I'll bet ye dinna see that one, did ye?" he boasted in a teasing manner.

"Well, kinda," Bibby said meekly, "It's just that sometimes I think it's better not to tell everything I know."

"Weel, lass, since ye've already learned that lesson, the rest of yer life should be a breeze."

Jane picked up on her husband's chagrin and suddenly felt brave: she'd speak up and change the subject to spare him further humiliation. "Our godson in America is about Wee Jim's age. When is his birthday?" she asked, then blew across the top of his head, tousling his curls.

"He just turned six months old. He was born May 1st," Bibby announced proudly.

"Aye, the boys are twins: zodiac twins. They were born of different mothers and fathers in different lands, but on the same day. They'll have the same traits if what the astrologers say is true."

"Do I have a twin in America? Do you have a goddaughter the same age as me?" Bibby begged hopefully.

Jane gave Benji a stern look that he could feel, even though he hadn't seen it. He smiled broadly and answered his niece, "Not that I'm aware of, or rather, not that I could even be remotely responsible fer." He added a nod to Jane. 'Nope,' he said with body language, 'not even a slim chance.'

"But, what about the other ones; the ones you were with last month?" Bibby asked.

Benji sighed deeply. He couldn't hide anything from this little psychic, so shouldn't even try. "That would be yer Great-Grandpa and Great-Grannie's youngest sons and yer Great-Grandma Bibby back in America. Wee Julian, Raymond, and Wee Bibby were all born on that same day."

Benji came over to Jane's side to play with his happy young nephew. He suddenly realized that, although all five bairns were born on May 1st and were all six months old, they were 231 years apart. He shook his head to clear his own confusion. It was only a few weeks ago that he was playing with this lad's ancestors. "Do I need to try and explain it to ye, or do ye have a handle on it, lass?"

"I," Bibby held up her arm and clenched her hand into a fist, "have a handle on it. But, I don't think I could explain it to anyone. I don't think they'd believe me, if I tried. But, we 'ken,' aye?" she asked with a smug grin. She liked her Uncle Benji and his wife. Her face fell quickly. But she was sad that they were going to leave.

48 Red-eyed Reunion

Benji looked up from his one-sided, ear-bending conversation with his enchanting and precocious niece. Jane was staring at the door, her brow furrowed, apparently wishing she were outside. Benji reached his left arm out and grabbed little Bibb Elizabeth the magpie around the waist, held her close, and spun her around in a tight circle, both of them giggling and dancing in an awkward pirouette. "How about if we take this ballet outside into the fresh autumn air?" he suggested brightly as he set her down, smiling broadly at Jane so she knew that she was the reason for the change in venue.

"Ooh, ooh; can we play basketball?" Bibby begged, jumping up and down, hands clenched together under her chin in the classic gesture of prayer. "Daddy put up a hoop for me. He was going to put it down low, but I told him I was going to grow up real fast and besides, I should learn to shoot at regulation height baskets. Do you know how to play basketball, Uncle Benji?"

"Aye, I do." He took his wife's hand and gently urged bouncing Bibby ahead of the two of them through the doorway.

"Over here, over here," Bibby called back.

"She sure reminds me of Jenny," he said to Jane as they exited into the brisk outside air. He sighed in memory of the courtyard. Someone had recently done a major renovation of the barren ground. The British had salted their historical rose garden during the Second Uprising. They didn't want the lowly Scots to have anything beautiful, especially a garden with such exquisite roses, so they ruined the ground with salt taken from the family's own larder. Two centuries of hauling out the spoiled soil and replacing it with fresh dirt hadn't worked. A concrete basketball court was evidently his parent's, or sister's, solution to the constant frustration at the eyesore.

"Now this weather is jest right fer playin' basketball. If it were any warmer, we'd get too hot. Now, Janie, this is the game I was tellin' ye of; jest perfect fer people like ye and me, people of height and with big hands. The object of the game is to throw this ball," Benji picked up the ball from the chair beside the court and twirled it around on the tip of his middle finger, "through that hoop; we call it a basket. But, ye see, ye have to start at one

329

end then move to the other. Now, ye canna jest run with it. Ye see, the other team—those are the others who are playin' and tryin' to get the ball from ye—will want to sink, that is throw, the ball through their hoop. Weel, I'll be," said Benji as he looked to the far end of the hard concrete court. "Ye have two baskets!"

"Uh, huh," Bibby said. "That's because Daddy's friends come out and play, too. He has lots of friends."

"Anyway," Benji said, as he started bouncing the ball, "this is called dribblin'. Now dinna get that confused with droolin'..." He wiped imaginary spittle off of his chin, and darted out toward the basket, bouncing the ball down the court, jumping up and releasing the ball to make a perfect basket. "Two!" he hollered, then looked back to see Jane.

"That's like you showed me the first day at the creek. But, you used a rock and threw it at a boulder," she said, grinning in recollection. She liked talking. Her days of staying mute and being afraid of speaking were over.

"Do ye want to try?" Benji asked as he tossed her the ball. "But, watch yer side. This game can get rough with the other team tryin' to grab the ball from ye."

Jane's reflexes were spot on as she caught the orange orb. She held up the ball to her nose and sniffed. "It stinks," she said, then dropped it. She saw that it bounced almost all the way back up to her without slamming it down. She picked it up with one hand and clutched it, and then turned it over, her long fingers enabling her to keep a grip on it even when upside down. This time she put force behind the ball as she threw it to the ground, copying Benji's smacking of the brown, bumpy ball to make it bounce back up to her. She continued pushing the ball down, and then realized she didn't need to use so much effort. She started giggling when she realized that she could walk and bounce it at the same time, just like Benji did.

"Come on over here and run a little. See if ye can dribble it down the court, that's the area here, and make, er, throw it through the basket."

"Do I use one hand or both when I *dribble* it?" she asked, bouncing it first left-handed then switching to batting it in a controlled manner with her right, getting faster and faster as she proceeded to get acquainted with the air-filled stink ball.

"Jest one hand at a time and dinna stop, hold the ball, and then start dribblin' again. If ye stop, then ye have to shoot, that is throw, the ball, either to another player or try fer the basket. But dinna throw it to anyone on the other team..."

Jane was already racing down the court, still giggling as she controlled the ball with a natural finesse. Yes, the basketball felt like it belonged in her hand. She looked up and saw her target: the chain curtained metal hoop. "Two!" she shouted as she tossed the ball with one hand, making her first basket without hitting the backboard or the ring.

"See, dinna I tell ye that ye'd be a natural," Benji crowed. "Now, there are a few tricks we can show ye, right Bibby?"

"Uh, huh. I can show you how to bounce it off the back, that's called a lay up, and Daddy can do a real neat trick. He can throw it down on the court, that's the ground, *so* hard that it bounces back up and makes a basket when it comes back down!"

"Looks like you have someone to play 'B' ball with, Bibby," Becky said as she strolled out with her son's dozing head over her shoulder, rubbing his back, trying to get him to burp. "Be careful now. We're just going to sit here and watch, so don't go making any of your crazy shots, okay?"

"Okay," Benji and Bibby answered at the same time, all four of them laughing at the obedience to the mother figure. Jim picked up his head from his mother's shoulder and joined in the chuckle, finally able to produce a hearty belch that got the group laughing all over again.

Ж

Meanwhile, down the road a bit...

There was never much traffic this far away from the main highway, but today two cars approached the side road from opposite directions at the same time. Gregg leaned his head out the window and hollered, "After you, son."

The dark-haired man in the red Toyota Hilux pickup truck waved the couple through and said, "Age before beauty," then brought his arm to rest on the window frame, his knuckles under his smiling chin to show he would wait patiently for them to proceed. "Besides, I dinna want ye eatin' my dust!" he added when he saw that they were willing to wait, too.

Gregg went ahead and pulled in, but rather than proceed down the drive, pulled forward fifty feet, stopped the car, and turned off the engine. He got out and opened the door for his wife, then waited for his son-in-law to approach.

"What's wrong," Jim asked, as he drove up behind the classic Renault Dauphine and followed Gregg's lead in shutting off the engine.

"Are you sure they're here?" Gregg asked, his arm reaching out to hold onto Mona. Ramona Pomeroy MacKay snuggled her face into her comfort cloth, the fist-held, wadded-

331

up, white and blue embroidered handkerchief. She wiped at her nose again, sniffing back the tears.

Jim got out of the truck and stood next to the nervous pair. "Weel, I can see ye doubtin' me and my waim, but it was Bibby who called ye, aye?" Gregg and Mona nodded at the same time. "And when was the last time she was wrong about seein' things before they happened?" he asked with a big smile of paternal pride.

He was excited and eager to meet his wife's brother, but also knew that this was a traumatic time for his in-laws. They hadn't seen their son in over twenty years and had no reason to believe that he would be here now other than their four-year-old granddaughter's prognostic proclamation.

"You're right," Mona said. "I mean, it was a lot of money involved flying back from Rome and canceling the trip to Greece and all, but if Benji is really here..." she said trailing off, the sobs beginning anew.

Big Jim reached into his truck and brought out a box of tissues. "Here, I dinna think yer hankie can handle all those tears. Now, I was told to be here no sooner than noon and," he paused and looked up to the sky and then pulled out his smartphone to verify the time, "it's half past twelve now. I'm sure they've had a bit of time to see Becky and the babies. Now it's yer turn," he said, as he ushered the anxious pair back to their car.

Gregg opened the door for Mona, then turned around to face his son-in-law. His mouth opened to speak, then shut without a sound. He tried again, but the words just wouldn't come out.

"Dinna worry about talkin' to him," Jim told his panic-stricken father-in-law. "Jest hold him and let him hold ye. And be glad he's here, even if he is about twenty years late!" he added with a grin. "After you," he said again, this time certain that they would proceed. After all, there was no turning back now.

Ж

Gregg pulled in next to the shiny silver rental car and felt the tears start. He had been able to hold them off so far— Mona had been crying enough for the two of them. He grabbed a double fistful of the tissues and stuffed them into his jacket pocket, then pawed another big handful and blew his nose. Nobody, but nobody in this region had a rental car. This had to be the one Benji came in. Normally, family would be called to pick up friends or relatives at the airport, and rentals wouldn't be needed. But, Benji hadn't called; at least neither Jim nor Becky had been told that he was coming.

It was the little big blessing, Bibb Elizabeth, named after her great-great grandmother so many times over on the Melbourne side, who was the reason they were here today. Bibby was foretelling events even before her words were intelligible. Mona was skeptical when her daughter called and told her that Bibby would point to the telephone and a couple of seconds later, it would ring. "Becky, it must have rung once or twice already, and you just didn't hear it. Ten-month-old babies can't have ESP," she said.

Becky tried telling her mother several times about her psychic sweetie, but Nana remained skeptical. Grandpa was less dubious. "I guess it is possible," he said. "I mean seers are real. 'The sight' is a gift that has been around since histories were shared, oral or written. I suppose it has to start sometime in their lives. It's just that I've never read about a toddler lettin' Mommy know that Nana is on her way over for a surprise visit."

Mona interrupted his cautious acceptance of their granddaughter's gift. "You must have slipped and told her something about us coming," she insisted.

"No, Mom, he didn't. I hadn't talked to Dad for a couple of weeks. And, you said yourself that it was a spur of the moment decision. I think you had just better accept that we have a little seer in the family. Now all I have to do is make sure she doesn't tell people more than they need to know!"

"Yes, and lots of luck hiding Christmas presents from her," Grandpa Gregg laughed.

Ж

Jim saw that his in-laws were an emotional mess and needed a guide for their re-acquaintance encounter. "Come on, I hear them at the basketball court. At least, I hope that's Benji. I wouldn't expect that Bibby's voice has changed that much since last week!"

Jim's joke was met with a couple of weak chuckles and a new wave of tears from Mona. Neither she nor Gregg had ever heard Benji's 'grown up' voice. He was still a squeaker when he was abducted. He was tall for his age, had a little peach fuzz on his cheeks, and his voice was in transition. His youthful singing voice broke and cracked at inopportune times, causing him to be bashful. He was his father's pride and joy with his love of song. He used to sing whenever he had the chance, but resorted to humming as puberty began, embarrassed at his unpredictable notes. Even his humming was erratic, but he refused to give up vocalizing his Beatles tunes. Benji wasn't a quitter.

"That, that has to be him," Mona said, her eyes red-rimmed from the tears that wouldn't stop. "He sounds like you used to," she said to Gregg, and turned into him for the comfort of his plaid sports coat.

"Hmm, I sounded pretty good, then," Gregg said stoically. He gave Mona a full body swing, picking her up as best he could to swing her back and forth like he did with Rebecca, his little Becky, when she was stressed about boys or zitz or a bad hair day. This was a major ordeal, and it probably wouldn't work for his tall wife, but it was worth a try.

"There, are you all better now?" he asked like a father to a daughter after setting her down.

"Yes," Mona answered meekly. "You always seem to know the right thing to do. I mean, if I'm acting like a child, then a child's remedy should fix me, right?"

"...*falling, yes I am falling...*" Benji's serenade to his dark-haired ladies continued in the background.

"Right, dear. Come on, we don't want to miss his finale. And, I want to see who he's singing to. Bibby did say he had a wife..." Gregg's voice trailed off as he walked up to the edge of the concrete court with his wife and son-in-law in tow.

"...and kept out of sight..." Benji quit his soliloquy when he saw his mother and father, realizing that the words he had just sung pertained to this moment like no others could. "But I kept out of sight to save ye," he said, his head hung down in shame as he walked slowly toward his parents, his arms slack at his side.

"What? You don't give your mother a kiss hello?" Mona blurted out, then rushed into his arms.

Benji's hands reached around to pull both parents into him, his eyes now just as wet as his mother's. The sobs continued for at least three minutes, muffled into each other's shoulders, faces moving side to side in attempts at wiping wet cheeks and snotty noses on each other's clothes, nobody caring about the saline and mucous messes they shared.

As the happy trio started to calm down and dry out, a sweet, high voice called out. "I told you so!" Bibby sang. "Aren't you glad I called you, Nana?"

"Oh, yes, dear," Mona said, and dipped down to pick up and cuddle her dark-haired little wonder. "We all are."

Jim dashed back to the car, grabbed the box of tissues, and handed it to the still entwined trio plus one. The adults all wiped eyes, noses, and chins, trying to compose themselves with the cellulose sheets.

"Ahem, ahem." Jim cleared his throat to get the group's attention. "I think that a few introductions are in order," he said boldly with a comedic twist, sidling over to the tall stranger who he assumed was the wife Bibby had foretold. "Hi, I'm Jim, yer brother-in-law, I assume. At least, I am if yer Benji's wife."

Jane was ill at ease with the close proximity of the stranger with the unbridled sense of humor and familiarity. She grinned as she realized that he reminded her of a dark-haired Benji. "Yes, I'm Jane, Jane MacKay, your sister-in-law."

Benji's eyes widened as he walked away from his parents to his newfound brother-in-law. "Jim? Jim Melbourne?" he asked, although he had figured it out from the last names of his sister and her children, and the man's short introduction to Janie. "Good God, man, yer tall!"

Jim couldn't help but laugh, bending over at the waist to keep from being too loud in his surprised reaction to the first words he had heard from his wife's brother. He stood back up and looked at Benji. "Well, ye'd ken a bit about bein' tall, aye?" he asked, as he neared the red head. "Not too many people I can look in the eye while I'm standin' up. Six seven?" he asked.

"Aye," Benji replied. "And my itty bitty wife is a mere six four," he replied dryly.

"And that's why they call him Big Jim," Bibby crowed. "We don't have to call my brother Wee Jim or Little Jim, just Jim, because Daddy's already Big Jim."

The group shared another laugh, then settled down. "Where's yer mother?" Jim asked, suddenly uneasy about her absence.

"She was just here," Gregg answered, then joined the frantic search. "I wouldn't think that she'd miss this for the world."

"Mommy!" Bibby screamed. She looked all around and then to her father for help. "Mommy, Mommy!"

"I'm right here, sweetheart. I just had to change your brother's diaper. Oh, I see your father has met his brother-in-law. Shoot, I missed it. And it looks like it was quite the wet reunion with you three. How about a refill? I made a big batch of lemonade and some scones earlier today on the advice of my daughter. That ought to hold us over until the ham is done."

Benji reached out for Jane's hand, then reached around his mother. "Shall we, Dad?" he asked the patriarch of the family.

Gregg sighed with contentment as he put his hand on his son's shoulder, "We shall."

335

49 Genealogy Lessons and Questions

"So yer a Melbourne," Benji said to his new brother-in-law, "but not from America, I take it."

"Nae, I'm from the line that originated with a James Melbourne who sailed from Great Britain over to Australia on *The Alexander* way back in 1788. He was one of the first white men over there. What a claim to fame: my ancestor arrived with The First Fleet, but he came over as a prisoner, not a marine or an officer. How ironic," Big Jim added dryly.

"Um, am I missin' somethin'?" Benji asked.

Big Jim snorted, "I'm a cop! Go figure. I mean, it canna be in the genes; I'm descended from a criminal," he said and chuckled.

"Weel, the Melbourne I ken in America is a cop, too. Hmm, I wonder if his adopted son—he's my godson, Mac—will be a cop? Genetics are only part of the equation. Environment makes a big difference. Was yer Da a cop, too?"

"Not really," Big Jim said solemnly, not wanting to speak of his father. Instead, he changed the subject. "What's that ye have there, Bibby?"

Bibby picked up her yard long bundle of yellow yarn strands and set it on her Uncle Benji's lap. "Mommy made this for me so I could learn how to braid. Can you braid?" she asked.

"Aye, but I'd like to use this fer something else. I want to talk about my family with this." Benji looked up and saw the confused looks on everyone's face, including the little seer Bibby. He definitely had their attention.

"Most people have a family tree, but keepin' track of our kin requires somethin' with more flexibility than wood. So here," Benji illustrated as he held up the bound end of the yard-long strings of yellow yarn, "the start of our kin, fer my purposes today, begins with Grandpa Jody's father Raymond."

"That's who Nana's named after, huh?" Bibby interrupted. "Oops, sorry," she apologized when she realized her rudeness.

"Aye, and one other, but I dinna want to get ahead of myself. Here's Grandpa Raymond. He had two children who lived to have bairns of their own," Benji split the hank down the middle, "Jody Pomeroy and Elly Kincaid."

Benji smoothed out the long pieces and continued. "Elly had four children who lived to have children of their own," he said as he split one section into four, "and Grandpa Jody has had five children, two of them who I ken have had children." He pulled out two strands and set them out.

"Five!" Gregg, Mona, and Becky all exclaimed at the same time.

"Weel, the first one, Hope, dinna make it. Then there's ye, Wallace, and the twins. But, I dihna ken about them havin' bairns; they were too small to be marrit when I left." Benji saw the shocked looks and realized that they didn't know about his wee uncles. "Ye dinna read about them in The Letters?"

All three heads shook back and forth slowly. "Ach, those must be The Letters they had in the second batch. Grannie did say somethin' about not putting all her eggs in one basket. Quick answer is ye have two more brothers: Wee Julian and Raymond. They're the same age, or were when I left, as Jim there. Zodiac twins, right Bibby?"

Bibby Liz bobbed her up and down rapidly; they had spoken of her wee uncles earlier.

"Over on this side, yer Great Aunt Elly's side, we jest want to be concerned with one of her children, Ian Kincaid." Benji pulled out the clump of yarn representing him, and tossed the other tresses back. "And, here is his son, Wee Ian."

"And, over on Grandpa Jody's side we start with Ramona and her daughter Becky and her two children, Bibby and Jim," he said, and wiggled the one strand that represented Bibby, winking at her. "Then her son, me, but I dinna have any bairns yet."

"Except for your godson, huh?" Bibby Liz interjected.

Benji shared a quick look of shock with Jane. She put her head down quickly and squeezed her eyes shut. Benji took a quick breath, ignored the remark, and then continued, "And, accordin' to ye, Miss Bibb Elizabeth, yer Aunt Janie and I will have six children, but we're not concerned with me and my line right now," he said, dismissing her embarrassing revelation.

Benji saw the look of shock on his mother's face and subtle smirk on his father's; they both knew something was up, but were genteel enough to stay mum.

"So next here," he said as he pulled out another length of yellow yarn, "yer Uncle Wallace who is marrit to Evie. They have, or had when I left, three bairns a little over a year old, an adopted daughter, Jenny, about eleven, and a grown up daughter, Leah, who was, is, marrit to James Melbourne."

Benji watched Big Jim's face fall as he made the revelation. During his little genealogical lesson, Big Jim was polite, but hadn't been rapt like the rest of the family. After all, they weren't his blood kin. Or so he thought.

"Melbourne?" he squeaked in shock, then cleared his throat and tried again, this time an octave lower. "James and Leah Melbourne?"

"And ye see," Benji started grandly, then took it down to almost a whisper as he asked his sister, "he *kens*, right?"

"He's been *told*," Becky said with a slight tinge of disgust and a glance at their parents. They nodded in agreement with what she was saying, "But he doesn't believe."

"He thinks we're a bit dotty," Gregg said with an eye roll and sneer. He didn't like being tolerated, but at least his son-in-law accepted that they believed in time travel and didn't try and make them feel small about it.

"Actually, James and Leah went *back* to Grandpa and Grannie's from this time, a little over a year ago. Their first child, Bibb Elizabeth Melbourne, was born six months ago in 1782. And since James and Leah were born in the mid 1980s, that means they were, what, negative 200 years old when she was born?"

"James Melbourne, my great-great however so many times grandfather, was born in the 1980s?" Jim asked softly, then pulled in his neck and scoffed. He had believed Benji for a split second, but no longer than that. This line of reasoning was creative fabrication, homegrown science fiction with a twist that included his family name in order to try and drag him into the fantasy.

Benji cleared his throat and looked first at his parents, and then at Jim. Gregg and Mona both had furrowed brows of recollection. They remembered the horrific pain they had endured traveling through the stones, the Stonehenge-type formations that were the portals to the past. They had gone through them to be with her 18th century parents, and then went through again to come back to the 20th century.

Big Jim looked curious, but was not convinced. Yup, he was probably a good cop, Benji reckoned, because he *wasn't* gullible. Hard evidence would be needed for this man.

"Yes, and that same James Melbourne's brother is the father of my godson back in North Carolina. So, how do you explain that one?" Benji asked with pride. "What kind of uncle is he to ye: yer great-great however so many times over, or just a plain uncle?"

338

Benji shook his head, dismissing the concept, then returned to his original subject. "Dinna fash; that's not what we're tryin' to show ye with the yarn. So, here we have Jenny, aye?"

"I know Jenny; she's real, huh?" Bibby asked, looking to Benji for validation. She knew her mother believed that she had a special connection with her—that she was real—but her father still believed Jenny was her imaginary friend.

"Aye, Jenny's real all right. And," Benji picked up the thread he had set aside as Wee Ian, "Jenny marrit Wee Ian. At least, that's what Wee James Melbourne told me."

Benji saw the curiosity in Big James's face and continued with a big grin. "Grandpa Jody called him Wee James because he was *only* six foot tall. That's as tall as yer Grannie, rather yer Nana as ye call her," he said as an aside to Bibby.

"Weel, Wee James traveled from this time back to 1781 to save a life. His wife, Leah, came with him because she loved him so much. It turns out it was the life of Wee Ian who was his great-great HSM times," Benji looked over at Jane and said, "that's short for However So Many," and then looked over at Jim, "grandsire's life. Ye see, if someone hadna saved Wee Ian, Wee James would have never been born. The story of *the fairy* that came and saved the elder Ian was in the Cherokee—that's Native American Indian—legend. But, the story should have been about *the fairy* that saved Wee Ian—or Scout, as Jenny called him."

Benji picked up the Wee Ian yarn from Elly Kincaid's side and joined it with the Jenny Pomeroy-Hart strand from Wallace and Jody Pomeroy's side. "And these two wound up being the HSM great-grandparents of my good friend James Melbourne. It's a bit of a Möbius strip. He had to be there—or at least he *was* there—so he could be born two hundred years later."

"Hmph," Big Jim snorted, suddenly ashamed that he had believed any of the tale, even for a moment. "Fairies, time travelin'... Weel, I guess if that's yer family's legacy, I'll not be one to dash it."

"So, where does yer family start? It may jest be coincidence that yer name is the same as my cousin's husband. Where did yer James Melbourne—the one who went to the penal colony in Australia—come from?"

Big Jim shut his eyes and sighed in resignation. He really didn't want to be a part of this discussion, but he was the host to his sister's newly found family members. "He was an American colonist, from North Carolina, who was arrested for—well, that part's fuzzy—in London in 1787. Rather than hang him, they let him go with Captain Arthur Phillip on the prisoner transport ship Alexander to New South Wales. He had skills. He had been a farmer and also knew how to read and do his numbers. The Captain petitioned to take him along. Word had it that his wife and three small children followed later and caught up with him in Parramatta in the early 1790s." Jim shrugged his shoulders and said, "That's the short story of my family's heritage, at least on the Melbourne side."

"Shit!" Benji exclaimed, then looked at Jane who appeared to be just as upset as he was.

Big Jim was taken aback by the harsh remark. He hadn't expected that. He looked over at his wife to see her reaction to her brother's cursing in front of their young daughter. What he saw was an expression twin to her brother's. He turned to his in-laws and saw that they were nearly as devastated as his wife. "Did I miss somethin'?" he asked, truly confused.

"Benji, there's nothing we can do. And, even if we could, you couldn't go back and warn him..." Becky said, then stopped in her explanation.

Her father picked up the thought. "Because if ye did, then Big Jim and my grandchildren wouldna, well, they wouldna *be*. It's already happened."

"Well, first off, I think you all know that I don't believe in predestination," Mona said firmly, rising to take on the moderator's role with her hands on hips, power woman stance. "And, I'm sorry if Wee James had to go through those trials and tribulations or whatever, but Leah did find him, right? I mean, didn't you just say that your great-grandmother Leah Melbourne followed him to Australia?" she asked Jim.

"Aye, but what does that have to do with anythin'? Yer not making any sense, any of ye," Big Jim replied with huff, trying to keep his rage in check.

"We were with James, Leah, and young Bibb Elizabeth Melbourne jest two months ago. They were alive and well in 1782 North Carolina. Leah had jest found out that she was with child again. Ye may not accept it, but we've all seen it. My wife, yer wife, and I were all born in the 18th century. I dinna ken how we can prove it, but it *is* true. And I ken the first of the James Melbournes. He is, was, a fine person and a more honorable man, I've never met."

"Ho kay. I think I'll go outside and make sure the gates are closed or the chickens are in or, or, excuse me; I need a moment," Jim said, and dashed out the door.

Now two more people in his life believed in that time traveling nonsense. It was a good thing he loved his wife so much. He'd tolerate her and her family's madness, even if they ate nothing but potato chips and dressed in purple polka dotted pajamas. It could be worse: at least they were all discreet with their insanity, and no one knew about it but the immediate family. After all, it wasn't as if he didn't have skeletons in his closet.

Ж

"I have to know, Benji: how did you handle the pain?" Mona asked when she was sure her son-in-law was out of earshot.

"Weel, I'd like to be the romantic and tell ye that I'd do anythin' fer my wife—and I would—but there was no pain. Not really, jest a queasy stomach. Wallace's wife, yer sister-in-law Evie, was sent through a different type of portal. She came back here fer jest a day after bein' shot with a musket. She got the needed surgery to fix her up, then went back to yer brother Wallace and their family the next day. And, then there was James and some maps and a smartphone and, and... Weel, there's enough to write a book about what has happened in the last year or two. But, before Big Jim comes back, I'll jest tell ye quickly that Janie and I came back through The Trees, Wallace is fine and verra happy with his big family, and Grannie and Grandpa are a bit younger than they should be, and that's why ye have two baby brothers. And I believe with all my heart that Becky's husband is from the same Melbourne line as Wee James and Leah. I jest dinna ken how to convince him."

"I know!" popped up Bibby. "He can look at The Letters! And can I see the movie with Great-Grandpa and Great-Grannie in it, please, please, puh-lease!"

"Geez, girl; I forgot you were even in the room. And what letters and what movie?" Becky asked.

"The letters that are in the leather briefcase with J.I.M. on it, and the movie that Grandpa Jody accidentally made. Did you bring it, Uncle Benji?" Bibby asked, although she already knew he had.

Benji went to the screen door and looked out. Big Jim was walking away from the house. Maybe they would have a few minutes together without him. The video might convince him, but it was such a personal item, he didn't want a non-believer to dismiss it, or even mildly scoff at it in front of his parents and sister. He looked back and saw all eyes were on him. He looked at Bibby. "Ye ken I have it," he teased. "Come gather around, everyone. This is jest for us right now. This video was taken with

Wallace's wife's smartphone. Grandpa Jody accidentally pushed the record button. Evie was still pregnant with triplets at the time, and ye dinna get to see Wallace, but, weel, here..."

Benji sat down in the big chair with Bibby on one leg and Becky on the other, each one laying her head on a broad shoulder. Gregg, Mona, and Jane leaned over the back of the chair and watched the little video from behind him. When Jody's face came into view, Mona whispered harshly, "Stop it; I mean pause it!" Benji did as he was told and held the phone up to her so she could get a closer look. "Oh my God, Benji, you *do* look like him. I thought so when I first saw you today, but, but... Here, take it back and let it finish."

When the mini-movie was done, Benji shut it off and Gregg spoke. "I'd like to make a copy of that. I mean, can I see it for a minute?"

"Here, Dad. Billy—that is Billy Melbourne, the cop in North Carolina who has become like a brother to me," Benji shrugged his shoulder at the word brother; he had always wanted one, "made about six different types of copies of it. Do ye think we should show it to Big Jim?"

Gregg had his smartphone in hand, took Benji's, and *bumped* them, instantaneously transferring the video file to his, and then gave the phone back to Benji.

"Hmph!" Gregg snorted. "I ken he's a sharp man, but he's also a bit close-minded. I dinna think he'd believe it. I mean, I'd have to watch it a few more times, but I canna think of anythin' in this that couldna been done on a movie set. Sorry. My vote is to keep it jest fer us who believe."

"I believe, I believe," Bibby squealed as she jumped off of her uncle's lap and started her own version of a victory dance. "I believe because I *know!*"

"Yes, dear, you know, but sometimes I wish your father could at least *suspect* that all of this is true. Hey, what about those letters and that briefcase—when are they going to show up?" Becky asked, suddenly remembering her little psychic's hint of things to come.

"Um, in a day, maybe sooner, I think. The bag used to belong to your friend James, who's my HSM great-great grandfather James Melbourne!" she bragged, and started jumping up and down again.

"I have twin brothers and Wallace had triplets? What's with all these multiple births?" Mona asked, as she walked up next to Benji and held his arm close to her, hugging him without being intrusive. "And you sure got tall."

"I ate my greens," he joked, then addressed her first remark. "Grandpa had been wounded and almost died from blood loss. James and Leah helped save his life. Actually, they searched the family out because Leah's mother is Wallace's wife, Evie."

Gregg and Ramona's eye's widened in disbelief at the remark. Mona started to interrupt, but Gregg cleared his throat and laid his hand gently on the back of her elbow, tactily telling her to hold back and let him finish.

"I guess there was a little tonic involved, or in the case of Evie, a lot of tonic. It caused age reversal and evidently enhanced fertility. Grannie had twin sons the day that young Jim was born, give or take a couple of hundred years," he laughed, then continued. "Grannie said they looked jest like I did when I was a bairn, all the way down to the red hair and attitude."

"I think she said smile, not attitude," Jane corrected. "They sure are beautiful. They look so much like Mac, you'd think they were related," she added with a chagrined smirk. She wouldn't tell her in-laws that they had another grandchild, but she had seen the look on their faces when little Bibby had mentioned Benji's godson: they knew. "Would you like to see his picture?" she asked demurely.

Benji gulped and started to say 'no, they dinna need to see him,' but realized that any godfather would and should be proud to show off his charge. "He's a brawly lad," he remarked, and pulled out his wallet to retrieve the snapshot. He held up the small bi-fold hemp folder and turned it over a couple of times. "Nae so good as a sporran, but I get enough stares as it is; a wallet is more discreet. Here, this is my godson, Billy Burke Melbourne, Jr."

Mona and Gregg looked at the snapshot of the little red haired boy, grinning broadly, showing off his two new bottom teeth. Their heads bobbed back up in tandem to stare at Benji, then nodded back down again to recheck their suspicions: the child looked just like Benji as a baby.

Benji volunteered an explanation to their obvious deduction, "His mother had red hair. And, since his name is such a mouthful, his parents honored me, his godfather, by callin' him Mac." He shrugged his shoulders, rolled his eyes once, and then looked at his parents sheepishly. He dropped the attitude and forced smile.

"I couldna love him any more if he were my own," he said. "His mother died jest after he was born, but he has wonderful parents now, and a dotin' grandmother who lives

343

with them. We all live in the same, big house when we're there. It's our home, too."

Becky looked around her mother's elbow at the picture of Mac and smiled at the beautiful child. Now her children had a cousin, sort of. "If everyone will excuse me for a moment, Jim and I are going outside to look for his father. I don't want him to feel left out. I'm sure he'd like to see your godson, the other six-month-old Melbourne child, and besides, dinner's almost ready."

50 A History Lesson

Big Jim needed to get away from his wife and in-laws for a few minutes: the emotional atmosphere around them was choking him. Checking the gate was a lame excuse, but now that he thought about it, it *was* probably open. He walked out past the yard and saw that, yes, the gate hadn't been shut. Right, he had forgotten to close it with all the excitement about Benji's arrival. Benji, his wife's brother who was supposed to be dead, shows up more than 20 years after his supposed incineration—and with a new bride.

Yes, Bibby had been right about his brother-in-law's wife and what she looked like. Who would have guessed that she'd be so tall and so black? Jane was very polite, even if she was quite reserved. And that smile: yes, he could see how Benji was smitten with her. But, she was probably a simpleton, easily led astray, willing to accept whatever they suggested just to fit in. She hadn't said a word when everyone was going on about Grandpa Jody and Grannie and *going back* in time, and actually looked like she believed it, too.

Hmph! Fairies! More like fools. It had been easy enough to disregard Becky's insistence that time travel was real. But, now that they had two children, he was going to have to put a lid on the casual remarks that came out of her and her parent's mouths when his daughter and son were around. Bibby having an imaginary friend was normal, but he didn't want her fantasy to be fed.

It had all started innocently enough years ago. They were at his place and had just watched the 'Star Trek' movie that came out a few years earlier, the J.J. Abrams version. It was that one-worded casual remark, "rubbish," he had uttered that got the conversation rolling.

"Really," she replied in agreement. "There's no way that Spock could be in two places at one time."

"Yeah, well, that, too. There's no way he could travel back in time, anyhow. A time rift: yeah, right."

"You don't know that. I mean, we don't know much about lots of stuff: outer space, time travel. Anything is possible," she suggested, then bit her bottom lip in that enchanting way that meant she wanted more, but wanted him to make the next move.

But this time, it was to engage him in more conversation, not to start snuggling or, hopefully later, necking.

"What? Aye, space travel is possible. I mean, they put a man on the moon and have sent out probes to other planets. Sendin' satellites into space is pretty common now. Yer right, space travel is a reality," he said, then bent in to kiss her neck. That move always got her wound up, and he was starting to feel frisky.

"Not space travel, the other thing: time travel." She inched away, telling him 'no, not now,' with her body. "I believe it's real. It's a part of me and my heritage," she said decisively, then sat up straight, pulling away from him and the comfy couch.

"Ye werena smokin' anythin' funny, were ye?" She had admitted months earlier that she had tried marijuana once in college, but that she wasn't a 'user.' Her eyes were fine, and she didn't smell of smoke, but she did seem a little distant all of a sudden.

"No! I told you it was only once and I didn't inhale!" She turned away and stood up to compose herself, then spun back and glared at him. "So, what do you want from me?" she demanded, her hands on her hips, her eyes narrowed in annoyance.

"What do ye mean?" he asked, at a loss on how to answer. "I'm sorry about the smokin' joke. It's jest that yer talkin' crazy. I mean, we're jest sittin' here, watchin' a movie, and all of a sudden yer all touchy about time travel and 'Star Trek.'"

"What I mean is, I need to know where we're going with this relationship," she said coldly to clarify her question, "and I don't care a flip about the 'Star Trek' movie."

"Uh, um," he fumbled, then looked up at her, lording over him with a scowl. He got up from the couch and stood in front of her to answer. He knew it was awkward; he was so much taller than she was. She had to crane her neck back to look up at his face, but just the fact that she was doing it was the answer he needed. Yes, she was a bit loopy at times, but he couldn't imagine not having her in his life. He'd ask her tonight.

"Will ye marrit me?" he asked sincerely, then bent down on one knee as he realized that he hadn't assumed the traditional matrimonial beseeching position. "I mean, that's where I'm goin' with this," he said, stumbling on his words as he fumbled with his body to get down on his other knee. "I mean, I'm getting' old and gray and need someone who's young and healthy and skilled to take care of me..." he continued in jest, making an exaggerated frown as he looked up at her with sad puppy dog eyes.

"Oh, Jim, I'd love to tell you yes," she answered, the tears welling up from both happiness and fear. "But, we really need to talk..." *Becky sighed heavily then pulled his head into her chest. She clutched him to her so hard that his nose was smashed into her bosom.*

"I really like where I am right now, but I canna breathe," he puffed through her shirt and breast. *She released her grip and let him get to his feet. "Now yer scarin' me,"* he said as he held her hand and led her back to the couch. *He patted the cushion as an invitation for her to sit next to him. "Tell me. I dinna care how big or bad or ugly or scary it is. I'm a big man and can handle it,"* he said with a mixture of seriousness and levity.

"How old do you think I am," Becky asked plainly. *It was a simple question and hopefully would be an easy way to start the difficult conversation.*

"I thought ye were 23. Yer not gonna tell me yer only 15, now are ye?" he asked with a mock frown, trying to get her serious attitude to brighten.

"Well, I'm either 23 or 236, depending on how you calculate it. You see, I was born in 1772."

Jim gave the response she was expecting: a dropped jaw, mouth opened, monosyllabic question of, "Huh?"

"I could keep it from you, but sooner or later, you'd find out. There are lots of little, scratch that, lots of 'big' secrets in my family. You've been to my parent's place, Barden Hall, right?"

Jim nodded his head slowly, but his blank eyes didn't blink. He hadn't a clue as to where this was leading.

"Remember the slash marks on the stairs from the Second Uprising? I know my Dad showed them to you. He's a real history buff."

Jim nodded again, this time blinking once to get some moisture into his eyeballs; they were drying out. Oops, shut the mouth, Melbourne, it's drying out, too.

"Well, my grandfather was alive when those were made."

Jim's one word remark totally bypassed his brain and came straight from his gut. "Bullshit."

"See, I knew you wouldn't believe me! Oh, crap! I guess I wouldn't believe me either if our places were switched. Do you want to hear the whole story or just rescind your offer of marriage right now and be done with it?" She hoped he would let her explain—she really did love the big man.

Jim put his head down, putting his index finger up in the air indicating that he needed a moment. He dashed into the kitchen and filled a tall tumbler with water, drank it down quickly, refilled the glass, and brought it out to her. "I dinna care to take back my proposal, so unless yer a murderess or a devil worshiper, start talkin'."

So, that sweet little dark haired angel told him her family history—or as much as she could until the water she had consumed during the story begged to be released. "Excuse me a moment," she said, and went to the bathroom.

Jim could hear her through the door. Yes, she was peeing like a wide-opened faucet, but he could hear the sobs, too. He heard the water running as she washed her hands and face. She came back out, sans makeup, but still the most beautiful woman he had ever seen. He gazed at her with the look of love and asked, "So, if we're marrit, does that mean I'll get 200 years older after our weddin' night?"

"No," she laughed, then started crying again. "Does that mean you still want to marry me?"

"Weel, I dinna recall hearin' anythin' about ye murderin' anyone or worshipin' Satan, so if ye'll have me, I still want ye—two extra centuries and all."

Two weeks later, she took him back to her parents and let them know that she had accepted his proposal. "Her grandpa," he said softly, as he touched the scarred wood, wondering how it could be possible. He could tell that the wood was at least a hundred years old.

"She told ye?" Gregg asked. He had been standing behind Jim and heard his comment.

"Yes, she did," he said simply, then turned away to go outside and get some fresh air. All of a sudden, he was feeling claustrophobic in the historic home.

Gregg somberly followed him outside to talk to him about it. He stood next to Jim, close enough to be sociable, but not so close as to invade his space. "Do ye believe her?" he asked without preamble.

"No, not really," he replied. He turned to Gregg and saw the ire in his eyes. The man was too mad to speak. This was his daughter who he had just called a liar, or at least a taleteller. Jim clarified his comment. "I canna believe it, but I ken she does, if that makes any sense to ye."

Gregg sighed and said, "It's true," glad that Jim's reply left an opening for more discussion. "Ye see, my wife's mother, Sarah, accidentally fell through standin' stones in Scotland—similar to the ones at Stonehenge—and wound up in 1744. There she met and marrit a young local man, the verra opinionated rascal, Jody Pomeroy. He fought in the Second Uprising. Ye do ken about it, aye?"

Jim nodded. He knew his world history, was actually fascinated by it. He nodded again, silently asking his prospective father-in-law to continue his story.

"Sarah had told Jody that the first battles would be won by the Jacobites, but then there would be Culloden. What came after it was worse: General Cumberland, the Butcher. The man rounded up the Jacobite soldiers and sympathizers, and their families, and killed them, either right away with a bullet or a blade, or slowly, starvin' them, takin' what little they had. Ye see, she knew her English history. She was from England, by the way, but we dinna hold that against her."

Gregg smiled and continued. "Jody sent Sarah back through The Stones to her old time in the 20th century and stayed behind to fight. He managed to 'lose' the men in his company on the way to the last battle, meanin' to save their lives by sendin' them off in the wrong direction. But him, he meant to die; he dinna want to live without her. He fought bravely at Culloden, was seriously wounded, but survived and later wound up a prisoner at Fort William. Sarah made it back to her own time where she went to school and became a doctor.

"Twenty years later, she came back to Scotland with Mona to do genealogical research. That's when I met them. Ye woulda loved Sarah, Becky's grandmother. Anyway, she had me check on the status of a list of men in a regiment. They were a tight knit group—neighbors and ancestors of a friend of hers who she wouldna name. She wanted to ken if they survived the battles. They did. As I was researchin' the records, I noticed the name Joseph Pomeroy, their captain, kept comin' up. I asked her why she dinna want to ken about him. That's when she told me."

Jim nodded a couple of times: he wanted to hear more. Gregg saw him, but waited. He wanted to be asked to continue the story. "Okay, okay, ye got my attention. What did she tell ye?"

"That Joseph, Jody, Pomeroy, the captain who had fought at Prestonpans, Falkirk, and Culloden, was Mona's biological father."

Gregg looked away for a moment for his words to settle in for Jim. He turned back and saw not a reaction from his son-in-law to-be, but a non-reaction. "You ken, the only other man I've ever seen who could carry off such a blank look was Jody Pomeroy. Remind me not to play cards with ye, aye?"

Jim shrugged his shoulder, but didn't speak, too angry to allow his gut reaction, 'What, do you think I'm a fool?' be verbalized or shown on his face.

Gregg paused in the story. "Do ye want to hear more?" He hoped he could reveal the rest of the history. There weren't many people he could share it with. Actually, Jim was probably the only new person he could tell; his family already knew it, and anyone else who heard it would probably put him in the nut house. Well, if this lad was going to be married to his daughter, he would be family, too.

Jim nodded unemotionally in answer, but still didn't say a word. He was curious about where this was going, but was also sure that anything he said would be wrong. This was his first meeting with her parents; he didn't want to leave the family gathering indignant, insulted, or with harsh words.

Gregg was enjoying the history lesson. "Floyd—the man who Mona had grown up thinkin' was her father—had told her on his deathbed that he wasna her real father, that Joseph, Jody, Pomeroy had sired her. He wouldna tell her more than that, only that if she asked her mother to tell her the story, she would. He warned her that it would sound fantastic, that she probably wouldna believe her, but that her mother would never lie to her. Mona never let her mother ken what Floyd—she insisted he was her real father since he was the one who reared her—had said. Regardless, Mona had been forewarned, so as outlandish as it seemed, she believed her mother right away. I, on the other hand, was skeptical.

"So, after more research, we found out that Jody hadn't died in the battle or in prison. He had become a teacher in Edinburgh. She never got over him." Gregg sighed. "Imagine, lovin' someone fer twenty years who ye thought was dead, and then findin' out he was alive. What would ye do?" he asked rhetorically.

Jim answered without thinking, "I'd go back." He gulped as he realized that he had just believed what Gregg was saying, on an emotional level at least, but let it slide, eager to hear more.

Gregg chuckled briefly then continued. "So, Sarah got her affairs in order. She had become a surgeon—the good 20th century American-trained kind—made sure Mona was well taken care of financially, secretly bought this place, and had it set up so Mona would get it when she was ready to move to Scotland. Oh, if ye couldna tell already, Mona was born and reared in the United States. Still, Sarah hadna decided on whether to go back to Jody or not. Ye see, there is a great deal of pain involved." Gregg saw Jim's eyebrows rise. Yup, the young man was intrigued. "Sarah did go back at Mona's insistence. She kent how much her mother loved Jody. She had her mother by her side for nearly twenty years; now she would give her back to him.

"All went well, we guessed. Ye see, there was no way to ken. But, a year later, Mona decided she wanted to meet her biological father." Gregg took a deep breath and his eyes glazed over in recall. "I loved Mona from the very start. I think she had decided she'd marrit me, but wanted to 'go back' to meet Jody and see her mother one more time. She dinna want to tell me about it because she kent I'd say nae, or at least she believed I would.

"But, I found out, convinced her that if I went with her, that we could get marrit in front of her parents, and then come back here. Weel, things got crazy with not bein' able to find family right away and poor communications, even face to face. We finally found her parents; got marrit, and things went well, fer a bit. We dealt with the British soldiers, the Indians, the untamed land, and usually came out ahead."

Jim swallowed hard, trying not to give an indication of his feelings about the story. He was listening with an open mind, sort of. It was too fantastic, but Gregg was such a great storyteller. He wanted to hear how the tale ended, but also didn't want to appear too eager.

Gregg could see that Jim was going to be a hard sell: he needed to add a visual to his story. "See this," he said as he pulled his collar down to reveal the faded, but still ugly scar around his neck.

Jim gasped when he saw the jagged scar that went all the way around the man's throat. His stomach knotted up in revulsion; he couldn't help but visualize what it must have looked like when it was fresh.

Gregg saw the shocked look and was empowered by it. "I was attacked by a crazy, truly insane, British officer who accused me of hidin' gun powder in our springhouse. It was totally ridiculous, I mean, powder is meant to be dry, it wouldna be any good if it was damp. But, he wouldna believe me. He called me a Patriot sympathizer, a Seditionist, and worse. Then he declared that he was gonna hold my wife hostage until I told him where the powder was or gave him gold. Well, I became belligerent: cursin' and throwin' punches. I stumbled in the fight, and the next thing I kent, he was gone and my wife was kneelin' above me, doing her best to staunch the flow of blood from my neck. He dinna get out unscathed, though. Mona managed to hit him in the back of the head with a sizable rock as he fled. He left a bloody trail for half a mile, at least. She said she woulda torn his head completely off, but she had a more important task: savin' me. Woulda served him right if she had gone ahead, chased him down, and caught him: her a hostage? Bah!"

Gregg turned his head and showed Jim the side of his neck. "He missed the carotid artery, but did so much damage to my larynx that I couldna speak for months. Of course, I dinna look too pretty either, but I survived, we survived."

Gregg took a deep breath and continued. "But I digress. It was hell back then. No real medications, surgeons were a bad joke: they believed that leeches and bloodletting were cures for everythin' from the common cold to venereal disease. My wife's first aid saved my life, my mother-in-law's healin' skills mended the gash and kept an infection from startin', and my father-in-law's counselin' saved my sanity. We built a house, then Mona had Benji. Life was good for a few years, tough, but lots of love and usually enough to eat. Then Mona had Becky."

Gregg paused for effect again and got the anticipated response. "And, and…" Jim asked. "Don't stop now; yer getting' to the part about my fiancée."

Gregg smiled in recall. "She was beautiful, so different than her red heided older brother. She's always had the black, curly hair. She gets that from Jody's father, but that's nae important. She was beautiful, but remember I told ye that Sarah was a surgeon?" Jim nodded, saying hurry up with his body language. "Weel, Sarah kent there was a problem. Becky couldna nurse well, she tired easily, had the blue lips and fingernails— somethin' wasna right. There was a problem with a valve that dinna form between the chambers of the heart. It was a simple surgical procedure to repair, but it couldna be done there, back in 1772. We came back together, got her fixed up right and proper, and stayed here. So, if it werena fer a bad heart, ye never woulda met yer future bride. That is, if ye still want to marrit her."

Jim grinned as he recalled that moment of truth. "Yes, yes; I still want to marrit her. Jest because she had a bad ticker when she was a bairn, that doesna make a difference," he said lightheartedly.

Gregg shook his head and groaned with eyes shut at his reply. This man would take his daughter and her crazy history in stride. He loved her, and that was all that mattered to him. Gregg opened his eyes, looked at his potential son-in-law, and asked, "Well?"

Jim shrugged his shoulder and presented his gut feelings about the incredulous story he had just been asked to believe. "If I was a Jew, would ye try and convince me to be Protestant or Catholic?"

"No," Gregg told him sincerely. "I'm Protestant and am marrit to a Catholic. I understand that there are some subjects

with little common ground. My wife and I have been able to have a good marriage because our life has a huge acreage of common ground. I'll respect yer disbelief as long as ye dinna try and convince me that what I ken to be true is a fantasy. Sound good to ye?"

"Aye," Big Jim replied with a huge, honest smile and shook his soon to be father-in-law's hand firmly.

"Okay, so I'll let you marrit my daughter—as if I could stop her from doing anythin' she had set her mind to do—but I'd appreciate it if ye'd at least try livin' in Scotland. She's the only family we have left."

So, Big Jim found the climate better than tolerable, the fishing great, and had no trouble getting hired with the Scottish Police Services Authority. His experience and training in SOCOM, Australia's Special Forces Command, was an asset in any country.

51 The Box

"Hey, Big Jim," called the lanky, freckle-faced youth. "Thanks fer the recommendation. They hired me! I'm yer new postal carrier now."

"Weel, no thanks needed, mate. If ye hadna cleaned up yer act by yerself, ye'd never been in the position to even apply fer the job. Whatcha got there?"

"Oh, there was a man—shoot, he was every bit as tall as ye and with flamin' red hair—who was in town earlier today. He heard me askin' the boss about this," the ponytailed teenager indicated the dilapidated carton in his delivery vehicle. "This box has been sittin' in the back room fer, shoot, years probably. There was this much," Ethan indicated a quarter inch, "dust on top of it. The boss said that it was addressed to a Jody Pomeroy. Since there wasna a Jody Pomeroy at the address of record, Parcelforce returned it to the sender. Weel, there was no such address at the sender's end either. At least they said it was a vacant lot now, so they sent it back to our outlet. I guess this has been goin' on fer quite a few years. I'd say the box and these bindin's look older than me. Here, look at this one postal stamp. It looks like it says 1969, aye?"

"Aye," Big Jim said. He looked at, but didn't touch the rumpled cardboard box covered in yellowed tape and sisal twine. He had heard about Jody Pomeroy from his wife and in-laws and really didn't want to get involved with the alleged 18th century man.

"So, anyhow, this big red heided dude said that Jody Pomeroy was Becky at Barden Hall's grandpa. He offered to bring it out here, said he was her kin. I dinna believe him, though, and neither did the boss—sure dinna look like her. So, after he left, I told the boss I'd come out here myself and see if I could pawn it off on ye. I wanted to come out here and thank ye in person fer the job, anyhow. So, do ye want it?"

"Aye, I'll take it," Big Jim said reluctantly, afraid that if he didn't, he'd be drawn into a long conversation about who was this Jody Pomeroy fellow, or even what business did the tall, red headed stranger have at Barden Hall. He took the offered box, put on his amiable law enforcement officer face, and said,

"Thanks fer comin' all the way out. I guess I'll be seein' more of ye then."

"Aye, ye will," Ethan said happily. "And on the right side of the bars from now on, I promise."

Big Jim tipped his head in farewell and started the trek back to the house, the bigger than a breadbox carton balanced on his hip. "Jody Pomeroy," he snorted. "Looks like yer mail is a bit late, nearly fifty years late."

"Daddy, Daddy," Bibby screamed as she ran out the screen door, unintentionally letting it slam in Benji's face. "Is that the package for Great-grandpa Jody?"

Jim rolled his eyes, shook his head, and huffed in amazement: she had seen this one coming, too. He'd never be able to keep a secret from her.

"A *package* for Jody Pomeroy?" Benji said. "So that's what they were talkin' about in town. I thought it was a letter." He looked down at the ground and said softly, "Thank God it wasna a letter."

Becky, Jane, and young Jim joined the little gathering. "Do ye need a knife fer the string?" Benji asked. "Although it looks like its so auld ye could jest about blow on it and it would fall apart."

"I got it handled," Jim said. He pulled out his Leatherman and snipped through the frayed cords, then flipped the tool around and sliced through the yellowed and peeled tape. "Now what do we have here?" he asked as he pulled out a second box, this one constructed of lightweight wooden slats. "This is jest about as light as cardboard. It looks like it was sent over water. Look at all these stamps: Sydney, London, Tripoli."

"Where's Tripoli?" Bibby asked.

"That's in northern Africa," Becky said, then turned her attention to the carton. "Okay, nice crate, but I want to see what was sent to my, our grandfather. Do you need a pry bar?"

"Nae, I got this," Jim said, and flipped out the multitool again, using its broad blade to slip between the wooden strap and the box's body. He forced it in, then tweaked the handle slightly, prying off the crosspiece. "Jest a couple more," he said softly, and bent to his task, getting the lid off quickly.

Becky peered around her husband's elbow. "A wool blanket?"

"It's jest a wrapper." Jim lifted the musky bundle out of the small crate. "What we have here," he said grandly, feeling better at being in control of the situation instead of on the outside as he was earlier with all of the chatting about the family history, "is an old leather briefcase."

Big Jim frowned as he saw that it wasn't anything exceptional. It was a contemporary styled, high dollar, well-constructed leather valise. It *did* look as if it had spent a fair amount of time in the desert air, or in an oven, though. The tanned leather was hard and cracked and in desperate need of a healthy rubbing with saddle soap. However, the design looked newer than the forty plus year postmark.

"That's Wee James's bag!" Benji exclaimed. "Look: his initials are right there, and if ye turn it over, ye'll see they're also on the bottom. James Ignatius Melbourne, J.I.M."

Big Jim turned it over and saw that Benji was right. "What the fu... I mean, ye've got to be kiddin' me! How did ye ken? Did ye see this at the post?"

"Hey, yer the one who jest opened it, not me. Do ye think that I coulda sneaked it into that box then resealed it with fifty-year-old tape? Yer the cop; go have the tape and string tested and dated. I'll wager that they arena current goods."

Big Jim rechecked the crate; it was solid. He turned the ratty cardboard box over and closely inspected it for signs of tampering. No, it was still sealed, and the only opening was the one he had just created. "How did ye ken about the initials? Are ye psychic, too?" There had to be a reason Benji knew about the engraving.

"Nae, I havena *the sight*, but I did *see* this two months ago. Wee James showed it to me. Look, there's a special lock here." Benji pulled away the now stiff, leather tab covering the hidden high tech lock. "See, ye put yer thumb here, and if yer the rightful owner, it pops open. See," he said as he touched the black disc, "I'm not the one. James had it set up for his thumbprint. Hmm, I wonder if his brother's print would work. They're kin and...hmm."

"I doubt it," Big Jim said, as he looked at the black disc, checking it for weathering or wear. It appeared to be in better condition than the leather it was seated in. He doubted that it had been added later. "The odds are one in 64 billion that two prints are the same. At least, that's what they told us in cop school." He set his thumb on the black composite.

Click. Click.

"Weel, ye jest found the one!" Benji walked up next to his brother-in-law's elbow. "Mind if I look inside?"

"Hold on, hold on," Becky said. "I want to make sure Mom and Dad see this. I mean, it was addressed to Jody

Pomeroy, and he *is* her father. Where did they go? They were just here."

"I'll take this in the house, then help ye look. They couldna gone too far, their car's still here." Jim loosely rewrapped the valise with the undyed wool shawl and placed it back into the wooden box. He threw the lid back on and set the weathered cardboard container on top. There might be a few clues in or on it, too. If he didn't know better—and he didn't—he wouldn't doubt that the leather had aged two hundred years. But, the thumbprint recognition technology was twenty years old, at the most. Suddenly, he wanted a drink in the worst way. "Not a chance," he said softly, "no way."

"Mommy, Mommy!" Bibby screamed in terror.

Jim dropped the boxes on the table and ran to her voice. She sounded terrified. He found her near the cars, all alone and shaking. Her grandparents rushed in to join her just as he got there. "What's wrong, honey?"

Now Benji and Jane were there, too. Only Becky and young Jim were missing. Bibby was mute as she looked at each family member, trying to read their thoughts, but all she could see was their concern for her. The bad man had her mother and baby brother—she knew that—but she didn't know *where* they were.

And then they were there; she could feel them, but still couldn't see them.

"mmph!" The muffled scream was slight, but they all heard it and ran to the source.

Big Jim started to tell Bibby to stay back then gulped, choking on his words. Instead, he opened his arms and let her run into them. If someone had snatched his wife and son, he wasn't going to let him take his daughter, too.

"Ooh, so ye made it back, did ye?" the leader of the group called out when he saw Benji.

Atholl Grant MacLeod the Seventh—Sept as he liked to be called—the man who had kidnapped Benji when he was twelve years old, was back. And, he had his two sons, Eight and Niner, with him.

Becky took advantage of the man's pride causing him momentary distraction. "Catch!" she screamed, and threw her son into the air in an act of total faith.

Janie saw the toddler toss from her position on the sidelines and leapt out, caught the squalling child, clutched him to her chest, and barrel rolled on the ground away from the vile trio toward her husband. Benji grabbed the pair and ushered them behind him. Now how was he going to get his sister back?

"Smart move, woman," Sept said snidely, his grimy fist grasping the military surplus bayonet, waving it at her threateningly. "Ye'll not get another chance like that again." He grabbed her free arm, the one that had held her son, and wrenched it up and behind her back, bending her forward, almost to the ground. "Bitch!" he growled.

"We're ready, Pa," Niner called from behind the opened car door. "Ferget the bairn; he'd probably be more trouble, anyhow. We gotta get outta here quick!" Eight revved the engine and Niner moved around to herd the reluctant, writhing hostage into the backseat.

All three of Becky's kin rushed the gang. "Stop where ye are!" Sept shouted. He stuck the bayonet blade next to Becky's throat. "I'll send ye a note—to the right address this time—with where to send all the money, gold, and gems. And dinna be slow in collectin' it. Ye might want to start emptyin' yer savin's accounts and safety deposit boxes right now." Sept grinned lecherously and leaned into Becky's hair, rubbing his face into it. She shook her head, trying to be rid his unwanted advances. "She'll have good company while we're waitin' fer ye," he said, and entered the car, trying to pull her along with him.

Niner shoved hard and forced the struggling, contorted Becky, her one arm still twisted high behind her, the rest of the way into the back seat of the vintage station wagon. Eight took off, wheels spinning in the loose gravel, as Niner fumbled to get the front passenger door opened, finally opting to climb in through the opened window, his feet pedaling furiously to gain complete access.

"Daddy, Daddy!" Bibby screamed, as she pounded on her father's shoulder. Jim was focused, intent on trying to see the license plate number of the getaway car, and was ignoring her thumps.

"Jest a minute, sweetheart," he said. Still holding her close to him, he ducked down to get a better look through the dust being kicked up by the tires.

He got back up from his crouched position and turned to her. "It's gonna be all right," he said, his lips pulled tight in anger. The gall of those men, kidnapping his wife, and almost his son, right in front of him, a police officer, and all of her family.

"Daddy, Daddy," she said again. This time, she pulled his face toward hers, her small hands clutching his cheeks to make him look at her, "You *have* to open the briefcase. It has the letter in it that tells where they're taking Mommy."

"What?" he asked.

Benji, Gregg, Mona, and Jane—young Jim held close to her chest—joined the pair. "Are ye okay?" Jim asked Jane as she neared.

"He's fine," she said.

"I mean ye," he said, nodding to her dusty and scuffed up blouse.

"Just a little dirt and maybe a scrape or two; I've had worse. Bibby, what are you talking about?" Jane asked the frantic girl since her father was ignoring her request.

"The letter! There's a letter in the briefcase that says where they took Mommy!" she repeated with exasperation. Everyone was acting like idiots and they had to hurry up, or they wouldn't be able to rescue her.

Gregg heard her and sprinted back to the house, the rest of the family close behind. Gregg dug into the open briefcase. "This one?" he asked Bibby, holding up a folded piece of yellowed paper that read, OPEN ME FIRST in a broad, brown-colored script.

Jim walked in, looked around and said, "Weel, get on with it! I may not believe any of what ye say about yer time travelin', but I'll believe anythin' my daughter says. Does it say where Becky is?"

"It's addressed to Jim Melbourne..." Gregg said, and looked up at his son-in-law who had suddenly gone ashen at his name. "It says, 'Jim, if your wife was just kidnapped by the MacLeods, then get to Swona Island as fast as possible. Take a helicopter, spare no expense. You and Benji together can take them. They're headed to the old house with red doors. Use the rear, ocean side entrance and watch out for loose rocks. Love, J.I.M.'"

"What the fu...I mean, what's goin' on here?" Jim asked angrily. "I should be on the phone to headquarters, not listenin' to this nonsense!" He snorted in disgust and reached for the phone on the wall.

"Daddy!" Bibby screamed, once again grabbing her father's face in her hands. "Just do it, please!"

Jim rolled his eyes then nodded his head to Benji. "Are ye ready fer this? I mean, I can take the truck and get us to the station in no time, but damn. Sorry, sweetheart," he said as he looked to Bibby, apologizing for the cursing. He turned back to

Benji. "We have a helicopter in town, but the pilot is out on holiday. I suppose we can drive to Gills Bay and take the ferry."

"If ye can get me to the station, I can fly the chopper. Jest call ahead and make sure it's fueled and everythin' that isna needed is tossed. I dinna ken the size of the bird, but with the both of us in it, it's sure to be pushin' maximum load."

"Ye mean, the two of us and Becky," Jim said, and handed his daughter to Gregg. "Take care of each other," he said to the group, "Benji, Becky, and I will be right back."

The End

Watch for FAIRIES DOWN UNDER

Fifth in THE FAIRIES SAGA

Release information at www.danihaviland.com

OTHER BOOKS IN THE SERIES:

NAKED IN THE WINTER WIND, the first book in THE FAIRIES SAGA, tells the story of Dani Madigan, a plump and perky older Alaskan lady who takes a vacation to Greensboro, North Carolina, to visit her daughter, Leah. Through an accident involving the mysterious Master Simon, she falls through time on October 31, 2012, and awakens in 1780, without her memory and in a younger, thinner body. She rescues a mountain man, Ian Kincaid, who names her Evie, and claims her as his wife. Months later, Ian takes her to visit his aunt, the time traveling fairy, Sarah Pomeroy, and then abandons her there. Many events and people impact the rejuvenated woman's life, including the generous Little Bear and the evil, renegade British Captain, Atholl MacLeod, a rogue who shoots her in cold blood. Critically wounded, Evie is sent on an emergency medical trip back to the 21st century where she reencounters Leah. Moments later Evie is kidnapped and taken back to the 18th century before she can explain to her daughter what has happened, where she's been the last year, and why she now has a youthful body.

AYE, I AM A FAIRY continues the story with Leah finding clues about her mother's whereabouts in a misplaced smartphone. The reportedly gay James Melbourne, the British Lord her mother met the day she disappeared, contacts Leah. He has more information about her mother's disappearance in his bundle of ancient Letters. The first of The Letters explains where Mom is, that the characters from *Lost*—the historical romance novels by Lisa Sinclaire—are real, and that some of these people are now her new family. Leah and James become friends then suddenly have to ward off attacks by the numbered heirs of Atholl MacLeod who are searching for The Letters and the treasure they lead to. Another old letter is received, apparently from Marty Melbourne, asking James to go back in time to save his ancestor. But, it looks like he won't be traveling solo—Leah wants to go back, too.

DANCES NAKED transpires at the same time as THE GREAT BIG FAIRY but in different centuries (it's a time traveling thing). Marty Melbourne has helped others in the 18th century but now wants to get back home to the 21st century. On his way to The Trees, the magnetic time portal through the centuries, he is robbed by Grant MacLeod, the callus brother of Atholl

MacLeod, who is dragging his reluctant younger sister and her baby cross-country, robbing, and pillaging at every opportunity. Marty escapes with his life but little else. No horse, no shoes, and no sense of direction thwart Marty's homecoming to 2013. A small Cherokee hunting party finds Marty and decides that the crazy white man in strange clothes could be of use to them. The group continues to grow when two very different women join the micro tribe. But Marty must wait until Chief Red Shirt is done with him before the brave will lead him to The Trees, and he can go home to Bibb, the woman he should have married, and Billy, the son he never knew he had.

FAIRIES DOWN UNDER, the tale of one of our time travelers who winds up on the First Fleet, is still under development. Watch for the latest excerpts and release information at www.danihaviland.com.

Follow us on Facebook:
The Fairies Saga Fans

And Twitter:
@chilloutdani

Thanks in no particular order:

Thank you, Leatherman Tool Group, Inc.®, for having such fantastic multi-tools that they're worthy of mentioning by name. Everyone in my family has at least two of them.

Thank you, Carhartt® clothing, for having the toughest work pants around. You also have great jackets and other gear, but my characters didn't need them in their summertime scenarios.

Note: Up here in Alaska, we refer to "Carhartts" and "Leathermen" by name so my former Alaskan characters do the same.

Thanks to my husband, Marty, and youngest daughter, Bibb, for being patient, supportive and ignoring the messy house while Mom writes and rewrites, cuts and pastes.

Thank you, Cathie Woods, the gifted body worker, for the many hours spent reading, suggesting, and editing this book.

Thank you, America and our valiant protectors, for securing my freedom of speech along with so many other rights and privileges still promised in our Bill of Rights. Because of them, I can share my wandering, imaginative mind without fear of repercussions. I have fun, fearlessly time tripping, knowing that there *really* is a way to travel in time; it's just that we haven't discovered how to put the science and hardware together. Then again, the secret of time travel may already be known by a select few. I know *if* I knew how to bounce back and forth between the centuries, I'd keep it to myself, too (grin).

And remember: always be nice to one another,

Dani Haviland
www.danihaviland.com

Cast of Characters

Amy ~ young, pregnant woman with Down syndrome, 21st c.

Autumn ~ teenaged runaway, 21st century.

Becky ~ Benji's sister, born in 18th century, living in 21st c.

Benji ~ 6'7" man, born in 18th century, grew up in 21st c.

Bibb (in 21st century) ~ older woman, married to Marty Melbourne, mother of James and Billy

Bibb Elizabeth ~ James and Leah's daughter, 18th century

BibbyLiz ~ young girl born in 21st century to Becky and Jim

Billy Burke ~ Greensboro cop 21st century

Big Jim Melbourne ~ husband of Becky, 21st century

Eight ~ Atholl Grant MacLeod the 8th, 21st century

Evie ~ 20th century born older woman, transported back to 18th century, has amnesia, now in young body due to an overdose of Fountain of Youth Water.

Gregg MacKay ~ Benji's father, former time traveler, 21st c.

Ian Kincaid ~ 18th century backwoodsman, Evie's first husband, biological father to her triplets

JB aka James Bradford ~ aid at The Club, London, 21st c.

James Melbourne ~ 21st century man, transported back to 18th century, son of Bibb and Marty, husband to Leah

Jane ~ 18th-century born 6'4" female slave

Jenny ~ Evie and Wallace's adopted daughter, about 11 yrs old

Jody Pomeroy ~ 18th century patriarch, Wallace's father

Mr. Jonathan ~ 18th century bad guy

José ~ Julian Hart's partner, 18th century

Judah, Leo, and Wren ~ Evie's infant triplets, 18th c.

Julian Hart ~ Wallace's stepfather, 18th century

Leah ~ 21st century daughter of Evie, now in 18th century

Mona MacKay ~ Benji and Becky's mother, time traveler, now living in 21st century.

Niner ~ Atholl Grant MacLeod the 9th. 21st century bad guy

Peter Anthony ~ Billy's domestic partner, 21st century

Sarah Pomeroy ~ Jody's wife, 20th century-born time traveler, healer, living in 18th century, Mona's mother

Scout Kincaid ~ Wee Ian, about 12 years old, 18th century

Sept ~ Atholl Grant MacLeod the 7th, 21st century bad guy

Wallace ~ Jody's son, Evie's husband, 18th century

Wee Michael Callahan ~ Benji's friend, 21st century